WHERE DEATH MEETS THE DEVIL

L.J. HAYWARD

RIPTIDE
PUBLISHING

Riptide Publishing
PO Box 1537
Burnsville, NC 28714
www.riptidepublishing.com

Where Death Meets the Devil

Cover art: L.C. Chase, lcchase.com/design.htm
Editor: May Peterson
Layout: L.C. Chase, lcchase.com/design.htm

ISBN: 978-1-62649-717-7

First edition
February, 2018

Also available in ebook:
ISBN: 978-1-62649-716-0

L.J. HAYWARD

RIPTIDE PUBLISHING

TABLE OF CONTENTS

ONE — THEN

Fuck.

Fuck, fuck, fuck. This wasn't how a guy was supposed to celebrate his thirty-fifth birthday. He was supposed to be in a pub, listening to a drunken rendition of "Happy Birthday," or at a BBQ being introduced to so-and-so's cousin with the great personality, or out to dinner with a slice of wheat-free, dairy-free, taste-free cake. Hell, anywhere but *here*.

Here was a twelve by twelve of raw cinder block, roofed in rusted, corrugated tin and in the middle of God-knew-where. The only furniture was the folding chair in the centre of the room, bolted to the cement floor. The chair Jack was tied to by wrists, ankles, thighs, and chest. They hadn't gagged him, which meant there was no one to hear him scream; hadn't blindfolded him, which meant what he saw wouldn't matter.

It was cold, but not as cold as it got closer to dawn, so only a couple of hours had passed since he'd been jumped, at least. The shivers running along his spine aggravated the shallow knife wound under his left kidney, to say nothing of the potentially broken ribs creaking each time he moved. His right wrist was either badly sprained or fractured; the plastic restraint was biting into the swollen tissue. All of it hurt enough to make his teeth ache. Or maybe that was from the repeated blows to his jaw.

"Hey!" Jack couldn't help but try. "What's going on? I didn't do anything. Come on, what's the deal?"

Like before, no response.

The icteric light of a dozen fluorescent glow-tubes hanging overhead gave everything a sickly yellow tinge. Behind him, the wall with the door. To his left, a wall with a set of shackles. It was easy to imagine himself strung up, hanging there defenceless, while the tools on the wall to his right were taken down and used. Knives, pliers, straight razor, a shock-stick, what was possibly a cat-o'-nine-tails. All of them were hung on a backboard, the type with an outline of each tool so you knew where to put them. Someone had made sure each tail of the whip hung in its precise place.

Still, it was a nicer scene than that on the wall in front of him.

A poster stuck up with aged, yellowed tape. An expanse of turquoise water, a curve of golden sand, a row of perfect palm trees, a peerless blue sky arcing over it. On the beach, four young ladies in bikinis played volleyball.

It had a caption: *Wish you were here.*

The truly disturbing thing, though, the one thing in the entire room that really concerned him, was that someone had used what was probably blood to smear a question mark at the end of it. That one, perhaps joking, addition did what nothing else in the room could.

It made Jack think he wasn't going to get out of here alive.

He really didn't want to die *here*. Not in this goddamned place, not for this bloody job.

Jack closed his eyes. The darkness he found there suited the cold, but it didn't stay dark for long. It rarely did these days. Something always lurked behind his eyelids, waiting to pounce.

Tonight's bad memory was the compound. Walking from the barracks to the Big House, where Mr. Valadian stayed when he was in residence, he'd kept his hands stuffed in the front pockets of his jeans, shoulders hunched against the chill of the desert night. Thankfully, his jeans and wool-lined bomber jacket, collar turned up around his neck, had been enough barrier against the cold.

Jack had barely got one foot on the bottom step before Jimmy was there. Thinking it had been a routine summons, Jack hadn't been prepared, a telling fact of how bad things had become. Jimmy had locked his free arm around Jack's neck, pushing a knife up under his jacket, the point keen against his skin.

Then Robbo had appeared and things had gone from confusing to screwed very quickly.

Jack banished the new bad memory to the files in the back of his head, then slammed the drawer shut on his own foolish mistakes. Too cocky, too complacent. Too bloody tired of the job as a whole. God. He just wanted to go home and forget any of this existed.

He might as well be wishing for the moon, because he was stuck here, surrounded by nothing but extremely hostile, empty desert in all directions. The Great Sandy Desert was too hot, too dry, or for pitifully few days a year, too wet. Those brave enough to endure it were small, scattered Aboriginal communities and a couple of mining companies who poured money on the inherent problems—and organised-crime bosses with big secrets to hide. With no water, no weapons, and no friends for hundreds of kilometres, Jack had about as slim a chance on his own as he did right here.

Then he heard a deep humming sound. It Dopplered around the hut, growing louder as its source prepared to land. The double-thumping of the helicopter's two contra-rotating rotors pounded against the shack, making the tools clatter against their backboard, jerking them out of their neatly aligned positions. Chains rattled and the roof crackled under the new pressures.

Well, that was one thing confirmed. It *was* Mr. Valadian who'd ordered his capture. He was the only obscenely rich megalomaniac in Australia who had a Russian Kamov Ka-52 Hokum-B attack chopper. Which meant Jack probably wasn't getting out of this with his skin intact, let alone alive.

The bird eased down, and a moment later, the engines cut off. In the sudden silence, Jack heard voices.

There was the stately drawl of The Man himself asking a question. Robbo's glacially paced tone answered him. The Man again, then the eager-to-please nasal twang of Jimmy. The nasal twang was fresh that night, courtesy of the punch Jack had landed on the prick's nose.

The Ka-52 was a two-man aircraft, three if two of the people were willing to get pretty well acquainted. As none of these three could pilot the thing, Jimmy and Robbo had probably been outside all the while, hopefully freezing their pathetically small nuts off.

The door opened, and Jimmy's greasy, "This way, Mr. Valadian," was followed by a soft snort from The Man as he stepped into the hut.

"Watch the door," Mr. Valadian said, no particular command in his tone, just an air of expecting to be obeyed.

"Of course, sir," Jimmy gushed as the door shut firmly on his sycophancy.

"Turd of a man."

Jack almost laughed. Mr. Valadian was one of those charming psychos, sophisticated and polite, and supremely capable of cutting a person to the bone with a blunt summation of their flaws.

"I hope you haven't been waiting long," Mr. Valadian said as he strode into view. "I was delayed by business."

The Man was not tall, not short, not ugly, not handsome. Brown hair, brown eyes. Unremarkable. Unmemorable. Evolutionarily perfected for vanishing in a crowd or sliding right off the end of a lineup. He had a sheet of charges as long as Jack's leg—possession of illegal firearms; possession of stolen property; financial fraud; even one for supplying underaged prostitutes to a redacted third party. A few had stuck, resulting in a couple of short-term "holidays" in minimum security, but most had slipped right off The Man's well-dressed back with barely a hitch.

That wasn't why Jack was here, though.

"No problem, boss," Jack said, trying for cool nonchalance. "Gave me a chance to tidy the old torture shack up some. I'd offer you a seat, but..."

Mr. Valadian smiled. It was the tolerant one The Man turned on business rivals, usually ten seconds before they were taken out of the running for good. As if he were at one of those "business" meetings right now, he wore a tailored suit in rich, dark blue, an ultra-fine wool overcoat hanging to his knees, and leather dress shoes dusty from the ground disturbed by the landing chopper.

"Come now, Mr. Reed," The Man said. "We both know why we're here. Just as we both know you don't want to make this hard for yourself."

"Sorry, boss, I must be a bit slow tonight. I really don't know why I'm here. If I've done something to disappoint you, I'm sorry."

How far could he push it? Jack had certainly felt like he was in favour lately, being called out on several high-level meetings with Mr. Valadian, his opinion of this or that person's motives requested. He'd felt like he was trusted. Finally. And now *this*.

The Man considered him, eyes hooded. "Are you? I would like to think you really were, Mr. Reed. The worst part of it is I liked you. Smart, fast, perceptive." He snorted. "*Trustworthy*. But I suppose that was the job, wasn't it."

Then he lifted his gaze and nodded fractionally.

Another person moved into Jack's line of sight, startling him so the chair creaked sharply. He hadn't even suspected there was someone else in the small space. None of his senses had picked up the footsteps, the heat, the sounds of another's breaths.

It was a man, which wasn't surprising. Mr. Valadian had very antiquated views on the sexes. Women had their place, and it wasn't in his business, be it in the glittering towers of glass and steel in the cities or in secret, paramilitary compounds in the middle of God-didn't-give-a-shit-where. This guy was no taller than The Man, but built lean, moving with the light, gliding steps of a person confident in their strength and skills. He wore, oddly, dark sunglasses and a suit of deep charcoal, fitted but cut to conceal weapons, which he was unashamed to show off. Pushing back the side of his own long woollen coat, the newcomer flashed a compact webbing under his suit jacket and the butts of two large handguns. From an inner pocket, he took a small grey box and handed it to Mr. Valadian. Returning his hands to his sides, he backed into a corner. Under a shock of dark hair, the skin of his face was pale and smooth, closely shaven.

This man was a complete unknown. And that meant an unclassified danger. Jack's stomach clenched in anxiety, but he didn't let it show on his face.

"What's going on, boss?" He used what he hoped was the perfect amount of confusion. "Who's the pretty boy?"

Ignoring the second question, Mr. Valadian said, "What's going on is that I've been made aware of a spy within the compound. Care to tell me anything about that, Jaidev?"

Jack forced a startled laugh. "A spy? Shit, and you think it's me? Oh, come on, boss. I've been with you for how long now? Fifteen months. Why would you think—"

"Tell me your real name, Jaidev."

"Real . . . It's Jaidev Reed. Named for my grandfather. He was Indian." Jack let a touch of frustration into his tone.

"I'm sure he was," Mr. Valadian said. "His name may have even been Jaidev, but I sincerely doubt yours is. If you won't tell me your name, perhaps you'd like to tell me who you're working for."

"I work for you. I'm not a spy!"

"Are you from the military? ASIO perhaps? Maybe even the Meta-State?"

Jack frowned. "Meta-State? What in hell is that?"

The Man regarded him for a moment. "The Meta-State is a highly guarded secret agreement between Australia, New Zealand, Malaysia, Singapore, and various other Southeast Asian countries to share intelligence and resources regarding terrorism and international threats. Rumours say the Meta-State controls a hidden anti-terrorism operation spanning not just the members of the Meta-State, but several other, potentially volatile nations as well."

"Wow," Jack said. "That sounds cool, if a bit far-fetched."

"Trust me, Mr. Reed, it is real." Mr. Valadian held up the small box. "Do you know what this is? It's a signal jammer. It'll block my phone and the comms on the chopper, but it'll also screw with neural implants." Not waiting for Jack to pretend ignorance this time, he said, "Yes, another secret the government would prefer we know nothing about. They've been trialling neural implants in the military's elite forces for some time now. Given your age, if you were military, I'd say you have one, Mr. Reed." Mr. Valadian gave him a patient look. "Tell me, Jaidev, who are you working for and what interest do they have in me?"

Shit. Fifteen months. So close to getting everything he needed—proof of Mr. Valadian's association with terror groups in Russia, Egypt, and Argentina; development of smuggling routes into and out of the Australasian region; the reason for the secret paramilitary compound housing a small army and enough weapons to pose a serious threat to the security of the Meta-State—and it was all about to end in spectacular pain and disaster.

Jack tried one last time. "Got me, boss. I don't know anything about it."

"Hm. Wrong answer." The Man's thumb moved over the button.

Fuck fuck *fuck*.

TWO

NOW

Christ.

This wasn't how a man's thirty-sixth birthday was supposed to go. It wasn't that Jack particularly wanted a big celebration; it would just be nice if for once it was a possibility. The way things were going, he'd probably be lucky to get out of here before his *next* birthday.

Here wasn't quite as bad as the torture shack, but it ran a close second. The room was freezing, his chair felt as hard as rock, and the buzz of incessant voices was like the constant drip of water torture. Case review meetings with the director were their own special brand of cruelty.

"Alpha Subject was seen entering the building on the fourth at nineteen twenty-six. He didn't reappear until twenty-two forty-eight, when he left in a vehicle with Deputy Secretary John Garrett. They proceeded..."

Jack tuned out Unit Leader Lewis Thomas's voice. This was all information they knew backwards and forwards. Including Jack, and he wasn't even an official member of the team assigned to Alpha Subject and his dodgy acquaintance with the deputy secretary. He was just an "advisor," not that Lewis needed Jack's advice on a case he was handling well enough on his own. They simply didn't know what else to do with Jack. Hadn't known what to do with him for the past eleven months.

As Lewis droned on, Jack's gaze wandered in the direction of the main floor beyond the glass wall of his current prison.

They were on the eighth floor of the Neville Crawley Building in Darling Harbour. On public record, the building housed a federal financial services department, and while the first three floors were

7

stocked with fiscal analysts, accountants, and economists, the upper nine floors were full of data analysts, spies, and handlers. The latter groups made up the Sydney branch of the Office of Counterterrorism and Intelligence—known simply as the Office—created and run by the Meta-State.

On the main floor, his fellow Internal Threat Assessment assets were busy with their jobs, bustling between cubicles, staring intently at screens of information, flicking through reports from field operatives or technicians. They were productive. Useful. Making a difference. And here Jack was, listening to someone else's report on a job he was barely a part of.

He might as well still be tied to that chair in the torture shack.

Wish you were here?

Shaking off the clinging tendrils of that old memory, Jack focused long enough to hear Lewis ask his second, Lydia Cowper, for clarification on a certain point. Letting the woman's soothing voice roll over him, Jack hauled himself out of the mire inside his own head and back into the present.

". . . photographic evidence," Lydia was saying, flicking a series of shots from the screen in front of her to the big one hanging on the wall at the end of the table. The images showed two men in a car, leaning towards each other. One was clearly the deputy secretary. The other one was the mystery. "These are the best photos we've managed to obtain of Alpha Subject so far. Our operative delivered the raw footage and recordings to Technical for analysis this morning. Hopefully we'll get a positive biometric match to a known subject in the next couple of hours."

Which wouldn't stand up as irrefutable evidence in any court of law, but it would at least confirm the deputy secretary of a government department was dealing with shady unknowns so Lewis's investigation could move to the second stage. It was good progress, but not enough.

"Good." ITA Director Donna McIntosh tapped her tablet. "Keep me apprised of any developments. We can't afford to drop the ball on this one. It's already taken far too long to get even this paltry amount of information." Her tone was the not-angry-just-very-disappointed one she used so effectively.

"Yes, ma'am." Lewis began gathering up his folders and tablets, then paused. After a moment, he nodded to himself with a determined expression. "Ma'am, things would be easier if we could just get more cooperation from Intelligence. I'm getting a lot of excuses whenever I request something. A lot of bounce-back of things marked *urgent*. Someone needs to put a bloody bomb under them or—"

All it took was one of McIntosh's looks to stop him in his tracks.

Lewis had worked for ASIO, the Australian Security Intelligence Organisation, before sidestepping into the Office. He'd faced down Defence Force generals and two different prime ministers and walked away with his career intact. Still, Jack had been subjected to McIntosh's glacial stares enough to sympathise with Lewis's involuntary flinch.

"If you're making an official complaint, Lewis, I will expect the correct paperwork on my desk before close of business today." McIntosh didn't let up on the cool look.

For a moment it appeared as if Lewis might argue. Interdepartmental politics were murky enough most asset-level staff steered well clear of them. An official complaint and investigation could take years, and in that time, resentment would soar, cooperation would plummet—even further—and everyone would suffer. Thankfully, Lewis backed down with a shake of his head.

As they all stood, ready to leave, McIntosh said, "I'll talk to Director Harraway, Lewis. See if we can speed up the flow of information from Intelligence."

Tension falling from his shoulders like a heavy cloak, Lewis smiled gratefully at her. "Thank you, ma'am."

She returned the smile, then motioned him and Lydia towards the door. Jack, too, beelined for the exit.

"Jack," McIntosh said. "Stay back."

Groaning inwardly, Jack turned to face the director. "Ma'am?"

McIntosh was beautiful—long blonde hair he wasn't certain was natural, blue eyes that could go from warm summer sky to stark glacial ice in a blink, and a trim figure with what he would have called killer curves on anyone other than his superior. No one in their office knew her age; Jack guessed she was old enough to be his mother, but the pregnancy would have been a mildly scandalous one.

Overall, Jack had always got on well with his director. She was tough but fair and, on the rare occasion she took an interest in one of her assets' personal lives, sympathetic and accommodating. Things had been a little strained between them since Jack's return, but that was at least half Jack's fault. Still, as she gestured for him to resume his seat, the distant, chilly cast to her eyes reminded him of the few meetings they'd had before he was inserted into Valadian's group. Those objective discussions with McIntosh and his handler, along with the entire preparation for the job, had felt rushed. No sooner had Valadian appeared on their radar than Jack was being hastily debriefed and sent on his way. And no one, most especially not McIntosh, had bothered to tell Jack why they were moving so dangerously fast on this one.

No wonder the whole operation had gone tits up. Maybe if McIntosh had been upfront from the start, Jack wouldn't be in limbo right now.

Sitting, Jack braced himself for whatever was coming.

"I read your latest psych eval this morning." Leaning back in her chair, hands clasped over her stomach, she regarded him steadily. "You're a good asset, Jack. One of the best. It's been tough having you grounded these past months. I'm sure Lewis wouldn't be in quite the mess he's in right now if you'd been cleared for field work in his investigation."

Shit. This didn't have the sound of good news.

"Ma'am, I'm good to go. No flashbacks for nearly eight months. No nightmares, either. I know I passed my psych eval."

"You did. Dr. Granger notes marked improvement in both conscious and subconscious reactions. Your threat response has come down to an acceptable level. Your cognitive modelling is back up to par. Once you requalify at the range, you'll be fine to be reinstated as a full field operative."

"Great." Jack felt lighter than he had in a long, long time. "Glad we had this talk."

McIntosh pinned him with her gaze. "I'm keeping you grounded, Jack."

His first thought was, *So this is the flavour of torture this year.* Eleven months he'd spent convincing them he was fine, that he was back and whole and *ready*. Eleven months breaking free of the torture shack and the desert and . . .

Jack threw himself out of his chair and took a couple of steps away from the table. Away from those thoughts, away from everything that had happened back then. He put his hands behind his head, fingers laced together, to keep them from doing something stupid.

The director waited him out, undoubtedly judging his reaction. Passing a psych evaluation was piss easy compared to actually going back into the field. No matter how layered the questions or how deeply the psychologist dissected the answers, a test could never, ever, replace real life.

Several deep breaths later, Jack asked, "Why, ma'am?"

Not resorting to a simple answer like *Because you nearly flipped out just now*, McIntosh said, "Frankly, Jack, it's because I'm worried about you. Dr. Granger is willing to put you back in the field, and if it were just a matter of your mental stability, then I'd be happy to throw you out amongst the lions once more. But it's more than that."

Maybe she *had* learned a lesson from the hasty prep for the Valadian op, but her apparent caution wasn't something Jack could appreciate right now.

"What more is there?" Trying for restraint and missing it as it flew right past him, Jack flung out a hand to indicate the rest of the office beyond the glass walls of the conference room. "I'm going crazy out there. Cooped up in these walls, *advising* on operations I should have been working on, or leading. You promised me Field Leader after the Valadian operation."

McIntosh stood and looked at Jack until he stopped pacing. "Everything you've said is true, but the fact remains, you were fifteen months in deep undercover with Valadian. By your own report, you began to sympathise with the subject of your operation."

"I didn't turn, ma'am. Yeah, he was a charming bastard and I guess I liked him, sort of. But he was a criminal. Terrorist wannabe. You know I would never have gone over."

With an almost sympathetic expression, McIntosh said, "I *want* to believe that, but honestly, Jack, I just don't feel as if you're *here* with the rest of us. You're a good operative; I don't want to lose you. But until I'm one hundred and ten percent convinced you're still loyal to the Meta-State, I'm keeping you grounded."

"Jesus. How am I supposed to convince you if you don't let me do anything?"

"I'm still working on that." McIntosh slipped her screen into a pocket. "I didn't expect you to pass your psych evals this quickly. Don't get me wrong, it's good progress, but you still have a ways to travel before I'm convinced. Why don't you take some time off? Wind down."

"Is that an order, ma'am?"

"No. Just a suggestion." Her eyes warmed a touch. "At least go home early today. Do you have plans tonight?"

Shoving his hands into his pockets, Jack shook his head.

"You should. It's your birthday."

As if he had forgotten. "Yes, ma'am. One drunken revelry coming right up."

"Stop by the tearoom on your way out. We got you a cake. Happy birthday, Jack."

McIntosh left, taking the shortest route through the maze of desks on the main floor. In her wake, Lewis turned to look back at the conference room, clearly wondering what had happened after he'd left.

Jack and Lewis had joined the Office at the same time, trained together, and worked several investigations together in the early years. Their paths had diverged when Lewis proved better at the administration side of operations and Jack had excelled in the field. Lewis directed a sympathetic grimace in Jack's direction and then, with a theatrical heave of his shoulders, tucked himself into his desk and kept working.

"Screw it," Jack muttered and pushed through the doors.

The hum of the office surrounded him, either the comforting sound of good work being done or pointless thumb-twiddling. Jack hadn't worked out which since he'd come back. It was one thing to tell Dr. Granger what she wanted to hear, another thing entirely to believe it. Sometimes, Jack found himself wondering if Ethan's views on bureaucracy had more merit than not, and that wasn't something he could exactly chat to Granger or McIntosh about.

Jack retreated to his desk and picked up his jacket. Then he hesitated.

Despite McIntosh's permission, and his general grumpiness with his role as *advisor*, Jack experienced a twinge of guilt for leaving Lewis's operation when it needed all hands to keep it from derailing completely. Working with too little information and too many variables, the operation had been languishing for some time. Jack should stay. He *wanted* to stay and do his job, even if he couldn't be in the field. In here or out there, red tape or no, Jack believed what the Office did was important. Vital. He should stay . . .

However, the very thought of being here right now, barely contributing, weighed on his shoulders. Wallowing wouldn't be good, but neither would sticking around and potentially getting pissed off enough to do something stupid.

Decided, Jack slung on his jacket and swung around the end of his little cubicle. Opposite him was Lewis's desk. The unit leader slumped in his chair, tapping idly at his touchpad, flicking through images, a worried frown creasing his forehead.

Jack almost changed his mind. Before he could decide, though, Lewis looked up and smiled tiredly.

"Going home?" he asked.

"Yeah. Birthday treat from McIntosh. If you need me, though . . ."

Lewis shoved dark-blond hair out of his face. "Nah, we should be sweet. Not expecting much action tonight. Not if the data from Intel keeps trickling in like it has been." There was a bitter twist to his words his outburst in the conference room had only hinted at. "Fingers crossed McIntosh can get Harraway to make things happen. Sorry I can't get away. Maybe we can have a belated birthday drink at the watering hole tomorrow."

"Yeah, maybe." Jack tapped his right temple. "If you decide you need me, I'm switched on."

As far as he knew, Jack was the only local Office asset with a neural implant. They didn't advertise the matter. Only those he'd worked closely with knew about it, or that he'd been SAS. It was an old tradition of the service—the only people claiming they were SAS, *weren't*.

"Thanks, man," Lewis said with feeling. "At least there's cake to keep me company tonight."

Forcing a chuckle, Jack left. Before he even reached the stairwell, his implant *ping*ed.

Half convinced it was Lewis, Jack said, "Need your hand held already, Thom-*ass*?" He could have only thought the reply, but that required a bit too much concentration at the moment.

"Excuse me, Mr. Reardon." McIntosh's icy tone cut through his head.

The chill combined with his surname meant he'd managed to somehow royally piss her off. And he didn't think it was just his unconventional answer to the call.

"Sorry, ma'am," he said contritely. "I was just on my way out. As you suggested."

"Not any longer, I'm afraid. Something's come up. You have a visitor. In the public foyer."

Jack's stomach dropped. Officially, he was employed as a Specialist Security Advisor to the International Security Office, which provided protection details for Australian dignitaries overseas. ISO HQ was in Canberra, and while being a fully functional organisation on its own, it was also the cover for a lot of Office assets. No one knew to look for him here.

"Who is it?" he asked.

"He gave his name as Paul St. Clair."

Jack went cold. Twelve months since he'd first heard the name. Eleven since he'd come back, hoping to never hear it again. Six since he'd stopped waiting for it and resigned himself to never hearing it again.

After swallowing a hard lump of panic, Jack whispered, "Happy fucking birthday, me." Then, all the tedium of the past months suddenly shattered, he said, "Code black. Lock down the building and get a security team to the foyer, now."

THREE THEN

The instant Mr. Valadian's thumb shifted over the button, Jack closed his eyes and slid *sideways*. It had to be the fastest transition to a trance state ever. Definitely a personal best.

Before Jack's inner eyes, the overlay for the neural implant grafted to his right temporal lobe appeared. His mission parameters and reports were filed in neat rows. Under them were his health stats, delivered via a subdermal device that monitored his blood components. There was an acute inflammatory response, the biochemical markers indicative of a broken bone, likely his right wrist, and the growing white cell count of a possible infection.

While equivalent to a smart phone, all the implant had done for the past fifteen months was ping home base on a randomised schedule. No one had picked up the signal—or so he'd believed.

In the lower corner of the overlay was a red dot. A kill switch for the implant, because they couldn't risk valuable intel falling into the wrong hands.

All this Jack surmised in the split second before Mr. Valadian's thumb depressed the button on the jammer. There was an instant of lightning between the jammer turning on and Jack flicking the kill switch, but that was all. No crippling static burning through his head, nothing to cause his limbs to spasm or make him scream. Nothing to rip away his cover of lies.

Jack opened his eyes. Mr. Valadian was pushing the button on the jammer over and over. He kept glancing between it and Jack, clearly looking for, and not finding, a response.

"What was supposed to happen again?" Jack asked.

Mr. Valadian glared at him, then he half turned and tossed the jammer to the other man. "This thing doesn't work. Or the information was wrong."

Pretty Boy caught the small box and tucked it away again. "The information isn't wrong." His voice was surprisingly low and husky, and British.

Mr. Valadian sneered at Pretty Boy. "You said he's military."

Was military. Their info was six years out of date, which meant they weren't looking at ISO or the Office for his handlers.

"I said it was highly probable, not definite," Pretty Boy said. "We had to test it."

Scowling, Mr. Valadian fished his phone from a pocket and tapped at it, cursing under his breath when he apparently couldn't get a signal. The jammer was working, just not on Jack.

Jack continued to look contrite and confused. No matter what The Man thought about his supposed loyalty, Mr. Valadian couldn't let him go now. Still, Jaidev Reed would keep insisting on his innocence.

"Come on, boss, you know I'm good. Didn't I deal with Rindone exactly how you asked?" Executions didn't sit well with Jack, but ridding the world of psychopaths like Link Rindone had its own brand of justification. Still, the sight of Rindone sprawled on the carpet of Mr. Valadian's Hong Kong office, back of his head blown outwards by a bullet from Jack's gun, took up a drawer in his mental filing cabinet. "Let me go and I'll do anything you say, no questions." Feeling the timing was right, Jack added in a level of desperation. "*Anything* you want, sir, I'm your man."

Swinging back to face him, Mr. Valadian managed to calm his expression into a bland nothingness that could see him vanish in a crowd. "What I want, Mr. Reed, is to know what you've passed on to your real employer."

"How many times can I say it? Nothing! I swear!"

And it was God's honest truth. He hadn't passed any intel back to the Office. They couldn't risk anything more than a location ping. All the information Jack had gathered was in the implant. Even if something happened to him, the implant had enough independent battery life to store the data until his body could be retrieved. A comforting thought for his handler only.

The Man merely looked at him. Then he straightened his cuffs under his coat sleeves. "Someone sold out Yakim Nikonov to the Russian FSB. Two years and two million dollars is not a loss I can just write off because you're willing to suck my dick."

Jack sat back, unable to keep the stunned look off his face.

Yakim Nikonov was—*had* been—a brigadier in the Krylov *bratva*, looking to branch out on his own. Mr. Valadian had targeted Nikonov as a potential ally and had spent the past two years courting him. Negotiations had been slow and expensive.

Jaidev Reed, however, wasn't supposed to know about Nikonov, and now he needed to cover that lapse. Morphing the shock into grudging acceptance, he said, "Not that I was gagging for the chance, but if that's what it takes to convince you I didn't sell anyone out . . ."

He had the grim satisfaction of seeing Mr. Valadian gape at him. Pretty Boy arched a dark eyebrow over the pane of his sunglasses.

"This is getting nowhere," The Man said firmly. "You played a damn fine game this past year. I never once suspected you." With a wave of his hand, he indicated Pretty Boy. "I'll leave you in the capable hands of my associate. He'll persuade you to tell him everything you know, I'm sure. Did I introduce him before? No? So sorry. Mr. Jaidev Reed, it's my pleasure to introduce you to Mr. Ethan Blade. I'm sure you've heard the name. Goodbye, Mr. Reed."

Jack didn't even note the final dismissal or watch Mr. Valadian leave. He was focused wholly on the figure in the corner.

Not Pretty Boy. Nothing so innocent.

Right from the start of this bloody op, Jack had feared it would go tits up. There hadn't been enough planning, nowhere near enough background information gathered on Valadian. They'd dropped Jack into this too fast and underprepared. He'd landed on his feet, though, and done the best he could, the best anyone could have done, given the lack of resources and intelligence on the subject. All that to the side, nothing could have prepared him for *this*.

Ethan Blade. Jack fought the urge to panic.

The somewhat ironically named John Smith List, updated by every intelligence agency around the world, catalogued all known assassins. The superstars of the paid-killer ranks held the top four or five positions, the wannabes filling out the lowest ones. It was, however, the mid-listers Jack feared the most. Those who calmly and methodically picked up tickets on targets, killed, and got paid. No flash, no glory. Ruthless and precise.

Ethan Blade, the seventh-ranked assassin in the world, didn't move or say anything. Just stood there and regarded Jack through the opaque veil of his sunglasses. A riddle wrapped in a mystery behind dark shades.

Whatever happened now, be it a miraculous escape or certain death, Jack's cover was shredded. He dropped the Jaidev Reed persona, squared his shoulders, and looked right back at those black lenses.

"Ethan Blade, huh? I guess there weren't too many professions you could go into with a name like that. International assassin or circus performer, really, they're your only options."

Blade didn't respond.

Jack dredged up one of Blade's most notorious jobs. "Those Marines in Colombia, found dead by poison inside their LAV. They never did discover how it was delivered. The men hadn't eaten together. There was no trace of gas, no injection marks. Come on, tell me how you did it. One professional to another."

Nothing.

"Okay, we'll come back to that one. How about the team of Afghani special ops forces walking into the Dashti Margo and never being seen again. They were tracked right into a salt flat, where their footprints just stopped. Midstride, then gone. I'd love to know how that one was pulled off."

"It wasn't me."

The reply was so unexpected it took Jack several seconds to process it, and even then all he could manage was, "What?"

"The Dashti Margo. It wasn't me." The corners of Blade's mouth turned up in a chilling little sardonic smile. "If you ever find out how it was done, let me know. One professional to another."

Before Jack's shock-dulled brain could catch up, Blade retrieved the jammer from his pocket, cracked open the case, and fiddled inside for a moment. He closed it and tossed it at Jack. It landed in his lap.

"When I say 'now,' hit the button."

"What?" Jack stared dumbly from the grey box to the man and back again. "What's going on?"

Blade reached under his coat and drew his handguns. They were Desert Eagles, visually impressive, but as a combat weapon, Jack had always thought them a bit too cumbersome. One had a laser sight attached under the barrel, and the small red dot danced across Jack's chest for a moment. Thankfully, it moved off him when Blade strode past him, coming to lean against the wall, head tilted towards the door, listening.

"Yell."

Straining his neck to look over his shoulder, Jack gaped at him. "What?" It was starting to sound like the only word he knew.

"Yell, as if I were torturing you."

"No," Jack snapped, tired and cold and too confused to care. "I'm not going to yell until you tell me—"

The laser-sighted pistol aimed at his head. Jack blinked as the red dot skittered over his face, following him unerringly as he tried to dodge.

"Yell."

So Jack yelled. He screamed and yelled, adding a few whimpers for good measure. Whatever Blade was waiting for happened a minute or so into the show. Waving for Jack to keep it up, he tucked one gun under his arm, took off his sunglasses, and folded them into an inner pocket of his suit jacket. Blinking rapidly, he grabbed the gun again and squared off against the door.

"Now," he said calmly and kicked open the door.

Startled, Jack coughed on a pretend scream and jerked his head around, trying to see what was going on. Blade was through the doorway the moment it opened. The Desert Eagles boomed, aimed in opposite directions, followed by the dull *thud*s of bodies hitting the ground. Two more shots and a cry of pain. Whatever else might have resulted from it was drowned out by the sudden whine of the chopper firing up.

Cutting through the drone of the chopper engine were the sharp retorts of return gunfire. The assassin dove to the ground and rolled out of sight, the Eagles answering in their deep, deadly voices. The door shut behind him, closing Jack off from the sudden combat.

Holy shit. More than Jimmy and Robbo out there, then. However many there were, they couldn't have all come in the chopper, which meant they'd been here all along.

Jack wished him luck against the unquantified enemy. The Ethan Blade legend suggested he would actually win. Which was a positive for Jack. Not a great one but better than the current situation. With Mr. Valadian's troops out of the equation, Jack would only have to deal with one man—Blade.

It even sounded as if it was working, the frequency of exchanges lessening, the screams of dying men coming further apart. Still, the jumbled cacophony was enough to start memories of nightmare combat flashing on the edges of Jack's perception.

Before Jack was lost to the memories, the door slammed open and a calm and affable British voice called, "I said 'now,' Jack, if you please."

Oh. Yeah. The jammer.

Spreading his thighs as much as he could, he let the box slide down between them, jiggling his legs so it landed on its side. Jack squeezed them together, depressing the button.

Outside, the night exploded.

FOUR

NOW

McIntosh stalked into the situation room. She spared a quick glance for the staff at the banks of monitors, then arrowed in on Jack. "Explain this now, Mr. Reardon."

Jack straightened from leaning over Technician Alderton's chair. "Flick it to the big screen," he told her, then turned to McIntosh. "The man who came asking for me."

One eyebrow cocked, McIntosh looked at the picture now spread across the big screen on the wall before them.

The foyer of the building was open and airy with glistening marble floor, tasteful abstract sculptures, and leather seats that were incredibly uncomfortable to discourage lingering. The long, curving reception desk was manned by four operatives. Stock-standard security personnel guarded the entrance to the elevators and the foot of the grand, sweeping staircase that didn't actually lead anywhere, but looked impressive.

Currently, the reception staff were barricaded behind their desk, bulletproof shields raised, assault rifles and handguns at the ready. The security personnel had been joined by a tactical squad taking positions behind all the convenient sculptures and suddenly not-so-superfluous staircase. The front glass wall of the foyer had darkened until it was opaque, the space now flooded by emergency lighting. What it showed seemed very unimpressive.

A single man knelt in the middle of the floor, dressed in a tailored suit, hands behind his head. Silent and obedient, he appeared to be the most unthreatening person in the world. With his arms up, his jacket gaped open, showing no signs of concealed weapons.

"Unless he's carrying the world's smallest knife, he's clear," McIntosh muttered. "What about the name he gave? Paul St. Clair."

"We have two hundred and seventy-five hits on that name, estimated age, and ethnicity, but haven't expanded the search outside of domestic databases yet," a tech answered, fingers flying over his keyboard. "We're eliminating them at a rate of five point two per minute, ma'am. We should have it narrowed down to three or four candidates in thirty minutes."

"Forget the search," Jack said. "The man doesn't exist in any database we can access."

McIntosh turned on him. "You obviously know who he is." Implicit in her words was that anything other than full disclosure would be viewed as highly suspect.

Jack studied the still figure on the screen. Nearly a year since he'd last seen him and even through the camera, he looked unchanged. Lean, strong, full of coiled potential. Lack of visible weapons didn't mean the man was unarmed. It just made him more dangerous. That old sensation of dread and excitement returned.

As if sensing him, the man in the foyer lifted his head and looked directly at the camera. A shock of dark hair fell back from his forehead. He wore sunglasses. Below the dark shades, his mouth was quirked up in a small smile.

"Mr. Reardon." McIntosh's tone hovered just above a snarl. "Explain."

"He's crazy," Jack said, completely honest. "He was working for Valadian when I encountered him."

"Just tell me who he is." McIntosh's glacial words broke Jack's shock like a dunk in ice water.

"He's Ethan Blade."

The announcement was met with silence, and then Alderton tapped furiously at her keyboard for a moment. She began reading from the file she'd pulled up. "Ethan Blade. Active assassin, working mostly in Eastern Europe, Africa, and South America. Preferred method of execution is a firearm; one instance of poison noted. Currently number seven on the JSL. Length of activity . . . sixteen years." As she finished, she looked at Jack with a mildly sceptical expression. "Are you sure it's him? The man in the foyer doesn't look *that* old."

How to answer that safely? "Well, he was working for Valadian, and Valadian always had the finest of everything. And I saw him in action." For good measure, he added, "If he isn't Blade, he does a very good impression."

McIntosh turned to Jack. "The unnamed benefactor in your report."

When he'd come in after four weeks dark, Jack had stuck to the truth as much as possible. Less likely to trip himself up that way. He'd reported the events at the torture shack as they'd actually happened, just left out the name of Valadian's "associate," saying his benefactor—a disgruntled Valadian stooge—had disappeared into the night after the explosion.

"Yes," Jack agreed.

"Everyone, get out."

For the second time that day—that *hour*—Jack found himself in private conference with Director McIntosh.

Damn Ethan for putting him in this position.

For a long moment, McIntosh ignored Jack and watched the unmoving assassin in the foyer of a building hiding one of the world's most well-kept secrets.

"You knew who he was when you wrote the report."

Heart skipping beats, Jack said, "I did."

It was too late for more dissembling. By showing up here, Ethan had effectively blown all of Jack's reports of that time to smithereens.

"Did you tell him about this building?"

"Jesus! Of course not. Valadian left him in the torture shack with me. For reasons of his own, Blade decided not to kill me and helped me escape. The man took out a small army of Valadian's troops to do so. When we parted ways, I said I wouldn't reveal his part in it, but if I ever saw him again, I'd bring him in." All true, as far as it went.

Now that reason was creeping back in, Jack couldn't believe it was happening. Not like this. He stared at the image of Ethan. Why now? Why like this? Ethan could have easily found Jack at home, at the gym, or *anywhere* other than here, somewhere they wouldn't have to deal with this shit. And yet it was classic Ethan Blade. So perfectly insane Jack wanted to laugh. Relief and anger swirled in a heady mix, making him a bit reckless.

He gestured grandly at the image of a captured, contrite Ethan Blade. "There you go, Director McIntosh. One less assassin in the world and another feather in your cap."

McIntosh cut Jack a look full of Arctic chill, then turned to the screen. "How did he find you then?"

"Who the hell knows? The man poisoned a unit of US Marines in an armoured transport without leaving a hint as to how. Pretty sure finding an Office branch wouldn't be beyond him."

"You sound almost as if you admire him." McIntosh's words hinted at Jack's unfortunate admission of coming to like Valadian.

"Not admire, as such," Jack hedged. "More . . . cautious about underestimating him."

Jack was torn. There could be a couple of reasons why Ethan was here, only one of which was worth more than Jack's life. In the months since parting in the desert, Jack had decided Ethan's theory hadn't panned out. There had been, after all, no fallout—and the fallout would have been unmissable. After so long, it couldn't still be viable, surely.

"Jack," McIntosh said softly.

Setting aside one potential trap, Jack focused on avoiding the other one. "Ma'am?"

"Promise me, *promise* me, he isn't here because you turned."

"God's truth, ma'am. I haven't turned. Would I have told anyone who he is if I had?"

"Honestly, Jack, I don't know." With a frustrated sigh, McIntosh tapped Alderton's screen, drawing the image closer to Ethan's face. "All right. What's our move?"

Given a bit of breathing room at last, Jack took a moment to seal away his mixed feelings about Ethan's appearance, putting them in the filing cabinet with all the other problems.

"Make sure he's not carrying," he said. "Get him into a secure room. Find out why he's here."

A full minute passed as they watched the unmoving assassin on the screen.

"He's here for you, Jack," McIntosh said. "You have the task of securing him."

Jack kept his expression schooled into something vague. Not an hour ago, McIntosh had said she didn't trust him fully. Now she was sending him into a very sensitive situation. On one hand, he could see why she might do it. Ethan was here for Jack, or at least, because of Jack. Who knew what results they'd get sending anyone else out there. Deaths? Possibly. A fight? More likely. Unnecessary roughness? Definitely. But if his director had recorded her doubts anywhere, this was skating too close to breaking policy for Jack's comfort. McIntosh was usually a stickler for the rules.

Except for when she'd broken land-speed records getting the Valadian job up and running and Jack inserted undercover, sidestepping several Office standard operating procedures to do so. Could her reason for throwing Jack into the op too quickly back then be the reason why she wanted him to deal with Ethan now?

Christ! As if wondering why Ethan had picked *now* to show up wasn't enough, he also had to think that maybe McIntosh had some hidden agenda as well.

"Jack? Are you up to it?"

If he didn't want to play McIntosh's game, he should say no. If he wanted Ethan brought in without blood being spilled, he had to say yes. His path split once again. It all came down to loyalty. He chose a path.

"Yes, ma'am," he said. "I'll do it."

FIVE THEN

The shockwave rocked through the ground under the torture shack. The rusted bolts holding the chair in place cracked, and it and Jack toppled over. He hit the cement on his left side. Pain snapped through him from the knife wound, blanking out the roar of the explosion for a moment. When he could make out nuances beyond the dull pound of blood through his ears, Jack heard the rising whine of a chopper straining against gravity. The pitch of the engines was wrong, too high, overly stressed, as if something had been damaged. Then the sound evened out and, with a burst of deep, thrumming noise, the chopper shot away.

So, the aircraft wasn't what had exploded.

In the wake of the vanishing chopper, Jack could make out the relatively quiet hiss and cackle of fire. Something out there was burning. A sudden flurry of gunshots signified some survivors.

Jack struggled against the plastic ties, hoping his new position had changed something. The metal of the chair creaked, and the armrest under his right arm shifted. Teeth gritted, Jack worked his arm back and forth and up and down, feeling the frame of the chair move. Feeling, also, a rather excruciating pain rip up his arm. Tears stung his eyes and he blinked them away. The plastic armrest cracked as he kept working. Sucking in a deep breath, he held it and twisted his arm savagely. The old plastic snapped all the way through and fell away from the metal frame.

The sudden relief whipped through him like a blow to the head, leaving him dazed. Continued gunfire encouraged him to keep going.

With the tie loosened around his wrist, Jack wriggled his swollen arm free of the plastic restraint. His situation had improved, if fractionally. He was still mostly tied to the chair, still surrounded by the enemy, still confused as to what Blade was doing, but he had an arm free. Albeit a broken arm, but he'd worked with less.

Jack began rocking, leaning forward, pushing back. Twisting his left arm, he managed to get some purchase on the ground, and used it to help lever himself upwards. When he had some momentum going, he shoved up and threw his weight sideways. The chair rolled over and he was on his back, legs higher than his head. Another little shove and he toppled onto his right side, arm out to avoid smashing it into the ground. Still, the impact on his shoulder jarred his wrist, and he couldn't hold back a cry of pain. Breathing through it, he reached out and, scrabbling at the cement, hauled himself towards the wall with the torture tools.

Time vanished somewhere beyond the pain, his whole being focused on his goal. Peripherally he was aware of the gunfight continuing outside, though the number of exchanges was reducing, now interspersed with panicky yells.

At the wall, he used the holes in the backboard to help pull himself upright, shuffling the chair back under him. Its rough journey across the floor had hastened its rusty deterioration, and it wobbled under his weight now.

The straight razor was at the very outer edge of his reach. Stretching his fingers towards it strained his broken bone and inflamed flesh, but when the slender tool slid off its hook and fell, it was all worth it when it landed in his lap. From there, it was relatively painless to pick it up, flip it open, and saw through the plastic ties.

"Good," Blade said behind him. "At least you're not totally useless."

Standing and spinning in the same move, Jack hooked a foot through the leg of the chair and kicked it in Blade's direction. The assassin sidestepped it casually.

Muscles burning from too long in one position, Jack held back even though he wanted to charge and hit and kick. He'd been knocked down one too many times tonight. Confusion and frustration made a sparking cocktail of his blood, but being injured and clueless made it the wrong time to go against someone of Blade's reputation.

Instead, Jack matched Blade's calm pacing around the walls of the torture shack. Blade watched him, expression part curious, part amused. He kept his Eagles down by his sides, with all the appearance of being nonthreatening. Jack carefully didn't laugh at the ridiculousness of the thought. Rather, he rolled his shoulders, flexed his arms, and tensed and relaxed his legs. The ache subsided and he warmed up in the cold night air. Blade stopped by the poster, waiting. There was dust on his coat and his hair was frazzled, but otherwise, he looked as if he'd just walked out of a meeting with his accountant, not out of a gunfight.

"What's the deal, Blade?" Jack asked.

"The deal, Jack, was to kill Samuel Valadian," Blade said blandly.

Jack should have pretended confusion at the name, but protecting a cover already shot to shit was pointless. "You know who I am?"

"Yes. Jack Reardon, former lieutenant of the Australian Special Air Service Regiment. Discharged six years ago for medical reasons I couldn't discover." Securing his right-hand gun in the underarm holster, Blade kept his gaze on Jack. "May I change mags? I'm almost out and there are still a few soldiers out there. It would be best to do this now, rather than in the middle of an exchange."

Jack was fixated on Blade's eyes. They were pale, unnaturally so, with pupils big and dark in the light of the fluorescent tubes overhead. Between that and the revelation Blade actually knew who he was but *hadn't* told Mr. Valadian, Jack realised just how painfully ignorant he was of, well, everything at the moment.

"Sure," he said, struggling for the one thing that seemed even remotely likely—Blade was planning on keeping him alive. Why? Jack had absolutely no idea.

Lips curled up in an unreadable smile, the assassin reached into an inner pocket on his overcoat and pulled out a mag for the handgun. "Catch." He tossed the mag at Jack, no harder than what was needed to get the mag to him.

Jack let it hit him in the chest. It landed on the ground at his feet.

"These are my favourite guns," Blade continued, hefting the Desert Eagle he still held. It had the laser sight. "I'd rather you didn't let this one hit the ground." He made as if to throw it.

"Why give me a gun?"

"You feel up to hand-to-hand combat? I'm impressed. Personally, I'd rather we didn't close with the remaining forces outside, but you were SAS. Your tactics probably differ from mine."

"Yeah," Jack muttered. "I'm not a murderer." It was hard to put honest conviction behind those words.

"Do you think to shock or shame me with that?" Blade advanced, holding the gun out to him, butt first. "I am what I am. And right now, I'm a lone man against superior numbers. It would be silly to dismiss a potential ally. At the very least, Jack, take it so you may protect yourself if I fall."

Jack adjusted his grip on the razor, keenly aware of how sad a weapon it was contrasted to the man before him. Within the military, the SAS were the elite forces. Jack hadn't been the most gifted in all fields, but he could hold his own against his fellows, which meant he could wipe the floor with just about anyone else. However, what he knew of Ethan Blade was enough to give him pause.

Shifting the razor to his injured hand, Jack accepted the gun. It settled into his hold with a satisfactory weight.

The moment the weapon was transferred, Blade backed off. He made a slow show of producing another mag and the other gun. After tucking his Eagle under his right arm, Jack crouched and picked up the mag at his feet. He worked his fingers over it to make sure it was actually full. It was. Standing, he locked his gaze on the odd, unsettling eyes of the man across from him. Together, they released the spent mags and slammed the new ones home.

Jack had the loaded gun pointed at Blade instantly, turning side on to present a narrower target. "Drop it, Blade." The red dot landed on Blade's chest.

Smiling, Blade held his own gun in two fingers, the other three splayed out. "Yes, Jack." He crouched and laid it on the ground carefully. "May I remove my coat?"

"God," Jack hissed, out of his depth with this strange creature. "How many more weapons do you have in there?"

"A few," the assassin said, amused. He shrugged out of the coat and spread it over the ground. "Would you cover the door while I assemble the rifle?"

"The rifle?" He was starting to wonder why he was even trying to get the upper hand. Blade was refusing to play the part. Lowering the Eagle, he nodded. "Sure. Got nothing better to do."

Blade smirked at the sarcasm and began tearing open the seams of the overcoat's inner lining.

Shaking his head, Jack turned his back on the assassin and crouched by the door. He expected his better judgement to put up an argument, but the usually finely honed sense stayed quiet, as if having a known killer at his back wasn't at all alarming. Frankly, at this point, a bullet in the back of his head would just be an end to the confusion. A hollow-point at this range would take out the implant, making the last fifteen months a pointless waste of time. Still, if Blade was serious about killing Valadian, then the problem was eighty percent solved.

Flickering orange light rimmed the door to the shack, the crackle of flames clear now he had the chance to listen for it. There wasn't much else to hear, apart from the tin roof shifting as it heated up. The air in the shack started to warm, smoke curling through the gaps in the walls. Whatever was alight was close by.

"They'll be closing in on us," Blade said as he worked behind Jack with a quick staccato of weaponry pieces snapping together. "I believe there are three snipers on the ridge to the east. At least five more mobile troops on the flat. How's your long-range aim?"

"Better than average."

"Brilliant. You can take the rifle then."

Turning enough to look at Blade, Jack shook his head. "You're a crazy bastard, aren't you."

"You're half right." The assassin stood and displayed the assembled weapon.

It was a sleek, lightweight sniper rifle known as an Assassin X. Made by unknown sources for people just like Blade, they were designed for easy concealment, quick assembly, and undetectability to most scanning devices. All those elements combined into a weapon that wasn't robust, had limited range, and only supported small-calibre rounds. The word that came to mind when Jack saw one was "flimsy." However, in the hand of Blade, it looked worthy of its name.

From inside his suit jacket, Blade produced a scope and clicked it into place on top of the rifle. "Night-vision scope. The mag holds seven .22 LR rounds, one in the breach." Which he loaded with a soft *clack*. "Headshots would serve us best, Jack."

"Right," Jack said with a sinking sensation. There was so much about the whole situation that was *wrong*, but he found himself agreeing all the same. It'd be a bloody miracle to hit anything with an unfamiliar rifle, let alone three headshots.

Blade joined him by the door, listening. "The trucks are still burning. Good." He paced away, head tilted as he looked at the roof in the corner over the beach poster. "Up, I think. Jack, your assistance."

Jack hesitated. He was an asset of the Australasian Meta-State, paid to protect its citizens from dangerous elements. Elements like Samuel Valadian and Ethan Blade. Right now, however, his best chance of stopping the former was to work with the latter.

With Blade on his shoulders, Jack stood steady while the assassin pushed the corner of the tin upwards. Done, Blade slid down and dropped to one knee. Making a stirrup of his hands, he said, "You first, Jack."

There was no point in arguing. With his injuries Jack wasn't getting up there without help. Judging the height of the wall, Jack stepped back a couple of paces. "Ready?"

Blade nodded.

Jack sprang forward, hit Blade's hands with one foot, and leaped. With a boost from the assassin, he grabbed the top of the wall easily. His broken wrist protested instantly and strenuously, but he threw his right arm over the edge of the cinder blocks, digging in with his left hand. Shoulders heaving, he hoisted himself up and out.

Slithering onto the corrugated tin, Jack kept low. The ground troops probably wouldn't spot him, but Blade had mentioned snipers on a ridge. The assassin was up and out seconds later. He'd left his overcoat behind and closed his dark suit jacket from neck to waist, eliminating the glow of his white button-down.

"This way," the assassin whispered and eeled along the edge of the roof.

As promised, the night was lit up by two merrily burning transport trucks, angled to block access to the shack. They were flatbed trucks with canvas coverings for troop transport. The fires were dying down, however, having consumed the meagre amount of fuel available in the material, the wooden benches, and the interiors of the cabins. Scattered around the two bonfires were the bodies of men from Mr. Valadian's army. Each transport could comfortably carry fifteen men, and it appeared they had been packed to capacity. About twenty lay unmoving, and then there were three possible snipers and a handful of troops still lurking beyond the fires.

Thirty or so soldiers, plus Jimmy and Robbo, all for Jack. He didn't know whether to be honoured or horrified.

Joining Blade at the front corner of the shack, bodies pressed tight side by side, Jack pushed away his misgivings and concentrated on the task at hand. This was no different from some of the jobs he'd run with the Unit. Trying to convince himself of that, Jack put the Assassin X to his right shoulder. After a second, he switched to the left. His right wrist wouldn't handle the recoil in its current condition. Jack settled the rifle, wriggled into a better position, and scoped the lay of the land.

The green-hued scene through the night-vision lens opened up for him. The land was arid; dry, cracked, dusty ground; low-growing spinifex; rocky protrusions increasing in size and number as the land swelled towards the ridge, the rock bed breaking free of the dirt in a jagged wall. The sky above was clear, no clouds, just stars—a perfect desert night. Jack scanned the top of the ridge. It was irregular with a sharp-edged cliff face, rounded mounds of dirt, straggly vegetation and, somewhere amongst it all, three bodies lying much as he was.

"Ready?" Blade whispered.

"No, but let's just get it over with."

With a soft chuckle, Blade said, "As you wish, Jack."

Then he stood up, a perfect target framed against the starry night, and got it started.

SIX **NOW**

"**S**hirt too," Gerard Maxwell, the head of security, commanded.

"Just don't cop a feel, sailor." Jack unbuttoned his blue dress shirt. His suit jacket already lay on the table in the small prep room off the foyer.

Maxwell grunted. "You aren't pretty enough, soldier."

Like Jack, Maxwell was ex-military. When they'd first met, there had been a spark of solidarity. Then Jack had discovered Maxwell had been a chief petty officer with the navy. Traditionally, army and navy weren't the best of mates, but Jack had been ready for a fresh start when he joined the Office. Maxwell, too, by the way he'd bluntly propositioned Jack a month into their working relationship. Despite Maxwell being neither physically nor intellectually attractive to him, Jack had considered it for about half a second because it would be sex and sometimes, casual sex could be great sex. The need to not screw up the new job, however, had made Jack turn him down.

Maxwell hefted a set of body armour off its frame in the corner. "I'll warn you, this shit's heavier than it looks. Thin so as to be concealed better, but dense. Latest hard armour evolution."

Shucking his shirt, Jack eyed the armour sceptically. "I'm pretty sure I'm not going to need it."

"McIntosh says you wear it, you wear it." Maxwell ran his gaze over Jack's torso, presumably to check for the fit of the armour. When he got to the small cluster of entry wounds where Jack's right kidney would have been if it had survived the bullets, he gave a short, impressed whistle. "That is some awesome precision. Who's responsible?"

"Taliban. Had a bee in his bonnet about something. Maybe he didn't like us raiding his weapons cache."

Maxwell gave an evil chuckle and nodded appreciatively. "Nope. They didn't like that much at all."

Jack lifted his arms to let Maxwell slide the armour on and wrap it around his chest and back.

"This one?" the HoS asked, coming around to Jack's left side.

"Thug by the name of Jimmy O'Dowd. Dirty knife. Looks small, nearly killed me though."

"Always the way." Maxwell buckled up the armour under Jack's left arm. "It's the small ones you gotta watch. Have a habit of creeping up on you, right?"

"Right." Holy Jesus. Maxwell wasn't wrong. For something almost as thin as his cotton shirt, the armour pulled down on his shoulders like a whole suit of cement. "You wear this stuff every day?"

Maxwell was built like a fireplug: sturdy, thick thighs, square shoulders absolutely bulging with muscles. Jack could understand it if this was what he carried every day.

"Nah. This here is the tuxedo of armour, special occasions only." Slapping Jack's back, hard, he added, "Don't be a bitch. You can handle it."

Jack staggered, wheeling his arms to keep his balance.

While Maxwell watched critically, Jack dressed again. He slung on an underarm holster and picked up his department-issued handgun. McIntosh had signed off on his firearm re-qual, trusting Jack hadn't let his skills atrophy during the eleven months he hadn't been allowed to carry. She'd handed over his Heckler and Koch USP and a mag with one bullet in it, her intention clear. *Betray us and you only get one shot. Use it wisely.* Wryly, Jack slapped the mag in and chambered his single round, then slid it into the holster. Over that went his jacket.

"Tie?" Maxwell asked, holding up the dark-blue cheapie.

"No. I've heard what he can do with one." He picked up his official ISO badge. "I will take this, though."

"Reckon he can't kill you with it?"

"Pretty sure he could, but I think this is sort of a formal occasion." Rapping his knuckles on his armoured chest, Jack smiled. "Got the tux and all."

Maxwell opened the door and ushered him out. "Good luck, Reardon. We'll be watching."

Jack nodded and started down the short corridor towards the foyer. Maxwell peeled off and entered a smaller version of the situation room. At the door to the foyer, Jack stopped and took several deep breaths. He still couldn't decide how he felt about this. Apprehensive, certainly. What would Blade say or do? One wrong word and Jack could kiss what was left of his career goodbye. Angry, possibly. How dare Ethan put him in this situation. After everything Jack had done for him, this was how he was repaid? Confused, ah, yes. When was he never confused around the crazy bastard? Upset? Scared? Annoyed? Yes, yes, yes. But beyond all the obvious emotions, one twisted from yes to no and back again with rollercoaster intensity.

Excitement.

Several more deep breaths. *Remember what Dr. Granger said. Emotions don't have to rule you. Don't act on them rashly. Think them through. Be rational.*

Ethan Blade was a wanted criminal. He belonged in prison. A high-security prison for the mentally unstable. He was nothing more than that. It didn't matter what he'd said in the desert. He couldn't be trusted. That was the rational path. And yet . . .

Operative admits to feelings of sympathy for the subject.

The one line in his initial psych evaluation upon coming back that put the brakes on his return to the field. Eleven months of inaction because of an irrational impulse to mention how he'd come to like Mr. Valadian.

Well, it wasn't going to happen again.

Jack opened his hand and looked at the badge. His ISO shield in gold-plated bronze looked spanking new, which it pretty much was. He only brought it out on official occasions, of which there had been a scarcity in his time with the Office. Still, he rubbed it with the tail of his jacket before clipping it onto his belt.

Then he pushed through the door and walked out. It closed behind him with a small *click* of finality. It was a one-way lock.

Jack emerged into the foyer at the back of the staircase, hidden from view. The leader of the tactical team waited for him.

"Sir." He wore armour of a much more bulky nature, and probably twice as light. "Subject has not moved, nor said anything. We've scoped him constantly; nothing's changed. I swear, he hasn't even farted once."

Jack snorted. "What did you expect? He's British. All right. I'm going out there. I'm not actually expecting trouble, but I wouldn't put a swifty past him."

The man nodded and thumbed on his throat mic, then informed his team the operative was heading out. He waved Jack out of cover and crouched, assault rifle at the ready.

Jack stepped out into sight of the foyer. Twenty metres away, Ethan showed no reaction, though Jack knew he saw him. The assassin's regard came with a certain predatory pressure, prickling the hairs on the back of Jack's neck, thrumming through him with a sharp spike of anticipation. He had no idea what to expect, and he didn't like the uncertainty. It didn't help that Jack had only ever found one way of getting the upper hand on Ethan Blade, a method he wouldn't be revealing. He could only hope that here, where he was surrounded by his allies, in a place he was confident of his position and job, he would have some measure of command over Ethan.

Yeah. He could hope.

Wish you were here?

Shaking off the doubt, Jack strode forward. Ethan kept still, hands behind his head, sunglasses trained on the floor about two feet in front of himself. Jack stopped precisely there.

"Ethan Blade. Well, isn't this the worst day of my life."

Ethan didn't reply. Didn't move, barely seemed to breathe.

"Really? You track me down, come all this way, and submit yourself to a dozen highly trained and heavily armed security personnel just to play the silent game? You're an insane bastard, Blade."

"Half right, Jack."

Ah. There was the bemused-tosser accent he hadn't missed. Now that Ethan was talking, however, Jack had to be doubly careful. Until he knew exactly what Ethan hoped to achieve by showing up here, Jack couldn't risk giving anything away.

"What's going on? Why are you here?" Frustrated with looking at the top of Ethan's head, Jack added, "Look at me."

Slowly, Ethan lifted his head. "Hello, Jack." He smiled, and it might have actually been genuine.

Breathing through the surge in memories, Jack said, "Just answer the questions."

Ethan's sunglasses finally angled towards Jack's face. "Unfinished business. To get this out of the way."

"Jesus," Jack hissed. "You haven't changed, have you?"

"No." Briefly, his tinted glasses dipped down over Jack's body and back up. "But you have. Nice suit, Jack. If a little cheap."

Mouth open to object, Jack stopped himself before he could. Arguing with Ethan was where the path diverged. One way was right, the other wrong. Veering onto the right path, Jack merely said, "On your feet, Blade."

Thankfully, Ethan complied without opening his mouth.

"Arms up. Feet apart."

More silent compliance.

Wondering when the other shoe was going to kick him in the nuts, Jack stepped up and, starting at Ethan's shoulders, patted him down thoroughly.

"I'm not carrying, Jack."

"You expect me to trust you?"

"It did cross my mind that there should be some level of trust between us."

Hands on Ethan's waist, fingers itching to dig in and hurt him, Jack scowled. "After what you did to me?"

"I apologised for that."

The urge to punch him didn't entirely go away, but it did subside a fraction. As far as he could tell, Ethan honestly believed saying "sorry" was all he needed to do. There was a level of innocence in Ethan somehow both at odds and perfectly aligned with his psychosis. A killer ignorant of just what his actions cost the world.

Teeth grinding, Jack lifted his hands to Ethan's arms and took his time. "This is so bloody typical of you. There's a sane, rational choice or a crazy-arse, do-or-die one, and you pick the one most likely to get you dead. Every single bloody time. You're insane."

"I have unarguable powers of reason."

Jack snorted before he could stop himself. He crouched and ran his hands down Ethan's legs. "Yeah. No one argues with your reason."

"Except you, Jack."

"Not anymore, Ethan. It ends here." He stood and, with only a moment's hesitation, ran his hands through Ethan's hair.

The assassin shifted fractionally under the touch, a slight tilt towards Jack, head dropping forward. He jerked back, however, when Jack drew his hands free, taking Ethan's sunglasses with him.

While Ethan blinked in the sudden brightness, Jack drew his gun. The barrel landed under the assassin's jaw, shoving his head back so he got an eyeful of bright white light.

"I'm going to inject you with a sedative, Ethan. It's the safest way to move you."

"As you wish, Jack."

With his free hand, Jack pulled the jet-injector from his pocket. As he put it to the skin over Ethan's jugular, Jack realised he felt guilty. It was a shitty thing to do. Ethan had come in voluntarily and had obeyed every order. He could be trusted to do as Jack said.

But no one would trust Jack afterwards, and if he was ever going to prove his continuing loyalty to McIntosh, he couldn't mess this up.

"I'll endeavour to make it as painless as possible," he said, and Ethan closed his eyes in acceptance.

Jack depressed the trigger and, three heartbeats later, the world's seventh-most-proficient killer crumpled in a heap at his feet.

SEVEN
THEN

Movement on the ridge. Jack tracked it and found the second sniper. Their position was about thirty yards south of the first one. Number three was proving very coy.

On the ground, Blade kept up his end of the bargain. He played tag with the remaining ground troops, evading them while drawing sniper fire. With a quick double retort, he took a soldier out of the game. Blade appeared from the flickering shadows cast by the burning trucks, Desert Eagle in one hand, a long-bladed dagger in the other. It gleamed red, thick drops of blood splashing into the dust at his feet. Silhouetted, he was a deranged image of Death come stalking. Echoing sniper fire rang out and Blade twisted, tumbling to the ground in a controlled roll.

The sniper fire revealed what might have been Sniper Three. Jack scoped the ridge.

There, higher than the others, further away. A brief hint only— could be a nocturnal animal. Ranging it, he found it right at the outer limit of the Assassin X's capabilities. Not great if he wasn't certain of the shot.

Blade flipped his knife, caught the tip, and with a negligent-seeming flick of his wrist, sent it spinning into the chest of the soldier creeping up beside him. That left three. Time for this to end. Jack had two definite snipers and one probable. If he didn't act now, Blade could make a fatal mistake and leave Jack with six against one. He liked those odds about as much as he liked taking Blade's help.

Jack lined up Sniper One. His finger caressed the trigger. He wished for his old SR-25, a solid, dependable sniper rifle. While he was wishing for things, he might as well conjure up Nigel Kruger, his squad's best sniper. Man could snipe the wings off a fly at range with a headwind.

Letting out a breath and sending up a fervent prayer, Jack squeezed the trigger.

Someone was listening, at least. Sniper One's head snapped back, a spray of blood outlined against the clear sky. Jack racked the bolt and swung to Sniper Two. Breathe out, fire. The shot missed, sparking off the rock beside Sniper Two.

"Fuck."

Sniper Two flattened himself and scoped for Jack.

After making an adjustment, Jack fired again. A small jerk and Sniper Two's rifle toppled over.

A bullet *ping*ed off the tin an inch from Jack's elbow.

Heart slamming, Jack aimed for Possible Sniper Three. The outcropping of rock he'd marked came into view, and clearly visible now was Sniper Three.

Jack racked the bolt at the same time Sniper Three did. Sending up another plea for divine aid, Jack fired and rolled. A bullet ricocheted off the tin where he'd been lying. Coming over onto his belly, Jack tried to locate Sniper Three again. Couldn't find the outcropping, so he rolled, the tin roof shifting under his weight. Found the right place this time and saw Sniper Three was down.

Someone opened fire on him from below. Jack shoved backwards, away from the edge of the roof. Five, six shots, then a strangled grunt and no more.

Warily lifting his head, Jack saw his attacker fall at Blade's feet, throat cut from behind. Blade stood there, a jagged offcut of metal in place of a knife.

Jack settled the Assassin X back into place and took aim. Squeezing the trigger, he took out the last soldier, who'd been creeping up behind the assassin.

Then the roof collapsed under him, leaving Jack dangling from the top of the wall. The sudden wrench jarred the wrist and knife wounds into painful life again.

Blade considered the impromptu weapon in his hand, then tossed it aside. He holstered his Eagle and regarded Jack calmly. "Do you require assistance?"

"No, I'm fine." Jack decided down was easier, and more beneficial, than up right then. Dangling by his good arm, he judged the drop acceptable and let go. He landed on his arse beside the rifle, sore and tired and just thankful he didn't land on the stupid thing.

The door opened and Blade came in. He surveyed Jack, the rifle, and the sheets of corrugated tin on the floor, then retrieved his overcoat from under the roofing and shook it out.

Jack cradled his broken arm to his chest, eyes closed. Bitching about his cold bed seemed like so long ago. No matter how many times it happened, it always stunned him how fast an entire life could change. One bomb going off in the wrong place at the wrong time and suddenly he was enlisting in the army. Four bullets fired in under ten seconds and he was one kidney away from needing a transplant. A half-hour briefing on Samuel Valadian and here he was. One shot and he'd saved the life of an unrepentant killer.

Ethan Blade. Horror-inspiring legend; willing to kill anyone, anywhere, for the right price; cold-blooded and calculating. And he stood before Jack, coat over one arm, cleaning his sunglasses on the hem of his shirt. Fresh from wading through a small army, he looked a little lost as he traced a tiny crack in one lens.

"What now?" Jack asked to break the mood, finding the sight of Blade being human disturbing.

Blade looked up, eyebrows raised. "Now?"

"Yes, now. The enemy's taken care of." He didn't want to indicate in any way he might also be an enemy.

"No, he isn't. Samuel Valadian got away."

Of course. "So?"

"He is my target. I have to finish the job."

"Right. The code of the assassin."

"There is no assassin's code. I've been paid for a job and I will do it. If that's a sentiment worthy of a code, then I suppose it's my personal one."

"And me? What I am to your code? Collateral damage?"

"No. You were bait."

Jack felt a sudden need to be on his feet. The adrenaline was ebbing, taking with it his will and strength. For a moment, he entertained the idea Blade wasn't a threat to him. He ignored it, got to his feet and, rifle slung over one shoulder, drew the Desert Eagle Blade had given him.

"Bait?" he enquired calmly.

"I needed to remove Valadian from the majority of his forces. I am good, but not that good. Revealing a traitor amongst his men was the most expedient means of doing that. Thus selling out Nikonov, to help prove there was a spy amongst his people."

Jack blinked. Blade had taken down a *bratva* brigadier just to get Mr. Valadian alone? Who the hell was this crazy bastard?

Blade continued. "Once I 'discovered' the spy, I knew he would have you brought here, and I would be asked along to interrogate you. Which I don't do, usually. Interrogation, that is. Once here, it was simply a matter of grounding him and doing the job." No change in tone, no hint of recrimination. "Had you detonated the charges when I first said, the chopper would not have been able to attain the height to escape. I will have to track him down again."

No. Blade was not going to make him feel guilty for letting Mr. Valadian get away. He went on the offensive instead.

"*You* broke my cover? Just so you could kill one man? Jesus *Christ*! Do you have any idea what you've done? Fifteen months gathering intel required to bring down his *entire* organisation, not just this one compound, or one piddling Russian ally, and now it's all screwed. We'll be lucky to get anything at all now. Mr. Valadian isn't going to wait around for you to find him. He'll be packing up and running. It'll set him back one, maybe two years, but it's destroyed any hope we had of taking him down before he makes his intentions known. Fuck me, you're supposed to be some sort of genius, and this is what you do." Piling on a mocking British accent, Jack ended with, "Brilliant, old bean. Can't wait to see what you do for an encore, old chap."

Blade stood through the entire tirade unflinching. At the end, he simply put on his glasses and coat before walking out of the torture shack.

"Oh no," Jack muttered. "Did I hurt the cold-hearted killer's feelings?" Either way, perhaps it wasn't smart to prod the assassin too much.

That thought in mind, he did a quick ammunition check. Two left in the rifle, a full mag of eight in the Desert Eagle. Enough to take down Blade?

"Jack?"

He brought the gun up to bear and aimed at Blade in the doorway, a white box in his hands. It had a familiar red cross on its top. An even more familiar red dot sat on the assassin's chest.

"I stole this from the chopper when we landed," Blade explained, supremely unconcerned about the weapon trained on him. "I thought there would be a good chance of you being injured and needing attention."

Nonplussed, Jack gaped at him for a full minute before lowering the gun. Totally bonkers.

With a twitch of his head, Blade indicated going outside. "There's more light by the trucks. I wouldn't want to miss something in the dark." He vanished once again.

Jack was following him before he made the choice to. Muttering, "Who's loonier, the loon or the loon who follows him?" he joined the assassin by the brightest of the burning trucks. The heat made removing his jacket bearable.

"Shirt too." Blade opened the first aid kit and studied the contents.

Grunting, Jack pulled the dirty and torn T-shirt off over his head. "Don't try to cop a feel."

"As you wish. Is your wrist sprained or broken?"

"Most likely broken."

"We'll splint it to be sure." Blade tore open a pack of antiseptic wipes. "Do you wish to do it yourself?"

Sneering, Jack grabbed the pack and pulled a wipe free. He cleaned up his arm. Grime and dust came away from his dusky skin, revealing a slight reddening around the inflammation. Every time he moved his hand, the dull ache sharpened into a throbbing pain that wore down his patience. It needed to be splinted.

Blade produced a roll of SAM splint and a knife. Knowing he couldn't do this on his own without a lot of hassle, Jack offered up his arm. The assassin measured twice, cut once, and moulded it around Jack's arm, then secured it with an expertly applied bandage.

"There's enough left for another splint," Blade said. "Just in case we need to change it."

Eyebrow rising at the "we," Jack was just grateful his arm was finally immobilised. Already some of the ache was easing out of it. He wiggled his fingers, making sure he had some movement.

"Any other wounds?"

Jack turned and leaned forward, showing off the knife wound in his lower left side. "It's just a flesh wound."

"It requires a bit of cleaning. Do you trust me to do it?"

"Don't have much choice, do I?"

"There is always a choice."

The tone of the words caught Jack's attention. A touch of sorrow? Regret? A hint of a conscience?

"Lie down," Blade commanded, back to his usual cool self. "I'm going to wash it with alcohol first. That will probably sting."

Resigned, Jack lay down. "Yeah, probably."

"Don't worry, Jack," he said. "I shall endeavour to make it as painless as possible."

EIGHT

NOW

"He hardly looks worthy of the fuss," Director McIntosh said.

The screen on the wall showed Ethan's cell. It held a bed of moulded plastic, unable to be broken down for weapons, and a similarly constructed table with two chairs. There were two buttons on the wall: one to dispense water, the other to reveal the toilet. The walls were pale grey, the floor one solid expanse of pressure padding, and the lighting soft, no exposed bulbs. The door was a smooth panel that retracted into the wall—nothing to grip and use to pry it open.

The assassin sat on the bed, head cradled in his hands, shoulders slumped. The sedative had knocked him around badly, the dosage set to ensure he didn't wake up en route. While unconscious, he'd been stripped, searched, washed, and dressed in blue scrubs. Any sign he was going to use the garments as weapons would initiate release of a tranq gas into the room.

Ethan's naturally pale skin looked sallow, his hair lank after being washed and left to drip dry. Out of the tailored suit and in the loose scrubs, he looked like a kid playing dress-up. His feet were bare, which had to be bothering him. Ethan didn't like bare feet. He kept scrunching them on the floor, a peculiarly endearing action, as if he had to keep reminding himself where he was. As if he'd realised he'd made a big mistake. There was a bruise on the side of his neck, where Jack had injected the sedative. He hadn't said a word since waking.

"I know." Jack leaned against the wall, weary now the mad panic and rush was over. "Believe me, it's required."

Those far-too-comprehending blue eyes turned on him. "It wasn't just one night you were with him."

Jack couldn't meet her gaze for more than a second at a time.

"Jack. Is anything in that report real?"

"Sure. Sheila. The homestead. The bit with the dingoes."

"But *he* was with you for those things?"

"Yes. About ten days total. The rest of the month I spent . . . working out how to get home."

McIntosh spun away from the screen. "What am I supposed to tell Director In Charge Lund? That an operative spent ten days careening around the desert with one of the most notorious killers in the world? You don't need to worry about whether or not I'll ever trust you again. Be concerned for your own neck, Jack." McIntosh crossed her arms, turning back to look at Ethan. "You met him for the first time that night?"

"Yes."

McIntosh regarded him closely. "You'll have to make new statements to reflect the added information. They'll come part and parcel of more restrictions on your activities on behalf of the Office until the conduct and disciplinary hearings about your actions are finalised. If you don't agree to them, you will be charged with conspiracy against the Meta-State, interfering with an ongoing investigation, and aiding and abetting a known criminal. Do you understand?"

Here he was again. His life could go one of two ways, all for a decision he had to make in the next thirty seconds. Delaying would only convince her of his guilt. *There is always a choice*, Ethan had said, and now Jack felt as if he understood the sadness in his voice.

The whole fiasco in the desert had been like a psych eval—layers within layers within layers. He'd given McIntosh the top layer upon his return. Now he'd given her another. Anything more and Jack might as well lock himself in the cell with Ethan.

"Yes."

"Good." Though it sounded anything but. "You'll be assigned a security detail and confined to the building until otherwise notified."

Great. A shadow with orders to take him down if he so much as sneezed suspiciously. "Yes, ma'am."

"I'll have that paperwork started. Then I'm going to talk to your friend in there. Feel free to observe."

She left then. After five minutes of not watching Ethan, Jack took the stairs from the sublevels to the eighth floor. Most of the office was empty. Only one operations room was lit up, where Lewis's team was keeping a twenty-four-seven watch on Alpha Subject. Jack avoided them and sat at his desk, contemplating the few personal items he'd brought in.

A photo of Sherlock, a goofy German Shepard with a floppy ear, dead of snake bite while Jack had been on deployment in India. A police-dog school dropout, he'd proven better therapy than most of the psychiatrists Jack had seen over the years.

A birthday card made by his niece, Matilda, when she was four. *Dear Uncle Jack, Happy Birthday, Luv Tilly!* She was sixteen now and hadn't sent a card for twelve years, not since her mother had decided she didn't agree with Australia's involvement in the conflict in Afghanistan. Even after his discharge, his sister hadn't wanted anything to do with him.

A frame with his service medals, kept here because he didn't think his apartment was secure enough and he couldn't imagine losing them. He'd been prepared to throw them, once, but his father had convinced him not to. One day, Dad had said, Jack might have kids of his own who'd like to know what their father had done to keep them safe. Or maybe Matilda would come to her own conclusions about her uncle's actions. So, he kept them.

A life in two frames and a piece of paper smeared with finger painting. Would Matilda ever reconsider if she learned about Ethan Blade?

Wish you were here?

"Reardon."

Groaning, Jack leaned back in his chair and eyed Maxwell, who'd come to parade rest beside his desk. "You drew the short straw, huh?"

"Not many wanted the job of taking down an ex-Special Forces." The HoS paused. "If required."

Hoping it was a good, I-don't-believe-you'd-betray-us pause, Jack forced a smile. "Hungry? There's cake in the tearoom." If Maxwell was going to be his personal bad smell, best to at least try to be civil.

Maxwell grunted and nodded. With the HoS trailing him at optimum tackling range, Jack went to the tearoom.

His cake was still on the table. About half of it was missing, a stack of plates covered in cream in the sink. The sight stopped him dead.

If his colleagues were willing to touch a cake meant in celebration of him, then they hadn't written him off just yet.

He and Maxwell had just sat down with coffee and cake when Maria Dioli burst in. She had been Jack's handler during the Valadian operation, and since his return, she and a couple of analysts had been wading through the intelligence Jack had discovered in the desert. Their main task was to find out why Valadian had gathered an army in central Australia. Jack and Maria had spent a lot of time together after his return, while she scoured him for every shred of information he'd had regarding Valadian. He hadn't exactly lied to her, but definitely hadn't told her everything.

She didn't look particularly angry with him at the moment. Rather, she seemed a trifle distracted, running hands through her unruly dark hair as she looked from him to the cake before doing a startled double take at Maxwell.

"Gerard," she said, her tone sternly neutral.

"Maria," he returned just as dryly.

That done, she sank into a chair next to Jack and ran a finger through the cream on the cake. "So, I got a call from McIntosh," she began, focused on Jack.

Jack braced for impact. "And?"

"Apparently I can expect some new statements from you regarding the Valadian op. That true?"

Here it came. He'd seen Maria go ballistic over incompetent work and had a good laugh at the hapless person in the line of fire. Karma certainly knew when to deliver a bitch slap.

"Yeah. Sorry."

Her dark eyes narrowed. Then she sucked the cream off her finger and went for seconds. "Because of Ethan Blade?"

Nodding, he dug a fork into his piece of cake, scooping out layers of sponge, jam, and cream. It tasted like cardboard. No. It was dry and gritty, like a mouthful of sand from the desert.

"Ethan Blade," she repeated, musingly. Then, "Ethan *Blade*. Shit, Jack, you must have balls the size of watermelons to bring in Blade."

Across the table, Maxwell snorted into his coffee and pushed his wedge of cake around the plate.

"I didn't bring him in," Jack told her. "He came in on his own."

"Because of something you did. I watched the footage from the foyer. He just stood there, let you pat him down and then inject him. I mean, shit!"

Maria's awe didn't make him feel any less rotten.

"From the tone of McIntosh's message, I guess she came down on you like the proverbial?" There was a dollop of cream on the corner of Maria's mouth.

Jack pointed to the offending smudge of white. "Two tonne."

"Shit." Maria swiped her tongue across the cream. "For what it's worth, no one on the floor thinks you're capable of a disloyal thought, let alone conspiring with someone like Blade." She carefully didn't look at Maxwell, though it was clear her statement was as much for his benefit as it was for Jack's.

A mouthful of cake stopped him from laughing madly. "Thanks," he finally managed. "And thanks for not being shitty with me for keeping it from you."

"Hey, I get it. If I had someone like Blade telling me to shut up or else, you wouldn't hear a peep from me about *anything*. Of course," Maria added, taking another scoop of cream as she stood, "if, when I read those new statements, I find something that could have finished this godawful operation six months ago, I'll be coming for you." She licked her finger clean, winked, and left.

Jack pushed away his plate, unable to stomach any more.

Maxwell mimicked his move. "Yeah, it's a bit too sweet."

The cake or Maria's support? If Jack hadn't rebuffed Maxwell all those years ago, would he be a bit more supportive now?

Jack eyed Maxwell. Regardless of the past, the man was all Jack had to work with.

"I don't mind the sweetness, actually," he said. "It's just not what I'm craving."

Taking a sip of coffee, Maxwell arched an inquisitive brow.

"There's this French patisserie called Gigi's on George Street. They do this salted caramel fudge I love. That's what I'd really like right now." Outright flirting would be laughed at, and deservedly. "I'd owe you."

Maxwell regarded him over the lip of his mug, expression guarded, then grunted. "It's that good?"

"It's that good."

"You *will* owe me," Maxwell promised.

Coffee finished, they headed down to the sublevels to observe McIntosh's interview with Ethan. On the way, Maxwell arranged for someone to get the fudge.

McIntosh and Ethan sat at the table in his cell, a plastic cup of clear liquid between them. It didn't look as if it had been touched.

"Aren't you thirsty, Mr. Blade?" McIntosh asked, tone politely enquiring.

He didn't answer.

"I promise it's not dosed with anything."

No response.

"All right. I'll leave it here in case you change your mind. Would you like to tell me why you came here today?"

Silence.

Jack winced. Ethan wasn't helping himself by playing mute. He had to know cooperation would be better than the alternative.

"I'm sure you're aware of the list of allegations against you, Mr. Blade. Not only here in Australia. We have extradition agreements with many of the countries where you've been indicated in various crimes."

If this bothered him, he didn't show it.

"Something made you decide to come in. Volunteering your surrender is a good start, Mr. Blade. It'll help us protect you. But only if you have something of worth for us." She gave him a suitable space to fill, which he didn't. "A man in your position is likely to have access to a lot of sensitive information. Is this why you surrendered yourself? Do you have something you wish us to know? Is it about Samuel Valadian?"

The questioning went on in this manner for another half an hour. McIntosh talked herself hoarse to no effect. All the while, Jack worried about Ethan's motives and, to a lesser extent, his mental state. He'd seemed all right in the foyer, but that was before Jack had destroyed whatever trust had been between them. Still, Ethan had known what would happen if he ever came face-to-face with Jack again. Could Jack be blamed for doing what he promised he would?

Finally, McIntosh changed tactics.

"Okay, Mr. Blade. How about you tell me what you want to get out of this? Protection? A pardon? Money?"

Ethan finally looked at McIntosh and smiled. The strangely innocent smile didn't reach his eyes, making the colourless orbs with their too-wide pupils all the more disturbing.

"Jack knows what I want."

McIntosh's shoulders tensed, only a fraction, but Jack saw it, which meant Ethan did as well.

"Jack's busy at the moment, so I can't ask him. Can you tell me what it is?"

"No. He'll get it for me." That smile again. "I trust him."

NINE **THEN**

"**W**e need to leave."

Jack sighed. Again, that "we," and he was starting to doubt it was the royal "we." He was lying on his belly, enjoying the warmth of the burning truck. Blade was right, but he was thinking sleep might also be right. The cleaning of the knife wound had sapped the last of his energy. He could barely work up the desire to wonder why Blade suddenly seemed to think they were in this together beyond the immediate situation.

"With the damage we caused the Ka-52, it will take them about an hour to get back to the compound." Blade was disassembling the Assassin X and tucking the pieces away in his overcoat. "Which means in half an hour he'll be able to mobilise more of his troops. He'll send a team back. They'll arrive within three hours. We need to be well away by then. It'll be dawn in another couple of hours, and we'll have to hide while they scout the area."

Again, Blade spoke sense. Jack really should care. He couldn't even trust in the Office coming for him. With his luck, the last location ping probably went off while he was still in the compound. Even if it had gone off here, before he killed his implant, it would take at least eight hours before they could get anyone out here. There was a very good reason Mr. Valadian had his compound in the square fucking middle of nowhere, and that was to stop people from sneaking up on him.

It didn't help that Blade was the reason he was here. Without the crazy bastard, his cover would still be solid. He'd be asleep in his warm bed. Possibly he could have found the intel mother lode within the next couple of days and gone home, at long last. He was sick of the desert. Sick of majestic sunsets and sweeping plains and sunburnt bloody vistas. Jack wanted to sleep in a bed big enough for his shoulders and not worry about falling out if he rolled over too enthusiastically. He wanted to run on pavement. To see a tree. A green tree. He wanted the hum of never-ending traffic to serenade him to sleep at night, not the distant howling of dingoes. He wanted to swim in the ocean. He wanted sand—*wet* Bondi Beach sand—in his arse crack and salt on his lips. What he wouldn't give to have a single piece of Gillian Golightly's salted caramel fudge.

"I did some recon before going to Valadian. I know a cave we can hide in. If we leave now, we'll reach it before dawn."

What would Blade do if Jack refused to move? Leave him? Shoot him?

Of all the information the Office had gathered on Ethan Blade, a firm physical description was not part of it. The only accounts they had were hearsay and third-hand stories. From such unreliable sources, he'd been described as a slender, dark-haired young man—such as the one with Jack right now—as well as a very tall, muscular blond and a stocky, dark-skinned bald man with missing fingers. Anyone who'd had a good look at the assassin was dead, or had a lot of incentive to keep quiet. Jack was a realist. He didn't think there were many people who could keep such a big secret. It was highly likely that when Blade decided he didn't want Jack around anymore, he would kill him. Which made Jack start to appreciate that "we" a little bit more. And if Jack was going to have any chance of not dying by Blade's hand, he would have to get to his feet, at the very least.

Groaning, Jack shoved himself to his knees. His splinted arm still ached, but it was manageable now. The knife wound stung from Blade's field surgery, but it was a clean, scoured feeling, which was better than the growing heat of infection. His T-shirt went back on. Bomber jacket over his shoulder, Jack stood.

Blade smiled encouragingly and set off, waving Jack after him. Jack wondered why the hell he was considering following Blade. The man would probably kill him at some stage. And yet he was here for Mr. Valadian. Which, if Jack couldn't get home with the intel, was about the best he could hope for. One way or another, Mr. Valadian would be stopped.

Tucking the Desert Eagle into the back of his jeans, Jack followed Blade.

They wound their way out of the field of battle, leaving behind about thirty corpses and the smouldering hulks of the two trucks. The scavengers would have a party until Mr. Valadian returned and took care of his dead.

Blade angled them to follow the ridge, and Jack trudged along behind him, studying the clear sky, finding the Southern Cross. They were heading southeasterly. With no idea where the torture shack was in comparison to the compound, Jack was firmly at Blade's mercy. Central Australia was big. And empty. Jack could have picked an arbitrary direction and died of dehydration, snake bite, or sheer loneliness before finding even a hint of human life. He might get lucky and find a dirt track. If the odds were truly stacked in his favour, he might even find someone driving along that long shot. In reality, though, it was him, Blade, the poisonous fauna, and a whole lot of absolute shit all.

The sky over the ridge was turning from black to satiny purple fringed in pale gold when Blade changed direction, heading over the rocky incline towards the ridge proper. Jack held back, watching the other man skip lightly over the uneven ground. Blade moved with the nimble, sure-footed ease of an experienced outdoorsman. How could he not, with those lean legs, narrow hips, and strong arms?

Crap. One sleepless night, a broken arm, and a piddly little stab wound and Jack was checking out the arse of an assassin with fuzzy-headed bemusement.

At the top of the scree, Blade stopped. He stood in the shadows of the ridge, overcoat drifting around his calves, looking both ways, up and down and then back at Jack. With a wave, he indicated they backtrack. While Blade scampered along above, Jack ambled over the relatively flat ground until the assassin stopped again. He climbed the final distance to the rock wall and vanished into a deeper shadow. A moment later, he reappeared, motioning Jack up.

By the time Jack reached the cave, he was thoroughly exhausted. His arm ached and his back was one big knot of tension. Squeezing in through the narrow opening, he half hoped Blade had outfitted his bolthole with a feather mattress and hot tub. Sadly, the light of the assassin's small torch illuminated a high-ceilinged, sand-floored space about half the size of the torture shack. The walls opened up briefly before narrowing into a tiny crawl space leading back further into the rock. There was the distinctive pattern of a snake track wriggling across the sand. Lovely.

Blade wedged the torch into a crack in the wall and removed his overcoat and jacket. "We'll wait out the initial search here. Feel free to sleep. I'll keep watch."

"What about you?"

"I'll be fine." He settled down by the entrance, balancing his Desert Eagle on an upraised knee.

"Right."

Jack took his own Eagle from the back of his pants and lay down, then pillowed his head on his jacket, gun held lightly in his left hand, resting on his chest. It was probably pointless wondering about Blade's intentions towards him now. Apparently, Jack wasn't destined to die by assassin just yet.

He dropped into sleep easily, a holdover from his service days. Soldiers learned to sleep when they could, never sure when they might have to get up and go. Still, he slept light and stirred when Blade left.

Bright light sliced into the cave from outside, meaning it was past midday and the sun at an angle to pour directly over the western face of the ridgeline. The assassin left his coat and jacket, taking only his Eagle and whatever else he had secreted about his body. He slid out of the cave without a backwards glance at Jack. After a couple of minutes, Jack rolled to his feet and went to the entrance. He cautiously looked out.

There was no sign of Blade, no sign of anything that had made him leave.

While it wasn't overly warm in the cave, the air drifting in from outside was dry and hot. The rocks outside seemed to vibrate in the heat, looking like a cooktop on high. In the distance, the flats shimmered with waves of superheated air; the world melted, beaten and forged into a deadly weapon by the unrelenting sun. The land out there would kill the unwary and unprepared as assuredly as a gun to the head. It just wouldn't be as mercifully fast.

Jack's mouth was dry, his throat scratchy with thirst. They'd have to find water soon. And, eventually, food. Right now, however, Jack wondered what Blade was doing. The man was clearly deranged. Was he prone to unpredictable actions? Jack snorted. Hadn't he just spent the night trying to keep up with Blade's unpredictability? He wondered what he wanted more—for Blade to return or stay away.

Two hours later he still hadn't decided, but Blade returned. He came out of the scree to the south. One moment, not there; the next, a lean shadow fell across the rocks before Blade appeared in its wake. Walking calmly, he approached the cave like a lost lawyer in his dress pants and button-down. He looked rather human and unthreatening with his shirtsleeves rolled up to his elbows, sunglasses on, and hair curling with sweat. Over his shoulder, he had two canteens of the style carried by Mr. Valadian's troops.

"You killed them for water?" Jack asked as Blade reached him.

"No. That would be counter to our purposes. Dead bodies would only prove our presence here."

Getting up to let him into the cave, Jack nodded. "Then how?"

"Human nature, Jack. People lose things. They forget where they put it, or it fell down behind the couch."

"Or it was stolen," Jack suggested wryly.

"Or it was stolen," Blade agreed with a small upwards curl of his lips. He handed a canteen to Jack. "Thirsty?"

Unable to stop it, Jack smiled, then regretted it. He was here to survive, not make friends. No matter how reasonable Blade sounded or acted, he was still the enemy. Right now, he might also be the enemy of Jack's enemy and therefore a potential ally, but definitely not one Jack should let himself get comfortable with.

He took the canteen and sipped. As much as he wanted to drown in the water, he didn't want to puke it all back up and waste what might have to last for days.

"You saw the search?" he asked as Blade settled opposite him.

"Yes. Standard procedure search pattern. They found our tracks but lost them when we hit the harder ground. A team passed the cave around midday. Didn't even look in this direction. They think we kept going, to get as far away as possible."

Taking another small drink, Jack shook his head. "Valadian has some very experienced ex-military types in his troops. They should be smarter than that, especially if they have any idea about you."

"And you. SAS, now working for a counterterrorism department. Should we look a gift horse in the mouth?"

Jack stared at him. "What do you mean, I work for a counterterrorism department?"

Blade's smile was wide and open this time. "Aha, so I was correct. You *do* work for the Office."

"I'm sorry?" Jack scrambled for some handle on the discussion. All he found was the old crutch of *he shouldn't know that*. It wasn't much support at all.

"The Office of Counterterrorism and Intelligence. Colloquially known as 'the Office.' I suspected but was far from certain. Samuel Valadian is a mobster, not a terrorist, after all. Organised crime, some high-stakes espionage, accumulation of troops and weapons, but no proven acts against Australia or your secret Meta-State agreement. However, he has the connections and alliances in place to make the shift into domestic terrorism all too easily. So, I suspected. As for you, Jack, all I knew was you *weren't* military intelligence. Since few other Meta-State departments would have the knowledge or ability to infiltrate Valadian's core group, I guessed you were an Office operative." He smirked triumphantly. "And you just confirmed it."

All true, and supposedly very, *very* secret information.

Neither confirming nor denying, Jack said, "You told Mr. Valadian you thought I was military intelligence."

"He didn't need to know the truth, just some semblance of it. That way, if things didn't go according to plan, he would go looking in the wrong place for you."

Jack blinked. "You used me, but at the same time, tried to protect me?"

"Of course. Your endangerment was never a goal, just a necessary risk."

"Did you really take down Nikonov just to convince Mr. Valadian he had a spy in the organisation?"

Blade looked up from holstering his Desert Eagle. "I wouldn't say 'take down' as such, but yes, I facilitated his capture by the FSB. At the same time, I spread rumours the leak that led to his capture came from somewhere in Valadian's territory."

Jack shook his head in disbelief. "All that just to get The Man on his own. Nikonov wasn't an easy target."

"Not as easy as some, no, but easier than Valadian." Blade checked his coat for damage. "He was also ticketed to a quarter million roubles."

"Fuck," Jack muttered. "I'm on the wrong side of this business."

"The money is nice," Blade said softly, not looking up from his meticulous work. "The freedom of choice is nicer, though."

There were enough tonal undercurrents in those words to sweep away the unwary. Tired and sore, Jack didn't have the mental capacity to navigate those waters, so he fell quiet. Unable to look away, he watched Blade go over the coat twice more before he was seemingly satisfied. The obsessive actions left Jack even more unsettled by this strange man.

Wish you were here?

He returned to the entrance. Outside, the world hadn't changed. Still hot, still hostile, still empty of help. If Jack wanted *any* chance at all of making it out of the desert, he needed Ethan Blade. He just needed to stay one step ahead of the assassin.

He snorted. Like he'd managed to do that so far.

"Is there a problem, Jack?" Blade asked.

A big bastard of a problem, but he said, "I don't get why the search team walked right past us. If I were leading it, I would have them scouring the ridgeline, looking for exactly this cave. I wouldn't care what I personally thought about the subjects of the search; I'd cover all possibilities regardless."

"Yes, but that's you. Not everyone is as thorough." Blade shuffled about behind him. "May I sleep, Jack?"

Turning, Jack frowned at him. "Why ask?"

Blade was lying down, head on his coat. "I wished to ensure you didn't object."

"Oh. I thought maybe you didn't trust me to keep watch." Or not kill him in his sleep.

"I trust you, Jack." He closed his odd eyes and, within moments, was asleep.

TEN

NOW

After submitting his amended reports, taking possession of two logs of fudge, and swapping Maxwell for an even more impossibly muscled security shadow, Jack wandered into one of the break rooms around midnight. His watchdog remaining outside, he found Lewis's second, Lydia, on the top bunk. She was curled around the pillow, so deeply asleep his arrival didn't even stir her.

After undressing down to his boxers, Jack lay on the lower bunk, hands under his head. In the dim glow of the light coming in under the door, he could just make out the frame and springs of the upper bunk. They felt about two inches from his nose, close and discomforting, as if they were about to fall in on him. He wished for the wide, impossibly high arch of a desert sky at night. The breathless expanse of stars curving over the world, jewels nestled on pillows of black satin. Out there, when he'd been walking towards that endless horizon, everything had felt so far away. Untouchable, unobtainable, inconsequential. As if nothing he did mattered.

If only that had been true.

Upstairs, the directors were meeting to discuss the situation. It was clear Ethan was only going to talk to Jack, and the upper echelons weren't sure if it was worth it. If McIntosh didn't back Jack, he'd never be allowed in the same room as Ethan again. It all depended on how much they wanted whatever the assassin might have to give them. Which in turn depended on just what Ethan hoped to achieve here.

With all the memories of those weeks returning, Jack's body was falling back into old habits. He dropped into sleep almost immediately, but woke when Lydia's phone buzzed, calling her back to the operations room. She mumbled apologies on her way out.

Jack grunted in what he hoped was a "no problem" manner and rolled over. Threat assessed and dismissed he fell back asleep the moment the door closed.

A *ping* from his implant woke him next time. Shocked by the immediacy of the sound inside his head, he shot upright, fumbling for a weapon and finding nothing. Dark-adjusted eyes scanning the break room, he breathed deep to ease the racing of his heart. Damn Ethan. Jack had just regained his equilibrium, and now he was jumping at shadows and reaching for a gun again.

Ping.

Jack groaned, then muttered, "Reardon."

"They're ready for you."

"Thanks. I'm on my way." He cut off the call and sat for a moment, elbows on knees, head hanging. Today wasn't going to be any better than yesterday. Why he thought it would be was beyond him right then. If history was to be trusted, he should never have expected otherwise. Birthdays. Fuck 'em.

A time check said it was 0537. Just about exactly twenty-four hours since he'd left home, thinking, despite the date, it would be a rather typical day. Head out to see Dad before work; come into the office feeling frustrated and angry, the usual issues after seeing his father; maybe a drink or two after work; a painful rendition of "Happy Birthday" and then home. He'd dared throw in the possibility of finding a companionable body to spend the night with. Never did the idea of seeing Ethan Blade again, of having to deal with the fallout of then, enter into his scenarios for how his day might progress.

Now he was expected upstairs to face whatever decision they'd come to.

Wish you were here?

Jack dressed in his slightly rumpled suit from the previous day, picked up his silent shadow at the door, and stopped by the toilet on his way upstairs. In front of the mirror he scrubbed at his teeth, pushed wet hands back through his tousled black hair, and dug the grit out of his eyes. He looked like shit. Drawn, red eyed, a decidedly grey undertone to his light-brown skin, ready to snap necks if he didn't get caffeine before attempting human interaction. There was no time for the niceties, though. McIntosh and her cronies were expecting him.

The halls of the building were empty but for him and his watchdog, their footsteps softened by carpet. Cool air cycled against Jack's skin, yet he couldn't help but feel like he was back in the desert, lost, on the back foot, heading into the unknown. The mix of dread and anticipation curled through his stomach, familiar and comforting for all that it made him sick with tension. He'd come to trust the sensation during his years with the Unit. It meant he was ready and alert, ramping up to that level of hyper-awareness needed to get him into and out of dangerous situations.

He took the stairs up two flights to the tenth floor and, at the door to the conference room, stopped, straightened his suit, brushed his hair back and, with a deep breath, knocked.

The door opened, revealing McIntosh. She stepped back and gestured. "Come in, Mr. Reardon." She at least sounded neutral.

While his watchdog remained in the hallway, Jack went in and took a moment to make a sitrep. Tasteful prints on one wall, a huge screen on another, floor-to-ceiling windows overlooking the harbour with its ferries and spreading wakes. High-backed leather chairs around the table. Each position had a small screen recessed into the tabletop, able to be pulled up, angled, and swivelled as needed. The vague lines of touchpads marked the smooth surfaces before the screens. Only one was activated, in front of the chair McIntosh resumed. Her fingers danced lightly over the keys, images and text flickering over her screen.

Around the table were the three Sydney Office directors. McIntosh from Internal Threat Assessment, of course; Glen Harraway from Intelligence; and lastly, Alex Tan from External Threat Assessment. He was McIntosh's opposite, looking outwards while she looked inwards.

Jack had never heard of a review meeting having all three directors in attendance—which could not be a good thing. This meeting was going to be three times as long and, most likely, three times as tedious. No matter the ideals behind the Office, it was a bureaucracy, and bureaucracies would do what they did best—drown the good work with red tape, endless forms, and committee meetings.

Shit. Jack was starting to sound like Ethan, now.

McIntosh waved him to a chair at the end of the table. "This is just a preliminary meeting, Mr. Reardon, to discuss the revised information in your reports on the Valadian operation. In the following days, we'll have more questions for you. I'm sure I don't have to remind you that your full cooperation during these initial talks will be beneficial during the official hearings, if it comes to that."

"Yes, ma'am." He sat, the queasy pre-combat feeling easing. The wait was over. He was in the thick of it now.

"As you are aware, the sudden appearance of the man calling himself Ethan Blade has caused quite a stir." McIntosh flicked her screen content to those before the other directors. "We have your amended statements, Mr. Reardon, but if you could once again tell us how you encountered Ethan Blade."

The constant repetition wasn't unexpected. Jack had been through enough operation reviews, objective assessments, and conduct hearings to be resigned to the endless recitation of facts.

Calmly and clearly, he once more explained his part in the Valadian operation, how his cover was blown, and the events of the torture shack. McIntosh and Harraway seemed keen on Jack's judgement of Ethan's actions during the fight at the shack, while Tan studied his screen. After nearly an hour and a half, Jack was about to move on to later events when Tan finally spoke.

"Why did you keep Omega Subject's identity from your initial report, Mr. Reardon?" he asked, fingers steepled over his touchpad. Tan was a small Singaporean national working in Australia as part of the Meta-State Agreement. He had grey swathes over his ears, stark against his black hair, skin a shade lighter than Jack's own mixed heritage, and a predator's mien. A lion sitting in plain view while the gazelles wandered by. Relaxed, bored even, but ready to pounce at the first sign of weakness.

Jack internalised a wince at the tag attached to Ethan. Clearly someone's idea of humour. "The man had saved my life. I felt I owed him. He'd also just taken out a vastly superior force. Anyone would have given him anything at that stage, just to keep him happy and themselves alive. I also told him that if I ever saw him again, I'd do everything in my power to bring him in. Which I did."

It went on in similar fashion for another couple of hours. By the time everyone seemed satisfied, Jack was hoarse and his head ached with the revelation of so many secrets—and still, he didn't tell them everything. If they didn't ask, he didn't say.

"Thank you for your patience, Jack," McIntosh eventually said. "I think we all have a clearer understanding of what happened. If we are ready to move on . . .?" She raised a questioning brow at the other directors.

It was a look Jack had been on the receiving end of countless times. Basically, she was only asking out of politeness, and any contrary opinions would be wrong. Jack did experience a little spurt of satisfaction as both Tan and Harraway agreed without hesitation.

"Right, our next point of discussion. How Omega Subject discovered us here."

Another hours-long grilling that went in endless circles. Jack managed to keep his temper under control even as his loyalty, intelligence, and training were dissected in painful detail. He simply kept reminding himself this would be nothing compared to what he would undergo if this mess escalated to formal hearings. Surprisingly, it wasn't McIntosh questioning Jack's anti-interrogation tactics or Harraway implying Jack was all brawn, no brains, that snapped his patience. It was Tan's occasional yet unsubtle intimations that Ethan wasn't *the* Ethan Blade.

"I'm sorry, sir," Jack said in the wake of Tan's latest insinuation, "but you clearly doubt who he is."

"Mr. Reardon," Tan said, "I honestly find little in your report worthy of any misconduct hearings. Your actions at the time of the events are, I feel, the best *you* could have done with the information available to you." Despite the supportive, if patronising, nature of Tan's initial statements, Jack felt like the man was about to pounce. "However, you appear to be unduly convinced this man is Ethan Blade, and while we have a man capable of serious damage in our custody, I see no real evidence he *is* Ethan Blade. Why are you so certain?"

It was a good question and Jack knew he couldn't answer it convincingly. He had to, though. "I saw him in action. He went up against thirty enemy troops and came out unscathed. He took me down, hand to hand. If anyone could be Ethan Blade, it's him."

"I think, son," Harraway said mildly, "that isn't what my colleague is questioning." Heading towards retirement, the Intel director looked like a genial grandfather—full head of salt-and-pepper hair, eyes that crinkled with the least provocation, and a personable management style. In his senior years, he had developed a laidback, nearly blasé attitude towards his job, but nothing got by him. "Perhaps there are other, less physical, reasons you believe Omega Subject to be Ethan Blade."

Jack squashed down a swell of guilt. "The psychology fits. He's a meticulous planner, highly intuitive, and has obsessive tendencies. Once he fixates on something, nothing stops him. Anything that gets in his way is removed without remorse." He suppressed a shiver at the memory of deliberately putting himself in Ethan's path.

"Any number of subjects fit that profile," Harraway said softly, as if letting Jack down gently.

"I know. There's also his knowledge of the hits attributed to Blade."

"Hardly top-secret information." Unlike Harraway, Tan didn't care about Jack's ego. His tone was dry and on the edge of condescending.

Jack pulled in a deep breath. "Yes, sir, I know. But there are things that we don't know. Things known only to the man who perpetrated the hits."

This caught Harraway's attention. He leaned forwards eagerly. "Such as?"

"Such as the US Marines in Colombia."

"We know those men were poisoned," Tan reminded them all.

"But not how." McIntosh turned to Jack. "He told you how it was done?"

Over the past hours, Jack had been under the microscope. His actions, his words, his thoughts, all cut apart and examined like a corpse on the autopsy table. However, right now, he finally felt as if he really had their attention. He resisted the urge to laugh.

"Well," he hedged. "Not exactly."

ELEVEN
THEN

They set out just after sunset, moving south. During his afternoon watch, Jack had seen no trace of the search party Blade had tracked earlier. Which didn't comfort him. It didn't seem possible, given that there were formally trained soldiers and officers in Mr. Valadian's army, that the cave had been missed. It was well hidden but not invisible to an alert searcher. Whoever was organising this search was acting like he knew nothing. Or, what he thought he knew was different than what Jack thought he himself knew.

He hadn't shared his thoughts with Blade. The other man certainly wasn't telling him everything. As much as Blade might assure Jack they were allies, it didn't mean he felt any sort of loyalty to Jack. Or that Jack should feel any towards him.

Hours passed in silence. Well, not true silence. A gentle breeze sighed through the stubby leaves of the scrub; a few hardy insects chirruped in the cold night; their shoes shuffled over rock and sand; dislodged stones clattered down the slope. It all had a dull, subdued feel to it, though. The vast space around them seemed to drink up the sounds—an empty sponge soaking up the spill of life, as if it had never been there in the first place.

It was an eerie sensation. During the day, the heat had made the world seem close and tight, like a fist curling around Jack and wringing him out. Now, the world had opened up, the jaws widening, preparing to swallow him whole. The flats spread out from the ridgeline, empty and endless. There was an almost hypnotic draw about all that open space, as if it offered the only chance of ever letting all his problems go so they'd drift away and get lost.

Over it all, a clear sky watched them through a million twinkling eyes, throwing the land into stark shades of silver and grey. The moon was rising, gibbous and bright, but cold, its light a mere reflection.

Jack recognised the moody thoughts for what they were and shoved them aside. He needed a hot shower, a cold beer, and a hard fuck. Not necessarily in that order, and possibly all at once. Fifteen months undercover, living and breathing a monumental lie, had left him tired.

Zipping up his jacket, Jack trudged after Blade, keeping his eyes on his companion's lean frame rather than the tempting emptiness to his right. He had to concentrate on getting through this alive. There was an implant full of information in his head that needed to get to the right people. Even if Blade succeeded in killing The Man, Jack had intel on his associates, weapons caches, and smuggling routes that was still valuable. And if Blade failed? Then Jack needed to know where Valadian ran to.

An hour or so off midnight, right around the twenty-four-hour mark into this madness, Blade turned them back towards the ridgeline and scrambled up the slope.

At the top of the scree, Jack saw what Blade had been aiming for. About thirty metres up the wall was a groove cut into the rock face by a long-dead creek.

"It'll take us over the ridge." Blade flexed his arms and fingers. "Save us a long walk or a higher climb. Do you think you can make it?"

"No sweat." If he hadn't had a broken arm. Still, he wasn't going to let that stop him.

"Good." Blade grinned. He didn't have his sunglasses on, exposing his strange eyes. The expression made them seem less weird, maybe a very pale blue if you were reaching for something normal to cling to. If anyone could be bothered to look past the incredibly long, thick, dark lashes. "Race you to the top?"

Jack wasn't given a chance to answer. Blade turned and, with barely a moment's consideration, reached for handholds on the rock face. He was several feet off the ground by the time Jack could swallow the sudden clot of confusion in his throat.

Shaking off the moment, Jack contemplated the ascent. He wasn't keen on rock climbing for work or pleasure. Jack had done it in training and the few times required on the job, but otherwise, if he could chopper up there, that was how he'd go.

He was hampered by the splint, his fingers unable to dig into small cracks with any sort of confidence, and any pressure on the wrist sent a spike of pain up his arm. It grew tiring after a while, forcing his way through the ache. The knife wound dragged on his other side, making reaching too high problematic. It all conspired to slow him to a crawl up the rock face, and it didn't help that his stomach had been cramping with hunger pangs for the past couple of hours.

He'd gone hungry for long periods during his time with the Unit, but had lost whatever tolerance he'd had for it over the last years. These days, if he missed a meal it was a colossal tragedy. Dinner the night before seemed a long way in the past.

Jack concentrated on the task at hand, forcing the hunger pangs from his immediate thoughts. He slowly and painstakingly made his way upwards. The burn in his left side increased, and he thought he could feel warmth creeping across the skin under the dressing. Fantastic. He'd opened the wound.

He kept an eye on Blade as they climbed, half to make sure he didn't try anything dodgy, half to watch for hand- and footholds. Blade sped upwards with stupid ease. His long coat billowed out behind him, looking for all the world like it would hold him up if he fell—residual wings on a fallen angel. Every now and then, Blade would stop and look over his shoulder, checking on Jack with a mix of worry and encouragement in his expression. It was hard to imagine him tearing his bloody way through twenty-five-odd enemy soldiers.

Everything from the night before had the sheen of distance on it already. A defensive mechanism, giving Jack the space to keep moving forwards without having to deal with the immediacy of the combat. It was getting easy to forget who he was with. Ethan Blade, the longest serving name on the John Smith List. Surely no one man could have done all the things attributed to Blade. Which the man above him had admitted to, sort of. He claimed no responsibility for the soldiers going missing in the Dashti Margo. Did that mean Ethan Blade didn't kill those soldiers? Or that the man with Jack now wasn't Ethan Blade?

Either way, the man calling himself Blade was an accomplished killer. It wouldn't pay to forget that.

At the top, Blade hauled arse over the edge and rolled out of sight. Jack scrambled up the last distance, not keen on losing sight of the man for too long. Who knew what was waiting for Jack out of sight?

It turned out to be an eastbound gully, which cut a gentle slope downwards, small-to-medium boulders cluttering the narrow space.

"This gully will take us down the back of the ridgeline," Blade murmured as Jack joined him. "Shortcut."

"And then?"

"We move north again. I have a stockpile of supplies a couple of day's walk south of Valadian's compound. We can resupply and then hit the compound."

Jack swallowed a snort of surprise. "Hit the compound? Two men against three thousand. You really must be Ethan Blade if you think that's doable."

Blade's forehead creased between his dark eyebrows. "You don't believe I'm Ethan Blade? Valadian told you, even."

"Don't get me wrong, your display at the torture shack was very impressive, and I guess somewhat convincing." Jack had no idea what suicidal impulse prompted the words, but between the questionable actions of Valadian's troops, the whole debacle at the shack, and the general over-the-top aspect of the Ethan Blade stories, he was starting to doubt a lot of things about the whole situation.

"Somewhat?" It was sceptical inquiry, not homicidal incredulousness, thankfully.

"Yeah. A lot of people are good in a gunfight."

"Truly, Jack?" Now it was injured disbelief. "I went against twenty-five opponents, and that's all you can say? Any gunman could have done that?"

Jack pressed his lips together. This was almost fun. "I guess not *any* gunman, but it's hardly a unique talent. What about that makes you Ethan Blade? I mean, your job, supposedly, was to kill Mr. Valadian and look how that turned out. We three were all alone in the shack together, perfect opportunity, and now we're having to walk across a bloody desert just so you can finish the job." Too late, he realised he may have gone too far.

Blade leaned away from him, eyes wide in disbelief. Then they narrowed and he shrugged, turning his attention eastward again.

"Killing Valadian wasn't the only objective. I am not responsible for your beliefs, Jack. I have no cause to lie to you, but whether or not you believe that is up to you. Can I at least trust you to help me track down Valadian?"

"Sure. It's in my best interests too."

"Thank you. I think we should keep going. Valadian may still have search parties out here." He started down the gully, clambering with barely a whisper over the rocks.

Jack wondered if he'd actually managed to penetrate the layer of crazy protecting Blade from reality. Probably best not to poke too hard, in case he did break through. He set off after Blade.

They'd gone perhaps fifteen minutes before Jack reached the top of a large boulder and found Blade waiting for him. He sat on the rock opposite, arms crossed, frowning.

"What?" Jack asked, looking around for something he may have missed.

"You don't believe me."

"Look—" Jack sighed "—if I turned up wearing a red suit and white beard, would you believe me when I said I was Santa Claus?"

"No. Santa Claus is not real."

Jack spread his hands in the universal *well-there-you-go* gesture.

"That's hardly proof, Jack."

"Neither is 'Mr. Valadian said so.'" Jack crossed his arms. "If it's that important, prove it. Tell me about the Marines in Colombia."

"One professional to another?" Blade smirked and got to his feet. Brushing down his arse, he surveyed the path ahead. "Guess."

Jumping from his rock to Blade's, Jack said, "Just tell me."

"Shall I give you a hint?"

"No. Tell me. Prove it to me."

"Ah, but I could tell you anything and that would be proof of nothing." Blade hopped to the next rock.

"Or, I could give you a feasible scenario and you could say that was it even if it wasn't." He jumped to a different rock, ahead of Blade.

Blade bounced past him, as if it were a game of checkers and he'd just snatched up two of Jack's pieces. "Also proving nothing."

"Except that you're a liar." Jack judged the distance, backed up, ran forwards, and cleared two rocks, coming to a shaky landing on the boulder next to Blade's.

"Or you have the mind of a professional assassin."

Jack rolled his eyes. "Or that I've been associating with one."

Blade's face lit up in a big smile. "You do believe me!"

"I believe you're an assassin, but are *you* Ethan Blade? That, you still have to prove." Jack kept going, suddenly enjoying himself.

Blade came alongside him quickly. "I'm not telling you."

"Fine. What's the hint then?"

"I knew you would see it my way." With a wicked tilt to his grin, Blade intoned seriously, "Your hint is this. What underrated commonality did the Marines all have in common?"

"That's it?"

"That's it." Blade snickered evilly and carried on.

"That is the world's worst hint, Blade." Jack scrambled after him. "They were a team of Marines. An easier question would be what they *didn't* have in common."

His only answer was an echoing laugh as Blade raced ahead.

TWELVE
NOW

"That's it?" Harraway asked, incredulously. "'What underrated commonality did the Marines all have in common?'"

McIntosh frowned as she considered it, and Tan, happily, looked just as stumped.

"Well?" the ETA director finally asked. "What's the answer?"

Jack chuckled. "I have no idea."

"And yet this is what convinced you that man is Ethan Blade?"

"Amongst everything else." Jack sobered. "I just know that whatever the answer is, it will stand up as proof."

None of the directors looked particularly convinced, but then they hadn't been there, hadn't witnessed Ethan in action. Hadn't felt the gut-deep, visceral reaction to his mercilessness. Hadn't experienced the man behind the assassin.

"We could argue for another year about whether or not our man is Ethan Blade," Harraway mused. "Short of matching him through DNA to one of his kills, we're never going to know for sure."

"Not even then," Tan interjected. "We have established that not all kills attributed to Blade are his."

The Intelligence director waved at Tan as if he were a rowdy youngster. "Regardless, according to the boy's testimony, hopefully complete and correct now"—he cut Jack a playful smirk—"the man we have locked up is an accomplished assassin. Even if he is simply operating under the guise of being Blade, he is very good at what he does. And a man in that position is likely to have information we can use."

Amongst the round of agreeing nods, Tan settled even further into his chair. "Then it appears we're all on the same page. The interrogation of Omega Subject will commence at once."

Jack fought down the instinctive reaction to the word "interrogation."

"Which brings us to the next item." McIntosh crossed her hands over her flat stomach. "Namely, negotiation of terms with Omega Subject. Usually we offer pardons in exchange for information. However, the subject is a professional killer. We have to consider the ramifications of releasing such a person back into the public."

Repressing a need to roll his eyes, Jack merely said, "He's not an uncontrolled psychopath. He doesn't kill for pleasure."

Tan steepled his fingers again and said dryly, "But he does kill for profit."

Jack swallowed the urge to bite back. "My point is that given the opportunity, Blade might surprise you."

Tan regarded him for a moment longer, expression unreadable. Jack didn't have a lot of experience of the man. The only other interaction of any significance was a job interview when Jack had been recruited for the Office.

Discharged, unemployed, and drifting, Jack had been headhunted by the Office. Courted, he sometimes joked. As such, he'd had some flexibility in where he ended up. His CV had been handed out to every division, and those interested had set up interviews. Tan had been the first taker, offering Jack pretty much anything he wanted in order to take a field operative position with ETA. Even without the benefit of any other interviews, Jack had refused the offer, and not just because the man had turned him cold with his calm description of the work and results he'd expect from Jack. Two days later, he'd met with McIntosh and had yet to regret the decision to join ITA.

Harraway cleared his throat. "Regardless of the outcome, any information gathered from him will have to be confirmed before anything can be granted." The Intel director sighed. "Which can take years, sometimes."

Christ. What had Ethan got himself into this time?

"The subject will have to give us something up front, in good faith," McIntosh said. "Once we have an idea of what he knows, we can begin to negotiate then. For now . . ." She turned to Jack. "I'm sure you know what we're about to ask you, Mr. Reardon. It's apparent

Blade will only interact with you. Of course, every interview will be monitored and behaviour patterns scrutinised."

Another piece in McIntosh's game fell into place. Less than twenty-four hours ago, Donna McIntosh had admitted she wasn't convinced of his fidelity to the Office and the Meta-State. Now she was trusting him with the sensitive questioning of an important subject. Was this just a test of Jack's loyalty? Or something more?

Jack wasn't an analyst. It wasn't his job to look for patterns. He just acted on what the analysts gave him.

"Well, son?" Harraway asked. "Are you willing to interview the subject or not?"

Jack wondered what they would do if he said no. He was sorely tempted to refuse, to see which way McIntosh turned, but decided against it. If he was going to work out what his director was up to, he needed more information.

"Of course. Anything to help."

"Will you require anything for the interrogation?" Tan asked.

Really disliking the man's continual use of that word, Jack shook his head. "No, sir. I already have everything I need."

McIntosh quirked a brow at him.

"A bribe, ma'am," he admitted. "Don't worry, Maxwell's already scanned it six ways from Sunday. Blade won't be able to use it for any nefarious means."

And if they believed that, then they hadn't been listening to his description of Ethan's skills.

He was dismissed then so the directors could argue in seclusion. Outside, his watchdog had morphed back into Maxwell.

"You really are a sucker for punishment," Jack said as they headed down the hallway.

"Yeah, and I like whips and chains, too," the HoS muttered sourly. "I have things I'd rather be doing than babysitting your arse, Reardon. Like paperwork."

"Hey, I was happy enough with the other guy. Feel free to send him back anytime." Jack smirked as he opened the door to the stairwell. "At least he didn't think Old Spice was the only cologne ever invented. Or is it the only one powerful enough to cover the smell of seaweed?"

"Not the time to be talking about someone else's personal hygiene, soldier." Maxwell added a pointed look up and down Jack's wrinkled suit. "Plan for today?"

"Right now, breakfast," Jack said, though he didn't really feel like eating. Not while he had a talk with Ethan hanging over his head. A potentially problematic undertaking at any time, but with McIntosh and the other directors watching for the slightest hint Jack was less than loyal to the cause? Queasy didn't begin to cover it. "Do you still smoke?"

Jack hadn't smoked in years. Had, in fact, only smoked while on deployment. The nicotine had become part of his pre-op ritual. Half a dozen chain-smoked just before going active. Outside of those times, he'd never craved a smoke, but if he missed it before an operation, he felt incomplete and dangerously underprepared.

"Not for years. Miller does, if that's your choice for breakfast."

Miller was two flights back up, sitting at his desk outside McIntosh's office. It was a flimsy excuse but good enough to convince Jack he didn't really need the nicotine.

"Coffee will do."

The eighth floor was buzzing with the usual workday chaos as Jack and Maxwell weaved their way to the tearoom. Lewis and Lydia were already in there, bickering over the last slice of birthday cake.

"But I'm hungry!"

Lydia slapped Lewis's hand away from the plate holding the lonely wedge of sponge, cream, and rather wilted-looking strawberry-half. "Cake is not breakfast food, Lew. Besides, it's a day old. Who knows what these slobs did to it overnight."

"I didn't touch it," Jack offered on his way to the coffee machine.

"I actually went home last night," Maxwell said as he sat at the table. He nonchalantly shrugged off three death glares.

While Jack waited for his coffee to trickle into a mug, Lydia snatched away the cake and handed Lewis an apple. The unit leader scowled at it, but bit in regardless.

"How'd the meeting go?" he asked when Jack sat opposite him.

"Same as usual. Endless repetition, couple of questions, and a 'thank you for now, mwhahaha.'" Jack cast Maxwell a sidelong glance. The HoS usually wasn't present for the asset-level dissection of these situations.

There were two nods of sympathetic understanding and one mildly raised eyebrow.

"Maria was here earlier," Lydia told Jack, wincing as Lewis crunched through the core of the apple. "Looking for you. She was wondering if she'll be given access to Blade."

"Omega Subject," Maxwell corrected.

"Eventually, maybe," Jack hedged. "He's not talking to anyone at the moment."

Lewis snorted. "So we heard. Apparently he won a staring contest with Tan last night."

Jack nearly spat out his mouthful of coffee, but managed to swallow it without choking. "Tan spoke to Blade?"

Giving Maxwell a wary side-eye, Lydia said, "Well, he tried. According to Maria it was a one-sided conversation."

"Yeah, for once, he didn't get *results*." Lewis snickered with a total disregard for Maxwell's presence.

The HoS merely gave him a withering look, then got up to get more coffee.

While Maxwell's back was turned, Jack leaned closer to his friends. "Did Maria say what Tan was trying to find out from Blade?"

Lydia shook her head. "She said she only saw some footage, no sound, but that Tan looked pretty pissed when he left the cell, too."

Jack suppressed a smile. Ethan could irritate a saint with nothing but politeness, and Tan was far from a saint. Of all the directors within the Office, Tan was the one with the biggest reputation for ruthlessness. He was the very embodiment of "the ends justify the means." While Jack had little experience of Tan personally, he had run afoul of the man's methods a couple of times. Namely ETA field operatives with job parameters so wide they were barely any better than the bad guys they were hunting, and anything short of open warfare on the streets in front of a dozen news cameras was retroactively approved. Basically, when Tan wanted something, he got it, with very little regard for the cost.

He probably would have gotten Jack when he offered him a job with ETA, as well, but for one very strong reason why Jack would never have accepted it.

"I bet," Lewis said, his voice lowered so much Jack had to lean even closer, "Tan's after something connected to the Valadian op. McIntosh got you inserted so quick no one else knew about it, and when Tan found out, it was like WW3 here. He claimed McIntosh's rash actions would endanger some of his own operations."

Lewis had a talent for intuitive leaps that proved correct, but this wasn't even a stretch for Jack to credit. Valadian'd had a lot of contact with criminal organisations outside of the Meta-State, and some of those organisations would be on Tan's watch list. Jurisdiction on such cases could get messy and usually required some level of collaboration between ITA and ETA. If Tan hadn't known about Valadian before Jack was sent in, that meant McIntosh had bypassed even more SOPs than Jack had initially suspected.

On top of that, if Tan had been so pissed off he'd abandoned his usually reserved attitude and confronted McIntosh openly, then whatever connection he had to Valadian had to be something very important.

While trying to work out what McIntosh's angle was, Jack now had to consider that Tan was involved in it all beyond sitting in on a review meeting.

THIRTEEN

THEN

"There's no other way," Blade whispered. "We'll have to take them out."

Lying beside him, looking through the night-vision scope from the Assassin X, Jack had to agree.

They'd continued their silly game down the gully, hopping from rock to rock, trying to outdo each other. Jack, happily, could jump the farthest. Blade, however, could make the tricky jumps with greater ease. After ten or so minutes of this, Jack had realised he was having a good time. His squad mates had laughed at him for running obstacle courses for fun. He preferred the courses that presented him with problem-solving tasks as well as physical challenges, and chasing Blade across the tops of scattered boulders had combined both aspects.

Then Blade had come to a stop, going still like an animal sensing a predator. Years working with a team had taught Jack to trust his fellows' skills and instincts. He'd immediately come alert, sliding into the deeper shadows on the walls of the gully. The Desert Eagle had settled into his hand with reassuring weightiness.

Slowly, Blade had moved forwards, forgoing the joyful bounds for a stealthy slink, disappearing into darkness just as Jack had. Jack waited, concentrating. The breeze had flurried, curling through the gully, bringing with it the scent of smoke. Lifting his head, he'd drawn in more of the smell. Not just smoke. His stomach had rumbled so loud he was certain it had given them away. There was definitely meat in there. Meat and potatoes. His mouth had watered desperately.

The most obvious conclusion was it came from some of Valadian's men.

Jack had crept forwards, noting Blade pacing him on the far side of the gully. After an eternity of excruciatingly slow movement, they'd come to the end of the gully. Before them was more flat land, a mirror image of what they'd left behind on the western side of the ridge. Except that here there was a small fire, dug into a pit in the ground. Four men lay around it, sleeping. Another two paced on sentry duty at a fifty-yard line. A darker shadow hulked behind the fire. It wasn't until Blade had passed over the NV scope that Jack had recognised it as a dune buggy, covered in a canvas to provide shelter for the men.

They'd been watching the camp for half an hour, tracking the sentries, detailing the landscape, and judging distances. It was impossible to sneak around them.

"We could wait here," Jack whispered, so close to Blade he barely had to give the words sound. "Going on yesterday's standards, they'll pack up at dawn and leave without searching the area."

"Maybe. We shouldn't trust to general stupidity, though."

"Probably not. We wait, see what they do. If they come in here, then we take care of them."

Blade studied the camp for several more minutes, then nodded. Wordlessly, they began to back up into deeper cover. They retreated past the point at which they'd first become aware of the search patrol, to make sure they were out of easy detection range.

Settling in to wait under an overhang, Jack watched as Blade began assembling the sniper rifle again, muffling the distinctive *click*s in the folds of his coat. Smiling, Jack had to admit the poncy thing was coming in handy.

"Don't laugh at my rifle," Blade said.

"I'm not. At least, not anymore. It performed better than I thought it would last night."

"Of course it did. You're just a weaponist, Jack."

Jack stifled a snicker. "A weaponist?"

"Like a racist, but against certain weapons."

"And you never met a weapon you didn't like."

"A couple, actually, but that was more personality differences."

"Hah! No. You're just a weapon slut. There's a difference. I'm a weapon monogamist." He considered that, then added, "Well, maybe a very limited polygamist."

"You haven't returned my Desert Eagle," Blade noted dryly.

"It's lonely out here and I'm a man with needs."

Blade scrunched his face against a laugh. His hands kept snapping parts together, though, working through muscle memory and long familiarity. When he was in control again, the assassin sat back, Assassin X resting across his knees. Hand out, he said, "Scope. And you're not comfortable with the Eagle. You think it's too big for our purposes."

Jack jerked in shock at having his private thoughts spoken aloud by this man. He didn't miss the "our," either. A progression on that "we," or an insinuation Blade thought they were on the same career path?

"Yeah?" Jack's attempt at blasé came off as slightly challenging. "If you know everything, tell me what pistol I prefer."

Blade regarded him with half-lidded eyes, as if assessing the real reason behind the question. "Show me your hands. Left hand, at least."

Cautious but curious, Jack held his hand out for inspection. Blade looked it over, turning it this way and that, curling his fingers, flexing his wrist. It was odd, having someone else touch him like this. Jack was not a touchy-feely person. Not because he was wary of people in his personal space—which he was—but more because, to him, hands were something intimate.

A lot of people paid no attention to what or how they touched, or just how expressive hands could be. A tender touch often said more than an entire speech. A slap expressed a deeper emotion than yelling. Reaching out to help or offer comfort or to give pleasure. Holding hands, a powerful image of solidarity. Flipping the finger, immediately satisfactory and insulting. A salute to show respect. Hands pressed together in prayer. Holding the scalpel that cuts out the tumour. A pat to reassure an upset animal. A final wave at the airfield to the soldiers departing on deployment. A silent signal for your squad mates to scatter, to find cover, to save lives.

On the other side of the coin, hands could kill, with or without a weapon, intentionally or carelessly. Jack had learned that very quickly in basic training.

Right now, Blade opened Jack's hand and pressed it to his, palm to palm, fingers aligned. The assassin's hand was slightly smaller, his skin paler. Jack contemplated the contrasts, fascinated as he always was by the different shades, by the definite line between his skin and Blade's. If he closed his eyes, those differences would be gone.

"Mm," Blade mused. "I would say . . . a Heckler and Koch. USP."

Jack took a moment to gather his thoughts. Hand still pressed to Blade's, he considered the similarities this time. Different colours, but sharing the same calluses, earned in the same way. Soldier, assassin. Both killed at the behest of another. Both were paid for doing so. Did Jack's belief he was doing it to protect his family and friends make it any more right? His sister didn't think so. From the moment he'd joined the army, Meera had been opposed. He'd believed she'd come around, that she'd just been reacting from grief. Dad had said she needed time to accept and understand. When Jack had been deployed for the first time, to East Timor, Meera had agreed to come see him off at the airport—only to be arrested for protesting their involvement in a foreign power's conflict. She hadn't called him an assassin, but "murderer" had rung in his ears throughout the entire deployment.

"Jack? Am I right?"

Pulling his hand back, Jack held out the scope. "Yeah. HK USP. How did you work it out?"

Blade smiled and clicked the scope into place. "Weapon slut, remember. I know them all intimately. It's easy to guess what a person would feel most comfortable with when you see their hands."

"Neat trick," Jack whispered.

"It rocks at parties."

Jack laughed silently.

There was nothing for it but to wait. Blade slithered out every now and then to check on the camp. Sentries changed, but little else did. The scent of cooked food kept drifting past, and Jack had the satisfaction of hearing Blade's stomach complain as well.

"I miss food." Jack moaned. "Like the thick, juicy steak I had last night. So good."

"For the right price, I can make it your last meal."

Jack frowned at him.

"Too soon for jokes? All right. I miss . . . wine. A sparkling Moscato. Or a rich, thick Muscat."

"Sweet wine? Never would have pegged you for one of those sort."

"I like a good cab sav, but it has to be *good*. Mostly, I have a sweet tooth."

"Honestly, me too. There's this patisserie I like, makes the smoothest, most delicious fudges you've ever tasted. Their salted caramel is divine. Perfect blend of sweet and salty."

Blade groaned. "I miss it too."

"You've never even had any."

Blade arched a dark brow at him. "How do you know that?"

"Well? Have you?"

After a moment, the assassin sighed. "No, I haven't. But," he added before Jack could smirk in triumph, "it is entirely possible to miss something you've never had."

It was said lightly, in keeping with the moment, so perhaps it was hunger causing Jack to imagine the hint of bitter undertone.

Real or fanciful, it vanished as Blade scrubbed his tongue across his front teeth. "Actually, I miss my toothbrush."

"With your tastes, I could understand that."

"Ha ha. But what I'd really like now is that buggy."

"Oh yeah, that would be nice."

"No, it would be *convenient*. *Nice* would be Raquel."

Jack goggled. "Raquel?" A girlfriend? Another assassin?

Blade smirked. "Yes, Raquel. A 1999 BMW Z8 Roadster. It took me a long time to restore her to her former glory. Most of that was tracking down the correct shade of blue paint. Interlagos blue. But she's a beautiful ride now. Races like a dream."

The only response Jack's addled brain came up with was, "You named your car."

"I've named them all, actually. Raquel is the newest, though, so currently my favourite."

"All?"

Which was an opening Blade had apparently been waiting a long time for. He launched into an obsessive recitation of his many cars, ranging from those Jack had a clue about—Camaro, yellow; Porsche, silver; Ferrari, red—to those he barely caught the model name of—Lamborghini Huracán, white; Maserati Quattroporte GTS, blue. Then he outlined various issues with restoring the older ones to pristine condition, admitting along the way he did all the work himself.

Most of it went right over Jack's head, and not just because he knew as much about cars as he knew about horses—how to steer them and what fuelled them, basically. It was more that as Blade spoke about his vehicular harem, he became animated. He smiled unconsciously, his hands gesticulated broadly, and his voice, already a pleasant husky timbre, got warmer. The man himself was simply more alive. More . . . human.

And that was where Jack's credibility dislocated.

Ethan Blade the assassin had been active for sixteen years, involved in work not suited for someone with a healthy conscience. Not at the beginning and certainly not after so long in a bloody, deadly game. It most definitely shouldn't leave a person so passionate about a topic that they talked excitedly about it for fifteen minutes straight. It shouldn't allow him to light up from the inside as if a fire had been unleashed in his chest. It shouldn't make him look young and innocent and completely honest. It shouldn't, but it did, and it made Jack reassess this odd creature with his lethal hands and small neuroses. It made him want to know more.

Finally, the assassin seemed to register the shocked expression on Jack's face. Sheepishly, he trailed off. "Sorry. I do tend to get carried away. It is very rare anyone shows an interest in my hobby."

Which Jack hadn't, really.

As if realising that, Blade laughed. In a more subdued tone, he said, "Of course, none of my cars would cope with the terrain out here. The buggy is the ideal transport for the desert." It carried the distinct tone of covering a lapse and being a distraction.

Disconcerted by the expression of humanity and his own wish to see more of it, Jack agreed. "Yeah."

What followed was a half-hearted attempt at making a plan to steal the buggy. They both knew it was hopeless, but it took them past the moment.

They fell silent. Somewhere on the flats a dingo howled. It was answered by the undulating chorus of its pack. They called back and forth for the better part of half an hour and eventually faded into the distance. Jack shivered, relieved. He didn't want to have to face a pack of hungry, wild dogs.

Blade went to check the camp again, and Jack considered the dark form disappearing into the shadows. He went over the conversation as he sat alone, looking for any hint it had been something other than two men talking shit. Not that he could see, or didn't want to see, perhaps. It wasn't that he hadn't expected Blade to be smart or have a sense of humour of some sort. It was that he'd never thought the man would be likable.

Crack!

Jack jerked to his feet, drawing the Desert Eagle.

Two more shots came in quick succession, followed by a frantic yell and then more shouts. Blade had been discovered. Even as he raced towards the camp, Jack had to wonder. Blade hadn't made one misstep so far. It seemed unlikely he would do so simply scouting.

Jack sidled around a large boulder and ducked into the cover of a smaller rock. Cautiously, he peered out. Three men crouched in the cover of the buggy, another lying under it, probably wounded, if not dead. Two bodies were sprawled at the sentry line. From his higher advantage, Jack saw no sign of Blade.

Damn it. Had Blade really bungled it? Or had this been his intention from the start? Six men, nothing for him to deal with. But they'd agreed to wait and see what the search party did.

And there was his problem. Trusting Blade.

No matter how open Blade seemed with his objectives, Jack couldn't know how much of it—if any—was true. Believing anything he said was a trap Jack couldn't fall into. Which made him question everything the man had said from that first word in the torture shack to right this moment, up to and including his prattle about the cars. Screw it. If Jack was that easy to fool, maybe he shouldn't be made a field leader when he got home. Probably shouldn't even have a job with an intelligence agency in the first place.

God. When had he become so stupid?

"Jack."

Twisting, Jack brought the Eagle up. Blade was pressed flat against a boulder just behind his position. He handed Jack the Assassin X and took off his overcoat.

"I need you to cover the camp," Blade whispered.

"We agreed to wait till morning." Jack couldn't keep the anger from his tone.

Blade stalled half in, half out of his coat. "They saw me. I had to act."

"Really? They saw you?"

"They fired first."

"Of that I have no doubt. You let them see you. You wanted to take them out right at the start."

"Yes, I did. We're on something of a tight schedule. A night's delay wasn't in our best interest."

Blade's calm words worked on Jack's doubts like the teeth of a saw grating over concrete.

"Neither is getting killed in some foolish fight that could have been avoided," Jack hissed. "Nor is alerting Valadian to our movements by leaving dead bodies behind. Isn't that why you *didn't* kill the search team yesterday? Or was that a lie? Did you kill them?"

Blade went still. Didn't blink, didn't twitch, possibly didn't even breathe. Those eerie white eyes pinned Jack to the spot and seemed to see right through him all at once.

Oh, God. This was it. He'd pushed too far, too hard. Jack just hoped that when they found his body, the implant was still intact.

Then Blade looked away and pulled in a deep breath. "I didn't kill the other team."

With absolutely no reason to, Jack found he wanted to believe him. He pushed that impulse down and, caution be damned, ground out, "Then why kill these men?"

It was a tense ten seconds before Blade managed, "The buggy—"

"Fuck the buggy. We agreed to wait."

"No." Finally, there was heat in Blade's voice, as if at long last he was actually expressing something real. "You wanted to wait. I allowed it because I thought it would make you happy." He snapped his arms free of his coat and balled it up. "And that was a mistake. As was being seen by the men down there."

"A *mistake*?"

"Yes, a mistake. I do make them, Jack." Blade's tone was both patronising and reproachful, as if he were angry with Jack and himself.

It had taken a while, and some heated provocation from Jack, but it was the recrimination he'd been expecting back at the torture shack. The "you screwed up by not blowing the chopper when I asked" in not so many words. And perhaps an admission Blade had revealed too much about himself to a potential target?

Blade checked on the camp. "Now they're getting in the buggy. If they get away and tell Valadian where we are, then this will all have been for nothing. I *need* that buggy."

I. Not *We*. An unconscious adjustment of his already perfectly settled webbing. A nervous tick, or something more? The implacable determination in his words implied a need beyond fast transport. Blade had fixated on getting the buggy, and anything in his path, Jack included, wasn't going to survive.

The deep chill of the night rushed into Jack's bones, banishing the warmth of his anger.

"Fine," Jack whispered. "I'll cover you, but that's it."

Blade barely acknowledged him with a terse nod before he faded back into the darker shadows, sublimating into the night.

Jack eased up to a rocky perch on top of a boulder. He didn't want to kill these men. Five minutes ago, he hadn't had to and he'd been good with that. If it had been a mistake Blade was seen, fair enough. If he'd revealed himself on purpose . . .

Jack wriggled into position, putting the rifle to his left shoulder. The circle of green-highlighted world came into focus as he breathed out slowly. One man was in the buggy already, one was dismantling their shelter, and the last one was scanning the space around them, looking for their enemy.

He could take them now. Three in close proximity, better odds than last night. His finger moved over the trigger. His doubts about just why this was happening stopped him, however. Blade had made the mess; he could get them out of it.

In the scope, the man finished pulling the canvas free of the buggy. He left it on the ground and jumped onto the running board of the vehicle.

"Come on," he yelled, waving to the sentry.

The sentry turned to look at him. A dark shape reared up from a patch of spinifex. A swift jerk of his arm and Blade slit the sentry's throat. To the sounds of stunned shouts, the assassin flipped the knife and tossed it. The blade sank to the handle in the driver's side. He grunted and slumped over, still moving, struggling to haul himself out of the far side of the buggy.

The last man shouted and opened fire on the assassin. Blade dove to the ground and rolled under the barrage. He came up in a fluid move, leaping and spinning, and kicked the gun from the man's hands.

Valadian's man had some training in hand to hand, but not enough. Not one of his punches landed on Blade, his kicks swinging through empty air as Blade danced around him. It felt like the fight went on forever, but it was over quickly. Blade's hand darted through a gap in the man's defences, and he jammed his stiff fingers into the man's throat.

Jack watched through the scope as the man crumpled to his knees, neck convulsing around his crushed windpipe, mouth working silently as he struggled for air. Sick, Jack aimed and was about to fire when Blade broke his neck.

Blade walked away from him. It took all of Jack's control to take his finger off the trigger as he followed the assassin with the scope.

The driver hadn't made it far. He was already dead, so Blade pulled his knife free, wiped it off on the body's clothes, and tucked it into an ankle sheath. Leaving the dead man with as little regard as he had the other, Blade returned to the buggy and dragged an appreciative hand across the roll bars. Turning towards Jack, he smiled, content now he had what he wanted.

"I don't need the armour, ma'am." Jack nodded to the thin body armour he'd worn the day before.

"You just spent the morning telling me how proficient a killer this man is," McIntosh reminded him.

"And nothing short of not going in that room with him will keep me safe. Armour or not, if he wants to kill me, he will."

His director pursed her lips. "Do you think he wants to kill you?"

There had certainly been times Jack had thought Ethan would kill him: in the torture shack; after the incident with the search party; in the cave; at the compound. Then there was the very real possibility someone had put a ticket on Jack, and Ethan was here to make a profit. Maybe he'd name whatever fancy car he bought with the money after Jack. No. Jack was flattering himself. He'd be worth a hot tub, maybe a pool at most.

Supressing a snicker, he shook his head. "I don't think so. Not enough return on it. Besides, he could have done me in the foyer and had an easier escape of it."

"I suppose. In case you were wondering, latest intel shows no tickets on you, Jack."

A little of the tension eased in his shoulders. "It is good to know." Picking up a small paper-wrapped log and putting it in his pocket, Jack smiled at McIntosh. It felt hollow and fake. Mostly because it was. "This is it."

"Good luck, Jack."

"Thank you, ma'am."

The walk to the cell was a short one, and Jack hadn't managed to get any thoughts straight by the time the guards came into view.

They patted him down as thoroughly as he'd patted Ethan down, one of them discovering the small package. The guard unwrapped it and cocked an eyebrow at Jack.

"It's a bribe," Jack said flatly. "It's already been approved by the HoS. Check with him if you want."

Maxwell had been given a break from shadowing Jack while he was in the bowels of the building. Security down here was nearly impossible to bypass without lots of explosives.

The guard did check and when the all-clear came back, the log was returned.

The other guard turned to the cell door. Beside it was a small screen displaying the room beyond. Ethan sat on the bed, legs crossed, eyes closed, statue-still.

Depressing a button, the guard spoke into a com. "Please go to the wall opposite the door. Spread your legs and put your hands on the wall."

For a moment, Ethan didn't respond. Then, just as the guard was about to repeat the instructions, he moved. Deliberately slow, the assassin did as told. They waited a full minute, and then the guard punched in the code to open the door.

It retracted with a quiet *whoosh*, and Jack stepped through before he could think twice. It closed before he could rethink his policy on not thinking twice, locking him in the room with Ethan Blade. He didn't move from the door, waiting to see what Ethan would do.

The assassin remained in his position against the wall. Jack considered seeing how long it took to get a reaction, then decided against it. Ethan could out-patience a saint.

"You can move, Blade."

"Thank you, Jack." He turned, an amused smile on his lips, eyes half lidded against the glow of the lights. "I'm glad they finally agreed to let you talk to me. I have—"

"Uh-uh." Jack had to get control of the situation before Ethan even had a chance of compromising them. "First, let's make things formal." He nodded to the table and chairs.

"Oh, of course. It would be a shame to upset the legal department."

They sat and Jack realised this was the only time they'd sat at the same table, like any other acquaintances. Like friends? Of that he wasn't sure. Wasn't sure he ever wanted to be sure. How many times had he come close to thinking he could like this man, then had that feeling ripped apart in some gruesome manner? Yet, every time it'd happened, he'd fallen right back into the same trap. Wasn't that the definition of madness? Doing the same thing over and over and expecting a different result.

He took a deep breath and began. "This and any subsequent interviews will be recorded—video, audio, and bio-data. Everything you say and do will be on permanent record with the National Archive and will be withheld from any statute of limitations regarding any information you may pass on, as well as the mandated release of private government records. Please state for the record you understand what that means."

Without hesitation, Ethan said, "I do."

"Also, anything and everything you say and do *will* be admissible in any court in Australia. Do you understand what that means?"

"Yes."

"Please state your name, age, and occupation."

"Ethan Blade. Thirty-two. Assassin."

"Please define 'assassin' in your own words, for clarification purposes."

Ethan smiled, tolerant and amused. "People pay me to kill other people."

"Mr. Blade, could you please state how you came to be a guest of the International Security Office." Since the Office didn't officially exist in public records and the Meta-State it operated under was an invisible entity, they used ISO as a cover for most of their intelligence-gathering actions.

Thankfully not bothering to tease Jack about all the secrets, Ethan looked around the cell pointedly. "Guest?"

Jack pressed his lips together. "Just tell us how you got here."

"Taxi. I was going to walk, but it was too warm out."

Jack raised an askance brow.

"I detest public transport for obvious reasons, and I was hardly going to bring my own car. I had no idea how long I might be detained and didn't want an exorbitant parking fine when I was finally released.

Besides, my local car is an Aston Martin. As if I'd leave her on the side of the road." He shuddered delicately. "What if they towed her?"

"Blade." A hint of impatience leaked out in Jack's tone.

"You never did appreciate my love of cars, Jack." Ethan heaved a long sigh. "I voluntarily surrendered myself into the custody of Jack Reardon of the International Security Office. It was entirely my choice. No one coerced or forced me. I am here willingly, to impart information I feel might be helpful to the security of Australia. Contrary to popular belief, I am not a heartless monster."

Jack gave him a cautioning look. "We're not interested in popular opinion, Mr. Blade. Just the facts."

"Aren't we all, Mr. Reardon."

Before things could get any more tense, Jack reached for his pocket. "I have a gift for you," he said, both as a warning and an announcement.

Ethan smiled. "I didn't get you anything."

"I know." Jack took the wrapped log from his pocket and set it on the table.

Eyeing it carefully, Ethan held back. "Is it . . .?"

Jack nodded.

His face lit up with a delighted grin. "Jack, thank you." Slowly and reverently, Ethan peeled back the waxed paper and revealed a short log of creamy brown fudge. Its top was covered with scattered flakes of salt. He licked his lips, fingers hovering over the confectionary as if scared it might disappear if he touched it.

"Go on," Jack murmured. "I didn't get it for you to drool over. Try it."

"Hmm. No knife to cut it."

"Jesus. Just take a bloody bite."

Ethan frowned. "Wouldn't you like to share it?"

Did he wonder if it might be dosed? Should Jack take him up on his offer and prove otherwise? Or should he simply put his cards on the table?

"It's not drugged, Blade."

Eyes widening, Ethan gaped at him. "I didn't think it would be. Taint something you love when gas or drugged water would do the job so much better? Have some faith in my reasoning capacity, please."

"You're right. Sorry. In that case, thank you but no. I already had a log to myself."

Ethan considered him narrowly for a moment, then relaxed. "Of course you did. I should have known you wouldn't share, Jack. In that case." He picked up the fudge and licked all along it, before taking a small bite from one end.

Jack kept his amusement off his face, watching as Ethan tasted the fudge.

The assassin sat for a moment, and then his eyes dropped closed and he slumped back in his chair. He didn't chew, just let the smooth substance melt in his mouth, no doubt spilling sweet and salty in perfect measure across his tongue.

"Well?" Jack couldn't help himself. He had to know.

Ethan swallowed, licked his lips, and finally opened his eyes. "You were right."

"Say it."

Clearly trying to hold back a smile, Ethan conceded. "It is the best fudge I've ever had."

"Now that you've admitted that, let's get to business. Why did your surrender yourself?"

Ethan carefully rewrapped the fudge and put it aside, but kept one hand close to it, as if in case Jack meant to take it away. "As I said before, I have information I think you might find useful. I am aware of your policy of trading pardons for information."

As expected. "You are aware the ISO is only able to address criminal actions taken within the borders of Australia? Any illegal acts performed outside of our jurisdiction are not submissible."

"Naturally. I may consider applying for political asylum. It depends on how the negotiations go."

Was that it? He was only here to share information? Jack couldn't bring himself to believe that. If he had another reason for showing up here, Jack was sure Ethan would find a way to tell him. Hopefully.

Resigned to playing the game, Jack said, "All right. Before any negotiations can begin, my superiors need something to prove you're on the up and up. Can you give us something relatively easily checked that might be of interest to us?"

Ethan sat back, head tilted towards the ceiling, eyes narrowed to mere slits. "Hmm. I do have something regarding Deputy Secretary Garrett of the Office of Transport Security."

Jack worked to keep his expression blank. John Garrett was part of Lewis's current operation. "Which is?"

"The man he's been meeting with over the course of six months is a high-class escort. Deputy Secretary Garrett thinks he's in love. He's actually being rather professionally seduced into giving inside information on upcoming changes in Australia's maritime security measures. The escort is working for Natport, a rather unimpressive import company."

It made sense. If Natport got hold of the new schedules and plans, they could easily circumvent them for any number of nefarious reasons.

"An escort?" Jack frowned. "That man has been under surveillance for nearly two months. We have yet to make a definite identification on him."

"I'm not surprised, Jack. The man isn't from here. He's technically a Spanish citizen, but generally works out of South Africa. He's more spy than prostitute. His fee rivals my own. Maybe if I were prettier I could branch out."

Silently warning Ethan off that path, Jack said, "You seem to know a lot about him. Got a name?"

"I have *a* name. Antonio Amado. I doubt it's his real name."

Jack snorted. "Me too. Isn't '*amado*' Spanish for 'love'?"

"'Beloved,' actually. It is a trend amongst the community, after all."

"Yeah. *Blade.*"

"I will take whatever advantage I can get. Will this information be enough to prove my good faith?"

Jack stood. "We'll have to check it out first. As soon as I know, I'll be back."

"I look forward to it."

At the door, Jack turned. "Don't eat the fudge all at once. The food here is pretty grim."

Ethan smiled. "Good advice. Thank you, Jack."

The intercom buzzed. "Please go to the wall opposite the door. Spread your legs and put your hands to the wall."

Complying, Ethan gave Jack a parting wink.

The door swished open.

"Don't go anywhere," Jack couldn't help but say as he stepped out.

The door shut on Ethan's laugh.

FIFTEEN — THEN

Along with the remains of the steaks and potatoes, there were protein bars, dried apples, and hydro-lyte. Jack munched on a bar while divesting the dead of their weapons. He'd taken a moment before entering the camp to put his concerns regarding Blade's actions—both ethical and psychological—into a drawer in the filing cabinet in the back of his mind. The poor thing was filling up fast these days. Compartmentalisation was essential to surviving war, and Jack had always been good at it. It was the decompressing afterwards he sucked at.

As if understanding Jack's feelings on the matter, Blade kept his distance. He rummaged through the cargo in the buggy, tossing aside equipment he had no need for, lightening the load. He looked like a kid on Christmas who'd received everything on his wish list. If Jack hadn't witnessed the cool, methodical killing of three men, he would have been amused by Blade's gleeful mutterings. He had to keep reminding himself it was an act he couldn't fall for.

Jack found a variety of handguns, knives, and two rifles. He stacked them all by the buggy, assuming Blade would want them. Amongst them was a single Glock 17. Not his preferred weapon, but he was more comfortable with it than the Eagle. Still, the Eagle would be staying with him until Blade asked for it directly.

Dawn was flirting with the horizon when Blade was satisfied with the buggy. The weapons were loaded in the back, along with an esky holding the food. While Blade fussed under the bonnet, Jack got behind the wheel. When he adjusted the seat for his long legs, the knife wound pulled sharply.

Jack sucked in a deep breath, the pain sudden and eye-watering. There was a burst of heat around the wound. Damn it! Bleeding again.

"What are you doing?"

Blade's unexpected voice made Jack jump, stretching the wound. The pain shot inwards, spearing his kidney and drilling into his spine.

"What the hell does it look like I'm doing?" Jack snapped.

"Getting ready to drive my vehicle."

There was no hostility in Blade's tone, but Jack was in such pain the words alone were goad enough to not regret a dose of "fuck you," even considering whom he was giving it to.

"Why is it *your* vehicle?" He growled the words out between the pulsing throbs in his side. It hadn't been lost on him the real reason these men died was for the buggy. He'd be damned if he'd let Blade be rewarded for the unnecessary kills.

"I did all the work for it."

"Work? How much do you get paid for killing six men just doing their job?"

Eyes narrowed, Blade regarded him with a level of intensity that challenged Jack's anger. The fact the assassin's hands were empty meant nothing. With or without weapons, the man was deadly.

Blade made a soft, derisive noise in the back of his throat. "And how much did they pay you to kill soldiers in Afghanistan? Weren't they just doing their job?"

"Oh, no you don't. You don't get to compare honest soldiers with yourself. At least we were killing for a good cause."

"Honest? Good cause? Do you really believe that, or are you just being an obedient little sheep and repeating what your COs told you to get you to jump out of the plane behind enemy lines?"

"Holy shit. When did you turn into my sister? I got enough of her bleeding-heart rhetoric back when she used to talk to me! I don't need it from some heartless fucking monster, as well."

The silence that followed was as cold as the night had been. A shiver crawled down Jack's spine, contrasting with the sweat beading on his forehead. The roiling anger, the doubt about everything that had happened in the last thirty-six hours, boiled his blood. Facing off against Ethan Blade was insanity. Yet, here he was for the second time inside an hour. Not a great life-plan on anyone's measuring stick.

As the quiet stretched out, Jack's fiery anger gave way to the growing ache in his side. It seemed to be burrowing in, like a nesting mouse.

What had he done? Pissed off an unstable professional killer while he wasn't in fighting trim. Sore and hampered by a splint, Jack stood less than a snowflake's chance. He dropped a hand from the steering wheel, hoping like shit he could pull a gun before Blade moved.

But Blade didn't advance. Jaw tight, eyes narrowed, he dragged his gaze off Jack with all the effort of crowbarring open a sealed lead box. Fingers flexing, he rolled his shoulders and said, "At least I get to pick my targets," so quietly Jack barely heard it. Then he walked around the back of the buggy and climbed into the passenger seat.

Jack eyed him as he buckled up his harness. What was this? Reprieve due to lack of interest? Or had Blade filled his vehicle-related quota for the day?

God. Why was he worrying about this? If Blade wanted him dead, he'd be dead. It was just that Jack had no idea why he was still alive.

"What were you doing under the bonnet?" Jack asked tersely.

"Disabling the GPS tracker."

"Okay."

There was no key for the buggy, just an ignition button. Jack jammed it into the console so hard it stuck. The engine started with a hiccup and then settled into a low, level rumble.

"Well?" Blade asked when they didn't go anywhere.

Hands gripping the steering wheel, Jack swallowed the lump of anger and sour doubt lodged in his throat. "Where are we going?" It bit hard to have to ask.

Blade snorted. "North, for now. Follow the ridgeline."

"Right."

Jack stomped on the accelerator and the buggy jerked forwards, tyres kicking up arcs of dust and rocks before catching traction. Jack slewed the vehicle around, then pointed them northward and depressed the pedal even further. The buggy bounced across the rough ground, engine whining as Jack abused it out of a sense of misplaced anger.

Mouthing off at Blade was not healthy. Men had died for the sake of this stupid dune buggy. Sure, there was a high probability they would have tried to kill Jack had they found him, but that wasn't a certainty until it actually happened. They were dead before they'd had the chance to make a move either way, all because they had this buggy—and Blade had wanted it.

The slowly brightening landscape blurred past in a streak of unrelenting brown, red, and grey. A small mob of kangaroos scattered in a chaotic burst of high bounds. The buggy jounced over rocks and skipped across holes and ditches, its suspension tested to its limits, and the engine strained until the whole frame of the buggy was shaking.

Blade had killed them without remorse or a second thought. For this buggy.

The sun rose over the horizon, and waves of heat rolled across the land, folding up the open expanse of the night until walls of hot, hard air towered over Jack and the narrow beam of the buggy's trajectory.

Blade put on his sunglasses and leaned slightly to the side. The wind caught his dark hair, flinging sweat-greasy locks back from his pale face. He slouched in the bucket seat, legs splayed in the footwell. A small smile played across his lips.

Fine for him to be happy. He had his fucking buggy and six more confirmed kills.

As the sun got higher, so did the temperature. There was only so much cooling speeding through the burning air could accomplish, which lessened the longer they barrelled across the barren land. The heat seemed to be crawling up through the tyres, into the chassis, and through the seat to claw at Jack's back. Sweat soaked his shirt. His hair was plastered to his scalp and neck in black curls. Despite drinking the hydro-lyte, his head throbbed and his spine ached from the constant jarring. Yet he didn't slow down. Couldn't stop. Those men had died, and it had to be for something other than Blade's madness.

"We should stop soon," Blade said, voice raised over the buzz of the engine. "It's getting too hot."

"Thought you had somewhere to be."

"We've already made up for the delay this morning. What good will the buggy do us if you burn out the engine?"

Right. That was all Blade cared about.

Jack tried to let it go. Lingering over the events of pre-dawn wasn't helping him at all.

His amazing compartmentalisation skills seemed to be failing. The filing cabinet was overfull, bursting at the riveted seams with fifteen months of witnessing the operations of a high-stakes mobster. But it had been more than just watching. Jack had done his fair share of contributing, with a smile and a "thank you, Mr. Valadian" at every opportunity. Raids on other illegal operations and military establishments. Guarding business transactions that funded the whole campaign, standing in on meetings between The Man and his associates. Hauling away associates Mr. Valadian no longer had a use for. The longer Jack did these things, the more he was trusted and the more things he was asked to do. Bigger things, worse things. Things like shooting Link Rindone through the head. All the while thinking he should be on the other side of the equation. His tolerance and patience wearing down over time, until it was hard to remember why he was going along with it all, why it was important he *not* pull a gun and just start shooting them all.

And here he was, with a man who seemed to have never understood why it was important to not pull a gun and just start shooting.

What was worse? Blade's lack of a conscience? Or the fact Jack had been feeling more and more detached from his?

"Jack?"

Jack shook his head, focusing on the landscape ahead of him. Nothing had changed. Empty and dry, life bleeding away under a sun that aimed to kill. Assassin in the seat beside him. Fifteen months of hard, terrible work made worthless if they didn't catch Valadian.

"Fine," Jack muttered and let the buggy slow down.

They stopped by a large patch of scrub bush and strung the canvas up between buggy and vegetation. The space it shaded was big enough for one of the dual-purpose sleeping bags from the search team kit. Blade spread it out, cool side up.

"Would you like to sleep?" he asked Jack. "I'll take first watch."

Preparing the little camp had reignited the knife wound, and it throbbed like a fresh brand, burning through layers of flesh to sear the muscles beneath. Jack gritted his teeth against the pain. "I'm fine. I'll take the watch."

"As you wish." Blade settled on top of the sleeping bag, sighing as the cooled, padded material moulded around him. "I'll sleep for a couple of hours. Then we'll switch."

"Whatever." Jack rummaged in the esky and pulled out a bottle of hydro-lyte. Raspberry flavour, not his favourite, but he suddenly felt too weary to look for another one. Maybe he should have taken second watch.

He settled into the buggy, facing outwards. The vinyl was hot under his arse, but not as hot as the ground would be. He drank, wanting some relief. Any relief. After a while, he pulled his shirt off. It didn't help with the heat, just exposed more skin to the searing air. He fanned himself with his shirt, then tied it around his head, a desperate measure to keep the sweat from blurring his eyesight. Gingerly, he touched the dressing on the wound. It was hot and damp, but what wasn't right then?

He took another sip, realised his bottle was empty. Tossed it into the back compartment.

The sun had settled directly overhead, burning the air with white-hot rays. Jack got another of the sleeping bags and wrapped it around his shoulders, cooling side in. The touch of the material on his heated skin was better than anything he'd ever experienced. Better even than all the accumulated sensations of all the blowjobs he'd ever received. How long had it been? More than fifteen months, that's for sure. The last one had been after the wind-up of his last operation, in New Zealand. The Maori with long hair he could curl around his fists, skin a deep, glistening brown. Jack had lost himself in the contrasting shades of skin, his half-Indian and the full-blooded Polynesian tones. The dark fingers curling around his hip, gripping his dick so he couldn't thrust too deep into the man's accommodating mouth. Not the best technique, but the visuals had been more than enough to tip Jack over quick enough to disappoint his helpful friend. He'd had better blowjobs, but it was the most recent, so it was right up there.

He snorted. Like Blade and his cars.

Damn, it was hot. He shrugged off the sleeping bag, shoving it away from his sweltering skin. Sweat rolled down his face and chest.

He hadn't sweated like this since . . . Cambodia. That godawful trek through the Cardamom Mountains. Rainforest, wet season, hot, humid, and a gang of human traffickers. Still, better than the other goddamned forest they'd been sent to. Jack shivered.

When had it gotten so bloody cold? Jack ripped his shirt off his head, pulled it on. Scrounged until he found his jacket and put that on as well. Still cold. He reversed the sleeping bag and curled it around him. His skin was damp, his clothes clammy. Just as they had been during that whole fucking job in India.

The Chota Nagpur plateau in Jharkhand, eastern India, in the wet season, and even in the rare moments it wasn't raining, everything was still soaking wet, including the SAS squad trying to move silently through the trees. The trees, nothing but trees all around them and Nigel's constant cursing of a clear line of sight.

"Can't see anything for the fucking trees."

Jack uttered a quiet, bitter laugh. He'd been happy to finally get to India, to confront those who'd torn his life apart. Hunting and eliminating Maoist insurgents was the ultimate goal of his service career. He'd waited so long for this moment, and now it was here, he hated it. Hated the near-constant rain, closed-mouth locals, and intelligence that had grossly underestimated their enemy's abilities. The insurgents were too bloody good at hiding, at striking out from cover and fading away before they could be caught.

Except . . . this wasn't right. This wasn't Jharkhand. It wasn't a spongy trunk at his back, and it wasn't clogging soil sucking at his boots. It was rock and sand and a heat so dry it felt as if it came straight off a blast furnace.

This wasn't India, wasn't the worst mission of his entire career. It was . . . somewhere else. Some*thing* else . . . so why was Nigel right there, shouting at Jack to dive for cover when the ground exploded right beside him?

Jack hurled himself sideways. "Down!" He rolled and came up on his knees, Austeyr rifle at the ready. Figures appeared out of the trees . . . *out of the scrub* . . . all around him. Instantly he opened fire, his squad a bare second behind him . . . but they didn't. It was just him against the enemy . . . just him against . . .

"Jack!"

This was wrong. It was a whole band of Maoists, not just one man. A whole group of insurgents who had opened up on his squad, scattering them into the trees where the bastards had waited to spring a dozen little ambushes. Not just a single guy approaching slowly with his hands raised. No. Not just one man, because one person Jack could have dealt with, rather than gathering the remains of his squad and running into the soggy forest . . .

. . . but it was dry. Everything dry and cracked and dead. This wasn't India. This wasn't . . .

"This isn't what intel said to expect," Nigel hissed.

"I know," Jack snapped back, but did he? He thought he *knew* what had happened in Jharkhand, but this wasn't it, wasn't what he . . . remembered . . . what he was remembering. This wasn't India. It was the desert, and he was . . . lost, burning up, shivering. India had been a nightmare, and this was . . . was . . . was *this* the nightmare?

Jack sank to the burning ground. Drew his knees up and rested his arms across them. Christ, he was tired. Sore and aching and his head hurt. So over this shit. What was the point of any of it? Had anything he'd done had the desired effect? There was still fighting in the Middle East, still civil war in India; Valadian was still running free. Had he managed to change anything at all? What was the point of anything he'd done over the past fifteen months . . . *fifteen years* . . . if nothing had bloody well changed?

The satisfying weight of a gun settled into his hand. Glock 17. Full mag. Enough to find Valadian and . . .

Glock?

"Mm, I would say . . . a Heckler and Koch. USP."

"Jack?"

Jack jerked back in surprise, gun coming up, aiming.

Blade stopped, hands up and empty. "Jack, please listen to me. You're sick. Heatstroke, maybe an infection. I think you're having a flashback. Can you hear me?"

Blade. Ethan Blade. Bad guy. Enemy. And Jack was sick and fucking tired of seeing the bad guys walk away while his own hands were tied by law and morals and fucking red tape. Well, maybe it was time for a change. Jack fired.

Blade dropped, rolled, and came back up in a slick move, pistols in both hands.

"Drop it, Jack." He was Arctic cool, like McIntosh. Steady as a rock. "You're in no shape for this. Your hand is shaking so much you're just as liable to hurt yourself as you are me. Let me help you."

"Help me? Right." He fired again.

Blade hit the ground and came up barehanded this time. Jack shifted aim and fired. The crazy bastard wasn't there. Then suddenly, he was behind Jack, pinning his arms and knocking the gun from his hand. Before he could think about defence, Jack was down, hitting the ground face-first. Blade landed on his lower back, using his knees to trap Jack's arms to his sides.

"Sorry, Jack," Blade said, arms coming around his neck in a sleeper hold. "It's for your own good."

Jack fought, but it was no use. He was weak and hurting, and Blade was too strong. His vision blurred and blackened, stars dancing in the growing darkness . . .

E than's information had injected new life into Lewis Thomas's investigation. With a name to start from, Lewis's team had rapidly collated so much data about Alpha Subject the list of aliases and jobs attributed to him began to beggar belief. He'd been a busy little "escort," gathering up an impressive list of clients across the globe, his latest target Deputy Secretary John Garrett of the Office of Transport Security. Natport, his current employer, had also shown unexpected depth when poked in the right places. With a plethora of dubious affiliations and dealings exposed, it was a short search to uncover an extensive smuggling network. People, drugs, animals, weapons—it seemed Natport wasn't too picky about what they transported, so long as whoever it belonged to paid handsomely for the service.

The information was perfect, just what they needed to break this case and convince the other directors Ethan was valuable. So perfect, in fact, Jack had to wonder. Not that he'd ever believed it entirely, but Jack now knew Ethan wasn't here just to share information. The problem with that was with the obvious out of the way, there were few other reasons Ethan would be here. Few enough Jack could only think of one.

At his cubicle, with Maxwell next to him catching up on paperwork, Jack tried to convince himself he was wrong. Tried to believe Ethan was only here to pass on information. No matter which angle he came at it from, however, he couldn't quite get there. The day Ethan Blade did something straightforward would be the day the Devil started knitting.

Wish you were here?

There were still moments, very infrequently in the last six months, more so in the last twenty-four hours, when Jack recalled the sick, fatalistic feeling he'd had in the torture shack, looking at that poster of the beach. No matter what happened in Jack's life from now on, that question would stick with him. Like the instinctive shudder he got whenever he thought about the soaking-wet forests of Jharkhand, the oppressive atmosphere of the Cardamom Mountains, or the invasive cold of Afghanistan in winter.

Jack logged in and called up the feed of the holding cell. Ethan was stretched out on the bed. He appeared asleep, but Jack wondered if he really was. The man had barely slept for three days after the incident with the search party. Too busy saving Jack's life.

God. Jack hated this. Knowing why Ethan was here hadn't answered all the questions. Had only introduced more questions—deadly questions.

His implant *ping*ed. Closing his eyes, Jack slipped *sideways*. The implant overlay opened up before him, showing a message in the corner. He tapped it open.

Meeting room 10B. Ten minutes. The ID tag was Director Tan.

Jack slipped out of the trance, then shut down the video feed from the cell and stood.

Maxwell stood as well. "Lunch time?"

"No. I need to talk to McIntosh." Jack set off to find her.

She was coming out of the operations room, a smug smile in place. The "Jack" she greeted him with was even warm and inviting.

"Ma'am." Jack fell into step with her. "Do you have a moment?"

"A brief one. I'm about to talk to the minister about Blade's custody."

Fingers crossed for a positive outcome of that conversation, Jack said, "I won't take up much time. I'll walk with you."

Jack waited until they were in the elevator, as alone as they could be with Maxwell's bulky body looming in the small space. "Tan's called me to a private meeting."

He watched her closely, looking for a reaction to Tan's request. McIntosh and Tan had been civil towards each other in the review meeting, so perhaps whatever had caused Tan to blow up when Jack had been sent undercover was all in the past. Yet Jack couldn't help but wonder.

All McIntosh did was nod tersely. "Not unexpected. He did express a great deal of interest in the situation. Don't let him threaten you, don't agree to anything he proposes, and come to me straight after."

Nothing she wouldn't have cautioned him about in any other circumstances. "Yes, ma'am." Maybe Tan would say something in the meeting to clarify why he'd acted as he had.

Maxwell kept his gaze straight ahead. As head of security, he wasn't subordinate to any of the directors, yet he wasn't their equal, either. He had sole responsibility for the Neville Crawley Building, but at the discretion of the directors in residence. If one of them ordered him to unlock all the doors, he would have to do so—within reason. The problem with Gerard Maxwell, however, was that while he was good at his job, highly trained, and perfectly discreet when required, he was also obedient to a fault. Jack could be wrong, but he was fairly certain Maxwell hadn't had a thought beyond performing his duty as ordered since joining the navy.

The doors opened on the tenth floor. McIntosh gave Jack a parting nod and headed to her office. Jack returned her nod, and then he and Maxwell went the other way.

Meeting room 10B was a smaller version of the conference room he'd been in that morning. Tan was alone when Jack knocked on the open door. He stood by the windows, looking out at a skyline decorated by streamers and painted flags flying from building tops, the result of a harbour-wide art installation.

"Close the door, please, Mr. Reardon." Tan turned around at Jack's knock. "Maxwell, you won't be required for this. Please remain outside."

The HoS nodded and turned, falling into a parade rest outside the door.

"I watched the video of your interview with Omega Subject," Tan said when the door was closed. "The man certainly appears to trust you."

"Don't believe it, sir. He *appears* to be a lot of things." Stone-cold killer; friendly comrade; attentive carer; innocent. "He's a superb actor."

"I'm sure he is. Intriguing, though, don't you think?"

"I suppose so, sir." Jack kept his eyes fixed firmly on the building across the street. The streamers twirled and twisted in slow chaos. Although Tan's voice had been rather dry, there was an undertone to it Jack didn't like. A touch too much . . . fascination? Whatever it was, it made Jack uncomfortable.

Tan leaned over the table and tapped a screen. It popped up from the table surface and came to life. "I've been reading through your amended reports regarding the Valadian operation and had a couple more questions. It's a very interesting read this time around." He scrolled through a couple of pages before settling on one, which he scanned quickly before looking up at Jack again. "However, I believe there is still more information you haven't surrendered."

"Sir?" Christ. Of course the new report *still* didn't contain everything that had happened in the desert. What the hell had Tan picked up on?

"Oh, don't worry, Mr. Reardon." This time, there was a definite suggestion to the words, a sly understanding that rippled down Jack's spine with chilly fingers. "I'm well aware of what's needed to get certain jobs done, and I have a far more . . . lenient attitude to the actions of my assets. As I said this morning, I'm quite happy with your behaviour throughout the Valadian operation. The new statements do not fundamentally change anything with the continuing investigation, so where is the fuss regarding your initial omission?" He cast a pointed look at the door, the other side of which was watched over by Maxwell.

"Thank you, sir," Jack murmured.

Tan smiled magnanimously. "Still, I'd like some clarification on certain things. For instance, this section." He read from the screen in front of him. "'A search party had established a camp at the far end of the gully. It was decided we would retreat and monitor the situation and only act if required.' You go on to say Blade was spotted while scouting the camp and that confrontation became necessary."

"Yes, sir." It was one of the more heavily revised parts of his original report. Excluding Ethan's presence in his initial debriefing had been difficult, but returning him to the action had been near impossible. Reliving those tense moments when he hadn't been sure if Ethan wouldn't kill him as coldly and swiftly as he had Valadian's men had only refreshed all the doubts he'd had about Ethan's intentions. All the doubts he'd had about his own actions in the desert. He'd made progress in the months after leaving the desert, getting past his own confused reactions to Ethan. And now he was right back there, feeling the same uncertainty, the same draw towards an unstable, enigmatic assassin.

Goddamn Ethan Blade for upsetting his life. Again.

"Your report on the confrontation is very thorough," Tan said. "Omega Subject comes across as a highly effective combatant, and very intelligent." There was a musing quality to his voice now as he regarded Jack pointedly. "Of course, one would expect that given the information we have on Ethan Blade."

"As I said in the meeting this morning, he's very convincing. So much so, it's hard to discredit his claim on the name. Sir."

Tan flashed him a predatory smile. "Regardless of the validity of that claim, however, Omega Subject is an extremely competent operator. Capable of pulling off jobs even some of our best operatives would have trouble doing. Nikonov, for starters. He was on our active watch list for years, and then within a matter of days, the Russian FSB had found him and had him in custody. Not to mention everything you say Omega Subject orchestrated with Valadian."

"He's very thorough." Jack was proud of his even tone. "He can read his targets incredibly well."

"And that's what I'm missing from your report, Mr. Reardon. What I'd like to know more about. You describe Omega Subject's actions and aims well enough, but not *him*. I'd like to know what you think of him. Not the assassin or meticulous planner, but the man himself."

Jack shifted his weight from one foot to the other, then back again. His breath caught on his ribs, which were suddenly too tight to let the air escape. This *wasn't* about Valadian at all. Tan was more interested in Ethan. "Sorry, sir?" He scrambled for time to understand, to wonder if Tan had somehow discovered the things Jack had left out of the report the second time around.

"It's not that hard a question," Tan said mildly. "I'd like your impression of Omega Subject's personality. His psyche. How he thinks."

"Jesus *Christ*." It was out before Jack knew he was going to say it.

Tan's only response was to lift an eyebrow, part quizzical, part reprimanding.

"Sorry, sir," Jack repeated, not really meaning it. "But you want me to psychoanalyse Blade, and that's a pointless effort. The man was playing a part the entire time I was with him." Except for those few moments when Jack had suspected he'd seen the real man behind the masks. The one who loved his cars; the control freak letting loose; the man who showed unabashed affection for animals; the one who wanted reassurance for the bad things he did.

Tan nodded. "As expected, yes. But you must have some idea why he does the things he does. For instance, why did he take the Valadian job? Valadian was a two-bit thug with no known agenda, political or theological. The most pertinent thing about him was the army he was hiding in the middle of one of the harshest deserts in the world. There are African warlords and South Asian drug lords with all that and more, and yet Blade shows no interest in them. So why Valadian?"

It was a pertinent question, and one Jack hadn't thought about back then. Too busy just trying to get through it without losing life or limb. Afterwards, that had been Maria Dioli's concern, not his.

"Think about it, Mr. Reardon." Tan shut down the screen and let it slide back into place in the tabletop. "I'd like to hear your thoughts about it and other aspects of Omega Subject."

"Other aspects?" Jack asked warily.

"Such as his feelings towards the Office. Is he a threat to us? Does he have any strong personal views on any of the world powers? Apart from his clients, is there anyone else he answers to? Anything, really, to give us a clearer picture of the man in the cell downstairs. You can go now."

At the door, Jack was stopped by Tan speaking again.

"Oh, and Mr. Reardon." He waited for Jack to face him before continuing. "If you ever get tired of Donna questioning your loyalty, come and see me. We'll work something out."

Jack left, more unsettled than he'd been going in. Maxwell fell into step beside him without a word, seeming to understand Jack wasn't in the mood to talk. Few people probably were after a meeting with Tan.

At McIntosh's office, Jack was asked to wait, as she was still on the phone with the minister. While they cooled their heels, Maxwell traded off with another subordinate. This guy was built like a swimmer—tall, lean, broad shoulders—and Jack observed that he had a habit of leaving his right hand on the gun holstered at his waist. Jack didn't bother pointing out he could probably kick the man's teeth in before the gun cleared the holster, even if he was clutching it like a toddler with a security blanket. Instead, he tried to find something in Tan's words that might hint at his overall agenda.

No matter which way he angled it, Jack couldn't see how Tan's interest in Ethan meshed with his reaction to the Valadian op. Valadian hadn't brought Ethan in until he was convinced there was a spy in his group, more than a year *after* Jack had been inserted. It was possible they weren't related, but it would be awfully coincidental if Tan just happened to have two different reasons to get involved in a single ITA operation.

Personally, the job offer meant less than nothing. Jack had no interest in working with ETA. If it ever came to be that he couldn't work for ITA anymore, then it would be time to leave the Office.

"Mr. Reardon, Director McIntosh will see you now."

Jack nodded to Miller and, when his knock was answered, entered McIntosh's office. It looked out on a similar view as Meeting Room 10B. The streamers on the opposite building twirled and small, darting sparrows played amongst the flying colours.

"The minister is pleased with our progress with Omega Subject," she announced, "but cautious about the long term. So long as we keep getting information like we did today, she'll consider his application for asylum."

If Ethan ever asked for it, which Jack knew he wouldn't. "Yes, ma'am."

Tapping at her screen, she asked, "What did Tan want?"

"More questions about Blade." He quickly took her through the conversation with Tan, leaving out Tan's parting comment about her trust in him, or lack thereof. "He's after something else, though. The interest in Blade's nature and motives felt too . . . personal."

McIntosh nodded along with his summation, but said, "And there was nothing else?"

Her steady tone would have given Tan's a run for its money. Just as with Tan, though, Jack didn't buy it. She'd found something in his words, some hint that worked into whatever game she was playing. Was it something about him? Or Tan? He hadn't been going to tell her about Tan's offer, but he was too curious now to pass up the chance to see her reaction.

"Well, he did offer me a job with ETA."

McIntosh's hands curled into fists, and her expressive blue eyes went Arctic. Assets transferring between departments wasn't rare, and this wasn't even the first time another director had made a play for Jack. It was, however, the first time he'd seen McIntosh react so strongly.

Then she blinked and the frost was gone. "He's always been interested in having your set of skills. What did you tell him?"

"Nothing."

She studied him for a long moment, then sighed and relaxed back into her chair. "Good. Now would not be a good time for you to contemplate a career shift, Jack. Your situation is rather . . . precarious."

An unnecessary reminder that his nuts were in her vice. If he made a move she didn't like, she would slam it shut faster than he could dodge.

"Yes, ma'am." He didn't bother to hide the dry sarcasm.

For a moment, the corners of her full lips hinted at a smile, as if they'd just shared something important. Then she was all business again. "Thank you for your time. You may go."

SEVENTEEN
THEN

Someone blew the biggest raspberry in Jack's ear. Warm spittle slapped against the side of his face.

Jack groaned and tried to push the offender away. His hand found hair and wet lips. Ugh.

"Piss off," Jack said, or thought he did. All he heard was a hoarse grumble that might have been his voice. He couldn't be sure.

A slobbery tongue tried to drill into his ear.

"Fuck!" Yes, that was him. He shoved out wildly, pushing himself away from the intrusion.

"Sheila! Bad girl. Leave Jack alone."

The tongue disappeared momentarily, then made a reappearance as the mysterious Sheila blew another raspberry.

"Bad girl," Blade admonished again, though not so stern. Instead, he sounded inordinately amused. "Oh, don't look at me like that. You're not supposed to be in here. Come on, out of Jack's room."

A disgruntled harrumph preceded a series of soft *plop*s that faded away, taking Blade's soothing voice with it.

What the . . .?

Jack pried his eyes open. All he saw was a dark blur with a fainter blur in the middle. He lifted his hand and tried to blink it into focus. Slowly, it became clearer in the dimness. Five fingers, hand, arm. All there, all more or less how he remembered it. Upon raising his other hand, he found an anomaly. Fingers, then red solidity. It looked like a splint.

He'd broken his arm. That was right.

A memory flashed. Standing outside, the sun blazing down, holding a gun in his right hand, pointed at . . .

"I put a new splint on your arm," Blade said softly from the doorway. "You'd managed to cut the other one off. Quite the feat given your state of delirium."

Jack lifted his head to look at him, then let it fall back to the pillow. A headache throbbed in his temples, a band tightening around his head when he moved.

"You're still dehydrated. Do you think you can drink?"

"Yeah." It didn't sound right, so Jack waved in an affirmative way. God, he felt so bloody weak.

Blade disappeared for a while, and then he was back. He perched on the edge of the bed and helped Jack sit up. It stung that he needed help. Propped up on several pillows, he watched as Blade opened a bottle of hydro-lyte. It might have been green, or yellow. Lime or lemon. At least it wasn't raspberry.

Jack refused to let Blade hold the bottle, taking it in his left hand. It horrified him when it shook as he raised the bottle to his mouth.

"Slowly," Blade insisted. "I've been trying to get fluid into you but haven't had much luck. I didn't think to bring the necessary equipment to set up a drip. Something to remember for the future."

A couple of shallow swallows were all Jack could manage. His arm ached from holding up the bottle, and he lowered it before he could drop it. Throat a little less scratchy, he asked, "What happened?"

"A nasty combination of heatstroke and an infection. I do apologise. I thought I'd cleaned the knife wound well enough, but apparently I didn't."

If he hadn't been two blinks away from falling asleep, Jack would have said it wasn't his fault. It was all Jimmy O'Dowd's fault. Bastard couldn't even keep a clean blade.

"Don't remember much." Jack took another small drink.

"That's probably for the best. If you did, I would be forced to defend my honour, and you're in no state to reciprocate."

"Shit."

"Yes. That too."

Jack closed his eyes. Things were better in the dark. "How long?"

"Three days. The first one you were lost in some sort of delirium. You were yelling in Hindi at one point. I don't speak the language, so I'm not sure what you were calling me, but it sounded thoroughly rotten."

"Great. That would be an India flashback."

"I wasn't aware you'd worked there." Blade took the bottle and screwed the lid on. "I managed to get you back in the buggy and drove here, where I've spent the past two days injecting you with some broad-spectrum antibiotics."

Grimacing, Jack muttered, "That's why my arse hurts."

Blade snickered. "Yes. I promise I didn't touch any more than absolutely necessary. You, however. Rather handsy."

"Fuck off."

"Repetition of that one has quite dulled its impact, I'm afraid. Come on, drink some more. Then I'll let you sleep again."

"Okay. Just don't let random tongues in my ears anymore."

Blade held the bottle this time. "Yes, Jack. Only specific tongues from now on."

All of his energy turned towards drinking, Jack let that one go by. When Blade was happy with his liquid consumption, he was laid back down and left alone. Jack tried to think through what he'd learned, but fell asleep before he could even remember why he shouldn't be relieved to see Blade.

The next time he awoke, it was naturally and he felt better. Still pathetically weak, but the headache had lessened, and he could focus further than a foot in front of his face. Levering himself up on his left arm, he managed a better look around. He was in a small room, bare brick walls, a long, thin window high on the far wall, covered with black plastic, little pinpricks of sunlight scattered across it. His bed was low and narrow, though solid and well padded. The sheets were fairly clean, if a little rank from his sweat. Except for the cast he was naked, which he'd be embarrassed about when he had the strength. An overturned plastic crate was a makeshift bedside table. A couple of hydro-lyte drinks sat on it, as well as a tray with an almost empty antibiotic bottle and a packet of needles and syringes.

Jack opened a drink and did his best not to guzzle it. Warm and raspberry, but it helped all the same.

"Feeling better?"

Blade stood in the open doorway, leaning against the frame. He wore his suit pants, shoes, and nothing else. Arms crossed over his lean torso didn't hide the finely honed muscles of his chest or abdomen. Wiry, but strong. His skin was pale, with a faint pink touch of being out in the sun. The colour made the scars stand out. A long slice over his left hip, another just under his right ribs, and the starburst of a large-calibre bullet between his sternum and left shoulder. Lucky shot for Blade. Probably highly unlucky for the shooter. Above his arms, his chest was bare of hair. Beneath them, a thin line of dark hair traced from his navel down into the top of his pants.

Jack hauled his gaze off him. "Yeah. Much." Teeth aching with grudging effort, he added, "Thanks."

"My pleasure. Do you feel like walking? You should probably start to move about."

As much as he wanted to just lie down and never move again, Jack nodded. The sooner he was ambulatory, the sooner he'd be able to hold his own again.

Blade approached him. "I'll take you to the other room. It'll give me a chance to wash the sheets, at least."

"Uh-uh." Jack waved him back. "Pants first."

"It's nothing I haven't already seen, Jack."

Jack glared. It hurt to do so, but he didn't care. "Pants. Now."

"As you wish." He left and came back a moment later with Jack's jeans. "Laundered and patched. I think you'll find I'm a deft hand with a needle and thread."

"Yeah, yeah, get out."

Blade got, but Jack could hear his evil little chuckle all the same.

Pulling his jeans on was an effort that almost defeated him. He was panting by the time he could do up the buttons. Lying flat on his back, exhausted, he stared at the ceiling. Exposed beams, corrugated tin. Too much like the torture shack for Jack's comfort. He rolled over, nearly fell off the bed, and caught himself in time.

"Are you decent, Jack?"

"Goddamn it," he hissed. Could the bastard get any smugger?

"Too bad, I'm coming in." Blade swept in and found him trying to stand up. "Do take it easy. I don't want to spend another two days tending to you."

Grumbling about the indignity of it all, Jack had to let Blade help him. He wouldn't have made it to the door if he didn't. He'd been badly injured before. Hard to avoid it in the service and with the Office, but he didn't think he'd ever been so weak. Hard, too, not to notice the texture of the skin under the arm slung across Blade's shoulders—smooth over solid muscle and warm from the sun. Harder, even, to ignore the pressure of the assassin's hand on his stomach, there to keep Jack from pitching forwards. The heat from Blade's hand, callus-rough and firm, seemed to sink right into Jack's gut. He made the mistake of looking down and seeing the assassin's pale skin against his darker shading. The stark and fascinating contrast made him so dizzy he stumbled. Which set off a little series of near disasters, resulting in him being draped over Blade more than he had been and *much* more of that smooth, warm skin pressed against his own.

Blade's huff of breathless laughter, combined with a gentle squeeze of his hands, went right through Jack like a blast from a jet engine.

"Are you steady now?" His breath shivered across Jack's neck. When Jack found answering impossible, he added, in a low, concerned tone, "Do you wish to go back to bed?"

Christ. Blade needed to stop talking. It wasn't helping Jack's efforts to keep his cool at all.

"No," Jack managed between gritted teeth. He scrounged up every scrap of energy he could and pushed off of Blade. Didn't get as far as he wanted, but at least he reduced the surface area of contact back to his arm over Blade's shoulders. "Just hurry up."

"As you wish, Jack."

He was light-headed by the time they left the bedroom. Vision swimming, he took in the other room through a haze of weariness. Slightly larger, it was open to the world along one side. Bright sunlight streamed inside, making Jack flinch, his lingering headache spiking.

"Here." Blade held out his sunglasses. "I think you need them more at the moment."

Absurdly grateful, Jack put them on and immediately felt better. He recognised the esky from the buggy, the scavenged weapons, and the sleeping bags. Stacked against the wall opposite the opening were several more plastic crates.

"This is your stash of equipment?" he asked curiously.

"Indeed it is. We're just lucky I always keep a well-stocked first aid kit with my gear." Blade leaned him against a wall. "Stay there. I'll fix you a seat."

"I'm good," Jack insisted.

"You're trembling all over. You're not good."

The seat consisted of several of the crates covered in one of the sleeping bags. As Blade guided him to it, he said, "I don't fancy lifting you off the floor, so please don't fall off."

"Try not to." Jack aimed for dry sarcasm and got to pained embarrassment. He hated feeling helpless.

"Call if you need anything."

Blade made sure Jack had a drink before stripping the sheets and disappearing outside with them. Jack dozed, waking at intervals to find Blade checking on him. At one point, Jack stirred at a loud blatting noise. He looked up and found a long, dusty face about two inches from his own. Large, slitted nostrils flared and the big, floppy lips quirked up into an absurd parody of a smile. Above that, huge black eyes blinked ridiculously long lashes at him.

"Holy shit," Jack gasped.

The camel grunted and lifted its head, exposing a long neck and shaggy body. It was huge, towering over him on four thin, knobbly legs. Jack was about eye level with the grossly callused knees.

Jack stared at it with something close to horror. This was the thing that had tried to shove its tongue in his ear. It returned his look with a gaze of dull curiosity, blinking and chewing absently.

"Not again, Sheila." The weary exasperation in Blade's voice caught the animal's attention. It twisted its neck and watched him approach, then lowered its head to butt at his shoulder when he was close enough. "Yes, yes, I know you've been lonely, but you can't keep bothering Jack. He's still sick."

Sheila blew a rude raspberry.

"Don't talk back. Now, come on, outside." Blade pointed imperiously to the opening. "Hurry up. Outside."

Groaning, the camel turned ponderously in the small space and lumbered outside.

Into the stunned silence, Jack muttered, "What the hell was that?"

"That was Sheila, my camel."

He was sick. Imagining it. Blade hadn't said what Jack thought he'd just said.

"She sort of came with the building, actually," Blade continued. "In truth, this is her home. Her stable. We did kick her out, so I can't blame her for wanting back in."

Maybe if he went along with the absurdity, it would be over quicker. "Stable?"

"Yes. This used to be part of a homestead. Abandoned some time ago, I believe, but Sheila seems to have stuck around. Even if she was very young when they left her here, she must be rather old by now, but still a sturdy girl."

"Jesus, it's an animal, not your old spinster aunt."

Blade laughed. "Not an animal lover, Jack?"

"I like dogs. Besides, it stinks."

"You're no bouquet, either. In fact, if I bring you some water, will you wash?"

God, yes. Yes, he wanted to wash, but the mere thought of it was exhausting. "Maybe later."

"All right. Are you hungry?"

Jack wasn't sure, but he nodded anyway. Anything to stop Blade gushing over his camel. His camel? Christ.

Food was watery porridge. It took Jack half an hour to finish his bowl, but he managed it. Needed a nap afterwards, but that was okay because when he woke he felt stronger. The sun was going down, blazing a red streak across the horizon. Jack staggered to his feet and tottered towards the outside world. He used the wall as a prop, stopping when it ran out. Leaning there, he took in the new landscape slowly.

Still flat as a pancake, but with less red dirt and more plants. Some even seemed to have a touch of true green to their leaves. To the south he saw the ruins of the homestead, a brick house with a crumbling veranda and caved-in roof. Weeds had dug through the foundations, sprouting from windows and through the gaps in the roof. The remains of a garden had gone feral, the surviving plants shrivelled, pale versions of their former glory. There were still touches of colours in a few flowers, violet and orange and yellow.

Between house and stable were the remains of a couple of holding yards. Old palings scattered in the scrub, rusting curls of barbed wire here and there. Not far away was an old hand-cranked pump on a bore. Blade worked it up and down, a bucket under the spout, while Sheila ambled around him, begging for pats, which he offered up happily. His body glistened under a sheen of sweat, catching the dying rays of the sunset, turning him golden. A fallen angel sans wings.

Jack growled at his wandering imagination. The absolute last thing he needed was to start feeling sympathetic towards Blade. He was an assassin. He'd purposefully set out to destroy Jack's cover with Mr. Valadian, used him as bait in a trap. He wasn't someone you started to like.

Still, Jack couldn't seem to stop watching the man. The man who might very well kill him when his reason for keeping him alive ran out.

EIGHTEEN
NOW

Jack needed some distance. Wished he could be back in the desert, under that vast dome of stars, feeling unattached. Here, everything was too close, too confining. He was trapped in this building, in the middle of something he didn't understand. And the one person he thought he might be able to trust was the one person he couldn't talk to.

After bumming a smoke and lighter off Miller, Jack, with Tall and Silent in tow, trotted up the three flights to the roof. They came out into a warm summer day. Finding a spot in the shade, Jack slouched against the side of a huge air-con unit, feeling its vibrations creep into his back. Tall and Silent stood guard several feet back, perfectly positioned to watch him. Drawing his knees up, Jack used them as a windbreak to light the smoke. On the first deep inhale, he tilted his head back and looked upwards.

Ribbons had been put up here as well. Colour had been abandoned, however. It was all black-and-white streamers over his head, twisting and turning, tying themselves in knots. A thick black ribbon had looped itself around a satellite dish. Stretched out, it would be decidedly longer than any of the others. No wonder it had become caught up.

Jack let out a long, smoky breath. The nicotine was doing nothing for him, not that he really needed it to. It was just an excuse to be here, outside, away from all the plots and secrets. He expected these sorts of games out in the field, not here in his home base. Here was supposed to be a safe place, somewhere he didn't have to be on constant alert, looking over his shoulder and searching for hidden meanings in every little move and word. He wasn't supposed to be used by McIntosh against their own people.

He took another long drag on the smoke and watched the black-and-white ribbons in their chaotic, uncoordinated dance overhead. One of them, a long, knotted white streamer, snapped sharply in a sudden gust. It broke free, then tangled briefly with a black ribbon before whipping away into the air. Jack tried to trace its flight for freedom but lost it quickly against the bright blue sky.

That was how he felt. Untethered. As if one more nudge might disconnect him from the only thing keeping him anchored. His loyalty was doubted and he had no operation to occupy his mind, no real reason to come to work other than to offer advice no one needed.

On top of that, both McIntosh and Tan had secret agendas, making them act contrary to what Jack knew of them. And the catalyst?

Ethan Blade.

Jack had a good inkling of why Ethan was here, but did McIntosh or Tan? If Jack's inkling was right, and the directors *knew* . . . then that meant Ethan was most likely right. It also meant that more than Ethan's freedom was on the line. More than Jack's career. The security of not just the Office was at stake, but that of the whole Meta-State.

If Ethan was right and *if* the directors were aware of it, then who did Jack trust? The man who'd betrayed him in the desert, or the people whose hands he'd put his life into countless times without a doubt?

This was it. Jack was back at the place where the path split. He'd been used and manipulated in the desert, and it had taken a long time to recover from that. He wasn't going to let that happen again, especially not here. Jack chose a path.

His first step was to talk to Ethan and find out what the plan was.

"What the hell, Munoz?" Maxwell bellowed from the doorway.

Tall and Silent jerked, hand going for his gun, then dropping guiltily when he focused on his boss. Not guilty for going for his gun, though, if the look he threw his boss was an indication.

"Does this place look at all secure to you?" Maxwell stalked towards his man, all but snorting and blowing like the charging bull he resembled. "Reardon's under building detainment. Is this what you call being confined *inside* the building, Munoz?"

"He was having a smoke, sir."

Jack held up his butt helpfully.

Maxwell grunted. "Get back inside, Reardon." He glared at Munoz. "You're relieved of guard duty. Go downstairs, hand over your gear, and keep out of my way for the rest of the day."

As Jack ambled back towards the door, Munoz loped past and went inside, head hanging. Maxwell was still growling when he caught up to Jack.

"Imbecile," he muttered under his breath as he closed the door behind them, making sure it locked. He even double-checked on the sec-tab on his belt.

The small security tablet allowed Maxwell to control most of the electronic security systems in the building. As a security specialist in his cover life, Jack was familiar with the functionality of the sec-tab. It took biometric confirmation, voice command, and an alphanumeric key-code to access. A dedicated hacker *could* break into it, but that would take longer than any rational person would like, and you had to be within a couple of inches of the device to access it.

"Don't be too harsh on him," Jack said as the HoS hustled him down the stairs. "He had me under close enough watch."

"Don't push it, Reardon. You knew better than to go out there."

"What can I say? I've been cooped up in here for too long. I just needed to see the sky. And have a smoke." He nudged his shoulder into Maxwell's. "You can understand that, can't you?"

Maxwell eyed his shoulder, where Jack had touched him, then Jack's, before snorting. "And don't try to pull that shit, either. You had your chance."

Jack laughed. "I'm not pulling anything, Gerard." He let a couple of flights go by before adding, "Though I have been locked up here for over a day now. And yesterday was my birthday."

Maxwell almost choked on a startled guffaw, stumbling to a halt on a landing between floors. "Seriously, Reardon? This is your big escape plan? Seduce me?"

"Not working, huh?" Jack patted Maxwell on his armoured chest. "Don't worry; you're safe from me. Can we stop by McIntosh's office? I need to ask her something."

Maxwell allowed it, though it was Miller Jack dealt with, as his director was otherwise occupied. However, Jack's request was granted so fast he guessed McIntosh had preapproved it. Within minutes, he was in the sublevels, outside of Ethan's cell.

"Please go to the wall opposite the door. Spread your legs and put your hands on the wall."

On the screen beside the door, Ethan rolled off the bed and obeyed. The minute between then and when he was actually allowed in dragged at Jack like an anchor. He was finally doing something, not for McIntosh or the Office, but for himself. As the minute drew out into what felt like an hour, Jack marvelled at how easily he'd decided the only person he could trust in this entire building was the one man they had locked up in one of the most secure cells in the world.

An eternity later, the door swished open and, once more leaving his second-guessing policy in the corridor, Jack went in. The door closed behind him.

"Hello, Jack. I didn't think I would be seeing you again so soon." Ethan turned and lounged back against the wall.

"It's not an official visit. It's all still being recorded, though."

Ethan made a silent *ah* expression. "If I'd known you were coming to chat, I wouldn't have eaten all the fudge."

"I told you to ration it."

"Do you think I didn't? In any other circumstances, that log wouldn't have lasted five minutes."

Jack smiled. "I'll have them bring you a toothbrush."

"It would be appreciated." Head tilted, he regarded Jack critically. "What's wrong, Jack?"

Trust Ethan to get right to the heart of it. Well, nothing else for it.

"I thought I should apologise," he began, trying for words that wouldn't be picked up by the analysts.

"For?"

"I feel like I've . . . betrayed you." Jack scratched his head with his right hand. "You helped me out in the desert. I would have died without you. I certainly wouldn't be back here if you hadn't nursed me back to health." A swipe at his face this time.

Ethan smiled. "Well, yes, as I said then, I was directed not to endanger you." He brushed at his sleeve. "I merely had a job to do."

Shit. Jack's inkling was right.

"Shall we sit?" Ethan asked.

Jack nodded numbly, and they settled into the same seats they had for the interview.

"So, tell me," Ethan said as if he hadn't just dropped a bomb. "How is Sheila?"

The question prompted a startled laugh out of Jack. "I don't know. She was good, last time I saw her. Little footsore, but okay."

Ethan chuckled. "She was a good ride. Not as smooth as Raquel, though."

"Remind me about Raquel."

"The BMW Z8 Roadster. Interlagos blue. I had her out on the track a couple of weeks back. She drove like a dream."

"You know, I still can't credit you as a rev head." He watched Ethan closely for a sign.

"Truly? I should think it rather obvious. I like going fast, and I like dangerous things. And I love fast, dangerous things."

Jack snorted. "You love being in *control* of fast, dangerous things. Gives you the impression you're in control of yourself."

"Haven't you grown tired of trying to psychoanalyse me yet?"

"Doesn't seem like it. And I'm right. You know it. It's why you nearly flipped out when I insisted on driving."

"Flipped out?" His tone was mildly condescending. "Your argument is flawed. I let you pilot the chopper."

"The half-crippled chopper. Sheila on a bad day was faster than that POS."

Ethan laughed. "True."

"If I remember correctly, you didn't so much *let* me as order it. Just something else for you to control."

Which was the wrong thing to say if Jack wanted to keep a level head during this conversation. With all the other issues from his time in the desert rearing their ugly heads, the last thing he needed was to remind himself how well Ethan had played him back then. Was potentially—*probably*—playing him right now.

Ethan's mask slipped a fraction, a quick hint of a deeper hurt, and then it was back in place, smooth and perfect. "If that's what you believe, Jack."

The silence was stilted. It had started out so well, as things with Ethan often did. Then they usually went pear shaped in a spectacular fashion. Jack had to steer this back on track. Praying Ethan was on board, Jack said, "You said your car here was an Aston Martin. I don't know much about them."

"She's a Vanquish S Coupe. Black. V12, six-speed transmission. Took me seven months to restore her." The assassin adjusted the cuff of his right sleeve. "I call her Victoria."

"And this is the car you put in one of the most traffic-congested cities in the western world. Seems pointless."

"Only because you don't know where to take a car like Victoria."

"And where's that?"

Ethan eyed him shrewdly. "Have you heard of a private race track at Kulnura?" His hands stayed still on the tabletop.

Jack frowned. "No. Should I have?"

"I suppose not, since you are a vehicular heathen. How about the Sydney Motor Sport Park?" When Jack didn't immediately exclaim familiarity, Ethan added dryly, "It's in Eastern Creek."

Working to not roll his eyes, Jack said, "Yes, I've heard of that one. What about it?" Again, no gesture. Did Ethan understand what was going on?

"I have raced at Kulnura. It's a nice track, but the SMSP is much more accessible. The last time I was there, I raced against a very good driver." Ethan drummed the fingers of his left hand on the table, as if trying to spark a memory. "Williamson, I believe his name was."

Now they were getting somewhere.

"You raced him in the Vanquish?"

With a little smirk, Ethan said, "Victoria, yes."

"Did you win?"

"That time." A brush of his hand over the table, as if clearing away nonexistent specs of dirt. "It was an eight-lap challenge. He dominated for the first four, but I caught up and was in the lead for the last three."

There was more than a touch of pride in Ethan's voice, and it distracted Jack momentarily. He found himself smiling at him, feeling that pull towards Ethan he'd experienced in the desert. The involuntary fascination with the human behind the coolly detached killer.

Before Jack could move on, Ethan did.

"Not all of my cars are race ready. Victoria is, of course. As is the Maserati. The Camaro's in about twenty different pieces at the moment, so she won't be running for a while yet. My favourite to race, however, is the Lamborghini, naturally." As he listed off his harem of expensive speed machines, Ethan absently flexed his right wrist, as if working out a kink.

"Naturally," Jack echoed, then leaned back in his chair and stretched his legs out under the table. "Would you like more fudge?"

Ethan smiled. "I would. Could I try a different flavour?"

"Sure. Any requests? Remember, I have to get it past the guards." He tapped Blade's leg twice.

"I am partial to mint."

"They do a great mint-choc swirl. I'll get you a log."

"Perhaps two?"

Snorting, Jack said, "How about four? Or five? Don't forget you can't exactly run up and down the stairs to burn it off." He tapped three times.

"No, two is enough. I promise to ration these ones and make them last at least five hours." He nudged Jack again, then with a quirk of his left eyebrow, added, "Actually, get three. Keep one for yourself."

"Gee, thanks for your generosity."

"You know, Jack, you do remind me of Sheila sometimes." Another raised brow.

Jack frowned, both at the words and the arch of that brow. "Hirsute and lumpy?"

"No." Though he did chuckle evilly. "Contrary yet reliable."

Getting it, Jack stood. "And on that insult, I'll let you get some rest. I'm sure there will be another interview soon."

"I look forward to it."

At the door, Jack waited while the guards told Blade to get against the far wall. When the door opened, he stepped out, resisting the urge to say "good luck."

Walking away from the cell, Jack tallied up the information passed between them.

A traitor. Here, in the Office. The target Ethan had truly been hunting in the desert, and that person was one of the directors.

Then there was the plan. Using two logs of fudge, Ethan was going to break out of the cell, then take out the two guards and however many more were between him and the door to the surface, three flights of stairs up. Jack's part seemed simple in concept if not execution. He was taking Sheila's place—a diversion—in this crazy scenario. Then there was the mention of seven, with no hint as to what it was. Williamson, eighty-three as the location. The cars as . . . transport?

And it was all going down in five hours. Five hours until Jack irrevocably screwed everything he'd worked so hard to get. All for Ethan fucking Blade.

NINETEEN THEN

The bucket of water was for Jack to wash with. As grateful as he was for the chance to sponge away the sick-sweat, he grumbled through the process, annoyed at how weary he still was. It didn't help that Blade stuck around, ostensibly fixing dinner, but in reality watching with a concerned eye, undoubtedly ready to catch Jack should he topple over. By the time Jack put his jeans back on, he felt as if he'd been through assault diving training again. Exhausted, he slumped onto the improvised chair and hauled the sleeping bag around his shoulders. The heat of the day was fading fast, revealing a sharp bite to the air that would soon turn into a bone-deep chill.

Blade had a small camp stove, and he heated tins of baked beans and canned vegetables. Jack ate with a desire to regain strength, not hunger, and afterwards dozed while Blade counted ammunition. It was when the assassin began assembling a frightfully diverse arsenal Jack remembered the world and all its issues beyond the walls of the stable.

He'd been out of it for three days, four including the one that had just passed in idle laziness. How had Blade handled that, considering his eagerness to get the dune buggy? There certainly appeared to be no resentment in him regarding the new delay, but then it had taken pushing Blade into a mild loss of control to get him to show some annoyance over Jack's screw-up at the torture shack. Was that the way to get anything honest from him? Needle and push until he got angry enough to break his rigid control?

One way to find out.

"How's the schedule looking?" Jack asked innocently.

Blade looked up, eyebrows raised. "Fine."

"Really? You've been nursing me for three days. Did you account for that in your plan? Are you that perfect?"

"I thought we'd already covered my ability to make mistakes," Blade said mildly, thumbing what looked like hollow-points into the magazine for the Assassin X. "But as it were, finding the buggy was very fortuitous."

Finding the buggy? Jack snorted. "Yeah?"

"Indeed. It not only allowed me to carry you here while your infection had you incapacitated, but reduced the travel time by exactly four days. We are perfectly on schedule." He dropped the filled mag into a bag and began on another. "That is, if you're feeling up to continuing on in the morning."

"Shouldn't be a problem. Will I get to drive?"

"You may if you wish. So long as you know how to steer a camel."

Jack gaped. "We're not taking the buggy?"

"Oh no, it's far too conspicuous."

"And two blokes on a crazy camel isn't?"

"It won't be, under the right circumstances." The twitch to his lips promised circumstances Jack probably wouldn't appreciate.

"I'm not getting on that stinking, spitting, devil-spawned creature."

Blade shook his head. "Devil-spawned? What has poor Sheila ever done to you?"

"Besides try to deafen me with its tongue?"

"Yes."

Jack floundered. "Well . . . I'm sure it's plotting something. It looks at me like it wants to step on me."

Blade put the second mag into the bag and stood, stretching his lean body. "Of course she wants to step on you. You took her bedroom. Not to mention my attention for two days straight."

"You're saying it's jealous of me?"

Blade patted his cheek as he passed. "Only a little. And please, she's a she, not an it."

Jack scowled but thought better of picking on the camel any further. "So, what's the next step in your plan, then? What will be expected of me?"

Clear in his memory was Blade saying they would "hit" the compound. Blade certainly had enough weaponry here to accomplish a halfway-decent assault, but Jack could only hold two guns at once, and he was fairly certain Blade wouldn't be able to handle more than that. Unless he was planning on arming the camel.

Jack shook that thought away before it could gather any momentum. Right at the moment, he couldn't be sure Blade *wouldn't* use the camel as an assault vehicle.

"Hopefully nothing too strenuous," was the reply as Blade stacked crates opposite him. "But just in case it goes haywire, I thought I could teach you a few things." He sat and faced Jack.

"Teach me what?" Jack eyed him warily.

Blade smiled reassuringly. "Nothing untoward. You needn't look so worried."

Jack looked away. It wasn't right, sitting here with this man, wanting to return his smiles and teasing. Maybe he'd spent too long amongst the snakes. Become a little too used to the relaxed morals of a criminal lifestyle. Hell, he hadn't had to force a laugh at Mr. Valadian's humour for damn near a year. Had, in fact, come to appreciate the wit and cunning insights.

Now, with Blade, he could see something similar starting to happen. The man wasn't what Jack had imagined when contemplating a highly successful assassin. He had a sense of humour dry enough for Jack to enjoy and, oddly, an approachable openness. Odd because the man was insanely cryptic at times, which drove Jack crazy. And it certainly didn't help that he had the sort of tight, trim body that usually drew Jack's attention.

Jack swallowed hard, then muttered, "What is it, then?"

If Blade noted anything awkward, he didn't show it. "A means of passing information while in suspect company. It's fairly easy, as it entails actually saying what you want to pass on, just mixed up in an otherwise unrelated conversation. The important words are signified with various gestures."

"Sounds complicated."

"It really isn't." Blade had put his dress shirt back on with the setting of the sun, and he presently unrolled the sleeves and did up the cuffs with quick, practiced motions. "Say I wish to pass on a location for us to meet up at later. I would start a conversation about, hmm, places I've visited in the past. For example, I do enjoy Johannesburg in autumn, but it has nothing on Darwin in the summer."

"Really?" Jack raised two sceptical brows. "Darwin in summer?"

Blade pursed his lips. "It's an example. However, I do like summer in the gulf. Wonderful fishing opportunities. Back to the matter at hand. Which city would we be meeting in?"

"I don't know."

"I'll repeat it, shall I?" He did so, shaking out the rumples in his left sleeve as he did so.

"Jo-burg?" Jack hesitated, thinking he'd detected a slight emphasis on the name.

"And again."

Naturally, Jack said, "Darwin."

"Yes, but without resorting to the process of elimination, tell me why you would have picked that one."

"No clue."

"Clearly." A patient little sigh, and Blade pointedly held out his hands. "I indicated the city I had chosen by motioning with my left arm. I did it all three times. Did you really not pick up on it?"

Jack gave him the finger. "I've been ill, all right?" Now it was pointed out, it had been rather obvious.

"Fine, Jack, I'll give you this one. Meeting places are signified by the left arm, be it gesturing with it, or stretching, or adjusting your clothes. Understood?"

"Yes. Just get on with it. I know what you're up to now."

What followed was several hours of instruction involving hand gestures, tapping fingers and feet, leg nudges, coughs, sneezes— though Blade despaired over Jack's fake sneeze, advising him to keep to coughing—and even eyebrow quirks. They followed it with practice conversations.

Finishing a story about fishing in the Amazon, Blade sat back. "Where, when, and how?"

"Rio, in two weeks, on a Tuesday at four p.m., and . . ." Jack hissed, trying to remember the sequence of taps and nudges. "Um . . . by goat?"

Blade laughed. "Goat? Honestly, Jack. Why would I want you to travel to Rio de Janeiro by goat?"

Waving his hand towards the great outdoors, Jack snapped, "You've got us assaulting a paramilitary compound on a camel! Why wouldn't you do something as crazy as hitching a ride on a mountain goat?"

"Please, I am not crazy. Just practical. If you'll recall, I rubbed my chest when I told you about the train ride across Colombia."

Which had diverted Jack's concentration for a moment. Scowling, he muttered, "I thought you were itchy."

"When having a circumspect conversation relying on hand gestures, best not to randomly scratch anything, don't you agree?"

"Shut up."

Blade smirked. "Your turn. Tell me something you think I need to know."

Eyes narrowing, Jack considered him for a moment. Blade sat with his back to the open night, his pale skin and white shirt picked out in stark lines against the blackness. The Milky Way, thick and creamy across the sky, haloed his dark hair. It was an entirely distracting image.

"Right," Jack said gruffly. "A story imparting something I think you should know." He closed his eyes to think, but mainly to eradicate the sight of Blade from his thought processes. "Okay, try this one. I'd just been accepted into the SAS, and my first deployment was part of a training exchange program with a couple of commando units from the 911 Special Forces Regiment of the Royal Cambodian Armed Forces. We were on manoeuvres in Sre Ambel, in the southwest of the Cardamom Mountains, when we heard about several girls being taken from a village nearby. The mountains used to be a safe haven for the Khmer Rouge, but it had been years since there was any trouble. The locals said the girls had probably been taken for sex slaves. Our CO thought it would be an interesting training opportunity, so we went after them. Straight into some of the wildest rainforest I've ever experienced."

Blade leaned forwards, elbows on his knees, expression intent. Whether he was just looking for Jack's signals or actually interested in the story, Jack wasn't sure, but he found it scary to have the assassin's undiluted attention. Scary and . . . thrilling.

"I was on point, scouting ahead, when I got the sense I was being watched. Don't get me wrong; there were millions of eyes in that jungle. Birds, monkeys, insects, snakes, spiders the size of your head. But this was different. The feel of it was . . . heavy. Aware. Like there was a definite purpose behind it, as if whatever it was could understand what I was, and that I didn't belong there."

The memories rushed forwards as he spoke. The heat of the rainforest, the cloying moisture thickening the air. The constant rattle and hum of the insects, the eerie screeching of monkeys he couldn't see. Golden-green sunlight punching through the solid-seeming canopy. The scents of damp rot and verdant life. Towering tree ferns alongside delicate orchids. The hidden funeral site they stumbled across, a cache of ancient ceramic jars filled with the remains of the deceased, the atmosphere sacred and sombre, isolated from the chaos of the jungle by a sense of quiet eternity.

And the awareness of being not the hunter, but the hunted. Stalked by an invisible, silent predator. Knowing he wouldn't see it when it finally struck putting a near-constant shiver down his back.

Looking at Blade sent the same shiver along his spine.

"You know what I mean?"

Blade nodded. "I do."

"We had no idea what it was or why it was stalking us. We just knew it was always there. This went on for six days while we tracked that group deeper into the mountains. We set traps at night and checked for prints every morning and found nothing. But it was always there, keeping pace.

"Our stalker stayed with us as we got closer to the abductors. Was right there when we attacked them and rescued the girls. All but one. She was dragged into the jungle by one of the kidnappers. I chased them. Lost the rest of the squad in the process. That was when the predator revealed itself."

Blade's breath caught in a startled gasp. "What was it?"

"A tiger. I haven't ever been so close to something that big, that deadly before. It was breathtaking. It just looked right at me with these golden eyes, like it knew me. Knew it could kill me quicker than I could run. It had watched me for days, was familiar with my habits, my weaknesses. Yet here it was, calm as you please, presenting itself to me, acknowledging another hunter passing through."

Jack recalled the regard of the tiger, the clear danger it presented, but also the gentle sense of companionship between them, the linked cause of hunting and protecting. The fear of this apex predator hadn't left him for an instant, but it had been modulated by respect and understanding. They knew each other, understood just what the other was and that they were the same.

The eyes regarding him now were silver, but the impression was terribly, and excitingly, familiar.

"The kidnapper lost his shit," Jack continued roughly. "He started screaming and panicking. He let the girl go free, so I had a clear shot. As soon as he was down, the tiger disappeared. Never saw it again, but I felt it following us all the way back to camp."

Jack took a drink to wet his dry throat. Blade was quiet for a long time, expression slightly awed, slightly perplexed, slightly sceptical.

"Was that true?" he asked.

"Every word."

The assassin frowned. "An animal will always leave behind spoor. If a tiger had been pacing you the entire way, you would have found *some* evidence."

"You calling me a liar?" Jack demanded. "Or just plain dumb?" That edge of thrill peaked when Jack taunted the current predator in his midst.

Blade jerked back. "No! Of course not. I'm just perplexed as to how . . ." He trailed off when he noticed Jack's smirk. "Oh, very amusing." After a moment's silent contemplation, Blade continued. "Either way, I thought the Cambodian tigers were extinct."

"So they say."

"Are you saying they aren't?"

"No. I'm just saying what I saw. What I felt."

Blade threw his hands up. "Then what? Are you saying it was a ghost tiger?"

"I'm not saying anything. Well, except for the information I thought you needed to know. Did you get it?"

Sitting back, Blade regarded him contemplatively for a long while, then nodded.

"So? What was it?"

Eyes narrowed, Blade recited, "'I don't understand you or why you haven't killed me.' Correct?"

Jack stood and grinned. "Perfect. Night, Blade."

Sleeping bag around his shoulders, Jack went to bed.

All the way, he felt those eyes on him.

TWENTY NOW

Maxwell wasn't taking any chances of another Tall and Silent incident and put two watchdogs on Jack when he left the sublevels. Thus sandwiched, Jack headed back up to the tenth and wheedled Miller into organising someone to fetch a clean set of clothes from his apartment. By specifying the particular garment bag he wanted brought in, Jack took the first step on Ethan's crazy plan, but an hour later, he was half convinced he'd made the wrong move.

There'd been no noise from either Tan or McIntosh. It was an ordinary day at the Office for everyone but Jack. He sat at his desk and tried to look busy, but was constantly distracted by every memo that flashed up on his screen. Only one had any sort of impact, sending him down to the first floor to pick up the requested garment bag.

In the toilets he undressed and did his best to wash down with damp towels. It reminded him of that day in the stable, still weak, trying not to reveal how his hands shook while he wiped days of sick-sweat from his body under Ethan's watchful eye. Of the lesson in subtle communications, the story of the tiger. Of the night that followed, the startling revelations and Ethan's confusing response to them. Jack still didn't fully understand it and suspected now neither did Ethan. Not a sociopath, but not given a chance to be anything else. The assassin's view of the world was fundamentally different to Jack's, to most other people's. No one had a chance of ever understanding him.

Leaning on the sink, Jack looked at himself in the mirror. The strain showed in his bloodshot eyes, in the tension in his temples and the straight line of his shoulders, the bunching of the muscles in his arms as he gripped the porcelain so hard it might have creaked under the pressure.

All this because Ethan said there was a traitor within the Office, someone who'd been protecting Valadian. One of the highest ranks, no less. It was a serious charge, and the consequences were even more serious. Someone at that level, with access to pretty much all of the most sensitive secrets in not just Australia, but within the Meta-State, could do just about anything: sell state secrets, cover up terrorist activity, derail Office investigations, pass on faulty information to the military so some hapless squad of soldiers was sent into a deadly situation dangerously underprepared.

If it was McIntosh, then it made her moves to get the Valadian op up and running without anyone else knowing understandable. With one of her own assets in play, *she* controlled the flow of information. She could deal with anything Jack might have uncovered before he possibly exposed her. Likewise, if Tan was the traitor, his ire at discovering the operation *after* it had been set up made sense. He would have been paranoid that McIntosh suspected him, or that she soon would.

Right then, Jack was doubly glad he'd lied through his teeth upon his return. If he hadn't been trying to hide Ethan, he could very well have said something to the wrong person and gotten himself in a tougher bind than he presently found himself in.

Of course, if Jack went ahead with Ethan's mad plan, he was effectively signing a death warrant for the guilty director. Ethan wasn't here to point a finger. He wouldn't trust any sort of bureaucratic system to do the right thing. He was here to do what he did best. Kill.

Jack *was* loyal. To his family, to his country, to the Office, even to the military hierarchy that had chewed him up and spat him out. He'd dedicated his life to making sure the madness in the wider world didn't impact Australia. A traitor inside the Office was just the latest enemy, and maybe this time, being loyal meant bypassing the red tape.

Slowly, Jack dressed, making sure each item was precisely the one he'd asked for. With every button he did up, he was confirming his commitment to Ethan's plan. When he pulled on the jacket and settled it on his shoulders, he let out a long breath.

This was it. Do or . . . die? Well, he hoped not.

He was leaving the toilets when he bumped into Maria Dioli. She bounced off him with a distracted curse and hurried past. Then she pulled up short and spun around. She was in the same clothes as the previous day, her normally ordered curls now a frazzled mess, and she had the overcaffeinated twitches common to active-case workers.

"Jack! I've been looking for you. Come on, in here."

She dived into a room across the corridor, waving for him to follow. When he didn't, she poked her head back out and frowned at him. "Hurry up."

Indicating Shadow One and Shadow Two, Jack said, "I'm not alone. And"—he pointed to the room she was in—"that's the ladies'."

Maria frowned at the watchdogs. "Why are they here?"

"To make sure I don't run away."

"Good, they can guard the door while I talk to you." She disappeared back into the toilets.

"Well?" Jack asked the Wonder Twins.

Shadow One sighed and ushered him into the ladies'. Shadow Two stayed outside, guarding the door. Inside, Maria was at a sink, hands cupped under running water, which she splashed over her face. Shadow One did a perfunctory check of the stalls, then settled into rest mode by the door.

"Can't this wait until you're done in here?" Jack asked, mildly amused as Maria did a horrified double take in the mirror.

"No, it won't take long. Shit, I look like the bride of Frankenstein."

"Frankenstein's monster, actually," Shadow One corrected.

Maria glared at him, then tried to tame her curls. "Whatever. Listen, Jack, I read through the new statements about your time with Blade."

She still didn't look pissed with him, thank God. "And?"

"And it doesn't really shed any light on what's been going on with Valadian's group since."

Jack snorted. "I know. If any of it had, I would have admitted it straight up."

"Right, but that doesn't mean it isn't interesting in its own way." Giving up on her hair, Maria faced him, leaning against the sink.

"I started looking into Ethan Blade's movements after he left you in the desert."

"Jesus, Maria. Have you been at it all night?"

She nodded. "Once I started, I couldn't stop. Not when I realised that I've pretty much been tracking his movements already."

That caught Jack's attention solidly. "What?"

"I've been tracking the remains of Valadian's organisation for the past year, and everywhere I've found a trace, Blade's already been there, or visits there not long later. He's after Valadian as well. Or what's left of his business, at least. You said he was there to kill Valadian and that you didn't know if he succeeded or not. I don't think he did, because Blade's still after him. He's got to finish the job. Some sort of assassin's credo or something, I guess."

"Or just a personal one," Jack muttered.

She had it wrong. Ethan hadn't been hunting Valadian. He'd been looking for clues about who had been protecting Valadian.

"He's fascinating, Jack." The glazed enthrallment in her eyes hit Jack like a gut punch. "I mean, I'm compiling data from over a hundred different sources to track Valadian's group. I have two techs working full-time on this and we're getting barely anywhere, and somehow, this guy has kept a step ahead of us. I no sooner got a hint of Valadian somewhere and Blade's already there, or so close it meant he had the information before I did. How is he doing this? Where's he getting his information? I need to talk to him."

Jack was shaking his head from about halfway through her speech. He didn't need this, not now. Not wearing what he was wearing, not after committing to a course of action he might be starting to doubt. How could he let Maria make the same mistakes he had? She was a good handler, a better unit leader. Tough, smart, dedicated. He couldn't let Ethan drag her into this, even if he didn't mean to. Jack had to steer her off this path before she went too far.

"Maria, don't do this."

She frowned. "Do what? My job?"

"No. Yes. Look, don't dig any further into Ethan Blade. Trust me, it's a one-way ticket to madness."

"What do you mean?"

"I mean he's not entirely rational. There are . . . circumstances that give him a skewed view of the world. You've seen his eyes?"

Maria nodded. "They're freaky, yeah, but what's that got to do with anything?"

"Are you familiar with the term 'Sugar Baby'?"

Sugar—an illegal synthetic dopamine-stimulator— had appeared on the market about forty years ago and quickly proved to be a cheap alternative to other, similar drugs. About five years after that, a flow-on problem had arisen. Namely, the babies born to female Sugar addicts.

"Sure, from about thirty years ago? Didn't they debunk a lot of the . . ." She trailed off as she made the connection. Eyes widening, she stared at Jack. "He's . . . Really?"

Jack hedged. "Not exactly, but he's not what we would call *normal*. He's been an assassin for half his life, Maria. That means he was sixteen when he started. At least that was when his kills began being attributed to the name 'Ethan Blade.' He doesn't look at the world and see it full of people. He only sees targets of varying degrees of difficulty."

"Even you?"

"Even me. Especially me."

Maria fiddled with her hair. "I watched the video of McIntosh's interview with him, and yours. He certainly appears to trust you. That would indicate he sees you as something like an equal."

"Believe me, he's a brilliant actor."

It sparked a sense of betrayal in him to say it. Ethan *did* trust him, with an innocent willingness that tore at Jack each time he doubted it. It didn't help that Ethan's first declaration of trust had been a lie, and that the second had been all but coerced out of him.

"You're saying because he's unstable, I shouldn't put any worth in his intelligence related to the remains of Valadian's group?"

Shit. "God, Maria, just forget about Blade. He can't help you. He doesn't help anyone. He just makes things worse. Look at me. Confined to the building, under suspicion." He motioned to Shadow One, looming by the door. "Watched even while I take a piss and change clothes. You're too good to be tarred by Blade's brush."

Maria regarded him with a blank expression that failed to hide the furious workings of her brain. Everything he said would be analysed and dissected, worse than Dr. Granger and her psych evaluations, and applied to Maria's agenda as she looked for links and insights.

She nodded slowly. "All right. Thanks for the advice, Jack. If you and your date could leave, I'd like to pee now."

Jack hesitated, then said, "I mean it, Maria. Stay out of it. I'm warning you."

He left then, hoping she considered his warning for what it was: an honest plea she back down for her own good. If he could keep everyone else out of Ethan's path, he would consider it a best possible scenario.

Back at his desk, he found the next part of the plan waiting for him. Two logs of mint-choc swirl fudge, dutifully fetched by Lydia Cowper this time.

This was it. The moment Jack delivered them to Ethan, the plan would be in irrevocable motion. Without it, Ethan wouldn't make a move and Jack could keep hold of whatever remained of his job. Maria wouldn't be caught up as collateral damage. Ethan would be a prisoner of the Office for as long as he served a purpose, after which it was doubtful they'd let him go even then. Ethan had come in knowing that, trusting Jack to not let that happen.

Wish you were here?

Swearing under his breath, Jack pushed back from the desk, not sure what he was going to do but knowing he had to do something.

Ping.

A message appeared on his computer screen. From Director Harraway.

Meeting room 10B. Five minutes.

Well. It would complete the set.

Watchdog front and back, Jack headed back up the stairs. Was that why Maxwell kept coming back on Jack-duty? His people were complaining about running up and down stairs all day? It amused Jack to think so, at least. The door to the meeting room was open when Jack and the Wonder Twins reached it.

Harraway, seated at the table, waved him straight in. "Leave the bodyguards outside, son."

Shrugging at his shadows, Jack closed the door in their faces, then turned to the Intel director. "More questions for me, sir?"

"Indeed. Sit, get comfortable. Not sure what Donna thinks she's going to achieve, having you trailed like that. Confined to the building should be sufficient punishment, I think, for preserving your life."

"Sir?"

"Ethan Blade. If I had him after me, you wouldn't see me for dust, I reckon."

"I get it, sir, but he's not really after me."

"Still, can't be comforting, being known to one of the longest-serving names on the John Smith List."

"It's a little startling. Is this all you wanted to talk about, sir?"

"No. I'll leave the Blade obsession in Alex's hands. I'm more interested in Samuel Valadian."

This was a new angle. "What about him?"

Glen Harraway smiled encouragingly. "Well, let's look at him. A somewhat ambitious organised-crime man with his hand in all sorts of illegal activities—nothing unusual, nothing to concern us. Then suddenly, he has this compound in the middle of the desert, a three-thousand-strong army, and a weapons stockpile large enough to threaten a city."

Jack shifted a bit uncomfortably. "It wasn't *suddenly*, sir. He'd been using the compound as a cover for years. We just weren't aware of his direct connection to it until ITA traced some of his weapons smuggling to it. And it wasn't until I got in there and was trusted enough that I saw everything he had going on."

Harraway waved aside Jack's correction. "You should know by now, son, if we haven't been tracking it for at least a year, preferably two, then it most definitely is *suddenly*."

"Yes, sir," Jack said dryly. Of course, *suddenly* discovering the full extent of Valadian's operations in the desert was thanks to someone here, in this building, covering it up.

True to his word, Harraway wasn't interested in Ethan. Instead he spent an hour digging deeper into Valadian's movements and motives. The Intel director didn't have a screen up or a tablet to refer to; everything he needed was already in his head. Another interesting point was that when Harraway had to mention Ethan, he used "Blade" or "the assassin," not Omega Subject. Either he found the tag a bit on the nose or felt Ethan wasn't that important to the overall situation.

After dissecting Valadian's ruthless solution to his Link Rindone problem—concluding Valadian had only done what was best for his organisation, even if it'd earned the ire of several Golden Triangle drug cartels—Harraway sat back in his chair with a little sigh. "I believe that leaves us just one more question, Jack."

Weary of the constant rehashing of events he'd worked so hard to leave behind, Jack asked, "Which is?"

"Why Blade?"

Jack blinked, surprised at the sudden turnaround in topics. "Why Blade what, sir?"

Harraway waved a hand as if to encompass their prior discussion. "Valadian wasn't a reckless operator. He did precisely what was needed, when it was needed. So why bring in such an expensive and notorious assassin to merely interrogate a spy? No offense to your skills, son, but it feels like overkill, and Valadian was too cautious to err on such a small thing. So . . . why Blade? You spent ten days or so with the assassin. Surely he said something about Valadian's plans for him."

"No, sir, he didn't. Nothing beyond finding out what information I may have passed on." Then, because in under three hours he'd have little left to lose, he asked, "Do you have a theory about it, sir?"

The older man contemplated him for a long moment. "Not a theory as such. More of a . . . curiosity. Something I was hoping you could help me shine a light on, Jack."

It was as far from a 'curiosity' as it could get. Harraway had a firm idea about why Valadian had secured Ethan's services. And, considering just what Valadian had done to do so, Jack had to admit Harraway was right. Valadian wouldn't have done *that* just so Ethan would interrogate a possible spy. As director of Intelligence, Harraway had access to every morsel of information moving through the Office. He undoubtedly knew far more than Jack, but what put the shiver down Jack's spine was that Harraway was probably leaps and bounds ahead of McIntosh and Tan, as well.

Over Harraway's shoulder, through the window, Jack fixed his gaze on the next building. Blue, yellow, and red streamers twisted together and apart, around and around. Once more, he felt like one of those ribbons, pulled against his will into a tangle of plots he had no control over.

Harraway knew something none of the rest of them did. Even if he suspected there was a traitor within the Office, even if he could help Jack puzzle out McIntosh's and Tan's motives without resorting to freeing Ethan from his cell . . . Harraway was still a *director*. He was still a suspect.

He focused on Harraway's hopeful expression. "Sorry, sir. I can't help you."

After a moment, the director shrugged casually. "Oh well. It was worth a try. Of course, if you think of anything, come to me with it. Thank you for your time, Jack."

TWENTY-ONE THEN

Jack awoke with a soft grunt of confusion. He hadn't meant to fall asleep. After his not-so-subtle declaration to Blade, he had wanted to wait and watch, see what sort of response he got. Instead, he had fallen into a deep sleep. Which, he had to admit, had done him a lot of good.

He felt much better. A dull ache in his lower back—probably more a result of the bed than anything else—and a lingering thirst, but that was it. Praise be to Blade's nursing capabilities and his stock of antibiotics.

The room was dark, only a faint brush of light falling through the doorway. It was also unusually warm—and pungent. Both of which were probably symptoms of the snoring, camel-shaped lump taking up the other half of the room. Apparently, Blade had lost the argument with Sheila about where she would sleep.

Jack snorted softly.

Lifting his head, Jack found Blade. He was sitting in the outer room, in sight of the door. The assassin was curled up on the improvised chair he'd made for Jack, wrapped in a sleeping bag, mug of something steaming in one hand, worn and dog-eared paperback in the other. A small torch cast gentle silver light across him so he could read. The light cut the curve of his cheek out of the darkness, softening the shadow of his unshaved chin. It sparked in his strange eyes as they darted back and forth across the page. Glinted off the tin mug as he raised it to drink, then didn't, caught up in the story. The mug lowered, rose, then was put down so he could turn the page.

Jack couldn't remember the last time he'd read for pleasure. Couldn't even remember the last book he'd really enjoyed. Growing up with a modern-lit lecturer as a father had pretty much ensured Jack's fate as a reader. His strongest childhood memories were of sitting on Dad's lap, lost in a haze of imagined worlds and characters as his father read him *The Jungle Book*. It hadn't just been the stories, either, for Dad, but the books themselves. The texture of the book, the smell of the paper, the tactile pleasure of turning a page. He hadn't eschewed e-readers, just preferred a printed book. With the clarity of hindsight, the first sign of his father's illness had been when he took his beloved books out into the street and set them alight.

Shoving those memories into the bulging filing cabinet, Jack focused on Blade. He seemed to have forgotten his drink, free hand poised at the top corner of the book, ready to turn the page as soon as he'd finished reading it. Jack couldn't see the title of the book, but it had to be good.

Not the image of a bloodthirsty assassin.

Could the two sides of Ethan Blade—the entranced reader, animal lover, and dedicated carer; the remorseless killer and deadly warrior—exist within one body?

Jack hoped so. With the flick of a switch, he'd killed thirty-six Taliban soldiers in a barracks. Two days later, he'd been celebrating Lionel's birthday in camp. It wasn't as if he'd set those charges for purely personal reasons. He'd just been doing his job.

Two weeks later, back in Australia, he'd gotten so drunk he started a brawl and ended up decompressing in a holding cell on base.

How did Blade decompress? With a cup of tea and a good book? Did he *need* to? Or was he really an unfeeling, cold-blooded killer?

Jack had been in the service for nine years, and the accumulated psychological trauma was still a thick layer of scar tissue over every inch of his life six years later. They'd been an intense nine years, though. First East Timor, then Cambodia, followed by three tours in Afghanistan and ending with the epic clusterfuck in India.

Blade had been in the business for sixteen years. Half his life. At least, that was how long the name Ethan Blade had been active, whether or not this man so entranced by his book was actually *the* Ethan Blade. How did anyone cope with that much scar tissue?

Scar tissue.

The term sparked something in Jack's memory. He curled up on his side, watching Blade, and explored the thought. Scar tissue . . . Something to do with eyes. A condition that left the eyes all but colourless, covered in a coating of tissue that had to be cut away from the iris. Which, in turn, stopped the iris from expanding and contracting as it should.

Shit.

"I know what you are." The words were out before Jack realised he was even going to speak.

Blade looked up from his book, dark brows raised. "Pardon?"

Struggling up, sleeping bag held as a buffer against the cold night, Jack repeated, "I know what you are."

The assassin smiled tolerantly, an adult patiently listening to a child's wild theories. "And what is that, Jack?"

"A Sugar Baby."

Blade went perfectly still, as he had moments before killing three men.

Continuing the theme of this entire madcap experience, Jack carried on recklessly. "A child born to a female Sugar addict, one who doesn't inherit a dependency on the drug but is born with a thick film of tissue over the eyes." He was pretty much quoting the text from memory. "Surgery to correct the defect often leaves the child permanently blind. Those who retain their sight are unable to adjust to extremes in light gradients, but develop a heightened night-vision capacity. You're a Sugar Baby."

The other man remained motionless for a long minute, then slowly looked back down at the book in his hands. His expression remained blank, but he blinked several times in succession, the only reaction to the revelation. Blade closed the book, smoothed down the cover, and put it aside.

"And does that explain everything about me?" he asked calmly.

Wondering, once again, why he dared push this man, Jack shrugged. "Not everything, but it clears a few things up."

"Such as?"

"Such as . . . I think I heard somewhere a recent study debunked one of the more common beliefs about Sugar Babies. About thirty-odd years ago, when the affliction became relatively well known, it was thought Sugar Babies were also sociopaths. Some with violent tendencies, but all with certain . . . incompatibilities with normal social behaviour."

Suddenly, Blade was on his feet. Throwing off the sleeping bag, he stalked into the inner room. His eerily colourless eyes picked up the faint light of the torch, burnished predator-bright and silver.

"Is that what you think I am? A sociopath incapable of normal social interaction?"

Shit. Jack had to learn to keep his mouth shut. He scrambled to his feet, feeling the stinging need to be ready to fight.

"No." He kept hold of the sleeping bag, to be used as a weapon if necessary. Or to at least cushion him from anything Blade might try.

"Then what? I know you don't trust me or believe me. So tell me, Jack, what am I?"

"I don't know. I know some things, but not what you *really* are. Or even who you are. I'm at a disadvantage here, Blade. You know everything about me."

"Not everything." His tone was frosty but held a touch of hurt that, like everything else he'd seen of Blade, confused the hell out of Jack.

"All right, I'll bite," Jack said tersely. "What don't you know about me?"

Blade dipped his head and looked at him through a veil of long lashes. It was oddly coy, but the glittering white of his eyes was a chilling contrast.

"There is one thing," the assassin said softly, and then he was moving, coming for Jack.

Jack reacted on instinct. He tossed the sleeping bag and, before Blade could knock it aside, followed it. Jack crash-tackled Blade, the sleeping bag between them. Blade twisted in mid-fall, getting a foot against Jack's hip. They hit the ground hard, Blade on the bottom, but with leverage. He shoved Jack off and rolled clear of the bag, but Jack was ready for him. Scissoring his legs, Jack swept Blade off his feet. The other man turned the fall into an elegant flip so he landed, perfectly balanced, crouched on his toes.

On his feet, Jack backed up, wary. He was, at present, outclassed. Still weakened, hampered by the low light and, plain and simple, bloody impressed by Blade's moves.

Blade didn't press the attack, watching Jack with a closed, icy expression.

"You made the first move," Jack reminded him.

"I did," Blade agreed.

Getting it now for what it had been, Jack lowered his hands, forcing himself to relax. "Did it tell you what you wanted to know?"

"Yes." Again, that hint of hurt. But it was quickly banished as Blade stood. He flexed his fingers, shoulders losing tension, shifting from kill-ready to calm as quickly as he'd gone the other way. He waved at the bed. "You should sleep. We'll be on the move again tomorrow." He turned and went back to his improvised seat.

And Jack was left in a stable, with a soundly sleeping camel and no more information than he had at the start.

Christ!

Muttering under his breath, he wrapped the warm bag around his body and shuffled out to Blade.

"I'm sorry." Though he didn't know why. He certainly didn't owe Blade anything.

As if he could now read Jack's mind, Blade asked, "What for? Everything you said is true. I'm a Sugar Baby. I spent the first six years of my life blind, and even now I can't see in direct light. And ever since I was old enough to understand, I've been told I'm a monster-in-waiting. A psychological time bomb. Even I believed it for a long time. I can't blame you for thinking the same thing."

Jack leaned against the cold bricks. "I suppose not. For the record, I don't think you're a sociopath. I mean, you have a camel for a pet."

"Sheila's not a pet," Blade said blandly. "More a casual acquaintance."

Suppressing a snort of laughter, Jack muttered, "Not doing your reputation any good by admitting that, Blade."

Lips twitching, he looked up at Jack. "I guess not."

The touch of humour fled as Jack met those strange but now explainable eyes. "I mean it. I don't think you're a sociopath. But I still don't understand you."

Blade stood, putting him closer to Jack than he had been when he attacked. "Do you really want to?"

Swallowing the sudden tightness in his throat, Jack could only shake his head.

Shockingly, Blade smiled, a surprisingly innocent expression that nearly reached his eyes. "Then stop trying to psychoanalyse me. It'll get you nowhere and only cause you grief."

There was truth in those words, and Jack vowed to live by them.

Being this close showed him a new side of the unstoppable killer. There were dark smudges under his eyes and a stretched quality to the skin of his temples.

"How long since you slept?" Jack asked.

"Three days, give or take. I didn't want to leave you unattended in your illness. Sheila offered but her bedside manner is rather deplorable."

"Yeah, that's what I thought." About both statements. "You go sleep. I'll keep watch."

"You're still not—"

"No arguments. I'm fine. You need to sleep."

"But—"

"Shut the fuck up and get into bed!"

Blade took a startled step back, eyes wide. "I have a sudden urge to salute." It sounded only about half joking.

"Blade." Every ounce of warning Jack could muster turned the name into something closer to its literal meaning.

"If you insist."

Blade slid past Jack and entered the inner room. Jack snatched up the sleeping bag the assassin had left behind and tossed it in after him. He was rewarded with a muffled gasp of surprise when it hit Blade in the face.

Jack had settled into the crate-chair, his own sleeping bag around his shoulders, when Blade spoke.

"May I ask you a question, Jack?"

Jack looked into the other room but couldn't make out much past the pale oval of Blade's face. The tone, however suggested a quiet seriousness. After the night's revelations, Jack was more than willing to entertain the idea.

"Sure. I reserve the right not to answer, though."

"As you wish. Do you like your job?"

Nowhere near what he'd thought it might be. Nonplussed, Jack took a moment to consider his answer. "Today? Not particularly. But generally, yeah, I do."

"Why?"

"Why?" he repeated to give himself a bit of time. "I guess, because it's good work. We're protecting people. Safeguarding freedom."

"And you see what I do as wrong?"

"You don't?" It was out before Jack considered how it sounded.

"I asked you first."

Jack took a deep breath. "All right. Justify one of your kills for me."

"Easy. Valadian. You're after him yourself."

"Not to kill. To neutralise. And he isn't dead yet. Pick again."

Blade didn't answer straight away, and all sounds from his side of the room—soft rustling, low breathing—stopped. When he did speak, it was quiet and low.

"They were part of a smuggling group, taking women out of Colombia for transport to Argentina, where they were sold as sex slaves."

"Who?" Jack had guessed but he wanted it confirmed.

"The US Marines."

"Can you prove it?"

"I can. The investigative team looking into it couldn't. Their progress was stymied by political red tape and military cover-ups. The longer the powers that be tried to deny it was going on, the more it happened."

"So you took the matter into your own hands. Vigilante justice, Blade?"

A hint of dry humour in his words this time. "Not vigilante. I was paid by the person who decided to bypass the bureaucratic nonsense."

Jack shook his head. "Are you saying all of your kills are equally worthy?"

"No. But if I have a choice, then yes."

What had Blade said when they argued about the difference between soldiering and assassination? *At least I get to pick my targets.*

"So, to answer *your* question," Blade said. "Yes, what I do is wrong. But for me, I'm doing it for the right reasons."

Crap. When was Blade going to stop tipping Jack's preconceived notions on their heads?

"All right," Jack conceded. "Tell me this, then. Do you like your job?"

Blade smiled. "Today? Yes." He rolled over and snuggled the sleeping bag around himself, and within moments, his breathing lulled into a relaxed, easy rhythm.

Jack picked up Blade's mug, sniffed a strong tea blend, and put it down with a disappointed grunt. Before he picked up the book, he tried to think of what Blade might find so fascinating and came up with nothing. Resigned, he turned it over and read the title.

Ice Station by Matthew Reilly.

Not immediately familiar. Curious, Jack read the first page.

Half an hour later he was no clearer on his impression of Blade. The book read like an action film—fast paced, wildly imaginative, highly improbable, and chock full of clichés. Jack couldn't quite mesh this with what he knew of Blade.

An hour after that, he still had no clue but he was thoroughly hooked by the book and had no intention of putting it down.

By the time dawn crept around the edge of the building, he was only a couple of pages off the end.

"Please, whatever you do, do not spoil the ending for me."

Not even looking up at the sound of Blade's voice, Jack muttered, "If you don't see the end coming a mile off, then you're not as smart as you want the world to think you are. I didn't think leopard seals were that vicious."

Blade put his hands over his ears and stalked away.

Smiling tightly, Jack finished the book in peace.

TWENTY-TWO

NOW

Thanks to the meeting with Harraway, Jack had lost his last doubts by the time he reached his desk. Barely pausing, he picked up the fudge and descended to the sublevels and Ethan's cell, Shadow One and Two dutifully following him.

"Again?" Shadow Two asked wearily.

"Dropping off another bribe." Jack brandished the confectionary. "I won't be long."

They went through the whole rigmarole again and it dragged out, time expanding around Jack so every movement of the guards seemed absurdly slow. He watched for a sign they suspected him or Ethan, hyperaware of anything that might escalate into a threat. It saddened him that this place he'd once believed to be safe suddenly seemed hostile, like he'd been dropped behind enemy lines in a foreign land.

Finally the door opened and Jack entered. It was getting easier to leave his doubts at the door the more times he did this. Each time reinforced the idea Ethan really was here, was truly back in Jack's life, making it as perplexing and dangerous as he had in the desert.

"Another visit so soon," Ethan murmured. "I'm flattered."

"Not a long one." Jack put the fudge on the table. "As requested, two logs of mint-choc swirl. Do try to make these last longer. I can't keep bringing you stuff like this."

Leaning against the wall, Ethan nodded, those predator eyes glinting. Like with the tiger in Cambodia, there was an intimate understanding in his expression. Ethan knew exactly what Jack was doing, knew why he was doing it.

"I'll do my best. Thank you, Jack." No hint of teasing.

Jack could only nod in acknowledgement, his throat suddenly tight. He reached behind himself and knocked on the door. The minute passed in silence. Ethan held his gaze the entire time. Conversely, time seemed to speed up, the sixty seconds flying by in a single beat of his heart.

Time is relative, Dad used to say. A minute surrounded by the enemy felt like an hour. An hour with your loved ones felt like a minute.

The door opened, and Jack forced himself not to race out.

He wanted to go back to the roof. Needed to see the open sky, breathe the free air. But he couldn't, not after Maxwell's earlier tirade. He ended up running the stairs, up and down. Told the Shadows he needed the exercise or he would go crazy.

At one point, he managed to lose his watchdogs. They'd taken to handing him off at the halfway mark, but as he was sprinting upwards towards the roof, Shadow Two dropped back, swearing breathlessly. In the confines of the stairwell, Jack managed to evade his watcher for nearly three minutes. When he was caught again, he got an earbashing from Maxwell and was further confined to the eighth floor. Apparently trusting the Shadows had performed better than Tall and Silent, Maxwell left them with Jack, but tasked them to keep him under better control.

By the time he reached his desk, they were down to two hours. He'd been sitting there for several minutes before he realised what he was looking at.

The photo of Sherlock sat crooked on the desk. Jack knew it had been square when he left his desk earlier. He always took a moment to make sure the frames lined up when leaving his desk. It was one of those little rituals everyone had, unconscious habits that became conscious only once they didn't happen, or someone else messed with them.

Jack checked on the Shadows. One leaned on the wall of Jack's cubicle, reading something on his phone, while Two surreptitiously checked out the female tech at the desk behind Jack's. She was pretty, but exuded a you-could-be-on-fire-and-I-wouldn't-care intensity that deflected friendly overtures and left come-ons broken in the dust. He wished Two good luck and turned back to his own dilemma.

While Sherlock's goofy canine grin laughed at his extreme caution, Jack carefully picked up the medals and Matilda's card and secured them in his top drawer. He contemplated the lone frame for a long moment, wondering if he was being stupid. Perhaps someone had bumped his desk in passing, knocked the picture over, and put it back carelessly. It could be nothing. Or it could be something.

He had to check it out.

Casually, he picked up Sherlock's picture, suddenly missing the big doofus. He'd come home from that last deployment, on medical leave, certain he was going to be court-marshalled, and all he'd wanted was to see his dad and play with Sherlock. Only to find his dad in hospital, confused and convinced his only son was KIA, and his dog dead.

Shaking off the memories, Jack ran his fingers over the back of the frame, looking for anything out of place. All he discovered was a piece of paper, folded and tucked into the corner. He pulled it free and slipped the photo into the drawer with his medals. While his hand was in the drawer, he unfolded the paper and glanced at it.

Rooftop. 1730. Ditch your dates.

Maria. It had to be. Only she had called his watchdogs "dates." And in an hour, one hour before the deadline, she wanted to talk to him privately. This didn't bode well for her staying away from the whole mess.

And just how the bloody hell did she expect him to ditch the Shadows?

He needed coffee. Well, he wanted bourbon, but coffee was all he had access to, so coffee it was. Lewis and Lydia were in the tearoom. Jack could think of no excuse to not sit with them, so he did and pretended to pay attention to their ponderings over their investigation. They were still turning over rocks and finding squirmy double-dealings thanks to Ethan's information. They had a list of questions for Jack's next interview with Omega Subject. He did his best to contribute as he would if he weren't planning anything untoward.

Then it was time for his mysterious meeting on the rooftop. Time to get some answers. If he could somehow ditch his dates.

When he stood, Shadow One came on point. "Where are you going?"

"Toilet. Coffee wants out."

Falling in front and back, the Shadows escorted him to the toilet, One informing Maxwell of their movements. They both came in with him this time.

Before Jack could get any further through his plan for ditching the Shadows than curling his hands into fists, the door to the toilets snapped open and Maxwell barrelled in.

"Sir!" Two exclaimed as the HoS sailed right past him.

Jack barely got out a grunt as he was rammed face-first against the wall by the urinal. Maxwell landed a knee in the small of Jack's back, reaching for his wrists with thick-fingered hands.

He reacted on instinct. Every nerve had been on edge since his second talk with Ethan that morning, his body primed for combat. Twisting his left arm, he broke Maxwell's hold, and then he jabbed his elbow backwards. He hit nothing but armour, pain slamming back up his arm. It distracted Maxwell, however, making him jerk to the side. Jack stepped back, getting his foot between Maxwell's legs, and buck-twisted at the same time. Maxwell went down with a heavy *thud* and an angry growl. He was fast, though, catching Jack's leg with his calves and bringing him down beside him.

Then there were fists and knees everywhere as the Shadows joined in.

"Fucking hell, Reardon!" Maxwell reached through the mad scramble and caught Jack by the collar of his jacket. "Give it up. I've got a whole team here. You can't win."

Not because Maxwell was right, but because Jack suddenly found himself in an interesting position, he stilled. Jack's head was in very close proximity to Gerard Maxwell's groin. And he hadn't had to orchestrate some other awkward scenario of getting close to the sec-tab on the HoS's belt. His plan to distract building security just might work.

How long things would go in Jack's favour remained to be seen, though, because frankly, *this* couldn't be good.

"All right, all right," he gasped, freeing his hands and holding them up in surrender.

While the Shadows secured his hands, Maxwell held him in place with that tight, unforgiving hold on his collar. With a slight tilt of his head, Jack's teeth would be in a position to cause some terrible pain for the HoS. Right now, however, escape wasn't in the cards.

Jack slipped *sideways*. His implant flared to life and he worked fast. He didn't need to access the sec-tab on Maxwell's belt, had no need to bypass the biometric, vocal, and key-code locks. All he needed to do was *skim* the device's radio frequency identification.

The implant *ping*ed a successful read just as Jack was wrenched away from Maxwell. Coming back to himself, he pretended to be dazed from the punches as they hauled him to his feet. Shaking his head, he managed to focus on Maxwell. There was a red patch on his chin where Jack had got a lucky hit.

"Sorry," Jack said, nodding towards the baby bruise. "I didn't mean it."

Maxwell rubbed at it gingerly, scowling. "Right, because innocent men always punch first."

"They do when they're shoved face-first into a wall in a men's toilet. I was scared about your intentions."

Shadow Two snickered, then cut it off the instant Maxwell glared at him.

"You should be, Reardon," Maxwell snapped. "This way."

Cuffed and subdued, Jack was frogmarched out of the toilets and back into view of all his fellow ITA assets. The entire floor went quiet as the security team fell in around Jack, escorting him to the elevators. Lewis charged out of his operations room, looking like he was prepared to tackle six armed people singlehanded. Thankfully, Lydia caught him before he got more than a couple of paces. Jack wanted to reassure Lewis and Lydia, but he didn't risk it. Anything he did, even a small shake of his head towards a friend, would be used against him and Lewis, and Jack didn't want anyone else dragged into this mess. Maria was already mixed up beyond being salvageable. He just hoped a security team hadn't been sent to the roof to get her, as well.

Jack was herded into the elevator and, in tense silence, taken to a meeting room on the tenth floor, where McIntosh was waiting for them. Maxwell came in with him, but left the rest of the team outside.

Donna McIntosh was in full Arctic mode, standing by the window, arms crossed, expression tightly controlled.

"Ma'am," Maxwell said respectfully. "The suspect."

Suspect? What had given him away?

She glanced at Maxwell, then Jack. A shiver rolled down his spine at the pure anger that flashed through her cold blue eyes.

"I had doubts, Jack," she said. "I didn't like it, but I had to address them. I can honestly say I didn't expect to find anything."

"Ma'am, I don't know what you're talking about." It was an honest statement. There was so much she could have discovered. What had she found?

"For a period of three minutes, you evaded your security detail in the stairwell," McIntosh said coolly. "Where were you?"

Oh fuck. "On the stairwell. Running off excess energy from being cooped up in this building. Is it my fault his"—Jack snapped a nod in Maxwell's direction—"staff can't keep up?"

Maxwell growled but McIntosh held him back with a cold expression. Then she turned to a screen on the table.

"I want you to listen to something, Jack." She tapped at the touchpad and Jack heard his own voice.

"Can't this wait until you're done in here?"

His watchdogs had been recording his conversations. He wasn't entirely shocked, having expected something like this. But still, he couldn't help but feel a little betrayed as his conversation with Maria in the ladies' toilet was played through. When it ended— *"I mean it, Maria. Stay out of it. I'm warning you."*—Jack had a chilling suspicion about why he was really here.

"What's happened?" he asked, dreading his suspicions being confirmed.

"What's happened is you disappeared for three minutes at 1622 today somewhere between the tenth floor and the roof. You had more than enough time to get to the roof and back down."

Jack blinked. "The roof?"

"Yes, the roof." She called up a file and turned the desk screen to face Jack. "She was found five minutes before you were secured."

On the screen was a picture of the roof. Maria Dioli sprawled awkwardly next to an antenna. Her sightless dark eyes were clouded in death as she stared at him.

"Her neck was broken. No sign of a struggle, so it was someone she knew. Someone she trusted to get that close." McIntosh didn't give him a chance to deny it. "Jack Reardon, I'm arresting you for the suspected murder of Unit Leader Maria Dioli."

TWENTY-THREE
THEN

"**W**e're leaving now?" Jack looked out at the burgeoning day. The sun had just cleared the horizon, but already the heat was building. Inside the brick stable, the cold of night was trapped, but it wouldn't last long against the brutal assault of the day.

"We won't be going far to start with," Blade explained. "And Sheila will be doing most of the work."

The beast in question honked happily and shoved her head at Blade's back. He stumbled forwards a few steps, almost dropping the hefty saddlebag he held.

"In a moment," Blade muttered, pushing her away.

"Christ, you're like an old married couple." Jack snickered and retreated to the back of the outer room, reluctant to go out in the unfiltered sunlight. His memories of his last effort were hazy, but those of the result weren't. He didn't want to suffer another bout of heatstroke, clean of bacterial infection or not.

Blade gave him a withering look, then pointed to a pack. "If you could secure that to the other side of the saddle, I'd truly appreciate it."

Grumbling out of a sense of obligation rather than any real frustration, Jack did as asked. In truth, he was keen for this to get underway. It was time to get back to work, to find Valadian and put this whole mess to rest. That, and he had a burning curiosity to see what Blade had planned.

Sheila knelt neatly in the middle of the outer room, her long, knobbly legs tucked up under her belly. While Blade had decked her out in her gear, she'd sat quietly and serenely. Now that Jack approached with the pack, she twisted her long, sinuous neck around and spat at him.

Jack glared at the thick camel-phlegm on his shirt, then gave the ugly creature a discreet kick in her shank.

The camel grunted and bared her teeth.

"Jack," Blade said wearily.

"What? She started it."

Blade stroked Sheila's neck. "If you treat her nicely, she'll return it in kind."

Things progressed slowly, with Jack having to dodge the camel's sneak attacks. Finally, Blade ordered him away and finished it up himself. When he was satisfied, he clambered up into the big, awkward-looking saddle.

"Come on, Jack. Up here, or you'll be walking."

"Don't know why we can't take the non-spitting, toothless buggy," he muttered, but hauled himself up behind the assassin.

"As I said, it's too conspicuous." With a gentle tap of his foot to Sheila's neck, Blade said, "Hup, hup."

Groaning so loud it echoed in the small space, Sheila heaved herself to her feet. Jack shouted in alarm as the beast rocked back and forth violently. He nearly slid right off, scrambling for a hold on Blade to stop himself from taking a tumble.

Blade laughed, then announced, "Duck," as Sheila hit her top height.

Jack swore as his head came an inch off smacking into the beams of the roof. Blade only laughed harder.

"Fuck you, Blade," Jack growled. "And the camel you rode in on."

"I apologise, Jack. Camel riding is a bit startling for the first-timer." He patted the arm Jack had wrapped around his waist. "I promise, it gets easier. Until we stop and she sits to let us off."

Jack didn't know what blocked the foul litany of curses he wanted to let loose—anger at being laughed at, embarrassment at clinging to the other man in surprise, or extreme embarrassment at clinging to the other man and then forgetting to let go when the chaos settled. Whatever it was, he released Blade with careful deliberation that didn't speak of shame, and reached back to clutch at the rear of the saddle instead.

"Ready?" Blade asked, amusement still in his voice.

"Just do it."

"As you wish, Jack." He tapped Sheila's neck again. "Let's go, Sheila."

The camel blinked her long lashes at him, then padded out into the day.

Blade had found a spare pair of sunglasses, which Jack had taken gratefully. Out in the brilliant sunlight, he was also thankful for the hat from the assassin's stocks. A flap draped around three-quarters of the brim, protecting his neck and the sides of his face from the sun. He wore a camel-pack of hydro-lyte under his shirt to keep him hydrated. Within half an hour, he was sweating profusely, especially where the swaying motion of the camel rocked him against Blade's back. The only good thing about it was seeing Blade sweat as much as he did.

They travelled northward, the sun to their right. Sheila moved at a steady pace that carried them over the burning ground at a good clip. After a while, Jack learned to move with the beast. It wasn't unlike horse riding, just a little less smooth. And a bit more stinky. And higher. Jack didn't have a problem with heights, but the ground did look awfully far away from camel height. He found himself reaching for Blade whenever Sheila's stride hitched.

"Just hold on if it feels more secure," Blade said.

Removing his hands again, Jack mumbled, "Wouldn't want to hinder you."

"You grasping me and then letting go is very distracting, Jack. One or the other, please."

He settled on holding the back of the saddle. There was already enough incidental touching going on. He didn't need to add to it purposefully.

A towering escarpment of red rock appeared on the horizon in front of them an hour or so later. Jack was sucking deeply on his hydro-lyte by then, feeling the heat crawl into his skull. His shirt was soaked with sweat, his jeans also starting to fill up. It was a wonder he had enough fluid left to fuel the half-mast erection he was desperately trying to hide from Blade.

It was an involuntary response to the motion, the occasional push against Blade's back, and his body rejoicing in no longer being sick. It didn't mean anything.

"Not much further," Blade announced, steering Sheila towards the cliffs. "Then we'll stop until the worst of the heat passes."

"Thank God," Jack said.

It took another hour to reach the rocks. Blade directed Sheila along the foot of the edifice. There were no shadows to be found, the sun blaring at them from their side of the cliffs.

Thankfully, a narrow opening in the cliff face appeared not long later. Sheila scrambled over crumbling rocks, as eager as Jack to find some relief. Inside the cliff, the passage meandered, barely wide enough for the camel and her passengers to pass through in places, the packs scraping against rock.

Jack loved it. The temperature began to drop, shadows crowding the narrow space and, eventually, he thought he felt a touch of moisture in the air.

"Where are we going?" he asked, unable to wait.

"You'll see." Blade's tone was smug.

Before Jack could demand a real answer, the passage opened up and they spilled out into a . . .

"A rainforest?" Jack gaped.

Under a partial overhang of rock high above, plants flourished in a vibrant burst of long-missed green. Honest-to-God trees and giant ferns, grass and flowers, vines and creeping moss. Somewhere, water fell into a pool, misting the cool air.

"Not a rainforest." Blade eased Sheila to a stop. "Just a haven from the desert where plants can grow unmolested by the extreme temperatures."

"Shit. Why didn't we come here sooner?"

"Because I couldn't get you on Sheila while you were delirious."

Jack considered that for a moment. "Sounds like you tried."

"One of my more foolish ideas, I'll grant you."

About to snark a response, Jack let out a startled yelp as Sheila rocked her way back into a sitting position. When things were relatively still again, Jack threw himself off the animal with a grateful moan. Sheila immediately twisted her neck to spit.

Dancing out of the way, Jack gave her the finger.

Blade took a couple of bags from Sheila's packs, then slapped her on the rump. The camel humped her way back to her feet and, saddle swaying ponderously, padded off into the trees.

"She'll be back," Blade assured Jack.

"I wasn't worried."

Blade smirked. "Of course not. Breakfast?"

It was cool enough to eat, so Jack agreed. Cold beans and tinned fruit under the beautiful green canopy. His back to a lumpy tree trunk, Jack felt much better. This was what he'd been missing. Life. The desert was barren, hollow. A vacuum waiting to pull him into its emptiness. This gorge reminded him of the Cardamom Mountains, of the beauty he'd found in the thick, tangled lives of plants, animals, and humans. If a tiger stepped out of the trees right now, he'd probably throw his arms around it in relief.

Between a full belly and the cool air, Jack dropped into a light doze. He was vaguely aware of Blade puttering about, organising packs. Sheila wandered back occasionally, for a pat and a quiet word, before disappearing again. Then Jack could ignore the growing pressure no longer.

He stood and stretched. "Gotta piss."

The assassin nodded and kept doing whatever he was doing.

Jack ambled off a ways, took care of business, then went in search of the waterfall.

He found it rather close by. A roughly circular pool at the bottom of the cliff, full of green-hued water, filled by a respectable-sized waterfall emerging from the cliff face about two dozen yards from the bottom. Small fish zipped through the clear water. Across from him, a white-plumed heron stood on a rock, watching the water intently.

The water was deliciously cool, so Jack stripped in record time and waded in. The first few minutes he spent splashing about, simply happy to be immersed in water after so long. The heron didn't appreciate the noise or him disturbing its hunting, so it launched on a wide spread of pristine white wings and ghosted away through the surrounding trees.

Wish you were here?

No, because *here* was near to bloody perfect.

"Are you having fun?"

Jack startled and sank below the surface. He came up spluttering to hear Blade laughing. Blinking water out of his eyes, he found the assassin on the bank, calmly stripping. Jack's erection made a comeback at the sight of so much pale, taut skin over sleek muscles.

"I was," Jack groused, turning away and swimming for the waterfall.

Under the spray, he found a ledge that lifted him mostly out of the water. It proved no respite, however, because Blade followed him out with strong strokes. Seemingly unashamed of his nakedness, Blade hauled himself up beside Jack. He handed over a cake of soap and proceeded to work his own into a lather.

"Think of everything, don't you," Jack grumbled.

"I do try, and I have a lot of experience to draw on. Of course, now I know to bring packets of saline in future, as well."

Jack snarled silently, then washed because getting properly clean would be so damn good. When he tried to rub the soap through his hair, though, he encountered a problem.

"Goddamn splint." He wrestled his broken arm free of a tangle of curls.

Blade lifted his own freshly washed head out from under the waterfall. "Do you need a hand?"

"No. I'm fine." His words were belied by the splint catching on more strands and making him wince.

"Here." Blade came up behind him. "Let me."

Keenly aware of how it would look to refuse, Jack stood still while Blade lathered up his soap.

"Could you sit? You're a bit taller than me."

Jack sat. Blade crouched behind him, knees to either side. The touch of his fingers against Jack's scalp was gentle as he kneaded the soap through knots and snarls. Jack had to work to hold down the shiver in his shoulders. It had been so long since anyone touched him like this. Well, that he was aware of. Blade had presumably taken care of him while he'd been sick, and Jack was so bloody grateful he'd been out of it, because if he'd felt like this then, who knew what he might have done while not aware.

He was highly conscious of Blade's proximity, of the heat of his body so close to his bare back, the fact they were both naked. The memory of moving against him during the ride was sharp and clear and hard to dismiss. The lean body, the firm muscles of his thighs, the sinuous way he'd rolled with the animal's gait.

All the tangles worked out, Blade dragged his fingers through Jack's hair, drawing it out straight and chuckling as it pulled back sluggishly into sagging curls. Then he dug his strong fingers into Jack's head, massaging his scalp.

Christ! Jack almost moaned. It was harder to hold back when Blade pressed two fingers into his temples and rubbed in circles.

"You need to relax," the assassin murmured. "You're very tense."

How else was he supposed to be when a slight shift in either of their positions would reveal his hard dick to Blade? Jack couldn't reply. If he unclenched his jaw, he wasn't sure it wouldn't be to groan in pleasure.

When Blade stopped the massage, Jack stupidly thought the trauma was over.

"I like your tattoo." Blade's nimble fingers skimmed down Jack's left shoulder blade. "It's very beautiful."

Jack almost laughed. No one who'd seen it before said that. Mostly, they asked what it meant. If he was truthful and said it was a reminder of his mother, it generally sent the inquisitive man running.

"It's a Saint Thomas Cross," he said softly. "Symbol of my mother's religion."

Blade made a quiet, appreciative noise, his fingertips tracing the outline of the cross, from the lotus flower base to the dove at the top. It took every ounce of strength and willpower to sit still for it, even more than when Blade had washed his hair. This was . . . was . . . intolerable, frustrating, personal. Wonderful. Arousing.

No. What it was, was ridiculous. This man was Ethan Blade. *Ethan Blade!* An assassin. He was the man who'd willingly broken Jack's cover for his own purposes, who'd torn his bloody way through thirty soldiers and calmly played doctor minutes afterwards. He was a cold-blooded killer. Not someone to lust after.

It wasn't because of Blade. Anyone touching him right now would probably generate a hard-on.

Still, when Blade finally stopped, Jack couldn't help a small sound of disappointment.

"Rinse off," Blade said, somewhat subdued. Was he annoyed Jack hadn't been able to relax while Blade was touching him? Would the truth of the matter make him angry or . . .

Jack pulled back from that avenue of thought and twisted to thrust his head under the waterfall. Behind him, Blade dove off the ledge into the pool. When he surfaced, he swam directly for shore.

"We have fresh clothes back at the packs," he said loudly so Jack heard him over the rush of the water. Then he gathered up his dirty clothes and walked away, naked.

Jack scrunched his eyes closed against the sight of those toned legs, that muscular arse, and that lean back. Fuck. This wasn't happening.

Except that it was, and his dick wasn't listening to reason. It didn't care how many people Blade might have killed. It just liked the way he'd touched Jack. And the way he looked. The way he could make Jack laugh. The way he appeared so young and innocent when he slept. The feel of his body shifting against Jack's. Even that accent.

Jack didn't know the exact moment he'd wrapped a fist around his dick. Even when what he was doing registered, he couldn't stop, too caught up in the sensation of heat building in his stomach, in the coiling tension in his guts. Even the harshness of his rough palm against the aching head of his dick worked, making him think of Blade's hand pressed to his, of the similarities between their gun-grown calluses.

Jesus. He was wanking to the memory of Blade touching him. Maybe he was still delirious. This was just the fever having its cruel way with him. Which made him pull forth the image of Blade helping him from the bed to the outer room. The sight of his hand against Jack's stomach. Pale skin against dark, the contrast fascinating and amazingly arousing.

Jack came with a startled gasp, his orgasm taking him by surprise. It rocked through him in successive waves, tremors lingering long after he'd fallen back on the rock, water splashing over his heated body.

"Damn," he whispered when he'd caught his breath.

Wanting to put it behind him as quickly as possible, Jack rolled off the ledge and into the pool. After washing thoroughly, he made for shore. He scrambled back onto dry land and shook off as much water as he could. Not particularly fancying strolling back to Blade naked, he bent to put on his jeans.

And froze.

A pair of boots stood back in the ground cover, partially hidden by a tree. Blade? Come to spy on Jack wanking? No, those weren't his boots, but they were familiar.

Slowly, Jack straightened and found himself looking down the barrel of a rifle, held by one of Valadian's soldiers.

TWENTY-FOUR
NOW

Maxwell pushed Jack down into a chair and stood over him. McIntosh woke up each screen in the table and angled them all towards him. They held pictures of Maria's body.

Was this his fault? Had she been killed just to frame him? Or had she found something she shouldn't have?

"You liked her, didn't you?" McIntosh asked quietly. "It was why she was chosen as your handler for the Valadian operation. Did you know how worried she was when you went dark? Quite the stressful time for Maria. She thought you were dead, that she hadn't seen the danger coming and left you there to die."

Jack shook his head in mute denial.

"Is that why you killed her? Because she left you out there alone?"

"I wasn't alone."

"No, I guess you weren't. You were with your new ally, Ethan Blade. Did Maria find something out about your relationship with Blade that required her being silenced?"

"No."

"Really? How can I trust anything you say now, Jack? You've already lied about so much."

He clenched his jaw over the angry response, waiting until it passed. "I'm not lying about this, ma'am. I didn't kill Maria."

"Her neck was broken in a single move. Something I know you are capable of. You said it yourself, in your report about your time in the desert."

The fog of shock was fading fast, leaving Jack's head clear and sharp. A spike in adrenaline flowed through him, his body trained to respond to threats.

"I didn't do this," Jack said calmly. "You know I wouldn't do something like this."

McIntosh studied him for a long moment. "Convince me why you had no need to silence her. Explain why you didn't want her looking into Blade's movements during the past year."

"You listened to the conversation we had. My reasons were exactly as I said to her. Digging into Blade's life is dangerous, even from a distance."

"Are you saying Blade had something to do with her death?"

"No. He's locked up."

"By your own words, Jack, the man's a meticulous planner. Couldn't he have planned for this? Perhaps he has an accomplice." McIntosh eyed him keenly. "Does he?"

"I wouldn't know."

The questioning continued in this manner for a long time, circling around the accusation Jack was working with Blade, coming at it from all directions. They were still trawling through the mountains of information Maria had on Valadian and Blade, yet McIntosh all but said she was convinced they'd find the proof in there. Jack kept up a deadly calm throughout it all, the anti-interrogation training he'd had with the SAS and the Office working against those who'd once benefitted from it. McIntosh didn't resort to anything as crude as threats, though, using repetition as her main weapon. Asking the same questions over and over, couched differently, in random order, trying to trip up his answers.

All the while, Jack searched for clues in her words. Was she the traitor? Had she killed Maria and questioning him was a cover for her own actions? Had he played ever so sweetly into her hands by avoiding the Shadows on the stairs? Jack could only hope his answers were as innocent sounding as her questions.

Five minutes to the deadline, the door to the meeting room clicked open.

Startled mid question, McIntosh snapped her ice-cold glare onto the newcomer.

"So it's true," Director Tan said blandly. "You have taken Mr. Reardon into custody."

Great. Two out of three suspects were here. Maybe Jack could goad them into a revealing argument.

"Not now, Alex," McIntosh ground out. "This is none of your business."

"Isn't it? A murder within the building is everyone's business." Tan stood beside her and perused the images of Maria as if idly reading a catalogue. "Certainly looks damning. Don't forget, Donna, we have a building full of specially trained people who could have done this. Not just this one man."

"No one else is on record as threatening the victim. No one else has motivation."

"No? Not even the proven assassin we have locked up downstairs?" Tan tapped at one of the touchpads. "Let's just make sure he's still in custody, shall we?"

Perhaps Jack didn't need to do anything to provoke an argument. Tan was walking a very thin line in regards to McIntosh's anger, but she maintained a neutral expression as the images on the screens switched to the feed from Ethan's cell. The assassin sat on the bed, legs crossed, eyes closed. On his knee rested a half-eaten log of green fudge.

"Well, well," Tan murmured. "Looks like you have some explaining to do, Mr. Reardon."

Before Jack could espouse his innocence, once *again*, movement on the screen caught everyone's attention.

Ethan wasn't on the bed anymore. He was up and stalking for the table. Gripping one of the chairs, he stood still for a moment, then picked it up and threw it at the door.

Alarms blared throughout the building, the abrupt *whoop whoop* of trouble. In his cell, Ethan ripped off his scrub top and twisted it into a thick wad with a couple of flicks of his wrists. Moving as if to wrap it around his face, he hesitated.

Sitting in a room thirteen floors overheard, Jack saw Ethan's chest hitch as if he couldn't catch his breath. He jerked silently, hands flexing in the material of his top as he staggered against the table.

They'd flooded the cell with knockout gas.

Jack's chest was tight with tension and fear and surging adrenaline. This was it. The low-level nausea that had been curling through his guts for the past several hours vanished, replaced by the steady calm that meant he was in action, his training kicking in with almost violent force.

"Get him out of here and locked up," McIntosh snapped at Maxwell, gesturing to Jack.

The head of security grabbed Jack by the collar of his suit jacket, then hauled him out of the chair. Roughly, he spun Jack towards the door and gave him a hard enough shove it threw Jack off-balance.

"No," Tan growled. "Reardon stays right here, where we can keep an eye on him."

Maxwell hesitated, torn between the orders of two directors.

Jack used it.

He transformed his stumble into a turn and delivered a double-barrelled kick to Maxwell's armoured stomach. The security head *oof*ed in surprise and staggered backwards two steps, then recovered. Drawing his Glock, he dodged Jack's next kick, defending with an upraised arm. Jack twisted, momentum and speed driving his kick into Maxwell's ribs. The HoS crashed back against the table. Jack's foot throbbed from the hard connection with Maxwell's body armour, but he ignored it in the rush of adrenaline.

Backing off, Jack worked his bound hands downwards over his arse. Maxwell charged after him. He came in with a low sweep of his leg, taking Jack off his feet and sending him crashing to the floor on his back. In the moment it took Maxwell to lift the gun and aim, Jack had slid his cuffed hands along the length of his legs and brought them back to his front. All in one smooth motion, he rocked back and up, throwing himself off the ground and right into Maxwell. They crashed into the table, chairs skidding away.

Across the room, McIntosh was shouting into her phone. Tan simply stood back, watching the fight with something close to curiosity.

Jack ignored them, concentrating on Maxwell. The head of security twisted out of Jack's awkward hold, sending a flying kick towards his gut. Jack shoved himself backwards, his heels hitting one of the fallen chairs. Jumping over the chair, he scooped it up with a foot and tossed it at Maxwell. Not bothering to wait for the outcome, Jack repeated the move with another chair, rewarded with a satisfying grunt of pain from Maxwell as it smacked him in the face. He picked up the first chair in his bound hands, then slammed it down over Maxwell's head. The chair broke. After adjusting his hold, Jack slapped the remains of the chair against Maxwell's gun arm. The Glock spun away.

Maxwell growled, lunging forwards with the suddenness and strength of a dump of adrenaline into his system. He ploughed his armoured shoulder into Jack's ribs, lifting him off the floor and slamming him into the wall. His big meaty fist pounded into Jack's stomach.

"Fuck . . . you . . ." Maxwell snarled between blows.

"Sorry, sailor," Jack gasped, his abdomen tensed so hard against the punches he could barely breathe. "You never were my type." And he brought his knee right up into Maxwell's nuts.

Christ! They were armouring their junk now. Pain whipped through Jack's knee and thigh from the hard connection to the solid cup. Still, it distracted Maxwell enough Jack could get his leg back between Maxwell's. He hooked his knee around the other man's and shoved at his chest.

Maxwell went over backwards, Jack coming down with his knees in Maxwell's groin.

Armour was great at absorbing kicks and punches. Not so great at deflecting the entire weight of a tall, well-muscled ex-SAS soldier. While Maxwell shouted in pain and shock, Jack grabbed the sides of his head, lifted it, and slammed it into the floor. Maxwell struggled, his motions becoming wild as Jack repeated the move. Dazed, the HoS couldn't defend when Jack punched him. Bone snapped and blood gushed from Maxwell's nose. Before the HoS could recover, Jack swiftly bound him with plastic cuffs from his own utility belt, which Jack unfastened and took with him when he straightened.

McIntosh and Tan were by the window, both with pistols trained on him.

"Stand down, Reardon," Tan said, cool and collected. "This isn't what you want to do."

Jack smiled. "Isn't it?"

He feinted with the belt, and they both jerked in reaction. Jack hit the deck just as McIntosh fired. He rolled under the desk.

The door burst open, and security personnel poured into the room with fluid coordination. Before Tan or McIntosh could alert them to his position, Jack kicked two chairs out from under the table and into the front ranks. They went down in a tangle of leather upholstery and limbs. Jack rolled out into the mess.

People were shouting. McIntosh commanded them to use whatever force necessary; Tan countered with demands for Jack to be kept alive; security people tried to keep track of Jack within the melee.

Jack used the belt to block blows, to snap guns from hands, to trip his opponents. He kicked and punched and headbutted, almost revelling in the freedom of it, of being surrounded by the enemy. Every body closing in on him was a target, and he let his training move him.

Then suddenly he was free, falling out of the meeting room into the relatively clear corridor. Another security team appeared around a corner, so Jack sprang to his feet and sprinted in the other direction. A shout gave him warning, and he tucked himself into a roll as the newcomers opened fire. Even as they redirected their aim downwards, he rocked up to his feet and jumped clear of the floor as bullets ripped into the carpet. His move propelled him into a wall, and he pushed off it before hitting the floor again and rolling around a corner. After coming back to his feet, he ran.

Alarms continued to blurt. The building would be in automatic lockdown by now, all external entrances sealed tight, the windows going opaque to keep out curious eyes. There were always loopholes in any security system, however, and Jack happened to have one handy.

He slammed through the door to the stairwell and stopped, pushing his back against the door. Going *sideways*, he activated the copy he'd made of Maxwell's sec-tab RFID. Instantly, the lock on the door behind him lit up in his implant, recognising the signal. Once all the electronic locks linked to the sec-tab—which was all of those aboveground, bar one—answered Jack's signal, he overrode their programming with an old one he'd used years ago on a mission with the SAS. Its encryption was military and wouldn't take long for the Office techs to crack, but it would give him, hopefully, enough time to do what was needed.

Throughout the upper twelve floors of the Neville Crawley Building, every electronic lock opened for one second, two, then shut with a new command. The building was, for about the next ten minutes, Jack's.

Working fast, he went through the utility belt until he found the key to the handcuffs. After a few twists of his wrists, the cuffs fell off with a clatter. Jack grabbed Maxwell's phone from the belt, then pocketed it and the key and cuffs, just in case.

As Jack took the stairs two at a time, heading down, he ripped open the secret folds in his suit and pulled free the components he'd sewn into the material.

TWENTY-FIVE
THEN

"**S**hit," the soldier muttered, a strangely worried expression crossing his face. "What are you doing here?"

Jack stayed still. "Having a bath, clearly."

The soldier looked his dripping, naked body over quickly. "Yeah, I can see that." His gaze flickered away and came back, narrowed. "Is that mad bastard with you?"

"He's around."

"Shit," he hissed. "Shit, shit, shit." The rifle wavered slightly.

This obviously wasn't going the way the soldier thought it should, which confused Jack. Mr. Valadian was looking for him and here he'd been found, but his discoverer didn't seem at all pleased by it. Unless...

"You alone?" Jack asked.

The soldier glared at him, jaw clenching tight, rifle steadying.

It all screamed *yes*. So that was his issue. Alone, and somewhere out there was Blade. Jack wouldn't want to be in this guy's position.

"Don't move," the man snarled, finger caressing the trigger of the rifle. "Don't open your mouth, either."

Jack simply spread his empty hands and obeyed.

This was going to be a waiting game, then, between the soldier and Blade. Would the man panic and shoot Jack before Blade came looking for him?

Jack didn't have the patience for either outcome. His orgasm had left him jittery and eager to move, to work through the last of the endorphins. Coming once always filled him with energy, usually to fuck again. But this would do as an alternative.

Jack dropped under the field of fire and rolled forwards. He came up under the rifle, knocking it aside before the soldier could even shout. Twisting the man's rifle arm under his own, Jack spun and put his back to the soldier's chest, arm and weapon trapped between them. He elbowed the startled man in the face twice, in rapid succession.

Jack found it almost too easy, despite his recent illness. Even when the soldier regained some wits and fought free of him, trying to sweep Jack's legs out from under him. Jack flung himself out of the way, then came back in immediately, double-barrelling his foot into the soldier's chest, then his face. Advancing again, he wrenched the rifle from slackening fingers and tossed it away.

Jack was burning to use his hands, to feel in complete control again, to know he could rely on his body. To reassure himself he wasn't a slave to its mindless lusting. So he forced the hapless soldier back into the trees, kicking, punching, weaving through the feeble return blows. Blood splattered the man's face and the front of his clothes. He fumbled for a knife, and Jack knocked it from his hold before he could raise it past his belt. Jack realised somewhere between one kick and the next punch he was playing with the man, taking out his frustrations and anger on him.

This wasn't the SAS way. Fight when necessary and within mission parameters. They didn't abuse their opponents, just eliminated the danger they posed.

Giving up his anger, Jack moved swiftly, closing with the soldier. Sensing the fight had changed, the man redoubled his efforts, blocking blows and dodging kicks. Now that Jack wanted it over, the man was finally fighting for his life.

Jack backed off, as if now wary. Snarling, the soldier shook blood and sweat from his face. He swayed on his feet but dragged in deep gulps of air, preparing for the next bout.

After feinting one way, Jack spun around and leaped onto his back as the soldier turned. As they fell, Jack twisted and got the man under him when they hit the ground. Knees clamping the soldier's arms to his sides, Jack grabbed his head and wrenched it up and to the side.

The man's neck broke with sickening *crunch*.

Jack knelt there for a long time, breathing hard. Whether it was a lack of oxygen to his brain or the swamping waves of adrenaline, Jack couldn't form a firm thought until his heart slowed from rapid-fire pace to something a bit more normal. Even then, the only thing that sang clear through his mind was *Blade*.

Jack raced back to their little camp. At his approach, Blade, who'd been kneeling by a pack, twisted and rolled. He came up on his knees, the two Eagles aimed directly at Jack. The instant he recognised Jack, the barrels of the guns jerked skyward.

Flowing to his feet, Blade tossed a gun to Jack. "What happened?" He immediately began scanning the surrounding trees.

"One of Valadian's men. He was alone, though others can't be far away."

"You neutralized him?"

"Yeah." Jack breathed it out like it was a humiliating defeat. Still, he let the gun settle into his hand with a little sigh of relief.

"I suspected it might happen this close to the compound. Get dressed." He indicated a pile of material where he'd been kneeling. "I'll keep watch."

Edgy, Jack dressed swiftly, donning a DPDU the same as Blade was wearing. The uniform had been meant for Blade, being too short in the legs and sleeves and a little snug across the chest, but it was better than careening around naked. Clothed and armed, he joined Blade in scanning for enemies.

"What now?"

"Now, I fear we'll have to take the long way around," Blade said calmly.

Blade whistled shrilly for Sheila, and by the time she lumbered back into their clearing, they had the small packs on their backs and Jack had added tough combat boots to his ensemble. Blade strapped the big bags upright on the saddle so that from a distance they would look like two people riding the camel. Jack watched bemusedly until he worked out what it meant.

"You're sending her off on her own? She's our transport!"

"A secondary benefit only. Her real purpose is as a decoy. We didn't bring the buggy because it couldn't drive itself home. Sheila, however." Blade stroked her neck, then stepped back and slapped her sharply on the rump. "Home, Sheila. Home!"

With a startled grunt, the camel jerked into a trot, heading for the narrow path they'd arrived by, her fake passengers wobbling. Blade watched her go with a small worried frown.

Jack grudgingly admitted it was a good idea. When Valadian's men came looking for their lost fellow—and found his body—they would see camel tracks leading into the gorge, camel tracks and theirs inside the gorge, and camel tracks leading out. If they followed and caught sight of Sheila in the distance, it'd look as if Blade and Jack were fleeing back the way they'd come.

"We go this way." Blade indicated further into the gorge.

They backtracked to the pool, and Blade moved them onto the rocks surrounding it so they wouldn't leave any footprints. On the far side of the waterfall, they clambered over damp rocks and squeezed through a very narrow gap in the cliff, coming into another opening a few minutes later. Unlike the previous one, this space wasn't fed by an underground stream and it was drier, the plants brittle and hard. The floor was sandy and Blade avoided it, jumping from rock to rock, even swinging between the thin, papery trunks of the stunted trees. It was warmer here, the heat of the desert not held at bay by a curtain of moisture.

Neither of them spoke beyond Blade warning Jack about a wonky rock or cracking branch. They fell into a natural rhythm of working together, Blade on point, Jack constantly checking their six. Jack had only ever felt such symbiosis with other military-trained personnel, people who'd had the same commands and actions drilled into them. Occasionally, Jack found himself falling into military hand signals, and Blade responded in kind. He supposed it shouldn't shock him, but tallied up with everything else, and the whispering echo of Blade's voice—*I have a sudden urge to salute.*"—Jack didn't like the conclusion he was drawing.

He kept his thoughts to himself. Right now wasn't the time to confront Blade about his past.

They kept moving through the narrowing and expanding gorge for several hours, leaving behind all hints of life and returning to the dead nothingness. The further they went with no sign of trouble, the more Jack wondered what the hell was going on. Valadian's army wasn't a sternly disciplined, regimented group, but it wasn't a stupid rabble, either. Jack and Blade *shouldn't* be getting away with this. And yet, it seemed as if they were.

Darkness came quickly in the gorge. The moment the sun dropped out of sight of their narrow view of the sky, shadows crawled down the walls and spread like ink over the ground. Jack put his sunglasses away and took the hat from his head, needing as much light as he could get. Ahead, Blade removed his hat but left his glasses on for longer. He finally took them off when the sun was over the horizon, leaving them in true darkness.

"No torches," Blade whispered. "Keep close to me."

Cold flooded down the gorge on the heels of the shadows. The sweat pooling at the base of Jack's spine began to cool uncomfortably.

Abruptly, Blade stopped, looking up at the rock walls closing in on them.

"What is it?"

Blade gestured. "There's a cave up there, big enough for us to bunker down in. I'm wondering, however, if we should keep going. There's another shelter at the far end of the gorge. I think we can make it by dawn. Or not long thereafter."

Jack considered. Night had barely bloomed and he much preferred travelling in the cold than the heat.

"Easier to warm up than cool down," was his offering.

Blade grunted agreement, and they continued on.

An hour later, Jack had a nice level of exertion going to keep the cold at bay. However, it didn't stop the chill of a dingo howl rippling down his spine. The damn thing sounded like it came from just in front of Blade.

The assassin froze, crouched on a rock slightly above Jack.

"Blade?" Jack hissed the name.

"Shh."

Another howl, sounding closer, and as it faded, another canine voice rose in response.

In the eerie silence that followed, Jack heard it. The soft pad of paws, the distinctive *click* of nails on rock.

Fantastic.

"Jack," Blade whispered. "Back up."

Not really needing to be told, Jack crept backwards, Desert Eagle up even though he could barely see anything beyond fifteen feet in the darkness. Blade was a paler shadow in front of him, sliding off the rock and moving in Jack's wake.

They'd gone perhaps a dozen feet when the dingo appeared, bounding to the top of the rock Blade had abandoned. It stopped there, glittering eyes focusing on them. Jack had heard they grew big in this part of the country, but this was ridiculous. The dog probably reached halfway up Jack's thigh at the shoulder, weighing nearly thirty kilos. A person would definitely feel it if this thing hit them full on. Otherwise, it was lean and sleek, a strong-looking animal, with a beautiful array of teeth it proudly showed them when it snarled.

"Jesus." Jack didn't know if it was a curse or a prayer. He'd always liked dingoes. At least conceptually. Here and now, he'd rather not have to reconsider his opinion.

The dingo lifted its head and howled, a long, undulating sound that rippled down Jack's spine and threatened to liquefy his bones. From the darkness behind the wild dog came answering howls, a chorus of savage hunters eager for the chase.

The red point of the laser sight on Jack's Desert Eagle was brilliant against the shadowed chest of the dingo.

Blade shoved Jack's arm up. The bullet cracked against the rocks of the gorge. On its boulder, the dingo crouched, snarling at the unusual sound. Its pack mates yipped and yowled, the sounds echoing between the narrow walls until it felt as if they were surrounded by hundreds of animals.

"What the hell?" Jack hissed, trying to wrestle his arm free of Blade's hold.

"It's just a dog," the assassin ground out. "He's only protecting his—"

The dingo leaped, flying towards Blade.

TWENTY-SIX
NOW

Four floors down, the Assassin X fully assembled and slung over a shoulder, Jack stopped and fished Maxwell's phone out of his pocket. He keyed up the video feed from Ethan's cell.

A body lay sprawled on the floor of the cell. One of the armoured and gas-masked guards. The door was closed and there was no sign of the other guard, or Ethan.

Jack quickly flicked back to when the gas had been released. Heart slamming against his heaving ribs, he watched as Ethan collapsed to the floor, hands clutching at his throat. A full minute passed—Jack sped through the footage at five times normal—before the door opened and the gas-masked guards came in. One crouched by Ethan, the other covering them with a tranquilizer gun.

From his prone position on the floor, Ethan spun and took down the first guard with a series of insanely fast sweeps and punches. Then he flipped to his feet, the downed man's tranq gun in hand. The second guard backed out of the cell, yelling for help, reaching for the door lock. Ethan fired through the rapidly narrowing doorway, then dove through.

Ethan was out of the cell, but he wasn't completely free yet. Putting the phone away, Jack kept going.

By the time he encountered opposition, he was three floors off his destination.

The only lock the sec-tab couldn't access was on the door to the sublevels, where the cells were. It was guarded by six security personnel and two key-code locks with randomised codes generated by an isolated system in the sublevels. The three guards on the outside of the door knew one code, those on the inside the other. Both codes were needed to open the door, which had undoubtedly happened to allow through the security team that had set up a barricade on the fourth-floor landing. They crouched behind a line of bulletproof shields, firearms at the ready.

Jack studied them from the landing above. A team of six with rifles modified to fire rubber bullets. Painful, but survivable. Either way, he couldn't afford to get caught up here. The techs would be hard at work on cracking his encryption. He only had about eight minutes left.

Settling the Assassin X to his shoulder, Jack rested the end of the barrel on the staircase railing. The height advantage gave him a line of sight over the top of the shields.

Jack sighted his targets, then fired once, twice. Both point riflemen went down, the little black tufts of tranq darts all but invisible against the black of their uniform sleeves. The Assassin X wasn't a tranq gun, and the darts hit with close to the force of a real bullet, but his victims would survive. Jack adjusted position and took out another.

"Stand down, Reardon," one of them shouted. "You can't get past us all."

Ignoring the effort to delay him, Jack fired two more wild shots as he flung himself over the railing and dropped to the lower stairs.

Shields worked both ways. He ducked into the cover they offered from those crouched behind them. They'd now have to lean over their protection to get a shot at him. Feet against the bottom of the nearest shield, he grasped the top of it with his free hand and pulled it over on top of him. Lifting the bottom up with his legs, he fired between his feet, taking down the last three people.

Jack shoved the shield away, stood, and kept going.

Barrelling down the final flight, he ejected the magazine from the rifle and slammed in another one. This one held only a single round. He racked the bolt coming around the final turn. Another team waited for him. No attempt at negotiation this time. They just opened fire.

Scrambling backwards, Jack crouched behind the railing. A bullet cracked off the cement so close to his head grit flew into his panting mouth. Spitting, he risked a quick look.

With more room to work in, this lot had crafted a dead end with their shields. If he charged, they'd hit him from both sides. There was no time to take them out, however. He had only the one shot available.

Jack breathed deep, reaching for a level of calm. The tactical moves were coming back with all the unconscious precision of muscle memory, but the emotional detachment hadn't quite kicked in. Another fallout of the desert. His ability to compartmentalise had been tested and broken on the sun-blasted rocks.

Damn it. He had to get his shit together. If this didn't work, the results didn't bear thinking about. So he didn't.

Another peek and he saw what he had to do. He waited out the volley of shots, pulled out the empty mag and, rolling out into the open, tossed the empty mag at the gathered guards.

The small black projectile looked enough like a grenade the guards didn't wait to make sure it was. They scattered, leaving the door to the sublevels exposed. The door standing between Ethan and relative freedom. The one with the lock Jack didn't currently command.

Coming up on one knee, Jack slammed the rifle to his shoulder. "Fire in the hole," he shouted and pulled the trigger.

The Assassin X took .22 LR rounds, a small bullet that generally did comparatively little damage. A .22 LR modified into a high-explosive incendiary round, however, was just enough to take out a lock.

Jack didn't wait around to see the results. There was barely three minutes left on his timeline, and he had to climb back up twelve flights. He took the stairs three at a time. His part in the plan was done. The rest was up to Ethan.

On the tenth floor, his implant *ping*ed. Trusting his body to keep going, Jack checked the message. His encryption was crumbling before the combined might of the Office techs. He had mere seconds left.

He was going to make it. He had to make it.

The lock to the door to the roof flared in his implant. He unlocked it an instant before he body-slammed it. The door opened just as the encryption failed and Jack's command of the electronic locks vanished.

He fell through the doorway and hit the cement of the roof hard. Rolling, he kicked the door shut, and it locked under the command of the Office. Hopefully it would take them another couple of minutes to realise he was on the other side of it.

Jack leaned against the door, dragging in massive gulps of air to help soothe his burning lungs. Blood pounded through his ears, deafening him to the quiet hum of the air-con fans, to the gentle whipping of the streamers, to the voice in the back of his head telling him he'd really screwed up this time.

No going back now. He had no idea how many people he had hurt. People he'd worked with for six years, who'd accepted him into their ranks after the military abandoned him. This building had been more of a home to him than his own apartment. For God's sake, he kept the few things truly precious to him here, and now he'd left them behind.

Ethan better be right about the traitor.

Ping. An incoming call. McIntosh's ID.

"Jack." McIntosh had found her inner ice-queen again.

"Ma'am."

There was silence for a long time, then softly, *"You promised me."*

"Yeah, I did. And I didn't lie about that."

"All evidence to the contrary."

Jack huffed. "I suppose that is how it looks. I guess you'll just have to trust me on this."

A sudden gust of wind snapped the streamers taut, stretching them out like spindly fingers reaching for the sky. The black and white of the Office building's decorations gave way to a rainbow of colours on the next—red, purple, yellow, orange, and right on the far edge, a single blue ribbon. A vague connection sparked in Jack's head, but McIntosh interrupted before he could pursue it.

"How am I supposed to do that? You took out two security teams, broke the head of security's face, and let a proven killer loose in a locked-down building. You're not exactly behaving like a loyal asset of this organisation, Jack."

Jack wondered how this conversation would go if it were Tan on the other end. "Just tell everyone to stay out of Blade's way. Let him do what he's got to do. He won't hurt you if you leave him alone." Unless she was his target.

What was the order? Vanquish, Maserati, Camaro, Lamborghini. *"What he's got to do?"* The chill was starting to melt under a growing anger. *"What the hell are you talking about?"*

Jack almost laughed. "You see, ma'am, the man has his own code. Once he's hired to do a job, he does everything he has to until it's done. It's nothing personal."

Black, blue, yellow, white. Jack's means of transport out of here.

"This is about as personal as it gets, you fucking bastard." McIntosh never swore, which made this poisoned barb sink deep. *"He destroyed one of my long-term, vitally important operations. He turned one of my best assets. He led this entire building around by its collective nose for twenty-four hours and now, he's ploughing his way through my staff like a plague on nine different stimulants! How is that not personal, Jack?"*

"You forget one thing, ma'am. This is a job, for you, for me, and for him."

Another protracted silence. *"That isn't very reassuring."*

"No, it isn't." He could appreciate the sentiment. It hadn't been reassuring when he'd found out he was just a job to Ethan, too. "But it's better than the alternative."

That was when he heard it. A soft *click* close to his ear. He turned his head and it came again, muffled by layers of steel and wood. Someone coding through the locks on the door.

Shit. McIntosh hadn't called to talk. She'd called to distract him.

"Come in now, Jack, and it won't be so bad. No one's—"

Jack hit the kill switch on his implant.

Slinging the Assassin X over his shoulder, he trotted through the web of streamers, looking for the one he'd noted earlier. There it was, on the east corner of the building. Right where he needed it.

He'd just finished untangling the long black streamer when the door burst open. A heavily armoured strike team poured through it, laser sights converging on Jack like flies to a rotting corpse.

Jack thought of the dingo, the red dot of his laser sight glinting on its chest.

If only Ethan were here to tell these guys Jack was just doing what came naturally to him. Protecting his own.

No friendly warning this time. The team opened fire.

Jack raced for the edge of the roof, wrapping the streamer around his hands. The strands of high-tensile wire woven into the material gripped him back. Bullets chasing him, gaining on him, Jack threw himself up onto the edge of the building and kept going.

Behind him, the satellite dish screeched as his weight pulled it around sharply. The sudden movement flung him out further, snapping the streamer taut. At the peak of his flight, Jack shook free of the material. He landed in a controlled tumble on the roof of the next building.

Immediately, he was up and racing for the far edge, aiming for the blue streamer. On the next, lower building, he found the yellow one, and beyond it, a single white in an undulating sea of red. His last ride. He flung himself off the top of the building and arced out over empty space, a hundred feet up and nowhere to go but down.

Jack twisted in mid-flight, then hit the water of Darling Harbour like an Olympic diver coming off a very high board.

TWENTY-SEVEN
THEN

Jack shoved Blade to the side and dove after him. The dingo flashed through the space they vacated. Blade stumbled to the ground, unprepared for the move. Jack kept to his feet, half turning to get a boot into the snarling dog's face. Snapping, the dingo backed off, head lowered, watching them intently, its regard a weight that tugged on Jack's guts.

This was a wild creature, a beast seeing only a trespasser, a threat. A savage intellect, alien and yet relatable. Blade was right. It was only defending its territory, its pack. Didn't Jack do exactly the same thing? Hadn't he turned himself into a predator to defend his home and family?

He and the dingo were both the products of their environments.

Jack eased away from the snarling dingo and slowly put the Desert Eagle back in the waistband of his pants.

"Jack?" Blade was on his feet again.

"Back up," Jack murmured. "Slowly."

With Blade behind him, Jack took slow, cautious steps backwards, feeling for each placement of his feet. Respect the animal and its instincts he might, but that didn't mean he wanted to end up on his arse, unable to defend himself should it pounce.

Wary now, the dingo held back, but followed. It stalked them across the uneven ground with sublime grace, seeming to flow over rocks and dead branches like a sentient puddle of quicksilver. Its top lip curled upwards, a soft, steady rumble rolling out of its chest.

Yip!

All three of them froze.

Jack's heart thumped hard against his ribs. Blade sucked in a sharp breath. Before him, the huge wild dog lifted its head, ears swivelling to catch the sound as it was repeated. Then it tilted its head back, exposing its throat.

Yip! Yip!

Dogs spilled out of shadows and crevices, slinking over rocks and from between boulders. Jack wasn't sure how big dingo packs got, but the four adult animals converging on their leader were more than enough for him. More than enough to keep him and Blade from getting where they wanted to go.

"Shit," Jack hissed.

"Should we run?" There was a strange note to Blade's voice, and it took Jack a moment to realise what it was.

Uncertainty.

Finally, something Blade wasn't supremely confident about. Something that shook that unassailable control of his. If he weren't currently half-petrified himself, Jack would have rejoiced.

"No," he whispered instead. "That's what prey does. Keep moving, though. Slowly."

The dingo pack moved with them, silent now they were together but for snarls and huffs, and the clicking of claws on stone. Jack got the distinct impression they were being herded. Hopefully, just herded out of pack territory and not *towards* something.

Every nerve in Jack's body was jumpy, his muscles tight with tension. Stupidly, he began craving nicotine. This slow-building pressure wasn't unlike the hours leading up to a mission, when Jack would feel sick and nervous, sucking down at least half a dozen cigarettes in an effort to calm himself. Whether it was the nicotine or just training kicking in, when the squad got the go signal, Jack would turn steely calm and be ready to face anything with a clear head and grim determination. The waiting, though, got to him. Every bloody time. He was torn now between wanting nothing to happen and wanting, *needing*, the tension to break.

"Jack," Blade murmured, his hand touching Jack's back.

Blade left it there, a simple connection, a way of showing Jack where he was. A confirmation he was still with him. Absurdly, it curbed the sudden desire for a smoke.

They moved at an agonisingly slow pace for what felt like hours, but couldn't have been more than fifteen minutes. All the while, the dingo pack gradually closed the distance. The level of growls grew until it was all Jack could hear, confined and amplified by the tall rock walls hemming them in.

"Jack," Blade said again, this time with a touch of warning.

"I know."

It happened no more than a minute later. The lead dingo sprang forwards.

Jack threw himself backwards. Blade had already slipped sideways, blurring through Jack's peripheral vision. The assassin's boot connected solidly with the charging dog's ribs. Yowling, the dingo tumbled. It twisted on the ground and, suddenly, it was back on its paws. Snarling, it sprang at Blade again.

Released by the pack leader's attack, the rest of the dogs pounced.

Jack didn't quibble this time. As with the troops at the torture shack and the unfortunate man at the waterfall, it was him or them.

He fired into the pack. The forerunner yelped and crumpled into a heap, tripping up the one behind it. Two streamed around the furry pile, one coming for Jack, the other veering off towards Blade and the pack leader. Blade was trying, successfully so far, to keep the huge dingo from closing in nothing but his hands and feet.

Scrambling awkwardly over rocks, Jack fired on the dingo charging for him. His shot went wide, the dog cringing and jumping sideways. It slowed down, watching him cautiously, darting forwards in short, unpredictable bursts. Jack took a moment to aim this time, but the animal that had stumbled over the injured dingo wasn't so reluctant to engage. It leaped over a fallen tree and pounced on Jack.

The dog snapped at his face as they crashed to the ground. Jack hit hard, dropping his gun, the backpack protecting his spine, his head barely missing the jagged gorge wall. He got his left hand into the ruff of fur around the dingo's neck—his right, with the splint, he shoved between the slavering jaws. Fangs scritched over the splint as the animal tried to bite down and Jack tried to force it off him. The power in the animal's shoulders and chest was breathtaking, though, and it pushed back. Front claws digging into Jack's chest for purchase, it scrambled its rear paws at his legs.

Crack!

The dingo jerked in his hold, stiffening for a split second before sagging forwards, limp. A couple of huffs of fetid breath caressed Jack's sweaty face, and then it died.

In the chilly silence that followed, Jack slowly realised the rest of the dogs had scattered. He was alone with the dead dingo lying on him in a boneless mass.

"Jack?"

The name snapped him out of shock. Jack pushed the dingo off and flipped to his feet. His heart was still racketing around in his chest, dancing with adrenaline and fright and relief.

Blade stood several feet back, Desert Eagle in hand, breathing hard, eyes glittering. "Are you all right?"

"Yeah."

Gaze going to the dead dingo, Blade let his shoulders sag. "I don't like killing animals." There it was again, a touch of something lost in his voice, hinting at something deeper in his psyche than his stone-cold killer reputation could account for.

Jack didn't like it either, but when it came down to him or them, it was amazing how strong self-preservation could be. He hadn't thought he'd ever be able to kill another person, either, but he'd learned otherwise very fast.

"We should keep moving," he said instead of something patronising. "They won't have gone far."

Blade nodded and moved to put his gun back in its holster.

The lead dingo flashed out of nowhere and slammed into Blade. They went down in a tangle of arms and paws, the night exploding with the howls of the pack.

Jack pulled his Eagle, but the mix of man and dog was too confusing to get a clear shot. He leaped over rocks to reach them. By the time he got there, the dingo had Blade on his back, in much the same position Jack had been in moments earlier. The big, powerful jaws were locked over Blade's left wrist. Teeth stained red dug into the material of Blade's DPDU. Blade grunted and dug his other hand into the mouth, trying to pry the jaws apart.

Rather than risking a shot, Jack drove his foot up between the dingo's back legs. His boot connected hard with the male dog's bulging balls.

The high-pitched yelp would have been comical in just about any other situation.

Mouth springing wide, the dingo released Blade's arm. Free, the assassin swung a punch at the dingo's head. His fist cracked against the thick skull, knocking the dog off him. It rolled, whining, and staggered upright. Jack made to kick it again, and it jumped backwards. Head lowered, tail tucked, it turned and ran.

Not falling into the same trap as before, Jack hauled Blade up and they too ran. In the opposite direction, looking over their shoulders for pursuit that thankfully never arrived. Either they'd convinced the pack to leave them alone, or they'd moved far enough out of the dingoes' territory to be let go.

Wordlessly, Blade led them to the cave he'd mentioned earlier. It required a short climb up the wall, but Jack made it gratefully, wanting unscaleable distance between him and the pack.

The cave had a wide opening but narrowed towards the back and turned sharply, providing a reasonably sized pocket protected from the outside world. A coating of sand smoothed out the rough stone floor.

Blade balanced a torch in a small crevice in the wall, so its pale glow spread out in a fan covering most of the space. Then he tried to take off his pack. He moved stiffly, holding his left arm out gingerly. Jack helped him slip the straps down over his arms and lowered the pack.

"Side pocket," Blade murmured. "First aid kit."

Jack pulled it out and opened it while Blade attempted to unbutton his top. The fingers of his left hand fumbled, slicked with blood.

"Christ," Jack said. "Let me."

He got the top open and Blade shrugged out of it. The white undershirt was stained with blood down his left side. Three long tears in the DPDU top matched three in the shirt, curving down from just under his shoulder blade to over his hip. Grumbling, Jack hauled the shirt off Blade as well, ignoring the man's soft protests of pain.

Three long claw marks followed the pattern of rips. The middle one was deep enough to worry Jack as he lifted Blade's arm and turned him to study the wounds.

"Shit, Blade."

Twisting to look, Blade said, "It's not bad."

"It's not great, either. Look at the mess I got into with a small knife wound. An animal claw is bound to be dirtier than Jimmy's knife."

Blade huffed a laugh. "I'm not about to act all superhuman and ignore it. Unlike some of us."

"Fine," Jack said frostily. "If you're going to be like that, you can clean it yourself."

"I could, but I would prefer your help." Said contritely and hopefully.

Shaking his head, Jack rummaged through the first aid kit for the antiseptic wipes. He cleaned up Blade's wrist first. The teeth had torn through the top layers of skin only. There were no deep penetration points. Jack slathered his arm in antibacterial cream and wrapped a large dressing around it. Then he turned to the claw marks.

The outer two were shallow, scraping across the skin, raising long welts. The middle one, however, broke the skin towards the lower half. By the time it had reached Blade's hip, it had drawn blood, the claw digging through enough epidermis to expose red flesh.

"This could use some stitches," Jack mused.

"Hmm. I have surgical glue."

"That'll do."

Jack made sure to clean the open wound thoroughly, holding back snickers at Blade's muffled gasps and bitten-off moans. Blade had his hands on the rock wall, leaning on it, head hanging between his taut shoulders. The body under Jack's hands trembled as Blade strained to not jerk away from his rough ministrations. The assassin's reaction to the pain was oddly satisfying. It proved the man did feel, after all.

After applying a small amount of the surgical glue, Jack pinched the wound closed and waited.

The skin against his hand was warm and slicked with a sheen of sweat. After their impromptu bath, Blade's scent was clean, carrying a light touch of the soap, but mostly it was just that tang of hot skin and natural musk that coiled through Jack like an olfactory drug. It worked its way downwards, drenching Jack's mouth with want and his body with need, his dick warming with memories of a Blade-induced orgasm.

Resisting a sudden compulsion to drag his free hand down the curved arc of Blade's spine, Jack gave in to another impulse and looked. He'd watched Blade previously, had bit his lip at the tight lines of his body and the supple flex of his muscles, but he was closer now, and he let desire direct his gaze.

Jack had never found military uniforms sexy. How could something he'd sweated in, crawled through mud and scrub and sand in, be considered exciting? Not even a dress uniform on an otherwise mouthwatering body could get him more than intrigued. The uniforms had been just that: uniforms. They signified work, not play, and the last thing on Jack's mind when he'd been on a mission had been sex.

Right now, though, he was having trouble wondering what might look better than those DPDU pants curved over Blade's arse. No DPDUs? That was a no-brainer. He'd already seen that naked arse, but he hadn't been close enough to bite then.

Dragging his gaze and his lowering inhibitions away from that temptation, Jack was caught by the lean back beautifully displayed for him. Every muscle in Blade's back was tautened with pain. The shape of each one stood out on his pale skin, inviting fingers to follow the patterns from straining shoulders down to narrow waist. Jack couldn't find one skerrick of extra flesh, just firm skin over sleek muscle.

There were scars, as well, but they didn't so much mar the canvas as make it all the more intriguing. On his left shoulder, the entry wound of the bullet that had caused the starburst on his chest, a small dimple only. A thin, ropey knot of scar tissue just above his right kidney, a messy knife wound. And under them, older scars, faded with time. Many, many years of time, if Jack was any judge. White slashes reaching from his shoulders to his hips, from side to side, sunk into the flesh so they didn't disrupt the otherwise smooth skin.

Which Jack suddenly realised he was touching. His hand had escaped his control and was skating his fingertips over those old, old scars. They had a stretched quality to them, as if they'd been pulled over time, lengthened. As wide as his fingers in places, tapering off towards the bottom of the strokes.

Strokes. That was what they were. The leavings of a whip. Stroke after harsh stroke of leather biting into Blade's back. Blade's smaller body. Before he'd finished growing.

"Fuck," Jack whispered unable to take his hand away now he knew what they were. He spread his fingers wide, pressing his palm over the scars. "You were whipped?" As a kid? But he couldn't ask that. He knew it, but to hear it might just snap his control.

Blade froze. The trembling stilled and he even stopped breathing. After a long minute, he shook his head.

"Blade." Jack pushed for honesty.

His head came up, face turning slightly towards Jack. The curve of his cheek was a pale shape against the dark, his long lashes a smudge across his skin. Jack fought down the urge to lean in and taste.

When Blade spoke, it was quiet and cold, but aching with pain.

"They called it discipline."

Jack ground his teeth against an urge to growl. He wasn't entirely successful, a small rumble getting loose. At the sound of it, Blade made an involuntary move towards Jack, pressing his spine against his hand.

Jack let the now solidly glued wound go and ran his hand around Blade's waist, fingers crawling across his shivering abdomen. Jack closed the space between them, sliding his other hand with the splint up Blade's back, over his shoulder, and onto his chest. Blade arched against his hands. A low, purring moan came from deep in his throat, and it rolled through Jack with concussive force. He shuddered against Blade, his hard dick pressing into Blade's arse.

The hand on Blade's belly dipped lower. With a gasp, Blade sucked in his stomach, and Jack's fingers were invited to slip into the new gap between skin and waistband. He hesitated, then settled for cupping his hand around Blade outside of his pants, needing to keep some barriers from toppling over so fast. The handful of hard, thick dick and straining material, however, didn't help his restraint. Jack groaned, giving Blade a slow, firm rub.

"Jack," Blade moaned, his hips shifting in what felt like involuntary ways, pushing his arse into Jack, then forwards, rubbing against his hand. His shoulders strained, trembling with some great effort. Against the rock wall, his fingers curled and uncurled.

Jack buried his face in Blade's shoulder, dragging in a lungful of air that tasted like Blade. He pressed his lips to the warm skin, feeling Blade tremble at the touch. He opened his mouth and licked, intensifying the taste and texture. The coiling pressure in his guts tightened exponentially. His dick was so hard he could probably crush rocks, and he ached with the need to relieve the tension thrumming through his body. Unconsciously, he ground his groin into Blade. He closed his teeth over the salty skin and bit down.

TWENTY-EIGHT
NOW

wo days of cautious movements got Jack to Ingleburn. A suburb in Sydney's southwest, it had a history of commission houses, low education, and high crime, but in more recent times was turning into an attractive locale for new home buyers, young families, and the inevitable hipsters planning on a future investment in "I was there before it was cool." One thing Jack was grateful for, however, was the relatively large Indian population. He blended in as he headed to the meeting point.

Hoping he'd interpreted Ethan's code right, Jack made his way to Williamson Road. It proved to be a street of industrial businesses, and number eighty-three was a warehouse enclosed in a tall wire fence. In a secluded spot, Jack scaled the fence and approached the building. It was a long, low structure with very few windows, all of which held black-glazed glass that wouldn't reveal the interior no matter how hard Jack pressed his face to it.

At one end was a wide roller-door with no external lock showing. Next to it was a normal-sized door. This one had a keypad. Given enough time Jack could probably hack the lock, but privacy wasn't guaranteed, and he didn't fancy being seen breaking in. He was fairly certain he had the right place. The darkened windows seemed like Ethan's style, as did the location. Was he expected to wait outside until Ethan appeared?

Feeling like a dick, Jack knocked and waited. Nothing. He tried again, harder. Still nothing.

Hanging around like this would look as suspicious as hacking the lock. Jack cursed under his breath. Maybe he had it wrong. Williamson. Eight. Three. Was he wrong? Was Ethan waiting somewhere else for him, as worried as Jack was? What if Ethan had been caught?

Jack leaned against the door, wondering, for the hundredth time since hitting the water of Darling Harbour, if he'd done the right thing. Not just in terms of his career, or even his continued life outside of a high-security detention facility, but for Ethan as well. If there was one thing Ethan didn't need, it was Jack double-checking every decision he made. The man had made it through thirty-one years of life before meeting Jack, before Jack had begun to view him as something damaged and then set adrift. He was one of the best assassins, spies, warriors, in the world. And yet Jack worried. Would Ethan have been better off staying in custody? He might have never been released, but he would be alive. Or not. Without Jack's help, he may have continued with his original plan, and his chances wouldn't have been as good.

Going back through that conversation about racing cars, Jack searched for extra information, for a sign he'd misinterpreted.

Seven.

Ah. The one he hadn't been sure of.

The lock was a seven-digit key. Which seven though? And in what order? Why couldn't Ethan have given him more to go on?

Unless he'd given him everything he needed. Jack hit the number seven seven times.

With a soft *click*, the door unlocked.

Chuckling, Jack slipped into the warehouse. Trust that mad bastard.

Motion-sensor lights flashed on as Jack closed the door and took a step into the space beyond. Rows of gently glowing bulbs along the roof cast soft illumination over the wide-open interior—enough light to see by, but not enough to blind Ethan's light-sensitive eyes.

The floor was cement and bare, mostly. To his right, a long work bench, pitted and scarred, sat against the closest wall. There were vices of various sizes, several crucibles, tongs for carrying them, and racks of moulds. Ethan did like to custom make ammunition. Above it on the wall, a series of locked, steel cabinets most likely held weapons.

Along the far wall was a well-equipped home gym, including an area of sparring mats, a kick-bag, and a martial-arts dummy.

To the left, a large furnished area took up most of the remaining space. Rugs on the floor, dining table, kitchen, large chairs around a gas fireplace, a long wardrobe, a shower stall of frosted glass big enough for a party, and a bed for the partiers to crash in afterwards.

In between was a car under a canvas. Jack pulled the cover off and stood back to take a good look.

Low slung and sleek like a gliding shark, the black Aston Martin Vanquish S Coupe looked predatory as if it were simply giving its prey a head start before leaping into top speed to bring it down. It sent the same shiver down Jack's spine as seeing Ethan did.

Jack could easily imagine Ethan in the car. His face intent, hands skilful on the gear shift and steering wheel. Propelling it to its top speed just so he could reassure himself he controlled his actions, his decisions, his life.

If the idea of watching Ethan drive this thing weren't so appealing, the whole concept would have been too sad to contemplate.

Jack covered the beautiful car up and wandered over to the living area. In the kitchen he found a tiny but exquisite coffee machine and row after row of expensive coffee pods. There was milk in the fridge. Jack had made a cup and was about to sip when he remembered Ethan didn't drink coffee. He was a tea drinker to the core of his dented soul. The bastard had put this in especially for Jack. Confident Jack would end up here, one way or another. Or prepared, just in case.

Drinking liquid gold, Jack wandered around the rest of the living area. In a wall cabinet he found a large TV and shelves of books. A lot of the authors Jack had never heard of, but he recognised several Matthew Reillys, which made him smile.

The closet was full of all sorts of clothes, from jeans and T-shirts to casual suits to full-blooded, double-breasted affairs that would cost Jack's monthly wage. There were also several tuxedos, probably all with hidden compartments and long pockets for weapons. One section was devoted to various uniforms, including police, ambulance, army, nurse, and several others Jack had no idea about.

At the end of the long closet were clothes too big for Ethan. They were, in fact, Jack's size. Shaking his head, Jack pulled out a pair of jeans and a shirt, made sure they fit, then headed for the shower.

Inside the shower stall, he discovered why it was so large. It was actually the entire bathroom enclosed in the frosted glass. Vanity and cabinet at one end, toilet in the middle, and open shower at the other.

Surprisingly, there was an old-fashioned lion-clawed tub opposite the shower nozzle. In the cabinet, Jack found all the supplies he could ever need. He shaved eagerly. A beard might help to disguise him, but he'd probably rather go to prison than put up with the itching.

Bypassing the tub, Jack stood under the hot, massaging spray of the shower for a long time. When he finally turned off the water and looked around, he laughed. The entire bathroom was fogged up, steam curling out over the glass walls. He padded on wet feet to the vanity, then grabbed a towel from the cabinet, dried off, and cleaned his teeth.

Another coffee later and he was feeling the effects of four days of high stress, little to no sleep, and a shitload of emotional confusion and trauma. Despite the heady swirl of caffeine in his blood, Jack found himself aiming for the bed.

It was the scent of strongly brewed tea that woke him, however long later. It had never happened before, and yet it felt normal to roll over, lift his head, and find a steaming mug of black tea on the bedside table.

Pushing himself up further, he looked around, finding clouds of steam spilling over the top of the bathroom wall.

The last curl of tension in Jack's gut eased, and he flopped back to the mattress.

Ethan was here. He was all right.

The frosted glass, further occluded by steam, hid Ethan from Jack's sight, but it was all too easy to recall that body. What it looked like, how it felt, the way it moved against him. How Jack's own body responded to even the slightest hint of interest from Ethan. Rested and secure, it responded now, just at the mere idea Ethan was here. It wasn't even the thought of him naked and wet that did it. Just that he was here and safe.

Christ. Jack couldn't afford to think like that. It was a bad road to go down. He was already in enough trouble because of Ethan. Adding to it by giving in to his body's wants was a sure-fire way to ruin whatever he might be able to salvage of his freedom when Ethan invariably disappeared again.

Jaw tight, Jack refused to let himself do anything stupid. Like go into the bathroom, shove Ethan to the wall, and rut against him until all the objections were ground away and the only thing left was the here and now. Immediate gratification, delaying the inevitable betrayal. Feeling so bloody good that for ten minutes he forgot all the pain.

He thought of all the unpleasant things he could to banish Ethan and his lean, supple body from his head. Thought about what would happen if Ethan was wrong.

Being accused of treason. The trial sure to follow. A stint in prison. Unemployment afterwards. His sister's inevitable visit to simply confirm her first opinion—this was what happened when you waged war. You fucked with karma; it fucked with you.

The death of a potentially innocent person.

It worked all too well. By the time the shower turned off, Jack was out of bed, pacing between bathroom and kitchen, and incredibly angry.

Goddamn, if Ethan was wrong and whoever he'd infiltrated the Office to kill wasn't guilty . . .

The door to the bathroom opened. Jack, hands tangled in his black hair, chest heaving in an effort to calm himself, stumbled to a stop, thoughts dying mid rant.

Pale skin damp, hair tousled and glistening with water droplets, towel around his slim hips, Ethan was everything Jack remembered and a little more, right down to the socks. Jack swallowed hard against a resurgence of lust. Those strange eyes blinked at him sleepily, mellowed by the hot shower. His mouth turned up in a small smile. The smooth expanse of his chest tapered down to the low-hanging towel, muscles so well defined Jack didn't have to imagine too hard what it would feel like to touch them. All the scars he remembered, plus a small healing cut over his left eyebrow. As he twisted slightly to secure the towel, Jack saw the remains of the dingo-claw marks. Most of them were gone, faded over the intervening year, but a puckered red scar remained where the middle claw had dug in deeper. The wound Jack had glued closed, had held together while it dried, while he gave in to temptation and touched.

Shit. This wasn't going to happen. Jack spun away and kept pacing.

"Jack? Are you all right?"

Grinding his jaw against the need to yell, he shook his head. He didn't hear Ethan come up behind him, but he felt him. Could sense the proximity of his heat, smell his skin, the scent wafting off him with the steam of his shower. It happily duck-dived from his nose right down into his belly, setting about eroding every very good reason Jack had for not letting this happen.

"Are you hurt?"

"No."

Ethan fell quiet, watching Jack run a groove into the hard floor.

He couldn't think, couldn't rationalise anything while Ethan was so close. He'd thought he could control this. They were here to finish the job, nothing else. But he just couldn't go beyond the fact Ethan was here, happy to see him.

And that was his problem. He wanted to believe he'd betrayed the Office for the right reasons. For the chance to discover who the traitor was, expose them, and then watch justice being done.

What if that was just the excuse, though? What if he was really here because his dick liked Ethan Blade so much it was making all the decisions? It didn't want to hear about all the lies and betrayal. It didn't want to remember that Ethan had pointed a gun at him and pulled the trigger. Or that little display put on for his benefit in the compound, Jack tied to a chair, Ethan and Valadian before him, side by side.

All very good reasons to have left Ethan in the cell at the Office. And yet . . . here they were, and Jack had no idea why.

TWENTY-NINE
THEN

"**J**ack," Blade choked out, close to alarm.

It kicked some sense into Jack's head. Going still, he waited, both dreading and wanting a reason to stop this he didn't have to find himself. All he got was Blade's harsh gasps.

"Blade?"

"Mm." Blade sagged.

Jack tried to let him go and couldn't. Just . . . couldn't. "Don't you . . . I mean . . . I thought you wanted . . ." This was going to end in disaster.

After a stretched silence, Blade turned in the confines of Jack's arms. His unreadable eyes were focused on Jack's mouth with unmistakable intensity. "Yes, I want this. Just . . ." He swallowed hard. "Just not against a cold, sharp rock wall."

"Shit." The relief was almost enough to set off Jack's orgasm then and there.

Blade slid his arms around Jack's neck and his head tipped, aiming for a kiss.

Jack jerked his head to the side. Blade's lips landed on his jaw. The relief fizzled in an instant, both of them stiffening in surprise. After a moment, Blade kissed his jaw, then trailed his mouth up to Jack's ear. "Is this all right?"

It took Jack several seconds to comprehend the words, and then he nodded. "Just . . . not on the mouth."

Another moment, then Blade relaxed and rocked his hips into Jack's. "Hmm. I can work with that."

The implicit promise in those words broke the last of Jack's restraint. He dug his fingers into the muscles of Blade's back, assaulting the strong line of Blade's neck with his mouth. Blade gasped and clenched his fists in the back of Jack's DPDU top. He pulled back and undid the buttons, but when Blade tried to push it off, Jack simply *couldn't* let him go long enough to allow it.

"Jack." Blade wriggled in frustration. "Let go. I have to . . ." He trailed off into whimpers as Jack nuzzled into his hair. "I have to . . . Oh, blast it." He gripped the back of Jack's DPDU jacket and ripped it right down the middle.

Face pressed into Blade's neck, Jack shuddered with laughter. "Did you just say 'blast it'?"

"I wouldn't have to resort to such language if you would just cooperate and get naked."

"You first." Jack slid a hand between them, heading for the fastenings on Blade's pants. Once opened, he hooked his fingers into the waistbands of pants and underwear.

"Before you proceed," Blade said, "I feel I should remind you just how cold it is."

"Yeah, I don't think that's going to be a problem."

One, because the heat building between them could spark dry tinder. And two, Blade had absolutely nothing to worry about from what Jack could feel of the bulge in the man's pants.

Jack ripped the last of Blade's clothes down in one swift move. Startled, the assassin staggered, grabbing at Jack to keep upright. Jack wrestled his boots off in record time. As he was about to reach for the socks, Blade shuffled back a few inches.

"I don't like bare feet," he murmured ruefully.

With a snort, Jack divested him of his pants. "Fine. I'm not really interested in your toes, anyway."

Jack glided his hands up Blade's tight calves, tickling his fingers across the soft skin on the back of his knees. Blade made a strangled sound and gripped Jack's shoulders harder. Storing that one away for later study, Jack swayed forwards and kissed one lightly haired thigh, then the other, feeling strong muscles twitch under his lips.

He needed more, right now. Jack brushed his mouth along Blade's hard shaft. Blade's moan shivered down Jack's spine and encouraged him. Licking up the underside of the thick dick, he looked upwards and found those strange eyes fixed on him. They showed nothing of the man's emotions. However, the slightly parted lips, the flush on his pale cheeks, the heaving of his smooth chest, all shouted lust. Blade's fingers tightened in Jack's hair, which reminded him of the waterfall and hair washing and a bloody good orgasm. Mouth watering, Jack slid his lips over Blade's dick.

Abandoning himself to the pleasure, Jack drowned in the glory of hearing Blade gasp and moan, revelled in those long, dextrous fingers curling in his hair. God, he tasted so good, all salty musk, blood-heated skin, and an unclassifiable spice that was purely Blade. Jack could have so easily taken him all the way, sucked and licked and kissed until Blade came in his mouth, but for the fact Blade was shivering in the chilly air.

Jack reluctantly pulled back. Rising from his knees, he wrapped as much of himself around Blade's naked body as he could. Even as he dug into Jack's warmth, Blade growled, "You stopped."

Chuckling, Jack shrugged off his DPDU jacket to sling it around him, but found a gaping hole from collar to hem. Both of them looked at it for a moment, then at each other, before laughing.

"Get the sleeping bags." Jack pushed Blade away.

With a wicked snicker, Blade obeyed. Jack stripped while watching his tight, lean body, entranced by the silky-smooth flow of skin and muscles as Blade arranged the sleeping bags. When he was down to his socks, Jack took a moment to drink in the vision of Blade waiting for him.

He lay back on the sleeping bag, propped up on his elbows, knees drawn up, feet spread. Jack had to squeeze his dick to keep things from exploding way too soon. It was unfair just how beautiful this man was. Lean, finely sculpted, all but bursting with deadly potential even as he squirmed under Jack's appraisal. It was all too easy to remember Blade whipping through the small army at the torture shack or mowing down the scout team. It was, however, even easier to imagine how he might move against Jack, how he would sound and feel.

Jack lowered himself into the inviting embrace. Blade pulled the second bag over the top of them, using it to draw Jack down. Enclosed in the warm bags, cradled between Blade's thighs, he felt the rest of the world slip away. All the second and third thoughts about having sex with this strange, dangerous man vanished. The need to find Valadian and finish this cursed job evaporated. Even the faint tug of caution warning him this could be a trap turned into the conviction that everything leading up to a possible betrayal would be worth it.

Jack tested every inch of skin he could reach for sensitivity and reaction, liking the way Blade shivered and arched and squirmed. The way he moaned and growled and both pushed Jack towards his most tender spots and wriggled away from the sensations he created.

Within the dark confines of the sleeping bags, the disparity between their skin tones was reduced to shades of grey. It was both liberating and frustrating, and Jack found himself sliding back into the light to see how his brown hands were perfectly framed on Blade's paleness, even as the barriers between their bodies dissolved in a mix of heat and passion.

Blade heaved and rolled them over. "My turn," he insisted, though any protests Jack might have had were surrendered when Blade ground his hips against Jack's.

Jack groaned, bucking under him, wanting more. Blade straddled his groin and rocked, stoking an already combustible situation with volatile friction. He kissed and licked Jack's chest, gun-roughened hands dragging over nerves sensitised to unbearable levels. His appreciative hums and purrs vibrated through Jack's already singing skin. The scent of their bodies, sweat and musk and a hint of blood to give it depth, intensified, caught within the shield of their warm cocoon. When Blade lifted his hips enough to slip a hand around Jack's dick and stroke slow and firm, Jack let out a low, rumbling growl.

He could be so bloody happy to rut and rub and come like this, feeling Blade all over him, his hand so amazing, his hips driving his dick into Jack's thigh. He grabbed Blade's arse and pulled him in tighter, harder, and Blade nodded frantically. They would come together. They'd dress, take turns on watch, and tomorrow finish what they were here to do, and it would be done. Because Jack was determined that when this was over, that was it. No more. Never again.

Which meant he wanted it all *now*. Not just this, as amazing as it was. He wanted to feel Blade under him, around him, writhing against him as Jack thrust into him. Yet, they were in the middle of God-forgot-where with no condoms or lube. Those restrictions weren't quite enough to kill the absolute need, though.

"God. I think I need to fuck you."

Blade went motionless, and Jack thought it really was over. As in he-might-become-an-Ethan-Blade-victim over. But then Blade lifted his head and gave a single firm nod.

Before Jack could comprehend the meaning of that, Blade rolled off him and slid out from between the sleeping bags.

"Please don't ask me why," he said as he rummaged through his pack. "If you do, this stops here and now."

Jack frowned until he saw what Blade produced. A foil-wrapped condom and sachet of lube. Holy shit. He had to ask. Needed to ask. Why the hell was Blade carting fuck supplies through the desert? His dick, however, put up a good counterargument.

"I don't care." Jack realised it was true as he said it. "Just get back here."

Blade settled on his belly beside him, trembling. Hopefully with uncontrollable lust, but just in case it wasn't, Jack gently took the packets from him and nuzzled into his neck.

"I'll make it good, but if you don't want to . . ."

Blade relaxed. "I do. It's just . . . been a while."

Laying a line of soft kisses along his jaw, Jack whispered, "We'll go slow."

"Not too slow, I hope."

Jack chuckled. "Crazy bastard."

"Half right, Jack."

Jack opened the lube and squeezed it onto his fingers, then slid them downwards. At the first hint of gentle pressure, Blade ducked his head into his arms, shoulders shuddering. Then, with a forceful sigh, he relaxed. Jack's finger slipped in.

Jack ground his steel-rod dick into Blade's hip to ease the overwhelming desire to just get on top and drive in before Blade was ready. Even when he had three fingers gliding in and out, he waited, torn between his desperate need to be inside him and wanting this to last as long as possible.

There came the inevitable moment, though, when he couldn't hold back any longer. Jack hastily rolled the condom on, then spread the lube with a couple of firm pumps. Sliding over Blade's back, Jack guided himself against his hole.

Slow, he'd promised to go slow. That thought firmly in mind, Jack pushed in. Slick pressure and warmth combined to send a shot of pure joy through Jack's dick and balls. It licked up his spine as he gently rocked into Blade until he was buried deep. A tremor rocked through Blade, tightening him around Jack, both of them groaning at the sensation. Braced on his arms, Jack began to move. Slow. Deep. Maddening. Wonderful.

So good. Jack sank into the incredible feeling of Blade under him, around him, against him. It had been so long and Blade was so hot and tight, Jack lost himself in the sensations. Lost himself so much it took him several strokes to realise the other man wasn't *with* him. Oh, Blade was there, under him, moaning with each thrust, but he wasn't moving, wasn't reacting. Hands curled loosely around the sleeping bag, head buried face-first in the soft padding, he was simply . . . receiving.

Jack was thrown out of the moment. Where was the man who'd moved on Jack to his own purpose, who'd taken as much pleasure from Jack's body as he'd given? He'd vanished, leaving behind this passionless vessel. Jack wanted that first man back, the one who gave up his control, who let the wants of his body move him. The one who'd driven Jack to the brink of orgasm with just the sheer beauty of his desire.

Determined to get that man back, to make this *one and only* time worth the potential fallout, Jack pulled out almost fully. Waiting a couple of seconds got the expected disappointed sound from Blade. It changed into a deep-throated groan when Jack thrust forwards, fast and deep. Jack repeated the move several more times. At first Blade only whimpered in response. Then his shoulders began to tremble, his spine arching. Jack increased the tempo, and Blade resisted only for a handful of rapid, hard strokes before he started to move. He squirmed and gasped, pushing his face into the cushioning of the sleeping bag as his thighs spread even further. His hips lifted in an unconscious plea for more.

Christ. This was it. This was what Jack had wanted, needed. He lay himself down on Blade's back, kissing and biting his tight shoulders as he pumped his hips as hard as he could. Every sense was flooded with Blade starting to let loose, the taste and scent of his heated skin, the sight of his long neck straining against Jack's weight, and the feel... Oh hell, the feel of him—hard and solid, smooth and satiny. When Blade started pushing and shifting for the angle he wanted, the pressure he needed, Jack nearly lost his mind.

With a massive effort of will, Jack lifted himself up and, one arm hooked around Blade's waist, hauled them both to their knees. The top sleeping bag fell off, but they were too far gone to care about the bite of the cold air. Face buried in Blade's shoulder, Jack rolled his hips in slow, delicious circles. Blade's head hung, enticing Jack to lick up his spine, into the locks of hair on the back of his neck. Letting out a strangled groan, Blade surged upright. Clamping Jack's hand to his chest with his own, he arched his back, pushing hips and shoulders into Jack. His head fell back onto Jack's shoulder, lips parted on a silent moan, long, dark lashes fluttering on his flushed cheeks.

"Jack, Jack," he managed between pants, "please."

"Yeah." Jack found Blade's hard dick with his free hand. "Yeah." He stroked him in time with his thrusts, deliberately slow and shallow.

Even as he mumbled, "Yes, yes, yes," Blade shook his head, writhing, clearly wanting this, but *needing* more.

Jack pushed in deep, straining for as much contact as he could, before he let Blade's dick go and shoved him to his hands and knees. Blade went with a startled gasp, the sudden tension in his body dissolving into liquid surrender as Jack rubbed his hands up either side of his spine. Caught by the contrast not only between his dark fingers and Blade's skin, but also by the white scars crisscrossing the reddened surface, Jack swept his hands from shoulders to hips and back. He slowly began to move again, utterly captivated by the way Blade dropped to his elbows, his body rippling as he pushed back into Jack, as he started to shake uncontrollably. When he reached for his dick, making incoherent pleas and shifting against Jack with frantic motions, Jack took pity on him—and himself, to be truthful—and really started to fuck. Hard, deep thrusts, fast and powerful. Jack lost himself in the furious wonder of it, of feeling another man moving so violently, so single-mindedly against him. Of seeing the blurring lines between their bodies, the contrasting skin tones twining together, chaotic and beautiful.

Whatever control Blade had left broke, one shoulder hitting the ground, his hand working furiously on his dick, all sounds barely audible now. His free hand curled into a fist by his head and thumped on the padded sleeping bag.

Blade was so fucking beautiful in his loss of control Jack needed more. More skin, more contact, more flavour. Pressing down on Blade's back, he shoved him onto his belly again, the hand around his dick trapped as Jack kept up the merciless thrusting. Jack caught Blade's other hand, curled his fingers around the clenched fist, and drew it close, wrapping around Blade, needing to hold him, encompass him, to feel him on every square inch of his skin. Mouth pressed to Blade's neck, Jack gave in to his own needs.

It went fast, then. Both of them straining against the other, grunting in their need to end it before they expired from exquisite frustration. Blade came first, heaving under Jack in wild throes. His orgasmic shout was muffled in the sleeping bag as his body convulsed, holding Jack fiercely until he too was coming. Jack strangled his own loud shout of pleasure against Blade's shoulder and then collapsed, their bodies shivering together.

"**J**ack?" Ethan tried again.

"Shut up," Jack snapped, striding past him.

Arms crossing, Ethan frowned. "Something's wrong. Please tell me. Maybe I can help." After a moment, he added in a soft tone, "I'd *like* to help."

"Shut up."

"No. What's the matter?"

Jack spun around and stalked towards him. "Shut up."

Ethan dropped his hands to his sides, body loosening, as if preparing for a fight. "Let me help you."

"Shut up." Jack kept advancing.

It was like the night with the dingoes. Ethan retreated, keeping a wary eye on Jack, who kept coming after him, predatory and crazy with confusion. The sound of that bloody accent wasn't helping the situation. Jack needed to make him shut the hell up.

"Jack." A hint of warning in Ethan's tone now.

"Shut up."

"Tell me what's—"

With a pleasing little gasp of shock, Ethan ran into the bed. He toppled over onto the mattress. Jack didn't slow down, crawling onto the bed between his legs, forcing Ethan to scramble backwards or collect a knee to the groin.

"Jack—"

Jack grabbed a handful of towel and yanked. He tossed it away and, satisfied with Ethan's position, caught his hips and pressed them into the soft quilt. Despite his shock, Ethan was hard, his body pushing up eagerly against the pressure holding him down. Jack rolled his body down over Ethan's, catching his hands and trapping them over his head. Lips parted, Ethan looked up at him. Those incredibly long lashes dipped to his cheeks, then up again. It was impossible to read anything in those abnormal eyes.

Ethan was too beautiful. Too damaged. This was most definitely the wrong path to take. It couldn't go anywhere good or healthy for either of them.

With a little shiver, Ethan freed his legs from under Jack. He wrapped them around Jack's hips, pushing up invitingly. The hiss of cotton socks on denim was absurdly arousing as Ethan rubbed his feet along the backs of Jack's thighs.

Goddamn it. Whatever measure of restraint Jack still had vanished in a puff of lust so strong it wiped every thought from his head. He lowered his face to Ethan's, their breath mingling, noses rubbing, lips tantalisingly close. Ethan made a soft, pleading noise that hollowed out Jack's stomach and made his hands clench around Ethan's wrists.

To stop himself from doing something even stupider than what was already happening, Jack burrowed his face in the junction between Ethan's neck and shoulder. He pressed his lips to the warm skin and vowed to keep them there.

In his ear, Ethan huffed a gentle laugh. "Still not on the lips, hmm?"

Jack lifted his head enough to mutter, "Shut up," before resuming his place. From there, he lipped his way across Blade's shoulder and up the quivering bulge of his biceps.

He slowly reacquainted himself with the smooth skin, the scattered scars, the most sensitive spots. Ethan squirmed under him, submissive and obedient. So different from that first time, when Jack had had to work hard to get something honest from him. Ethan had a pathological need to be in control, a product of history Jack didn't know—wasn't sure he wanted to know. But this right here, the sounds and shapes of him letting that control go, was a heady concoction that boiled through Jack like a dangerous mix of alcohol and a good dump of adrenaline.

Jack dragged his tongue, rough and hard, over one of Ethan's nipples. The resultant shudder and gasp was encouraging, so he repeated it, adding a flick with the tip of his tongue on the end.

Another involuntary shake and lower moan. Jack played, seeing how far he could push Ethan with this alone. When Ethan had to resort to broken-worded pleas for it to stop, Jack was pleased and moved on.

After thoroughly exploring his ribs, Jack devotedly outlined each rippling shape of Ethan's six-pack, going down one side and up the other. At the lowest point, the head of Ethan's dick butted against his cheek, hot and wet. Jack rubbed against it for a moment, then nudged it aside and kept going. Ethan's groan of dismay made Jack grin against the feverish skin of his belly.

At the first, deep flick of Jack's tongue into his navel, Ethan all but came off the bed. His spine arched into a long curve, shoulders and feet all that remained touching the bed, his stuttering yelp echoing in the cavernous space of the warehouse.

Shocked by the powerful response, Jack clutched the trembling body tight, face pressed into the heat of his abdomen. When the assassin collapsed back to the mattress, Jack let him go and sat back on his heels between Ethan's spread legs.

Ethan sprawled in boneless, careless disarray. He looked spent, though he hadn't come. Jack resisted the urge to take him then and there, enthralled by the utter vulnerability on display before him. Had anyone else ever managed to crack through the tough layers of control? Jack hoped not, because he wanted this vision of surrender before him to be his alone. Which in turn scared Jack to no end. He'd not thought "mine" in a long time, and if he was going to start again, the seventh-ranked assassin in the world was the wrong launching-off point.

Shaking off the unusually possessive thoughts, Jack unbuttoned his shirt, watching the man on the bed slowly recover enough wits to open his eyes and smile.

Ethan was so damn tempting, like a deadly sin offered free with a bottle of good bourbon—all but impossible to resist. The flushed heat in his cheeks and inviting part to his lips tugged Jack back down. He poised his mouth over Ethan's, then dipped to the side, kissed his jaw up to his ear, and puffed a breath into his hair. Ethan shivered and made a soft sound of pleasure. He found the last of the closed buttons on Jack's shirt and took care of them. One arm at a time, Ethan shoved the shirt off and tossed it. He ran his palms from Jack's shoulders to his chest, then down to the waistband of his jeans.

"Uh-uh," Jack murmured, shoving dextrous fingers away from the button fly.

"But," Ethan began, and didn't finish because Jack flicked a finger over a peaked, damp nipple and Ethan's voice turned into a strangled groan.

"That's not yours to play with," Jack said, fighting his own need to just give in, to let Ethan have his way. But he held back. Not yet. "Where do I find the gear?"

It wasn't quite a pout on Ethan's lips, but it was close. "Bedside table." He indicated the closest one with a nod.

"Prepared, as usual." Jack stretched out over him to reach the drawer.

Ethan huffed a little derisively. "Where else should I keep it?" He caressed Jack's torso as it hovered over him.

"I don't know." Jack's fingers found a foil packet and lube. "Just didn't think you brought too many men back to your secret lair." Gear in hand, Jack settled back on his knees.

"All right," Ethan admitted. "You caught me out. I did put it there when I was planning my incursion of the Office."

Jack shook his head. "I'm pretty sure no one else in the world considers condoms and lube when preparing to infiltrate a secret government building."

That made Ethan smile, slow and languid. "Oh, I don't know. It might be more common than you think."

Eyes narrowed, Jack asked, "Are you saying you fuck your way into a lot of jobs?"

All too clear he remembered what it felt like to learn he'd just been a means to an end. To have Valadian tear away his last hope with one of his brutally direct summations. Despite the desire still coiling in his gut and the pressure of his hard dick against his jeans, Jack would walk away from this bed in a heartbeat if Ethan said the wrong thing.

Ethan blinked. "No. You know that."

"Do I?" It bit hard how much Jack wanted to believe him.

Sitting up, Ethan reached for him, tentative. When he wasn't stopped, he slid his hands around Jack's waist and pressed his face into

Jack's chest. "I told you, Jack. What happened between us, when *this* happened, I hadn't planned for it. You took me by surprise, literally and figuratively." His lips stretched into a smile against Jack's sensitive skin. "I know I didn't appreciate it at first, but that was more shock than anything else. Thus the supplies in the bedside table in my secret lair."

Good enough? Jack's dick said yes. His higher functions were currently wallowing in the feel of Ethan's lips on his body and didn't care.

He grabbed Ethan's shoulders and pushed him back to the mattress. The desperate drag of Ethan's fingers down Jack's thighs as he went sent shivers up Jack's spine. Lifting up to his knees, Jack looked at the naked man. God. What was it about Ethan that made it so easy to take leave of his better judgement? No matter what had happened in the desert, the man was still Ethan Blade, killer for hire.

What was Jack, though? Once, he'd thought he was a loyal soldier, but his ideas of loyalty had shifted out of alignment with what the military thought, so they'd tossed him out. Then he'd thought he was a dedicated officer of the law, until he'd been thrown amongst the snakes and shown once again how wrong his perceptions had been. All along, he too had been a killer, but for all the right reasons, or so he'd believed. Now, knowing there had been a traitor within the Office, hiding and falsifying information that was the lifeblood of Jack's job, he didn't even have that belief.

So what did any of it matter?

Deliberately, Jack ran his hand over his own chest, watching Ethan watch him. Ethan swallowed as Jack reached the fly of his jeans. With a casual flick, Jack undid the top button. Moving as slow as he dared, Jack worked his way along, popping buttons. Each little release was like a small explosion against his dick, setting off rippling waves of pleasure through his body. He sucked in a sharp breath to keep from ruining the show by ripping his jeans off and just fucking Ethan into the mattress. He'd thrown caution to the wind, so he was going to take his time and pleasure exactly how he wanted it.

When his fly was open, he pushed the jeans down far enough to expose his dick and give himself some room to manoeuvre. He dragged two fingers up the underside of his shaft, his hips jerking forwards at the touch. Ethan bit his lip and propped himself up on his elbows, hands pressed into the mattress. Jack gripped his own dick and stroked, long and slow.

Ethan jumped as if it were him in Jack's hand. His hips shifted in sympathy, breaths coming in short pants. The sight of Ethan was doing more for Jack than the strokes on his dick. His plans for a good ten minutes of torture flew out the window. He dropped the lube onto Ethan's belly.

"Prep yourself."

Complying with almost amusing eagerness, Ethan lubricated two fingers and reached between his legs. He lifted his hips for better access, delivering as good a show as Jack was giving. It didn't take long before both of them were close to losing it, touching themselves, watching the other and hungering.

"Jesus," Jack hissed when Ethan pushed a third finger into himself.

Jack let his dick go before things got explosive, then fumbled for the condom. Ethan, making nonsensical but positive noises, grabbed the lube. Between them they got Jack out of his jeans, gloved up, and slicked in record time. Unable to wait any longer, Jack held Ethan's thighs to his chest and, his knees spreading to either side of Ethan's hips, eased in.

Spine curling, Ethen threw his head back as he moaned. The length of his exposed throat made Jack lean over and lick across his Adam's apple. Ethan whimpered as Jack began to move. Slow, gentle thrusts, bodies moving together as if it had been only moments since the last time, not twelve months.

Christ. Jack thought he'd remembered what this was like, but memory was a pale, shallow substitute for the reality. For the feel of Ethan against him, around him. For the heat radiating between them. Every inch of his skin ached with the need to touch Ethan, to press so close even the distinction between their colouring blurred into nothingness.

Jack released Ethan's legs. They snapped around his waist, knees clamping to his ribs, ankles locking together over the base of his spine. Jack moaned hungrily as he pressed back down, belly to belly, chest to chest. The hard shaft of Ethan's dick pushed into his abdomen. Ethan wound his arms around Jack's neck, bringing him closer, cheek to cheek.

"Jack."

The whispered breath of his name shivered across Jack's neck. Something warm and bright bloomed in his chest. He buried his face in Ethan's neck, breathing in deep of his soap, warm skin, and that particular musk that was purely Ethan. Jack's strokes inside him were controlled for now, long and deep, but the tension curling through his guts and tightening his balls was escalating at an alarming rate.

Under him, Ethan shuddered and groaned. "Jack," he managed, voice husky and low and desperate. "Please, Jack . . . I . . ." He fisted one of his hands in Jack's hair, the other grabbing the back of his thigh, strong fingers digging into the straining muscle. "Ngh! Jack . . . I need . . ."

The broken pleas snapped Jack's restraint. He needed too. Braced on knees and one hand, Jack rocked his hips harder and faster, driving deep. Ethan bucked, hands pulling at him, mouth open on near-silent gasps. His heels pushed into Jack's arse, hips rising to meet each thrust.

He was so wild and beautiful Jack wanted it to last forever. To witness this precisely controlled man so undone he was incapable of forming words, his aim so affected he grabbed Jack's ear instead of his hair. Wanted to keep him poised on the edge for as long as possible, just to feel how his body shook, to have that deadly strength clamp around him and hold him tight. The instant Ethan came, though, his dick stimulated between their rubbing bellies, Jack forgot everything. All he knew was this man, this moment, this overwhelming surge of heat and connection, and how it all made him come so hard his vision whited out.

THIRTY-ONE
THEN

When Jack felt steady enough, he pulled out of Blade and slid off him. He quickly took care of the condom, then rested his hand on Blade's back, feeling the other man struggle for air as much as he did. Little shivers racked Blade's body. He clenched his hands into fists in the sleeping bag, head turned away from Jack.

Jack stroked his back. "Blade."

Blade reacted with a hard shudder, which turned into a roll of his shoulders that knocked Jack's hand off. Swiftly, the assassin rolled over, taking the sleeping bag with him. Tossed the other way, Jack hit sand. Blade curled up, sleeping bag wrapped tight around him.

Shit.

Jack rolled to his feet, brushing off the sand. He tried to not be bothered by Blade's reaction. He obviously hadn't been as okay with fucking as he'd said he was, but this was a good thing, surely. In any other circumstances, after experiencing a fuck like that Jack would have tried for another. One orgasm usually left him initially sated, but still energised, wanting more. Right now, though, the presented back helped reinforce his "once only" decision.

Keenly aware of Blade only pretending to sleep, he scrambled back into his clothes. The DPDU top was ruined and he didn't have another. So, sleeping bag wrapped around his shoulders, he grabbed his Desert Eagle and a cleaning kit, and sat at the bend in the cave so he could see the outside world.

Hands moving instinctively, he broke down the gun and began cleaning it, staring out at the night.

There wasn't much to see, just darkness and the faint hint of the far wall of the gorge. He couldn't see the sky, couldn't look up at the stars and feel release. Instead of opening up around him and giving him the space to let his thoughts and troubles go, the night seemed to condense down, narrow in on the cave, isolate him—lock him in with his numb thoughts and raging doubts.

Even if Blade had cuddled or asked for more, Jack would have left. Well, he hoped he would have. He was already one-nil for giving in to bad decisions tonight. That didn't bode well for avoiding any more.

He couldn't even remember the moment he'd consciously decided fucking Ethan Blade was the only option available. Goddamn it. Jack had made some really dumb choices in the past, but this one was probably the dumbest. In the middle of the bloody desert with an unstable assassin, hunted by a crazy megalomaniac, and Jack let his dick make the decisions. The dick that, despite the sour turn in his thoughts, was still warm and content, hoarding a residual hum of pleasure that with very little encouragement could become something more active.

It had been good. More than good. Fantastic. When Blade had let go, had responded naturally, it had been mind-blowing. Jack hadn't come that hard in so long he couldn't remember the last time. Certainly not over the past fifteen months when he'd had to be satisfied with his hand in the shower. Not even the blowjob in New Zealand.

Pulling in a deep breath of the cold night air, Jack forced his thoughts away from the man rolled up in his sleeping bag. He pushed his own bag off his shoulders, hoping the chill, and actually paying attention to cleaning the gun, would take care of the growing hardness in his pants. Still took a while but thankfully, his body settled down. It would have been easier if he could have run off the endorphins, but he wasn't going out there with the dingoes. Then again, a frantic fight for his life might be just what he needed.

He emptied the magazine and cleaned it.

This was it. He was done. It was out of his system. He didn't need to wonder what it would feel like to bury himself in Blade. Or what sounds he might make as Jack moved in him. Or the way Blade's body would react to his touches. No more wondering because he knew now.

And Christ, he wouldn't be forgetting any time soon.

Gun clean, Jack stood and went back into the inner cave.

Blade was asleep, properly, not just pretending. In the soft light of the torch he looked much younger, an innocence at odds with the sated slackness of his body. The urge to roll up behind him, to wrap around him, rocked through Jack and obliterated a few of his hard-won convictions.

Jesus. Jack quickly found Blade's Desert Eagle and retreated.

He'd just slapped home the sparkling-clean mag when Blade appeared. He stood in the curve of the rock wall, in the shadows, sleeping bag around him.

"I'll take the watch," he offered, tone neutral. "You should sleep."

"Yeah, I guess." Jack stood, stretched, and held the assembled gun out to Blade. "Cleaned it."

Blade took it and checked it with the swift touches of a pro. "Thank you." He didn't look at Jack once.

Great. This wasn't going to be awkward at all.

Jack gathered up his bag, and when he eased past Blade, the other man visibly stiffened.

Teeth grinding, Jack ignored it and kept going. Was it his fault if Blade regretted the fuck? No bloody way. Jack had given him more than enough chances to refuse. Or was it because Blade had lost control and he really didn't like doing that?

Jack settled down in the sand, rolled up as securely as Blade had been. He didn't sleep though. An all-new set of disturbing thoughts worked to keep him awake and alert.

What if Blade was upset enough to want retaliation?

And there it was. The result he should have thought of before giving in to his base desires. Whatever truce he and Blade had come to, it was most likely over now. If the assassin decided he *really* didn't like what Jack had done, then Jack probably wouldn't even feel the bullet that killed him. Damn, he wished he'd damaged the striker in the Eagle now.

The remainder of the night passed in slow, agonising indecision. He'd been happy enough to dive right in when it was all about his dick. Now that it was about the ugly aftermath, he couldn't work out what to do. Say something? Apologise? Ignore it?

By default, he ended up going with the last option. When Blade stirred from his post and came back in, Jack got up and in silence they packed up their gear. Before they set out, though, Blade assembled a needle and syringe, then drew up a measure of broad-spectrum antibiotic. Syringe between his teeth, he unfastened his pants and shoved them down enough to expose part of his arse.

Swallowing hard, Jack offered, "Want a hand?"

"No, thank you. I can manage." Blade's tone was even. He jabbed the needle in, depressed the plunger, and then fixed himself up.

Uneasy quiet broken, Jack felt a bit better in asking, "What's the plan?"

Blade slung on his pack. "The plan is to get through the pack's territory while they're safely tucked away in their den."

"Right. And then?"

"And then, Jack, we will be making a two-man assault on Valadian's compound." He glanced at Jack, one corner of his mouth turned up. "Do you feel up for it?"

Jack carefully kept his expression neutral. Double entendre or unfortunate choice of words? With no clue, he just shrugged. "Shouldn't be hard." He internalised a wince at his own unconscious choice. "If the quality of the search parties is anything to go by, the gates should be wide open and everyone too drunk to care what we do."

"Cakewalk, then."

Still a little troubled, Jack followed Blade out, and they made the climb down without a hassle. Then the awkwardness of the morning after was put aside for the cautious trek through the gorge.

Dawn was rolling around as they started out, brushing the shadowed gorge with hints of orange and silver-grey. The air was still incredibly cold, their breaths puffing out as white mist, but Jack quickly warmed up.

Signs of the pack were everywhere. Shit, paw prints, tufts of fur caught on rocks or the branches of the scraggly scrub. The pungent stink of freshly marked territory was thick and rank. Jack wanted to hack out the taste of the smell, but silence was their best ally. Despite a desire to rush, Jack kept to the slow, guarded pace Blade set. The threat of alerting the dingoes did very well to distract Jack from thinking about Blade's reaction to the sex. By the time they reached the far end of the gorge, the relief he felt at making it through unscathed translated into an ease with Blade that seemed reciprocated.

They emerged onto another plain, more red dirt than sand, stretching out into the distance. There was more plant life here, and Jack recognised the general area. The compound was roughly ten clicks north.

This was it. Whatever Blade had planned would happen tonight.

Blade turned them northward. The sun hadn't risen over the top of the ridgeline, leaving the western front in shadows. Although the temperature was heading upwards, it wasn't as bad in the lee of the rock cliff. They covered a lot of land before they agreed with a silent acknowledgement it was too hot to carry on.

They set up a small shelter against the cliff face, and Blade put out tinned fruit and beans, again. It felt like years since Jack had eaten anything other than tinned peaches and cold baked beans.

"Maybe we will get steak tonight." Blade speared half a peach and contemplated it on the end of his camp fork.

Jack grumbled at his beans. "You read minds now?"

Blade snorted. "If I did, you wouldn't . . . have taken me by surprise last night."

It wasn't what he'd meant to say. Changed it at the last moment and, perhaps inadvertently, changed it to something worse, judging by the way he immediately pressed his lips together and looked away.

Shit. They were going to do this now?

Jack put his tin down. "You could have stopped it at any time."

Blade ate his peach half, slowly, methodically. He picked another one out of the tin, then put it back and sighed. "I know."

Several minutes of uncomfortable silence passed, and then Jack found himself asking, "Did I hurt you?"

"No." A firm answer. Then a little tremulously, "Not at all. It was . . . good. I'm just not . . . Blast it. Have you ever made a decision that seemed right at the time, but it turned into an utter disaster?"

Jack couldn't help it. He laughed. Hard.

Blade frowned at him. "You're not helping, Jack."

"You crazy bastard," Jack managed between gasps for air. "You've just described the last week of my life. Not to mention the fifteen months before it. And let's not forget the nine years in the military."

After a moment, Blade snickered. "Yes, I suppose so." Then he grew serious again. Swirling the last couple bits of fruit around in the juice, he asked, "How do you deal with it? The . . . emotional fallout, I guess you'd call it. When you realise it hasn't gone to plan and someone's going to get hurt?"

The last vestiges of humour drained away like water into the parched land around them. Jack focused on the far horizon, shimmering away like the world's biggest cooktop. Even in the shade, the heat was closing in, pressing down on him like God's stern hand. It was too hot to puzzle out Blade's words. He wasn't talking about the sex—that much seemed obvious—but just what it was, Jack couldn't fathom.

"I don't," Jack said. "Not right away, anyway. I'd push it aside, forget about it, and keep going until the mission was done. Then I'd keep going until I got home. Then I'd keep going until I found myself in a pub, three sheets to the wind, usually picking a fight with some poor bastard who just happened to get in my way. That's when I had to deal with it. In the local lockup or on base, depending on who got me first. Either way I'd be sent to the psychologist, and I'd talk about it, get it out in the open. The last time, though, I didn't go home or get to the pub. I just kept going right into the CO's office at base and, stone-cold sober, laid the prick out with one punch. Didn't help me deal, sadly. They said it was PTSD and gave me a medical discharge rather than a court martial and sentence. Really, they were just buying me off. That wanker put my squad into Jharkhand knowing the intel was bad, knowing we had a less than forty percent chance of surviving. I lost half my people and he lost some teeth. I lost my job and he . . . Well, as far as I know, he's still there, putting more soldiers into no-win situations and getting away with it." Jack sighed and tipped the last of the beans out, leaving them for whatever desert dweller might want them. "Sometimes, I wonder why I went back to the government for work."

Beside him, Blade made a noise of agreement and followed suit with the peaches.

"You really have a thing against any sort of bureaucracy, don't you." Jack said. "Why?"

Blade glanced at him. At least the dark panes of his sunglasses turned Jack's way, then back to the red expanse before them. "They have their place, I guess, but no, I don't like being in their control. It makes it too easy to forget why you do the things you have to do."

Taking another risk, Jack said, "You were military, weren't you."

Silence was an answer on its own, but after a while, Blade said, "If it makes you feel better, I wasn't navy."

Jack snorted a laugh. "Thank God for that. If you were, I would've had to knock you down a rank or two on the John Smith List."

Blade smiled. "Well, you'd try." Then the smile faded. "I don't regret last night. It wasn't . . . what I expected, but I don't regret it."

Unable to agree or disagree, Jack settled back and waited for the world to stop cooking itself so they could get this over and done with and he could go home and start not dealing with any of it.

THIRTY-TWO
NOW

Jack awoke to an otherwise empty bed. Soft murmuring assured him Ethan was somewhere out of his line of sight. Considering he was belly down, face in a pillow, that wasn't hard. He didn't feel like moving to find him, either. A pleasant lethargy weighed down his limbs, but a not-so-pleasant pressure in his bladder had other ideas.

Jack rolled over and levered himself up onto his elbows. Blinking his eyes into focus, he found Ethan.

The assassin stood by the car. He wore a pair of loose pants, the drawstring waist sitting low on his hips. Above it, the muscular curve of his toned stomach caught Jack's gaze, shown off as Ethan leaned against the car, one hand resting on the silky-smooth metal. Head tilted forwards, he spoke softly into a smartphone, nodding occasionally. Whoever he was speaking with did a lot of talking, not letting Ethan get too much out. The hand on the car curled and uncurled into a fist.

The call didn't look like it would end soon, so Jack scrambled out of the bed and hit the shower. The hot water sluiced away the dried sweat of the night's exertions and left him feeling like he had perhaps a modicum of control back.

Right. He'd believe that when he didn't bloody well jump Ethan's bones in the next twenty-four hours.

Towel around his waist, he left the bathroom and found something to wear. By the time he was buttoning up a flannel, Ethan was done with his phone call and was setting out breakfast.

"Who died?"

Jack certainly hadn't meant to start the morning after with such a topic, and by the way Ethan fumbled a plate of toast, he hadn't been expecting to talk bodies over breakfast, either.

Deftly catching a fleeing piece of toast, Ethan frowned at Jack. "Pardon?"

Grimacing, Jack decided to just get it over with. Like ripping out stitches. "At the Office. Who did you kill?"

Continuing to set out a breakfast—toast, bacon, poached eggs, mushrooms and, naturally, a pot of tea—Ethan said, "Hopefully no one. I do recall your objections to unnecessary loss of life, Jack, so I tried to inflict nonfatal injuries. It may be that I wasn't entirely successful, but I did my best, I can assure you."

Holy shit. Had Jack, in his deepest, darkest thoughts, really missed this?

"Not that, but thank you for trying, anyway. I mean, which director was it? Who was the traitor?"

Ethan beamed at him. "You believe me."

No. No, he hadn't missed this. Not at all. "What? Believe you . . . What?"

"About the traitor within the Meta-State."

"Jesus. Yes, I believe you. I think. I mean, you're here, aren't you?"

Ethan put an egg and bacon on a plate, then set it on the table in front of Jack. "Indeed I am. As are you. Thank you."

He was doing it intentionally. Making up for a year of not messing with Jack's head. Wondering if he should even bother trying to sort through Ethan's crazy conversational method, Jack sat and contemplated his food while Ethan fetched him a mug of coffee.

"You're welcome," Jack eventually muttered as Ethan sat opposite and picked up a piece of toast. "But what for?"

"For coming here." Ethan's lips fought some overpowering expression, but his cheeks nevertheless flushed as he added, "Twice."

Jack groaned, then snorted, then chuckled. "Smooth."

Ethan's smile was part shy, part wicked, and totally derailed Jack's thought train, so he spent several minutes just eating and watching the man across from him. However, reality intruded and Jack got his head back in the game.

"So, who was it?" he asked blatantly. "Tan?" *Please, don't let it be McIntosh.* She hadn't treated him so well lately, even before the Great Escape, but it wasn't as if it had been unjustified. Given how Jack's behaviour and actions must look from her position, he couldn't blame her for any of it.

"No one died, Jack. I don't know who the traitor is."

Jack's brain went offline again, though it was anger, not lust, induced this time. "What? You mean I helped you escape for nothing?" And yes, Jack knew "nothing" was unfair. Getting Ethan out for his own well-being wasn't "nothing."

"Not for 'nothing,' Jack." When Ethan continued, his tone was low, hesitant. "Even when you gave me what I needed to escape, I kept wondering if you would go through with it. Or if perhaps you were setting me up for a fall. I probably would have deserved it."

"No probably about it." Jack smiled to take the sting out of the words. "I considered it, though. Must have changed my mind about four times."

"May I ask what convinced you?"

"Wasn't any one thing. All of the directors were acting weird. None of them seemed too concerned about you directly, but more about what it meant for them that you'd shown up. Then someone killed Maria Dioli, the asset in charge of the Valadian operation. She found something about your involvement in the whole thing that got her killed."

"And you believe it was someone who works for the Office."

"Had to be. It's a secure building."

Ethan lifted his cup and sipped. "I got in."

"Only with a sensational display. Are you saying you killed Maria?"

"I was locked in an escape-proof cell."

"And yet you escaped."

"With help. Thank you for the fudge, by the way. Though next time, perhaps something that doesn't have chocolate chips." Ethan touched his nose gently. "One of the little blighters got stuck up there."

"Remind me, when this is all over, to go tell Gillian Golightly how her fudge, when stuffed up a nose, helps against gas attacks."

"When this is all over, you will be taking me to Gillian Golightly so I may apologise for the terrible uses I put her excellent fudge to."

"When this is all over, I'll be lucky if I'm not in the cell you escaped from."

Ethan reached across the table and touched the back of Jack's hand. "Do you think I won't keep you safe?"

"How can you? I broke a dozen laws helping you out of that cell and another half dozen just getting here, and I'm sure simply sitting here with you breaks at least three more."

"Not to mention trespassing on private property. I must thank you for accurately discerning the door code. A wrong one would have triggered the destruction of the building." At Jack's alarmed eyebrow raise, he added, "Explosives under the floor. The whole place would have come down, not to mention a good portion of the street. I'm glad you made it in successfully. I would have hated to lose ... Victoria."

"Guess you're going to have to change your brilliant code now I know it."

Ethan smiled, slow and reminiscent of the way he'd looked after the second fuck. "I trust you, Jack."

"You've said that before, then shot me."

"For which I apologised."

"Whatever." Jack took a gulp of coffee. The subject of trust was one that should have been addressed before he willingly walked into this building. *Well* before. "So, if not to kill the traitor, what was the purpose of infiltrating the Office?"

"The purpose, Jack, was to discover the identity of the traitor. On my way out of the building, I planted spyware that will send data to an outside server."

Jack frowned. "It's been four days. They will have found it by now, isolated it, and purged it from the system. We do have some of the finest software and techs available, you realise."

"I know. That's why I planted four different programs. The first two are fairly standard infiltration programs, which mimic each other. Your techs will find one and think they've contained it, while the second continues to work in the background." He held up a hand when Jack made to defend his co-workers' skills. "When they realise the second program is still running, the third piggybacks on their own efforts to isolate it, in the process giving the fourth program a back door into most of their systems."

Jack nodded. "All right, pretty thorough, but not foolproof."

"It's as close as it can be, though."

"How?"

"The final program. It's a Matryoshka program."

The mug Jack had half raised to his mouth hit the table hard enough to slosh coffee onto the smooth surface. "Matryoshka program. Isn't that just a rumour?"

Like the Russian nesting dolls it was named for, the Matryoshka program was layers upon layers of code that, when discovered by a host-protection program, peeled off the top coat as a distraction before escaping. It was hypothesised a perfect Matryoshka program could run forever and never be disabled. The downside was, they were supposedly very narrow-minded programs, specifically tasked with a single goal.

Ethan smirked. "To those who don't have the money to buy one."

Jack's gaze skipped off Ethan, to the expensive car, to the living quarters setup that must have cost more than a few pretty pennies, then down to the floor under his bare feet, laced with enough explosives to take out the building. Even considering that . . .

"And you have enough money for that?" he asked, wondering just who this man was.

"No. But my client does."

"Right. Your client. And this mysterious person cares enough about a traitor within the Office to buy a mythological computer program that can infiltrate any system?"

"Apparently so."

Jack slumped in his chair. "Fuck."

Ethan acknowledged it with a nod, then tucked into his food. Jack managed a bit of bacon, then had to stop.

"So, if this undetectable—"

"Not undetectable. Just unstoppable."

"Fine. Unstoppable. If this wonder program is digging through the Office systems, what have you got it looking for?"

"The name of the traitor, of course."

Jack snorted. "You really think they're dumb enough to leave something so obvious on the system?"

"Of course not. The program was given a defined set of parameters to look for, namely any information on Samuel Valadian. He was definitely being protected by this person and the data should show some evidence of that. It will send that information to an associate of mine, who will do a pattern recognition scan on it and, fingers crossed, find the identity of the traitor. It was my associate I was talking to earlier. She's not very happy with me at the moment." A touch of his earlier annoyance tinged his tone again. "Apparently, I did not accurately surmise the amount of data she would have to go through. It will take her some time."

"And in the meantime?"

Ethan pointed to the food between them. "I suggest you eat before it goes cold."

"Maria said she had information that you've spent the past year tracking down the rest of Valadian's organisation."

Ethan went still, like prey sensing a predator. No, a predator sensing discovery. "I'm sure she did."

Wondering what about his comment spooked Ethan, Jack pushed. "And? What did you find?"

After a long, tense moment, Ethan sighed and let the tension go. "Eventually, confirmation he was being protected by someone in the Australasian Meta-State, and precisely, a director in the Sydney Office. And that's all you need to know."

"Like fuck." Jack was starting to feel used and abused again. Just another means Ethan utilised to reach his desired goal. He'd been a fool to think otherwise, though. "I think there's a shitload more I need to know."

"Jack, plausible denia—"

"No! That's not what I'm talking about."

Tone calm, Ethan asked, "Then what, Jack? What else is there?"

The sheer ignorance in those words shot through Jack like a jolt from a shock-stick. Did Ethan honestly not realise what he'd done? Yes, a small part of Jack's mind answered. Ethan didn't think the same way as normal people. How could he when he'd been tortured as a child and killing for half his life? Jack shouldn't expect rational answers. Still, that voice was drowned out by rising anger, a surge he couldn't stop just as he hadn't been able to stop himself from climbing into bed with him.

"There's me, Blade," Jack snapped, as upset with himself as he was with Ethan but unable to hold back. "It's been a year. It took me three weeks to get my shit together and come home. Then I spent two months under intensive review, my entire life put under the microscope. I went through hell trying to convince them *I* wasn't a traitor. My own director still suspected me, right up to the day you waltzed into that building." Jack pushed away from the table, getting up so he could pace. "I spent the first six months so on edge, waiting for you to show up somewhere, I cannot, in all good conscience, blame them for doubting me. Then when I finally decided you weren't going to show, when I began to think you'd changed your mind, you appear. Right in my building!" He held his fingers a couple of millimetres apart. "This close, Blade. I was this close to getting my life back. And here you are, to fuck it all up again."

Ethan sat and took it, his gaze locked on the cup of tea between his hands.

"So, yes, I think... no, I *hope*, there's something more." Jack forced himself to stop pacing. He leaned on the back of his chair, gripping it so tightly his knuckles went white. "Is there, Blade? Is there something else?"

The assassin was still, barely breathing. "Yes, Jack, there's something else. Or at least, there was."

"What was it?"

Drawing in a deep breath, then letting it out slowly, Ethan stood. He began gathering up the breakfast plates. "It was . . . something I can't tell you about."

"Can't, or won't?"

"Right at this moment, it's can't." He sounded calm enough, but he wouldn't look at Jack.

It was like the night in the cave, when after fucking, Ethan hadn't been able to look at him. The man *needed* to be in control, of himself and his surroundings, and hadn't liked it being taken away from him. But more so, he hadn't wanted to admit that he *had* liked it, too.

He also hadn't liked that it had been Jack to do it to him. Jack, the man he'd been gearing up to betray the very next day.

"Fine," Jack muttered, shoving the chair under the table harder than necessary. "Here's a suggestion, though. This time, when you aim a gun at me, make sure you mean to kill me."

THIRTY-THREE
THEN

The compound that had been Jack's home for the past fifteen months came into view an hour before sunset. It sat in the middle of the great nothingness of the desert like a mirage, an illusion of safety tricking the unwary into veering off course. A high chain-link fence surrounded a twenty-acre parcel of dry dirt, lookout towers at each corner. It was filled with barracks to house the three thousand men, warehouses to hoard the weapons and vehicles, training fields, and in one corner, the small herd of cattle Valadian kept as a ready supply of fresh beef. In the middle of it sat the Big House, which wasn't really that big. Around the house was a hard-won patch of grass, which never attained a vibrant green colour, no matter the amount of water wasted on it.

There was absolutely no movement. It was as empty as the open, barren plains around it.

"This was your schedule?" Jack asked as Blade assembled the Assassin X. "To get here after they'd evacuated."

"Yes. We needed to give Valadian time to get his troops out but not enough time to destroy all the evidence. If we're to find where he's gone to, we need to get in before he does something drastic."

"Like what?" Jack demanded.

"Firebomb it."

"Christ."

The rifle ready, Blade handed it over. "It's partly why I wished the chopper taken out of commission. It would seriously delay his plans to destroy the compound. Sourcing another means of dropping the incendiary devices has given us a bit more time."

Jack raised the Assassin X and scoped the compound. "Why didn't he rig it all at ground level?" There was no sign of life amongst the buildings or in the towers.

"It's far too dangerous to have that much explosive on hand. Anyone could have walked in and triggered it while he and his troops were there."

"Anyone like you."

"Or you. Do you see anything?"

"Nothing. I think the chopper is still there, though. Something's shining behind the west weapons store. You sure it's grounded for good?"

"Fairly certain. The damage we caused it would have been compounded by the flight back here."

"Damn. I've been dreaming about taking it up since I got here. Ka-52s are notoriously awesome birds."

The look Blade gave him was pure surprise. "You can fly a chopper?"

Jack smirked. "Had to do something while recovering from getting shot up by the Taliban. Learning to fly seemed like a useful skill set. There is absolutely fuck-all movement down there."

"Charming. Shall we storm the castle?"

Jack put on a chipper accent. "Do let's. You first, old bean."

Blade snickered and broke cover. In his DPDU he wouldn't be immediately visible, but it was a bold move. He skittered down the scree with his usual grace, Desert Eagle in hand though it didn't have the range to hit anything in the compound. Neither did the Assassin X, but Jack kept the scope on the buildings, looking for any sign Blade had been seen. By the time Blade had crossed half the distance, Jack had seen no movement, so he followed the assassin. He caught up to Blade when they were almost at the entrance.

It was a large gate in the eastern side of the fence with an arching sign over the top, proclaiming it to be "The Saint Jude Retreat for the Hopeless and Despaired." Under it in smaller print was, *The faithful should persevere in the environment of harsh, difficult circumstances.*

This was Mr. Valadian's cover. A religious-orientated retreat for men needing help and direction. The face presented to the public said it was a program geared towards ex-military personnel trying to reacclimatise to civilian life and ex-cons requiring added rehabilitation. Rather than link Jack to the military, the Office had fabricated a history of assault, larceny, and drug possession for Jaidev Reed. It got him in as a general thug, leaving him to work his way up the chain to become a trusted bodyguard. It had been the perfect cover, and then along had come Ethan Blade.

The gate was locked with a huge padlock and chain. Given enough time, Jack could have picked it, but Blade didn't bother with that. Instead, he ran his hand through his hair. Thick locks got caught around his fingers, and he tugged on them forcefully. With a wince, he broke a substantial clump of hair free. It wasn't until Blade had picked off most of the hair that Jack realised it was a length of thin black wire. He repeated this action twice more, then wound the wires together to form a thicker diameter, which he then wrapped around the chain. After ejecting the mag of his Desert Eagle, Blade took a single bullet from another pocket. Chambering the round, he moved away from the gate.

"Look away," he cautioned Jack, lifting the Eagle.

Obeying, Jack turned his face away just as Blade fired. The bullet hit the black wire and exploded. An instant later, the wire flamed into intense life. The extreme temperature of the burning pyrotechnic melted through the thick metal of the chain in the space of seconds, glowing orange droplets splattering on the red soil.

"What the hell was that?" Jack demanded when the chain dangled in two pieces, ends melted and steaming.

"Thermite." Blade frowned, as if expecting Jack to know that already.

Recalling running his hands through Blade's hair the night before, Jack shuddered. "I got that bit, but that wasn't an ordinary bullet you ignited it with."

Blade grinned. "It was an HEI."

"Fuck me," Jack exclaimed, still a little shocked. "They don't make high-explosive incendiary rounds for handguns."

"No, so I make them myself." Blade leaned back and kicked the chain free of the gate. "Beauty before brawn?" he asked cheekily, then ducked through the gate.

Jack gaped after him. "You crazy bastard."

"Half right, Jack. Hurry along."

Muttering under his breath, Jack followed Blade in. The gunshot would have alerted anyone still here to the incursion. Rifle at the ready, Jack scanned the buildings as they moved.

The windows were dark in the lowering light of the afternoon, but no movement showed behind any of them. Shadows gathered between the long, low-roofed buildings. Blade cleared each space before they moved on. Jack scoped the towers constantly, looking for snipers and finding nothing. He did the same to the upper storey of the Big House, again coming up empty. If there was anyone here, they were keeping their heads down.

"Any information about Valadian's plans will be in the Big House," Blade reasoned as they drew closer to the central building.

"Yeah." Jack agreed even though he wasn't feeling right about this. He wasn't sure why, but it felt off the same way the clumsy handling of the search parties had felt off. The same way his encounter with the lone soldier had felt off.

Still, he followed Blade to the Big House, keeping his attention sharp and focused, his awareness spilling out around him as it did in combat situations. He was keenly alert, ready for anything, his back-brain working on what was puzzling about it all while his active concentration was on getting out alive and in one piece.

Crossing the dry, brittle grass before the house, Jack was sent right back to that night a week before, making this same journey. His back began to prickle, and he wondered if Jimmy's ghost might be coming up behind him, knife at the ready. Jack spun, tracking across the open space. Nothing.

At the front door, Blade keyed in the code for the lock. He eased the door open, then covered the interior before sliding in. Jack gave the compound another sweep. Sunset draped orange-and-red light across the buildings, lengthening and deepening the shadows. More room for someone to hide in, but again, nothing. He followed Blade into the house.

The foyer was high and airy, extending up both storeys. A curved staircase gave access to the upper floor, doors to either side led to the parlour and dining room, and a corridor heading deeper into the house went to the study and kitchen.

Jack covered Blade while he pushed open the door to the parlour. The curtains hadn't been drawn, letting blood-red light fall into the house. There was no way to keep any building in the middle of the desert perfectly clean, so motes of dust drifted through shafts of light and sand crystals sparked on the hardwood floors. The rugs were rucked up where hasty feet hadn't paid attention to where they stepped. One of the plush armchairs was pushed out of alignment. A painting of Uluru on the wall hung askew, the wall safe behind it left open and empty. All signs of a quick getaway.

"We should split up," Blade whispered. "Search the place quicker."

"You sure?" Jack led with the rifle into the dining room. It wasn't as disturbed, but then Mr. Valadian could get new crockery wherever he ended up.

"It would be the prudent thing to do. Unless you do know Valadian's schedule and when the bombing is going to take place."

"Fine. Let's separate."

Blade nodded upwards. "I shall take the upper storey."

"Whatever."

The assassin sidled out of the dining room and vanished from Jack's perception. The sneaky bastard was far too quiet for Jack's comfort.

Jack went back to the parlour and made a cursory inspection of the few things left behind, not really expecting to find a discarded phone with a set of flashing GPS coordinates, but unable to pass the slim chance by entirely. Judging by the shoddy search patterns, it was highly likely some dead shit had left his copy of the evac plan behind.

Jack stood in the middle of the parlour, suddenly suspicious. He let the rifle drop from readiness. It hung from his right hand as he turned around, looking at the room with fresh eyes, trailing unsettled thoughts as he moved.

It all felt unreal, flawless. The disruption to the room, the empty compound waiting for them, a dune buggy exactly where Blade needed it, the search parties walking right by them. Out of memory came Blade's response when Jack needled him about not killing Valadian in the torture shack.

"Killing Valadian wasn't the only objective."

What else was there?

Wish you were here?

Jack brought the rifle back up and eased out of the parlour, covering the foyer and corridor before pointing the weapon up the stairs. Was there something up there Blade didn't want him seeing? Was that why they had to split up?

Christ, he was stupid. If he got out of this alive, he should probably retire in all good conscience. He didn't deserve his job when he'd let Ethan fucking Blade lead him around by the dick for a week. How much of what Blade had said was real, and how much was meant to trick Jack into . . . what? Following him around the desert while he pretended to go after Valadian? Why? What reason could Blade have to do all this? And where, Jack couldn't help but think, did letting Jack fuck him fit into it?

Feeling his combat awareness start to be overtaken by anger, Jack forced his mind off unanswerable questions and focused on finding Blade. Wherever he was, there were bound to be answers, surely.

With slow, cautious steps, Jack ascended the stairs. The second storey was laid out much the same as the first floor: two rooms at the front of the house, the rest at the rear. The corridor ran side to side, though. At the top of the stairs, Jack crouched in the cover of the railing and tracked towards the north side of the house first. Mr. Valadian's room was that way. Nothing. Likewise to the south. Rising, Jack paced carefully towards The Man's bedroom. There were thankfully no nooks or embrasures to launch an ambush from, just the hallway and a couple of closed doors, prints of desert landscapes on the walls. A large window at the end of the hallway filled the space with fading orange light.

The door to Mr. Valadian's room was locked. If Blade had been in here already, he wouldn't have bothered to lock the door when leaving. Jack checked the hallway again, finding it as empty as before. Then he stepped away from the wall, reared back, and kicked the door open. As it banged inwards, Jack spun and pressed his back to the wall beside the doorway, prepared for an attack.

Nothing.

Leading with the rifle, Jack entered the room. As below, it was artfully disrupted with an unmade bed, a few clothes scattered across the floor, drawers ajar. Another picture shifted to expose a hollowed-out wall safe.

Too textbook.

Jack left the bedroom and, forgoing stealth, busted through the door opposite. A large bathroom, empty. The next door was another bedroom, no sign of life and no hint of Blade. Another bathroom, two more bedrooms, all the same.

"Fuck," Jack hissed. "Fuck, fuck, fuck."

Where had the mongrel gone?

Alert levels skyrocketing, Jack quickly backtracked downstairs. Swinging around, he scanned the corridor with the rifle and headed for the study, which was locked as well. It would take more than a forceful boot to open this door. After slinging the rifle, Jack took out the Eagle and aimed, then hesitated.

Blade definitely hadn't been here, either. Which meant whatever he was up to had nothing to do with what might be in here.

Jack left the study untouched. He made a quick recon of the kitchen, just to make sure it was empty, and then crept back to the foyer. Scanning around showed it to be as empty as it was when he left it.

Tension coiling like a snake in his gut, Jack reached for the handle on the front door.

"I wouldn't do that, Jack."

Jack spun, raising Assassin X, and pointed it unerringly at Blade. He stood on the staircase, several steps up. Whether he'd just come down or hopped up there from wherever he'd been hiding on the first floor, Jack didn't know. All he was aware of was the barrel of the Desert Eagle, aimed directly at him. Blade's white eyes were as unreadable as ever, but his hand didn't waver, his voice steady.

"What the hell is this, Blade?" Jack ground out, curling his finger over the trigger. "What the hell is going on?"

"It's complicated."

"Like fuck it is! Just tell me what you've been doing with me."

Blade didn't answer, just kept his gun trained on Jack, going as still as a statue.

"Jesus Christ, Blade," Jack snarled. "This is worse than when we fucked. How hard is it to tell the truth?"

The assassin flinched at the word "fucked," then firmed up again. "Remarkably hard at times, Jack. If you would—"

"No. No excuses. Just tell me."

"I can't."

"Can't, or won't?"

"Right at this point in time, can't."

Anger searing white hot through his veins, Jack took a threatening step forwards, the rifle never once moving off Blade. How pathetic he'd been. Played so easily. He felt gutted, ripped apart. Felt as he had in India, when he'd realised his team was never supposed to get out alive. Like he'd been betrayed.

Which was ridiculous, because that would mean he'd, somehow, come to trust Ethan Blade.

"What's outside, Blade?" he asked softly, calmly.

"Don't go out there, Jack."

"Why not?"

Not waiting for another nonanswer, Jack spun and kicked open the doors.

THIRTY-FOUR
NOW

"**Y**ou don't trust me." Ethan leaned against the kitchen counter, hands gripping the polished marble behind him. He looked innocent, a puppy kicked for something he didn't realise he'd done wrong.

"Shit," Jack hissed. "You just make it so damned hard. Keeping secrets from me, and when you do tell me something, nine times out of ten, it's a bloody lie. That first day in the desert, you said you trusted me, and that wasn't true. You were just waiting to see what I would do while you were vulnerable. All part of a job you care more about than you care about—" Jack cut that off before it got even more messed up. "More than you care about other people. You're an unrepentant killer, Ethan, who betrayed me. Why should I trust you?"

God, please, give him an answer that didn't involve Ethan pulling a gun and shooting him.

"You shagged me," was what he got. Softly said, no touch of heat in his voice. "You touched me with gentle hands, caressed me, kissed me. You did that knowing what I was."

"It doesn't take trust to fuck. Just a tight arse and fifteen months of abstinence. You were convenient. And willing."

Even as he said it, Jack regretted it. All those things had played a part, sure, but the biggest contributing factor had been the thought of having Ethan moving with him, sharing this amazing, brilliant thing with him. Not Ethan Blade the ruthless assassin, but Ethan the man who could make Jack laugh, who reassured with a touch and promised help when Jack was at his worst. The man who, with hindsight, had tried to stop Jack from walking into the ambush.

"Yes," Ethan said. "I was willing and, as I said the next day, I didn't regret it. And I still don't. *None* of it."

Jack huffed in exasperation, to which Ethan gave a pained wince and waved it aside.

"I think we talked about it enough back then to cover all angles, so let's move on. What I didn't tell you then is this." Ethan pulled in a deep breath, expanding his bare chest in an unconscious display of his lean, perfect body. "I don't have sex outside of jobs. You joked last night about me bringing men back to my secret lair, and I can assure you, you're the first, Jack. Sex is . . . *was* always just another skill to be used to get what I wanted, or to get where I needed to be."

So that was why it'd felt mechanical at first, because that was all Ethan had known before. No real passion, no lust. It was a small pinhole in the wall surrounding Ethan, but Jack felt it exposed so much more than his reaction to sex. Was *life* just another skill to Ethan? Mimicking the people around him, not really feeling a part of it, detached? All so he could go amongst them and kill without ending up like Jack did—burnt out and on the edge?

Not wanting to know, but needing to, Jack indicated the rumpled bed behind him. "That was part of the job too?"

Ethan smiled in weary amusement. "No, Jack, that was *not* part of the job. You know that. You're just fishing for compliments now."

"A few earnest compliments do make me more willing to trust."

Ethan came around the table. He walked right up to Jack, then slid his arms around his neck and pressed against him. "In that case, it was the most amazing, teeth-rattling sex of my life. If you'd let me, I'd kiss you until you believed me." He did kiss him, a brush of his lips against Jack's jaw, close to his ear. "And thus, you'd trust me."

Jack put his hands on Ethan's hips, initially to push him away, but the kiss had the bizarre result of tightening his hold and adjusting them both until things slotted together nicely.

"That simple, huh?" he asked.

"Why make it any more complicated?"

Spluttering a startled snort, Jack pulled back enough to look at him in disbelief. "Aren't you the one who goes out of his way to make things complicated? I refer you to that entire fuckup in the desert, for starters."

Ethan frowned. "It wasn't a failure. It was going perfectly swell until *you* complicated things. I refer *you* to the night in the cave."

Jack had two options. He could reignite the argument, or he could keep Ethan pulled against him, their dicks hardening at the contact between their bodies. The latter would, incidentally, keep Ethan's hands on the back of his neck, his fingers playing in his hair. Well, there was a third option, where Jack could rib Ethan for using a word like "swell," but he dismissed it in favour of option two.

Snugging Ethan a little closer, he lowered his head and breathed against his ear. "I say again, you were willing." Still was, judging by the soft moan escaping his throat.

"And I repeat, it was part of the job. At first." His arms tightened, then slid down Jack's back and up again, under his shirt. Hot skin against hot skin had them both drawing in sudden breaths. "You didn't let it remain professional for long. I resisted, but you . . . kept at me until I couldn't help it. It was the first time, *ever*, I felt that way during sex."

If Ethan kept talking, he was going to feel that way again, very shortly.

Resisting the urge, Jack said, "So, you could say, I was your first."

With a little gasp, Ethan stiffened against him. When he let the breath out, it was in a long sigh, relaxing his body as it went. "Yes, I suppose you could say that."

In the end, neither of them said anything apart from each other's names and pleas for more, harder, faster, for some time after. Ethan's grip on his control was nonexistent from the start, and Jack honestly thought he might expire from the sheer wildness of it, the lines between their bodies blurring and mixing until even the colour difference was lost to him.

"Well," Jack huffed when his heart slowed enough to let him breathe once more, "I think that cherry's well and truly popped."

Ethan, face buried in a pillow, moved enough to thump him on the chest.

Jack wheezed out a laugh and shoved his hand away. They lay in relative silence for a while. For once, Jack was satisfied thoroughly. He had no wish to try for another fuck. At the same time, it felt wrong to just lie there, happily spent, feeling the warmth of another body not far away, listening as Ethan's breathing evened out, softening towards sleep. Just yesterday, Jack had been running from the law. He shouldn't be here, like this, while the traitor kept betraying them all.

But if there was anything they had to do, Jack was fairly certain Ethan wouldn't have let them go this far. Surely. From the corner of his eye, he looked at the back of the dark-haired head, at the breadth of those shoulders, the faint scars crisscrossing his back. Maybe he would if, like anyone discovering the joys of sex, all he could think about was the next fuck.

No. Ethan Blade was too long in the job to be easily waylaid. He'd proceeded with his plan after that night in the cave, after all. The sex hadn't stopped that. Which made Jack wonder just what could have kept Ethan away for a year. He'd been hell-bent on finishing his job when he left Jack in the desert, so what had stopped him?

Meaning to roll off the bed, Jack found himself going the other way instead and landing half on Ethan.

Ethan grunted but didn't push him away. Rather, he turned his head to press his face into Jack's shoulder. "Hello," he said, voice muffled.

"Hi."

"This is nice."

"My man sweat?"

Shoulders shaking with silent laughter, Ethan shook his head. "No, you tosser. The cuddle. Almost better than the sex."

Jack huffed. "Remember what I said about compliments?"

Lifting his head, Ethan smirked at him. "I did say *almost*."

"Yeah, whatever." Jack mashed Ethan's face back into the pillow. He let him up before his stifled laughter suffocated him. "Ready to talk reason now?"

Ethan shook his hair out of his eyes and turned in the confines of Jack's hold, pressing against him, legs sliding between Jack's. He kissed his way along Jack's collarbone. "Do we have to talk? Can't we just . . . shag?" He punctuated his question with a wriggle of his hips that had Jack's eyes rolling back in his head.

"No." It cost him a lot to say it, even more to pry Ethan off and get at least a few centimetres of space between them. "I don't want to argue about this, but I'd like to know. Why can't you tell me about the past year?"

Ethan pulled back a bit further but kept one hand on Jack, his fingers rubbing lightly against his biceps. "It's complicated."

"How?"

"How is anything made complicated? By too much history, by too many hands in the pot, by too . . . By not having enough control over things you wish you did. Please, Jack. Don't ask me about this. It has little to no bearing on this job. Yes, it delayed me, far longer than I thought it would, but it was personal. And while I might wish to be able to share it with you, I simply can't."

The moment Ethan said "personal," Jack didn't need to hear more. Fantastic sex aside, betrayals and rescues forgotten, Jack knew he shouldn't be investing emotionally in this disastrous relationship. Enough hurdles stretched out in front of him without adding any sort of commitment to a mentally unbalanced assassin into the mix. Ethan could talk all he wanted about the fucking not being part of the job and Jack could believe it, but that didn't mean it wasn't encapsulated within the confines of it. Once the job was done, Ethan would leave and Jack would . . . Well, he'd sort that out when it happened, but he wouldn't pine for Ethan Blade. He hadn't last time. He wouldn't this time, either.

"All right," he conceded. "No more questions about it."

"Thank you. For what it's worth, I am sorry it upset you. If I'd had a choice, I wouldn't have stayed away so long." He rolled over, hauling Jack's arm across his chest as he did.

Sliding up behind him, Jack forced himself to relax. "So, you couldn't come here, but you could race all over the world looking for the remains of Valadian's group?"

"Jack." Said with more than a touch of warning.

"What? It's not about the other thing."

"Not directly. And stop doing that." He pushed Jack's face away from his neck. "You breathing on me like that isn't going to encourage 'reasonable talk.'"

"You're the one who wanted to cuddle."

Ethan harrumphed. "Must you always deflect blame?"

"Only when I'm blameless."

"Hmm, which seems to be all the time." He wiggled against Jack. "Either let me sleep or shag me again. Those are your options."

"Compromise. You answer the question, and I'll let you sleep afterwards."

Ethan pretended to consider it, then nodded. "As you wish. Yes, because I couldn't get here, chasing down Valadian's group seemed to be the best option. There was every chance someone else knew just who was protecting him."

"But you didn't find anything."

"Only that the traitor was within the Office. Hence, why I am here now. Good enough?"

"Is it the truth?"

Ethan didn't answer immediately. Instead, he burrowed into the pillow, pulling Jack's arm against him tighter. Jack had resigned himself to not getting an answer, and thereby *getting* one, when Ethan spoke again.

"Yes. That is the truth."

But not all of it. At least, that was Jack's interpretation of the guarded words. Christ. Ethan was going to drive him insane.

Within minutes, Ethan was asleep.

Jack tossed between staying or getting up. He closed his eyes and tried not to think how good it felt, right now, like this. It wasn't personal. It couldn't be. He should be annoyed at Ethan's refusal to tell him about the past year, not worried. But still his mind kept going back to that thought—what could stop Ethan Blade doing what he set out to do? The man had undertaken a dangerous trek across the desert to test Jack, had put himself at Jack's mercy to see what he would do. He'd convinced Valadian to give up forty of his troops to get the job done.

What problem, personal or otherwise, could be so great Ethan couldn't think, shoot, or sneak his way past it?

Then Jack made the mistake of opening his eyes and looking at Ethan. Curled on his side, the smooth expanse of his back pressed to Jack's front, chin tucked into his chest. Here and now, sleeping deep in this secure place, he didn't look as if he needed to think, shoot, or sneak his way past anything. Didn't even look as if he *could*. Ethan just looked young and innocent, peaceful.

In this quiet, safe moment, the masks fell away and revealed the man Jack had caught glimpses of in the desert. This was Ethan. Not Ethan Blade, assassin, but *Ethan*, a young man doing the only thing he knew how to do. This was the man Jack was drawn to, who attracted him, who made him listen and take risks. The man whom Jack wanted to protect and help. The man Jack trusted.

For the first time in what felt like forever, Jack didn't wish to be somewhere else. Here was the only place he wanted to be. And that was okay, he decided as he pressed a kiss to Ethan's shoulder. Okay, as well, to want this man, to want to be with him like this, as a friend and occasional companion. Outside, in the real world, it would be different, difficult and dangerous, but here, like this, it was good.

Still, Jack decided to get up. If he stayed in bed, tangled up with this man, he'd probably end up doing something incredibly stupid.

THIRTY-FIVE
THEN

Jack's first thought—an irrational grasp towards the hope he *hadn't* been betrayed—was that Blade had wanted to stop Jack from springing the trap so they could both escape. Reason, however, crashed back in almost immediately, and he *knew* this was where Blade had been leading him all along.

Mr. Valadian stood on the grass before the Big House, suit impeccable, not one hair out of place, smugly superior expression on his plain face. He looked absolutely nothing like a man who should be running for his life from an assassin. Of course, that could have had something to do with the army at his back.

It wasn't the full three thousand, but the hundred or so armed soldiers may as well have been for all the chances Jack had of getting through them.

"Put your weapons down, Mr. Reed," Mr. Valadian suggested, oh so urbanely. "While your death isn't entirely off the books yet, I'd hate to have the decision made for me."

Right then, an army-assisted suicide looked pretty inviting, but Blade was suddenly behind him, muzzle of the Desert Eagle pressed to the junction between skull and neck. Swiftly, he pulled the other gun from Jack's waistband and slid the Assassin X off his shoulder.

"I urge you to not do anything stupid, Jack," Blade murmured.

"Why should I stop now? Worked so well for me up to this point."

"Jack." The warning in the tone sounded honest, though Jack had to wonder if he'd ever had a real reading off Blade.

"Come on down, Jaidev," Mr. Valadian said. "We need to talk."

"Yeah." Jack tried to let go of the anger and open up for the cool serenity of detachment. It didn't work.

He had to get his head into the game, wanted that rush of calm he needed in order to dive head first into combat and get out the other side alive. It was too personal this time, too close to home. It was like the Maoists had just blown up the school and all he could feel was a towering desire to hurt those responsible for killing his mother. He looked at Valadian and saw the man who'd destroyed so many lives with his criminal empire, who'd ordered those who dissatisfied him beaten and killed, who'd built this place, put the name of a saint on it, and then defiled it with his careless cruelty. He hated that he'd come to laugh at the man's jokes. But mostly, he hated the fact Blade stood behind him, gun to his head, hand steady, ready to kill him if he so much as twitched the wrong way.

"Yeah," he said again, then, "No."

Before Valadian could question him, Jack reached back for Blade. Got hold of his arm and went down on one knee in the doorway, hauling the assassin over his back.

For whatever reason, Blade hesitated, the only reason Jack's gambit worked. He tumbled over with a startled gasp, which turned into an *oof* of pain when Jack slammed him down to the veranda. Jack twisted the arm he held, then caught the Eagle when Blade released it. Jack all but threw the assassin back into the house, followed him, and slammed the doors behind them.

Blade was partway to his feet when Jack caught him with a boot to his gut. Another kick sent him back to the floor, at the foot of the stairway.

"You goddamned little shit! What was that—"

Moving faster than Jack could credit, Blade flipped back to his feet. His expression was closed down, cold, full of the detachment Jack wanted but couldn't find. For maybe a second, he held back, then he was moving.

It took every ounce of skill, training, and luck Jack had just to keep up. Blade attacked with a fluid blend of martial arts, every move precise and infinitely controlled. All of it perfectly aimed to get inside Jack's defences. Jack held his own, barely. He used strength where Blade used speed, his kicks knocking the smaller man back, his punches getting satisfying grunts of pain, but Blade was always twisting back in, delivering driving jabs and lightning fast strikes.

Blade back-flipped over Jack's sweeping leg, coming down into a spinning kick aimed at Jack's gut. Staggering back, Jack turned away from the next hit, collecting it on his ribs, not his aching stomach. Catching the arm under his, he rolled with the blow, bringing his back to Blade's chest. Elbowed him in the face with all the force he could muster, then continued around, wrenching Blade's arm out at an unnatural angle, punching him in his bloody nose again.

Head snapping back, then forwards, Blade focused on Jack for a split second and there was nothing relatable in his unchanging eyes. No pain, no anger, no recognition. Maybe they'd been wrong about the Sugar Babies. Maybe they were unfeeling, insane, inhumane. Intelligent enough to mimic acceptable behaviour but that was all it was—an act.

"Blade." The mad thought he could get through this automaton and find the man he'd known was given a moment of desperate life before it died.

Blade threw his head forwards, aiming to smash his forehead into Jack's face. Seeing it coming, Jack pulled back enough to take the blow on his jaw. It knocked him back, his head ringing with the power of the impact. Blurrily, he saw the fist coming and tried to move. It slammed into his shoulder, pushing him further off-balance. The follow-up kick caught him on the jaw. He crashed to the floor. Blade was on him instantly, straddling his chest, knees clamping his arms to his sides.

Physical attack seemed to be inadequate, so Jack went with psychological.

"Huh," he managed, even though his jaw protested massively, "knew you didn't like getting fucked."

The fist smashed into his face. His body reacted without thought, thrashing off the floor, lifting Blade up. Twisting, he tried to topple the assassin off. Blade went with the roll, though, legs clamping tight around Jack's torso. One hand in the collar of Jack's shirt, Blade punched him again and again while Jack scrambled to get enough purchase on the slick floor to break free. He dug his fingers into the hard, straining muscles of Blade's thighs, hoping to find a nerve or two.

"Maybe I was wrong about the fuck," he wheezed. "You seem to like having me between your legs."

Blade snarled and squeezed with his thighs.

Coughing up the last of his air, Jack hooked his hands into the back of Ethan's DPDU pants and heaved, trying to break his hold. Blade arched his back, then snapped his legs out straight, tearing Jack away from his clothes. Before he knew what was happening, Jack was flung around again, ending up on his other side. One moment Blade was in front of Jack, the next he was behind him. Legs still clamped around his body, he wrenched Jack's head back and wrapped his other arm around his throat in a chokehold.

Jack's scrambling hands found Blade's arms, his sides, his knees, but nothing worked to loosen the hold. He rolled them into the wall, hoping to knock Blade off. He didn't budge. The assassin hung on like a parasite, draining the strength out of him with each airless gasp.

Wish you were here?

As his body weakened and his efforts faded away, Jack felt Blade move. He kept the hold firm, pushing him further towards the growing darkness, but pressed his mouth to Jack's ear.

"Shh," he whispered, almost soothingly. "It'll be all right. I'll protect you."

And, wondering if he was hallucinating from lack of air, Jack fell into the black . . .

. . . which was ripped away with a painful, strangled cough. His throat tore with the effort of pulling in a breath. Light sparked behind his eyelids, red and white. His head throbbed in time with the ache in his neck, the pulsing of blood through vessels poorly abused.

God. Jack hated waking up like this. Thankfully, it had only happened one other time outside of military training, and like that time, he came around with a startled gasp, body jerking against the bonds holding it tight to . . . another bloody chair.

He kept his eyes squeezed shut, didn't want to open them and see the torture shack again. It would do what nothing else had managed yet and tip him right over the edge. If he had to look at that fucking beach again, at those words that had emblazoned themselves across his mind, he would lose his shit once and for all.

"Mr. Valadian, he's awake."

That accent roared through Jack like wild fire. He snapped his head up, blinking in the sudden wash of bright light into his dark-adjusted eyes. He wanted to see that goddamned lying face and . . . and . . . kick it.

A door opened before he could see clearly and a shadowed shape entered the room. Valadian. He swam into focus lazily: his overcoat, his bland features, his smug, bloody smile.

The room around them was white walled, empty bar the chair Jack was tied to. No poster, no implements of pain. It wasn't the torture shack. That much Jack was grateful for. The rest of it could go fuck itself, including the two men standing in front of him.

As he had that night at the shack, Blade stood back, behind Valadian, containing himself to a very small portion of the room. He would have disappeared into the walls if they'd been painted the same camouflage pattern as the DPDU he still wore. Jack sneered at him, liking the look of the bloodied nose, the blackening eyes, the scratches on his cheek Jack couldn't remember inflicting. His own face probably looked worse, but he didn't care. He'd damaged Ethan Blade. He'd ask them to write it on his epitaph.

Valadian studied Jack for a long while, then asked, "Were you successful?"

Startled, it took Jack a moment to realise he was speaking to Blade.

"I was. His real name is Jack Reardon. He was with the SAS before leaving on a medical discharge. It was falsified, however, covering his move to military intelligence." Blade's cool, steady tone gave nothing away. The lie rolled off his lips as easily as the ones he'd spoon-fed Jack for the past week.

The Man snorted. "And you had to waste forty of my men to find that out?"

"It was necessary. He's been trained to resist interrogation. I needed him to trust me, and it was the most expedient way. By convincing him I was here to kill you, I made him feel he could confide in me."

Jack jerked at the words. How much of it was true? Blade was clearly keeping something back from Valadian. He knew Jack worked for the Office, not the military. That was one thing, but *was* Blade actually here to kill Valadian?

"Did he get any of the information he'd gathered out to his handlers?" Valadian asked Blade.

"No, sir. It's all stored in a neural implant. We should be able to wipe it easily enough."

Jack's head hurt, his throat ached, and there was a buzz between his ears slowly eroding what little control he might have begun with. Was Blade selling him out or not?

Whatever was going on, Jack didn't like it, and he was getting angry again. "You fucker," he snarled at Blade. "So that's what that was? The torture shack, the desert trek, the 'let's be the best buddies ever!' It was all part of the world's longest foreplay? All so you could fuck me over?"

Blade ignored him, keeping his gaze on Valadian's back.

Valadian regarded Jack with an almost sympathetic smile. "He's very good, isn't he? Came most highly recommended. I'm not even paying him. He asked for the honour of doing this for me." He shook his head sadly. "I almost feel sorry for you. You put up a valiant fight at the end there, but you were never going to win against Blade."

With a gesture, he motioned Blade over. The assassin moved without hesitation, coming close to Valadian's side. The Man cupped the back of his neck, pulled him even closer. With a wink in Jack's direction, Valadian kissed Blade on the mouth.

Jack's already jumpy heart skipped and slammed against his ribs. His breath caught in his throat.

Blade's head tipped back, his mouth opening under Valadian's. Eyes closed, he leaned into the older man, hands clutching at his coat, melting into the kiss. Soft moans escaped him, his mouth chasing Valadian's when The Man pulled back. Smiling at the utter submission, Valadian kissed him again, harder.

All the questions about Blade's actions spun into nothing as Jack watched the man he'd worked so hard to get a surrender from give himself completely to an arsehole like Valadian. They deserved each other, the lying, vicious pair of them. The way Blade moulded around Valadian, it was like they were alone, no witnesses, no crazy ex-SAS soldier ready to attack them both.

This time, when Valadian broke the kiss, Blade sighed and dipped his head into the man's shoulder, his body shivering with aftershocks.

"What the fuck?" It burst out of Jack on a tide of rage and confusion.

"Precisely, Mr. Reardon." Valadian's hand slid down to cup Blade's arse and squeeze proprietarily. "Go prepare the men," he murmured to the assassin. "We'll be leaving as soon as I'm done in here."

Blade's "Yes, sir" was breathy and thick with desire, but he left the room steady on his feet.

Valadian watched him go, a smirk on his well-used lips. When the door closed, he said, "Such a doormat."

A cutting summation, clearly, but in his addled state it whizzed by Jack.

"A what?"

Snickering, Valadian repeated, "A doormat. Some men are like doormats. Lay them right the first time, and you can walk all over them for years."

It had to be a lie. A game. Something Blade had concocted. But why? What did this all mean? Perhaps he was still unconscious and it was all a mad dream.

"You fucked him?" Jack had to know.

"Yes. I don't like men that way, though. Women don't have many uses, but they have *that* one, at least. Still, the man who recommended Blade to me said fucking him was an easy way to keep him in line. Totally submissive, which is a bit of a turn-on, I have to admit. And I get the services of an assassin for the price of a few fucks." He smiled, as if expecting Jack to laugh along.

"You're a sadistic prick," Jack said instead.

"And you're a pathetic fool."

Jack flinched. The Man had nailed it again.

Valadian adjusted his coat. "I am sorry it's come to this, Mr. Reed. I really did like you. I think I might miss you. Just a bit."

He turned and left, the door closing firmly behind him.

Alone and so thoroughly gutted he felt numb, Jack slumped in the chair. He didn't even fight against the restraints. Closing his eyes, he tried to shove everything into the filing cabinet. He got Valadian's parting words in there, and Blade's betrayal, but no matter how he tried, he couldn't get the images of the kisses in there. The shapes and sounds of Blade letting Valadian kiss him, of how the assassin had clung to the arsehole in a show of willing passion, of how Blade had blinked dreamily in the wake of the forceful connection, none of it went into the overstuffed compartments.

The harder he tried, the more they resisted, until his feet were drumming on the floor and his arms were twisting within the plastic ties.

And then it happened. The filing cabinet burst at the seams and all the shit spilled out. All the beatings, the delivered threats, the stealing. Link Rindone's head snapping back as the bullet ploughed through his skull. The pointless waste of lives at the torture shack. The men with the buggy. Giving in to his base desires. The memory of Blade moving against him. Of Blade holding a gun to his head.

All of it. All at once, spreading like a dark stain across his mind, pouring cold and hard into his heart.

THIRTY-SIX
NOW

Jack was restless, antsy. He paced, he ran on the treadmill, he spent a good half hour beating the stuffing out of the kick-bag. It was all up in the air and he couldn't even see the balls, let alone catch them. After the agonising indecision, then the chaos of breaking Ethan out of his cell and the frantic race to get here, suddenly it was all sit down and wait.

Ethan was being incredibly Zen about it all. He sat at his work bench and cleaned weapons, his hands and fingers deft and quick as they disassembled rifles and handguns with equal proficiency. Or he made pots of tea and cups of coffee. At one point, he stared into the fridge for a minute, then sat down and made a shopping list.

Watching the seventh-ranked assassin in the world be so domestic was amusing for only so long, and Jack was back to being jittery. That constant nag of pre-combat nausea was making him cranky, partly because he didn't have a go-time, and partly because Ethan didn't have any smokes and wouldn't let him go out for some.

So they argued instead.

"That's your plan?" Jack demanded.

Ethan, sitting at the table reviewing his shopping list, glanced up at him expressionlessly and then back down, tactfully adding *cigarettes* to the bottom of the list. "Yes, Jack, that is my plan."

Jack was back to pacing, along his preferred path between dining table and bed. "The vaunted and feared Ethan *Blade*'s great plan once he finds out who the traitor is, is to—" he waved vaguely at the Aston Martin "—and then—" making explosion noises, he mimed something blowing up "—after which, it's a 'simple'—" the world's most sarcastic quotation marks "—two-man, *no*-camel assault on the Office, where we'll have to face some very highly trained security personnel while trying to find the one person who'll be doing everything they possibly can to not be caught." He stopped pacing and gesticulating wildly. "*That's* your plan?"

After folding up his list and tucking it into a pocket, Ethan stood. "Yes, Jack," he repeated patiently. "That is my plan. We will, of course, try for minimal deaths, but it may be impossible, given the circumstances." As he passed Jack, he winked and patted his cheek. "Are you saying you're not up to the challenge?"

It was an entirely new sensation for Jack, this anger mingled with an arousal strong enough he knew he was going to act on it. He'd definitely been cranky and horny at the same time in the past, but never on this scale. Never in such a way he couldn't ignore either impulse.

"Minimal deaths? Not up to . . .?" He spun and caught Ethan around the waist from behind. "I'll show you *up to the challenge.*" And he wrestled a not-really-protesting man onto the bed.

"Jack," Ethan gasped as his shirt was pulled off roughly. "We need food and . . . and . . . your cigarettes . . ." The word trailed off as he *thump*ed back on the mattress, groaning as Jack began a two-pronged attack: lips and teeth against his left nipple and insistent hand on the quickly growing bulge in his pants.

"No," Jack growled, "what we need is a better plan." Bypassing all sorts of niceties, he wrenched open Ethan's pants and got flesh-on-flesh contact. "There will be *no* deaths. These are my people. Good people." He squeezed until Ethan moaned, then teased his thumb over the sensitive spot just under the head of his dick until Ethan was squirming helplessly. "Are we agreed? Absolutely no deaths."

Breathless, Ethan managed, "It may not be possi— Jack!" His back arched off the bed as Jack upped the ante.

Which was the wrong tactic. Not only did Ethan lose the ability to form coherent sentences, but Jack forgot his agenda at the sight of Ethan losing control. Things devolved in the best of ways until it was just the two of them in the bed, moving together. No plans, no traitor, no jobs, no world.

A long while later, Jack finally remembered why they'd ended up in bed in the first place. He lifted his head from Ethan's belly, dislodging the man's fingers from playing in his black curls, and studied him. Sprawled across the bed, so relaxed the hand that had been seconds ago resting on Jack's head now flopped boneless to the sheet. Eyes closed, breathing slow and steady, he could have been asleep. Asleep and innocent. He was, however, neither of those things.

Right then, Jack admitted something to himself.

The plan was dangerous. Parts of it, Jack could see the merit in. They had to get back inside the building and find the traitor before he or she escaped. The Office would be on high alert, security amped up to the highest level. A covert approach would take too long. Surprise was the best option they had, so that bit, Jack could get on board with. The rest . . .? The risk was too high, not just to Jack's fellow assets, but to Ethan as well.

That was what Jack had to accept. He wanted . . . no, *needed*, to protect Ethan. From the Office, and himself.

Ethan opened his eyes and looked at him. "Jack?"

"Let me do it."

"Pardon?"

"I'll take the evidence in and do it officially. If I go back alone, they'll be more willing to listen. You going back there now will only put them on edge, more so than they already are. Things will escalate needlessly . . ."

It wasn't working. As Jack spoke, Ethan stopped being the man he'd just fucked and became the assassin. He didn't move, but his post-orgasm, languorous mien morphed into the predatory stillness Jack had encountered in the desert, in those moments he'd wondered if he would truly survive. Those moments when Jack had gotten between Ethan and his goal.

"My job is to eliminate the traitor," Ethan said, cool and calm. "And I will do my job."

Shit. The reminder of just who Jack was dealing with was timely, but even as he held up a hand in surrender and said, "Okay. Just offering an alternative. We'll go with the shock and awe approach," he knew it wouldn't stop him from doing what he had to do.

Afterglow sufficiently dimmed, they got up and showered together, quick and perfunctory. While Ethan retreated to his work bench to check his gear with the tight, fastidious motions of someone working through a compulsion, Jack ran out his frustrations on the treadmill and devised amendments to Ethan's plan. In the end, it wasn't a vast improvement, but he was convinced it was less risky for everyone.

By evening, with Jack if not happy then content with his alternatives, and Ethan's psychological needs satisfied, they managed a civil dinner and in bed, even though they didn't fuck, Jack fell asleep curled around Ethan's willing and warm body.

However, as the next day dragged on with no word from Ethan's "associate" and Jack still had no cigarettes, he got grumblier and grumblier.

"How much longer?" he demanded at one stage, while Ethan lay under the car, doing something mystical and ritualistic to it, judging by the time and concentration it took.

"It will take as long as it takes, Jack." Ethan's voice echoed up through the engine, which was exposed, the car's bonnet propped open. "Could you hand me the nine-sixteenths wrench?"

"The what?"

"The nine—" Ethan cut himself off with a sigh, pushed himself out from under the car on a little wheeled trolley, and pointed to the tool kit by Jack's foot. "The wrench with nine-slash-sixteen on it. No, not that one, the other one. The *other* one. Bollocks. Just let me do it." He grabbed the tool and rolled out of sight again. "You need a hobby, Jack. Something to occupy your mind and hands."

Peering at the engine, Jack grimaced. "Some of us aren't rich enough to buy sports cars, Blade."

"There are other hobbies. I also enjoy fishing."

Jack rolled his eyes. "I can think of something else to occupy my hands."

"Pardon?"

With a squeal of tiny wheels, Jack pulled Ethan out from under the car. Before Ethan even managed a yelp of surprise, Jack was straddling him, Ethan's grease-streaked hands pinned over his head to the cement, the wrench clattering free. The trolley rocked as Jack leaned down and nipped at Ethan's neck. It seemed, deprived of nicotine, Jack's body was falling back on another chemical rush to ease the tension.

"I don't think this is an entirely appropriate hobby," Ethan murmured, but he tipped his head back to give Jack more access.

"I'm sure you're right." Jack hummed against the warm skin of Ethan's throat. "I'll undoubtedly be bored with it by the weekend and shove it in the cupboard, never to be seen again."

Ethan's chuckles vibrated against Jack's lips. "Undoubtedly." With a nifty little twist, he freed one hand and skated it down Jack's ribs and back up, bringing his shirt with it. His fingers ran over the exposed skin, making Jack shiver.

"You'll get me all greasy."

"And then I'll wash you off," Ethan promised in a low, husky voice.

"It's a plan." Jack sat up, reaching for the hem of his shirt.

Grinning, Ethan waggled his grubby hands in eager anticipation. Then his grin vanished, and he reached into his pocket and fished out a presumably vibrating phone. He tapped it to answer a call.

"Yes?" The sexy tease was gone from his tone, leaving it flat and businesslike.

This was it. It had to be.

An entirely different flush of excitement ran down Jack's spine. He got off Ethan, watching him as he listened intently. Phone caught between ear and shoulder, Ethan picked up the wrench and rolled back under the car.

Jack gathered the weapons from the work bench, then stripped and dressed in one set of body armour laid out on the bed. By the time he was done, Ethan was out from under the car, still on the call.

"Thank you. I truly appreciate this," he said on his way to the bathroom to wash his hands. "Yes, I understand. I'll be there in half an hour."

When he emerged, Jack cocked an eyebrow at him.

"We have an answer."

"And? Who is it?" Jack suppressed an urge to shake him until he spilled the answer. This was it. He was about to learn who had taken money from Valadian and kept him off threat lists for so long. He needed to know, to finally have an end to this. At the same time, he dreaded hearing the name. Whoever it was, it was someone he'd worked with, trusted, relied on. He didn't want to have that trust ripped away from him, not again.

Ethan quickly undressed. "I don't know."

Jack stared at him, not seeing the lean, beautiful body. Just another barrier. "Sorry? You don't know?"

"Not yet. My associate won't relay the information over even secure channels. We'll get the information when we see her in person."

Armoured and weaponed out, they got into the low-slung car. Ethan started it and the engine rumbled into a smooth, rolling purr, vibrating through the entire car in a way that reminded Jack of how Ethan shivered under him.

Ethan tapped a code into a keypad attached to the black console. As the big roller-door began to open, Ethan gunned the engine and it throbbed with a deep, throaty roar. Sunglasses on, he settled into the leather seat. "Hold on."

"To what?" Jack asked, then forgot his question as Ethan slammed the car into gear and hit the accelerator.

The roller-door was barely high enough for the car to squeeze under it, but they made it with maybe two inches to spare. Ahead, a gate in the fence was opening and it, too, was barely wide enough for the car when they slipped through. The tyres squealed as Ethan put the car into a tight turn that drifted its back end out alarmingly. Hands working assuredly on wheel and gear stick, the assassin straightened the car out. It responded fluidly, engine winding up and up in pitch, then dropping back as Ethan shifted gears, again and again. The industry of Williamson Road blurred by Jack's window.

Jack clamped onto the edge of his seat. "Holy Jesus fuck!"

Ethan laughed.

They careened south on Williamson Road, swerving around what traffic there was. Ethan handled the car with supreme ease, the sleek vehicle seemingly gliding over the road surface as if there were no traction on the tyres. Even through the closed windows, Jack heard shouts of surprise and alarm and the warning blurts of horns. Ingleburn might have had its fair share of hooligans and hoons, but none of them probably tooled around in an Aston Martin Vanquish S Coupe. It almost made him smile.

They quickly left the industrial area behind and joined the suburban streets. More traffic here but if Ethan slowed for it, it was barely perceptible. Still, they made it onto the Hume Motorway without anything more troubling than a sudden braking at a roundabout to let a bus lumber by. But once on the highway, Ethan gleefully made up for the lost seconds by unleashing the Vanquish fully.

Even though it was part of the plan Jack agreed with, he would have protested out of a sense of practicality, but he was too busy reassessing his earlier opinion of Ethan behind the wheel of his car. Appealing? It didn't even come close.

Ethan was moulded to the seat as if it were a part of him, as if the car were just another limb he controlled with exacting precision. The intent expression eased into something softer, something more like contentment melded with utter confidence. This, Jack realised, was the real Ethan Blade. Not the killer, or the abused child, or the man acting out a part, but a person who felt completely at ease with himself. He was in control of a fast, dangerous vehicle; he was in command here as he was nowhere else in his life.

Regardless of how the rest of the day turned out, Jack would remember Ethan this way.

Naturally, they picked up a cop. Coming from the north, the cop car turned its lights and siren on as Ethan and Jack zoomed by in the opposite direction. They'd passed a lane connection not far back and sure enough, the cop used it to get over to the northbound lanes and work on catching up.

On an open road, with no other traffic, there would have been no competition between the Vanquish and a cop car. As it was, there was barely one anyway. When it looked like they might lose their pursuer, Ethan slowed to make sure they didn't, and then it was on again. By the time the Hume became the South Western Freeway, their friends had tripled in number and there was a chopper overhead.

"What do you think, Jack?" Ethan asked as he took the exit for the M7. "Do we have enough eyes on us yet?"

All the pre-combat queasiness was gone, replaced with a perfect calm. Jack glanced at the flashing lights following them, and then at the shadow of the chopper pacing theirs on the road.

"Yeah. No doubt about it. The Office will know exactly where we are."

THIRTY-SEVEN
THEN

They left him alone for a long time. Far too long to spend surrounded by all the mess of the past fifteen months.

Valadian was spot on. He was a fool. Those words kept cycling back to the front of his thoughts, alternating with the memory of those kisses.

It shouldn't infuriate him. Jack had absolutely no claim on Blade. Didn't want one, either. They'd fucked; that was all. Blade had gone along with it out of a sense of duty to his job. Jack had simply taken an opportunity, nothing more. They hadn't kissed.

Kisses were like hands. Revealing, expressive, intimate—and, also like hands, most people didn't see how powerful a kiss could be. Several of Jack's partners had joked about his refusal to kiss their lips, likening it to stories of hookers who wouldn't kiss their johns. Jack couldn't disagree. Fucking was just genitals banging together. In mind-bendingly brilliant ways, yes, but that wasn't love.

Love grew out of hearts and minds, and those things were most eloquently, most purely, expressed with the lips. In the words a person spoke to show their thoughts, their opinions, their feelings; the way they smiled or pouted or grimaced; the subtle touch of a tongue to a lower lip; downturned at the corners often more expressive than a gesture or walkaway; a bitten lip to keep in a throaty groan. The mouth was the most intimate part of a person and, as with hands, the least guarded.

Seeing Valadian kiss Blade, seeing Blade kiss him back, twisted Jack's guts into irrational knots. Not everyone felt as he did. Very few people did, in fact. People would kiss before they'd fuck. Knowing his reaction was unreasonable didn't stop Jack from seething over it, though.

So when Blade slid into the room, Jack hissed and redoubled his efforts against the restraints.

"You fucking bastard," Jack snapped. "I'm going to kill you. I really am."

Blade had that blank look on his face again. He reached to the back of his waistband and drew one of his Desert Eagles. Calmly, he removed the clip, ejected the chambered round, and inserted a single bullet from his pocket. Then he levelled the gun on Jack.

Jack went still. "You're really going to do it, aren't you."

So this was how they'd wipe out the information in Jack's head. At least it would take all the bad memories with it.

Except Jack wasn't done. Fifteen months of living in the snake pit, of letting them wind around him and drag him down, and it couldn't all be for nothing. He had to try.

"Blade, don't do this. If this is because of last night, I'm so—"

"Shut up."

"No. I want to—"

"Shut up."

"Screw you—"

Blade glared. "Shut up."

Jack saw it that time. The finger along the side of the gun's barrel tapped the silky steel.

Oh.

Understanding lasted about as long as it took to blink.

Blade adjusted his aim and fired.

Pain exploded in Jack's chest, dead centre. He was rocked back so hard the chair tilted alarmingly. He saw the white ceiling blur and grow dark, the sheer agony in his body stretching the seconds out into hours. Time was relative, Dad used to say. The cloud of black grew and grew until it swallowed him whole . . .

Coming to this time wasn't so pleasant. His whole body hurt as if he'd gone ten rounds sans gloves. He felt pummelled and broken, every nerve end throbbing. Pain jolted through him as if he was . . . being carried, fireman style, at a steady jog.

"Stay still," that poncy accent murmured as Jack moved experimentally.

"I will if you will." But somehow he didn't think the words managed to leave his head, because Blade didn't respond to them. Just kept jouncing along as if he hadn't caved in Jack's chest with a bullet.

"Hey!" someone called from behind them.

Blade slammed to a sudden halt, jarring Jack even more in his uncomfortable position.

"What are you doing back here?" The tone had the cadence of command about it. One of Valadian's officers, probably. "Everyone's supposed to be in the main yard."

"Sorry, sir," Blade said, turning slowly. He'd lost his British accent and sounded so perfectly Australian Jack almost coughed in surprise. Lucky he didn't, because Blade added, "I'm just disposing of the spy's body, as per The Man's orders."

"Oh, shit," a new voice said. "That's him. Valadian's weird pet killer."

"What? No, he's a Pom and he's out—"

The guy never got to finish. With a startled grunt, Jack was dropped to the ground. He tried to roll when he hit, but the burst of pain across his chest pretty much collapsed him in on himself where he landed.

Blade was already moving, silent and deadly as he lunged into the midst of the soldiers. There were more than two of them, that was for sure, because Jack heard the distinct *thumps* of two bodies hitting the ground in quick succession, and yet the yelps, grunts, and shouts continued.

Forcing himself to move, Jack uncurled and shoved to his hands and knees. His chest hurt like a mule had kicked him. When he blinked his eyes into focus, he found the fight moving away from him. Blade's fluid shape and style was easy to find in the mess of bodies and flying limbs. He had three opponents. Two more lay in the dirt, not far from Jack. Valadian's troops usually moved in groups of six.

A knife blade slid across Jack's throat, not hard enough to cut, but so close to it Jack stopped breathing altogether. His captor's other hand fisted in the back of Jack's abused shirt and hauled him back onto his knees, the knife never moving from his neck.

"You're supposed to be dead," the man hissed. "The white-eyed freak was supposed to kill you."

Jack lifted his hands, fingers spread, to show he had no weapon. "The work ethic of assassins these days, huh?"

As he spoke, Jack grabbed the wrist of the hand holding the knife to his throat and pulled it down, locking the man's arm in place on his shoulder. Jack bit his hand. Hard. While he was distracted, Jack scrambled around the man, one forearm across his shoulders, forcing him to the ground, the other twisting the wrist of his knife hand until it gave up the weapon. Jack snatched it before it hit the ground and acted without thought.

Blade found him there, still crouched over the dead man, knife protruding from between his shoulders. The assassin took it in with a swift glance, then motioned for Jack to get up.

"We should hurry. I took care of the rest of them, but there may be another patrol through here soon."

The ache in Jack's chest wasn't just from the bullet anymore, but he heaved himself to his feet and trotted after Blade.

Around them, the world was turning to a lovely, soft bronze colour, pre-dawn in the desert. It was still cold, though, the warmth of exertion cooling rapidly. From somewhere ahead, a cow moaned irritably.

"The cattle pen?"

"No one's here," Blade answered.

"For now." Jack sagged against a railing. Adrenaline waned, letting the pain return. He sank to the ground, wincing as the motion pulled on his chest.

"Are you all right?" Blade crouched in front of him.

"What do you think? You shot me, you mongrel." He gritted the words out between pain-locked jaws.

"Only with a needle-tipped rubber bullet full of enough tranquiliser to knock you out fast."

"Tranquiliser?" Jack rubbed his chest, hissing at the depth and breadth of the sore spot.

"I couldn't very well have you waking up after I killed you." He peered into Jack's eyes. "I am sorry."

"For which bit? Betraying me, beating the shit out of me, or shooting me?" Or kissing Valadian?

"All of it." He sat back on his heels. "It's far too complicated to explain now."

"Try." Jack shifted and sat against a fence post. Behind him, cows rustled and farted. "And as you do, remember I'm only not strangling you because of crippling pain."

A corner of Blade's mouth turned up, then sank down as he took a deep breath. "All right. Condensed version. I was employed by an anonymous third party to not only kill Valadian, but also discover how he'd managed to slide under so many radars for so long. My initial search led me to believe there is someone, or a group, protecting him."

Jack made to protest, but Blade carried on.

"It makes sense, Jack. Valadian's been gathering troops and armaments for years. He's been looked at by various government agencies several times, and never charged with anything. Someone has been deflecting those investigations. Either one of Valadian's more powerful partners . . . or, more likely, someone from the inside."

Talking over him, Jack said, "You only think that because you have issues with bureaucracy and governments."

"I swear, Jack, it's true. I don't know who it is, or where they are, but it's the only explanation."

"All right, if someone's protecting him, why was I sent in?"

"Precisely. Why? My first thought was you were sent in as an added layer of protection for Valadian. Someone he wasn't aware of who could look out for other spies and eliminate them quietly. Why else would a decorated SAS soldier be sent in as a general thug, when inserting you in the military side of things would have allowed you to rise through the ranks much quicker?"

Things were falling into place at long bloody last. As much as Jack hated to admit it, it made sense. Valadian's operation here had been too well established when Jack arrived, too entrenched, and The Man himself seemingly very confident of his secrecy.

"So, you staged the whole torture-shack scenario as what? The longest, most complicated trust exercise in the world?"

Understanding didn't make it any easier to take. He'd been used. Tricked, manipulated, betrayed. Everything Blade had said and done in the desert had been a lie, aimed to discover if Jack was on the level or not.

"In a sense, yes." Either Blade wasn't aware of what was coming or he didn't care. "If I put you in a position where you believed I was going to kill Valadian, and then made myself vulnerable to you, you would expose your true purpose in being here."

"And did I?" Jack's hand curled into a fist at his side.

"Yes, Jack, you did. You didn't try to kill me. I know you're not protecting Val—"

Jack hit him. Punched him as hard as he could. Given that he was propped against the fence, aching abysmally across the chest, it wasn't as hard as he could have otherwise managed, but it rocked Blade off his feet.

Tumbling to his arse in the dust, Blade didn't retaliate. He just sat there, a smear of blood on the corner of his mouth, which sat open in shock.

"That's for betraying me." Jack shook out his hand. "You could have told me all this *before* we went into the compound."

Gingerly, Blade touched the corner of his mouth, then frowned at the blood on his fingertip. "I could have, but I still needed to discover who the protector was. My best bet was to see if Valadian would let it slip while talking to you. It would have been much more difficult if you were fully aware of everything. Sadly, the gambit didn't pay off. I know he didn't tell you. I watched the video feed while he was talking to you."

Which meant Blade had seen Jack go mental about the kiss and the fucking. Hopefully he didn't see the blush roaring up Jack's neck and cheeks.

He laughed, part in shame, part to deny it, but it hurt, so he stopped and settled for shoving at Blade with his boot. "That's all I am. Part of a job. It was all a lie. Everything you said and did. Just an act to suck me in."

Blade pulled in a deep breath, then another. "At first, yes. I needed you to think I trusted you enough to allow myself to be vulnerable around you. And then I started to like you."

"Like me?" Jack couldn't keep the derision from his tone. "Why? I think we can rule out the fuck, because you didn't really like that, did you?"

"Half right, Jack," Blade whispered. "It was before that night, yes. Why? Because you treated me like I was a person, not something to be scared of."

"I was plenty scared."

"Scared or not, it didn't stop you arguing with me or telling me how you truly felt. Most people, when they hear the name Ethan Blade, clam up out of fear. They don't want to upset me or provoke me. You didn't do that, and it felt . . . good."

Jack looked away. Damn it. "Yeah, well, it's hard to keep quiet when someone has a pet camel. That shit just has to be acknowledged."

"And you make me laugh, Jack." Case in point, the chuckle under the words.

Shaking off the moment, Jack scowled. "So, what next? You're not going to betray me again, are you?"

"No, Jack. Never again." There was an aching honesty in the words. "Now, we have to get you out of here before Valadian discovers I haven't done as he asked." He stood and offered a hand to Jack.

Jack contemplated the hand for a long moment, then took it. Blade helped him up.

"You've screwed up your own cover now, haven't you." Jack said softly. "Getting me out. Taking down that patrol."

Blade shrugged. "It was time. Valadian dies today."

"About fucking time."

THIRTY-EIGHT

NOW

The mad chase continued until Ethan veered onto an exit at the last possible moment, concerned about roadblocks. Two of their tails missed it and kept on going on the freeway. One, however, managed to follow them, but lost them when Ethan cut across two lanes and made a highly illegal left turn.

"Um, Ethan." Jack's hands tightened around his seat belt. "We seem to be going the wrong way."

Oncoming traffic was scrambling wildly to get out of the way of the speeding Vanquish.

"It would appear so." Ethan deftly swerved them around a confused hatchback. "We are, however, clear of pursuit for a moment."

Jack leaned forwards and peered up through the windscreen. "Chopper's still with us, though."

"It won't be a problem soon." With only a mild near miss, Ethan hooked the car into another left turn so they were going *with* the traffic, not against it. "Jack, in the glove compartment you'll find a phone."

He did and, under Ethan's instructions, sent a short message he didn't understand but which had to mean something to the person on the other end, because about thirty seconds later, *K* appeared on the screen. Short for okay? Or some indecipherable assassin code? Jack didn't ponder too long over it, however, as Ethan threaded them further into the heart of Sydney. With the chopper still overhead, it wouldn't be long before the police found the Vanquish again. If everything went to plan, even that wouldn't matter soon.

Sure enough, a couple of minutes later, Ethan cut across a rather busy intersection, swerved around a delivery truck, and entered the car park of a large shopping centre. They lost the advantage of speed but gained the cover of overhead sails.

Jack let out a long breath. Somewhere in the maze of the car park, Ethan's associate waited with the name of the traitor. One way or another, by the time the sun had set, this would be over. Hopefully with the traitor locked up and Jack not. And if meeting this mysterious associate gave him another insight into Ethan Blade, then that would just be a bonus.

Several turns later, they eased up a row of parked cars, and there, about halfway along, was a woman. She looked like she belonged exactly there, leaning against the back of an Audi SUV, in sunglasses and a flowery summer dress, waves of white-blonde hair falling beautifully around her shoulders, bags of shopping at her high-heel-encased feet. Phone in hand, she appeared to be waiting for someone. The moment she saw the Aston Martin, she slipped the phone into her purse and waved.

They pulled up beside her, and Ethan opened his door.

"What is this?" the elegant woman demanded while smiling brightly. "This wasn't the deal."

Getting out, Ethan said, calm and collected, "The plan changed."

She lost the smile and poked Ethan in the chest, sharply. "You were told, *specifically*, that this couldn't happen." She gestured at the interior of the car as she said it.

While she could have meant the car, Jack didn't believe that. For some reason, this person he'd never met before had decided he wasn't supposed to be here.

"This is my job," Ethan replied, no change in his tone. "I'll conduct it however I see—"

"That excuse is getting pretty thin." Though some of the hardness was gone, as if she were about to cave. "Remember, it was you who wanted this. Not me, not the others."

Now it was Ethan's turn to relent. "Yes, I remember. However—"

"No." She stopped him with an imperious hand. "I don't want to hear it again. This isn't the time. That chopper's still up there." She dipped a hand into the valley between her breasts and produced a data stick and a car key. "Here. Don't make any more stupid changes."

Then she slid into the Vanquish, taking Ethan's place behind the wheel. Before Jack could move, she turned and regarded him. Even with the sunglasses between them, he could feel the burning glare.

"Well?" she snapped. "I'm not here to babysit you. Get."

Every memory of failing to obey his older sister when they were kids fuelled Jack's hasty escape. Between him and Ethan, they piled the shopping bags onto the passenger seat and stood back while Ethan's associate revved the engine. The growling roar made her smile. She dipped her glasses and looked over the top of them.

"Don't get caught," she admonished Ethan. Then she was gone, burning away in the sleek car.

"Come," Ethan said. "We'd best get moving."

"Yeah," Jack muttered, still digesting the sight of her eyes. All white, with large pupils. Just like Ethan's.

She was a Sugar Baby. And if he chose to interpret her words one way, there were others.

Ethan was on the move, weaving between parked cars. Holding up the key, he hit the Unlock button, and a sedan in the next row blinked and beeped. In the sky, the chopper was circling, waiting for the Vanquish to reappear. Which it apparently did just as Jack reached the new car. Somewhere distant, horns blared, tyres squealed, and the thrumming of the chopper moved in that direction. Poised at the driver's side of the understated sedan, Ethan looked up, following the sound. He frowned worriedly, then got in.

Even though Jack wondered if the worry was for the Vanquish or the disturbingly big-sister-like woman, he jumped into the new car, which was refreshingly more his style. He might not have found any more answers to the puzzle that was Ethan Blade—had, in fact, been handed more mysteries—but inside this car was the answer to the most pressing question.

"So?" he pushed. "Let's look at the info on the stick."

Without a word, Ethan produced a small tablet and inserted the stick. Jack leaned over and together they watched page after page of data scroll across the screen. If this was a summary of what the Matryoshka program had found, he could understand the ire of Ethan's "associate." Still, that was a minor matter when they finally reached the end and a single name was highlighted.

"Shit," Jack cursed.

"Not who you were expecting?" Ethan pulled the stick and tucked it in the front of his armour.

"No." Settling back as Ethan started the car, Jack added, "But it makes perfect sense."

"Yes, it does. Shall we go do something about it, then?"

He didn't bother waiting for Jack's affirmative. Within minutes, they were out of the car park and, sans chopper, resumed their journey back to Darling Harbour.

As opposed to when they'd actively been pursued, Jack's tension now ratcheted up. He had a name at long last, a reason for all the trouble the Valadian job had caused him, both then and now. They were so close to ending it Jack worried about all the things that could still go wrong. None of them were anything he could fix right now, but that didn't mean he couldn't try.

"It's not going to work, you know."

Ethan glanced at him. "What isn't going to work?"

"Your plan. The other directors won't believe you. Not until they've gone through every skerrick of data. Which can, and *will*, take weeks, probably months. They aren't like you, Ethan. They have to follow the rules."

"They won't be able to keep me there."

Jack conceded with a nod. "You might get out. I probably won't."

Ethan's fingers flexed around the steering wheel. "Then come with me."

"I can't."

"Can't, or won't?"

Jack swallowed hard. He *could* do it. Ethan was fun and smart, occasionally endearing, and sexy as hell. Even his personality quirks were intriguing. The stone-cold killer thing was an issue, but it wasn't why Jack answered as he did.

If he ran, he would have no hope of convincing anyone he was still, and always had been, loyal, but that wasn't why he said what he said.

"Right now, it's won't."

Ethan kept his gaze on the road ahead, then nodded once.

It was on the tip of Jack's tongue to explain. To say something like, *It's because I'm finally home. Back from the desert. Out there I was lost and confused, wondering what sort of person I was if I could feel any sort of sympathy for a total bastard like Valadian. Or you. I was struggling to keep myself together. I wasn't fighting for a reason. I was fighting myself. But here, now, I've found a target again. Something to aim for. My job is to protect. My family might not approve of what I do, or remember me, but they're the ones I have to keep safe. And if you stuck around, I'd try to keep you safe, as well.*

But he didn't. Just kept his trap shut, let Ethan drive—and planned a betrayal.

A block away from their destination, Ethan pulled over into a loading zone. He left the car idling as they watched the building. Everything appeared normal—massive glass panes shining in the afternoon light. It was an illusion. No matter the distraction of the unmistakable Aston Martin, those inside the Office wouldn't be fooled. Security would be amped up, traps ready to spring around every possible ingress. They knew Jack and Ethan would be coming back. It was how they'd get in that was the mystery.

Jack's stomach tightened in a sudden burst of nausea, but it passed as quickly as it came, and the soothing calm he'd been missing since the desert finally arrived. Why it decided to return now, he didn't know. Didn't want to admit it was because of the man beside him.

"Are you ready?" Ethan asked.

"Let's just get it done before the building goes into lockdown."

"As you wish, Jack."

At the far end of the block, the lights at the intersection turned red. For a precious few moments, the lane opposite them was clear of traffic. Revving the engine, Ethan spun the wheel, and the car charged out of the loading zone, then crossed to the far lane in a cacophony of horn honks. The car leaped forwards down the empty lane. By the time they reached the Neville Crawley Building, they were doing nearly eighty K/hr.

Armoured gates were dropping over the façade of the building as the car bumped up over the footpath and aimed for the huge glass plates. Ethan floored the accelerator.

At the last moment, he spun the wheel and the car screamed, skidding in sideways, then backwards, then coming around as it shattered through the thick glass. The armoured gates *clang*ed shut just behind the spinning car. Another rotation and the car crashed into the foot of the pointless staircase in the middle of the foyer.

Head spinning, Jack pried himself off the caved-in door of the smashed car. In the abrupt silence after the crash, noise was slowly returning. The ticks of the hot engine, the faint *click* of something inside it still trying to work. The *woot woot* of the building alarm and the growing shouts of security converging on them.

Unfolding as much as he could, Jack reached for Ethan. "You okay?"

Ethan moaned. "I believe so."

This was it. According to Ethan, what happened next would be a protracted fight against the security teams converging on them. Then a running battle through the halls, looking for a traitor who would be doing anything to not be caught.

Or, they could do it the easy way.

"Good." And Jack punched him.

Stunned, Ethan crumpled against his door. Before he could defend himself, Jack hit him again. Gun pressed to the assassin's ribs, Jack scrambled for the handcuffs he'd tucked into the back of his pants earlier, cursing the tight confines of the car. He got them secured around Ethan's wrists before he recovered enough wits to retaliate. A furious search later, Jack found the data stick and slipped it into a secure place.

Getting out proved to be another minor disaster, ending up with Ethan's door popping open suddenly and spilling them both onto the debris-littered marble floor.

"Come on, you crazy bastard." Jack hauled Ethan to his feet, making sure to keep the pistol trained on him.

Blood smearing his mouth and trickling from a shallow cut on his cheek, Ethan wobbled. "Half right, Jack," he managed before his legs buckled.

"Stop right there," Gerard Maxwell commanded. "Put the man and weapon down and your hands up." He sounded like he hadn't forgiven Jack for smashing his face in.

Jack stalled in mid grapple with Ethan. They were surrounded, black-armoured security personnel closing in, rifles at the ready. Letting Ethan slide the rest of the way to the floor, Jack straightened. He didn't drop his gun, though, keeping it pointed at Ethan's back.

"This man is Ethan Blade," he announced clearly.

"We know who he is, Reardon."

"Good. Then I don't have to explain how he's a wanted criminal. I've brought him in to be put in custody."

Maxwell removed his helmet, revealing his split lips and broken nose. His cheeks were still puffed up but his eyes, in their pools of yellowing bruises, were clear and full of anger. "Only after helping him escape."

At his feet, Ethan groaned and tried to get up. Jack pushed down on his back with his boot, pinning him to the floor.

"Get Director Tan," Jack said calmly. "He'll straighten everything out."

Stepping back, Maxwell murmured into his phone low enough Jack couldn't make out the words. Under his foot, Ethan's shoulders tensed as he tested the strength of the cuffs.

"Quit it," Jack snapped. He quietly added, "Turnabout is fair play, you crazy bastard."

Ethan went still.

It was a tense wait. Five minutes, then ten, passed. Pinned by a circle of rifle barrels, Jack sweated buckets. It all depended on Tan now. If the man didn't live up to his word, it would get ugly fast.

Finally, the ETA director arrived. He entered from the back of the staircase, as Jack had when Ethan first showed up. Surveying the ruined foyer, the crashed car, and the prone assassin, Tan nodded. "Good work, Reardon. I have to admit, I'd wondered how you would manage it, and frankly, I was surprised with your methods. Still, the results speak for themselves."

"Sir?" Maxwell demanded.

Tan smiled smugly. "Stand down, Maxwell. Reardon's still one of us. He was just on special assignment." From a pocket, he took a jet-injector and tossed it to Jack. "To ensure he doesn't get free."

Jack caught it and crouched by Ethan. Belly down, breathing hard, the assassin lifted his head enough to peer at Jack. The wounded expression was a perfect image of betrayal and how it felt. Jack wondered if that was how he'd looked at the compound.

"Like before, Blade." He tapped the injector. "I guess we can both pretend, huh?"

Ethan swallowed, winced, and coughed. "I guess we can, Jack."

Jack pressed the injector to Ethan's neck and the assassin gasped, eyes rolling back in his head before he slumped boneless to the floor.

THIRTY-NINE
THEN

"**R**ight. Got a plan for how we kill Valadian?" Jack hated how easily he was throwing around that "we" now.

Blade scanned their immediate surrounds as he checked his Eagles by feel. "*We* don't, Jack. You're in no shape."

"Because you shot me." Jack, too, cast an eye over the cattle pen and sheds. The compound was quiet in the pre-dawn, their fight with the patrol not yet discovered. The calm wouldn't last long, however.

"It was simply the most expedient way of getting you out of the Big House. Come on, I have your escape vehicle."

Blade trotted away, leaving Jack to follow. Or not. Jack recalled those thoughts he'd had right back at the start of this whole mess. Why should he follow Blade? He was trained to deal with these situations. And surely he had every right to put a bullet or two into Valadian.

The first step he took, however, proved Blade right. The blow of the rubber bullet to the chest might not have killed him, but he wasn't in peak condition either.

Then he saw the direction Blade was going.

Seeing the possibilities, Jack followed.

"I thought you said it was grounded," Jack huffed as he caught up to the assassin.

"I have a half-dozen racing cars, Jack," Blade said smugly. "I've learned to maintain them myself. You'll find I'm something of a deft hand with a spanner."

The Kamov Ka-52 loomed above them, a sleek, powerful shape cut out in matte black against the glowing gold sky of dawn.

"I've fixed the damage I caused," Blade explained. "It'll get you up well enough, but the damage was compounded. It won't get you all the way home, I'm afraid."

Jack ran his hand along the side of the chopper. "As long as it doesn't blow up on lift-off."

"It won't."

Turning at the hint of sadness in Blade's tone, Jack was surprised by the assassin pushing against him, arms wrapping around his waist.

"I meant what I said, Jack. I don't regret the other night."

Still not sure if he did, Jack kept his hands to himself. Whatever Blade said now, Jack was highly aware of him also letting Valadian fuck him.

At the lack of response, Blade sighed and let him go. "Wait until I've distracted the troops, then leave."

Jack nodded. "Sure. Whatever you say."

Blade eyed him suspiciously, then turned and walked away. Jack watched him go, unsure of the mix of emotions in his sore chest. He didn't know how much of that soreness was from the bullet and how much from Blade's betrayal.

Alone, Jack looked up at the chopper. He'd logged a couple hundred hours between simulators and aircraft, but that had been ten years ago. Did playing sim-flight games count? They'd better.

Jack popped the canopy, heaved himself up, wincing with every pull on his abused chest muscles and broken wrist, and all but fell in. Arranging himself in the pilot's seat, Jack got reacquainted with the complex array of buttons, levers, and gauges. He'd never flown a Ka-52 before, but a chopper was a chopper was a chopper. Surely. At least the digital screen in front of him was in English, not Russian.

Ignoring Blade's advice to wait, he ran through the pre-flight, relieved at the hum of the batteries and, when he got that far, the whine of the engines. The coaxial rotors starting to turn overhead made him cheer. He might just manage to get this thing off the ground after all. Landing without crashing would be a problem for later.

He'd finally gotten the HUD up when whatever Blade had planned began. Shouts, gunshots, truck engines roaring.

Valadian had had about a hundred soldiers with him when he'd ambushed Jack. Blade was good, but was he *that* good?

Jack needed up, now. The rotors were thumping beautifully, kicking up dust in a rolling wave around the chopper. If Ethan had misjudged his repairs, Jack would find out very soon. Slowly, the aircraft lifted up, ponderous and awkward at first, swinging too far left. Overcompensating, Jack nearly drove the rotors into the storage shed on the right.

Across the compound, towards the entrance, there was an explosion and a fireball rolled into the sky.

"Fuck," Jack shouted. He had to get his shit together, or it was going to be too late to do any good.

Finally, memories kicked in and Jack found his rhythm, lifting the chopper steadily. Once he was above the surrounding buildings, Jack pushed the stick forwards. The nose dipped and the Ka-52 shot away.

Leaving the compound behind, Jack took the chopper through its paces. Thanks to the coaxial rotors, it was one of the more manoeuvrable craft around. Thanks, however, to Ethan's previous sabotage, it was sluggish to respond, engines whining as Jack forced the chopper into a near-vertical climb. When the vibrations got a bit too scary, Jack tipped it over and dived for the ground. Aware now of his aircraft's abilities, Jack banked wide, easing the chopper through the turn, and then charged back towards the compound.

His first pass showed him a blazing truck, so reminiscent of that night at the torture shack he almost had an attack of nostalgia. The second, coming in slower, showed several bodies lying across the dirt, a pitched gunfight between soldiers taking cover behind an overturned truck, and Blade, making his way across the rooftop of a barracks.

A third truck was hurtling towards the gates of the compound.

Jack whizzed by it all, swinging out in a long, curving arc. He checked the Ka-52's weapons and found them fully stocked.

Coming back around, he dropped the chopper down until it skated so close to the ground it left a veritable sandstorm behind it. Hoping the poor thing held together, Jack arrowed for the front gates of the compound. He armed the side-mounted guns and, from a distance of several hundred metres, began firing.

Two great plumes of dust blew up in lines ahead of him, driving straight for the truck presumably carrying Valadian away from his compound and the assassin intent on killing him.

Jack held on until he saw the truck swerve sharply, come up on two wheels, teeter, then topple over. At the last moment, he wrenched the stick back and around.

The chopper screamed through the tight turn, its belly scraping the top of the fence. Then it was clear and hurtling back over the compound. Jack let out a wild yell of surprise and victory.

Another wide arc and he came back in, this time aiming for the troops holed up behind the second truck. He hovered over them, nose down, turning in a slow circle and laying down a carpet of bullets. Bodies scattered, and on his roof, Blade waved his thanks, then raced on.

Jack concentrated on pinning down those soldiers who survived his first attack. As he drifted through the air over the compound, feeling the chopper start to shudder and shake more and more, he kept an eye on Blade.

The assassin was back on the ground and calmly ploughing his way through the soldiers protecting Valadian. He moved with that singular purpose Jack had witnessed the first night, every motion precise and controlled, perfectly targeted and flawlessly executed. It was a terrible kind of beauty.

Jack emptied his guns just as the last of the soldiers dropped their weapons and surrendered. Amidst them, Blade stopped his dance of death and said something. Whatever it was, the soldiers moved, and as Jack swung by on a slow pass, they dragged a protesting Valadian out of the truck.

He made another low fly over. Valadian was on his knees before Blade, his once-loyal soldiers hightailing it out of there as quickly as they could. Blade stepped up to Valadian, saying something, to which The Man shook his head furiously. Then he surged to his feet, rushing Blade.

Feeling the chopper jitter uncomfortably, Jack left. He couldn't stay and watch what happened next. If he had any chance of getting home, he had to take it.

He made it as far as the homestead, and that just barely. The groaning aircraft landed with an ungainly series of thumps and crashes. Even after he shut down the engines, the whole thing vibrated so much Jack didn't waste time getting out of it.

Taking shelter behind the stable, Jack waited. The chopper didn't explode.

Blurt!

He even managed not to kill Sheila out of shock. In fact, he was so grateful to see the ugly beast he patted the long, smelly neck. Which apparently was all it took to gain a camel's friendship for life.

FORTY

NOW

Maxwell didn't let anyone else near Blade, taking the job of divesting him of weapons himself. Jack he left in the unkind hands of an entire team of security personnel, probably hand-picked from those Jack had torn his way through the last time he was here. They certainly seemed to have several bones to pick with him, judging by the way they went about locking his wrists together at the base of his back. It didn't seem to matter that Tan had vouched for him. No. It probably did. If he hadn't, Jack had no illusions he wouldn't be lying next to Ethan right now.

Jack just hoped Ethan understood why he'd done it.

While Jack was hauled away under the mildly amused eye of Director Tan, Ethan's limp body was hoisted onto a stretcher and, under the growling countenance of Gerard Maxwell, was carried off in the midst of a ridiculous amount of guards.

Half expecting to be taken to a meeting room on the tenth again, Jack was aversely pleased to find himself being shoved and pushed through the now-fixed door to the sublevels. Down one flight of stairs only and all but kicked through a door to an interrogation room. Inside, he was tied to a chair and then left alone.

As far as intimidation tactics went, it had nothing on the torture shack. Or perhaps it was more the fact that right then, Jack wasn't exactly worried about himself. No matter what happened now, he'd live. Possibly in isolation in a high-security prison for the rest of his life if things didn't go well, but he'd be alive. He could do some reading. Ethan, on the other hand . . . One wrong move on his part and the official report would say "fatal accident," if a headshot could ever be called an accident.

They left him alone for an hour. Jack spent the time imagining what they were doing to Ethan. Stripping him, washing him, full-body search, another set of scrubs, and then back into a cell. The tranq usually lasted several hours. If the directors didn't start moving this along, then things would get tricky.

Thankfully, McIntosh, Tan, and Harraway came in just past the hour mark. McIntosh faced Jack directly, eyes Arctic and gun prominently displayed on her hip. Of the three of them, she was the only one openly carrying. She seemed prepared to deal with Jack however she deemed necessary. Tan stood off to the side, watching Jack with a bland expression, giving nothing away. His hands were on his hips, jacket pushed back to show he wasn't packing. Harraway held back, leaning against the wall, apparently disinterested in the proceedings. Arms crossed, he could have a hand on a concealed weapon.

"Jack," McIntosh said coldly.

He nodded to her. "Ma'am. Sir," he said to Harraway. Then he addressed Tan: "Sir, the job's complete."

Harraway jerked and looked to Tan. "Job? What job?"

Tan didn't answer immediately, taking a moment to study Jack. The longer the ETA director kept quiet, the more sweat gathered between Jack's shoulder blades. They'd taken his armour, leaving him in a long-sleeved black T-shirt that stuck to his clammy skin. Tied to the chair with cuffs more secure than the plastic ties Jimmy and Robbo had used in the torture shack, Jack was totally vulnerable. He couldn't fight, could barely dodge. And he was putting his life—and Ethan's—in, of all people, Tan's hands.

"The job," Tan finally said, removing a small key from his front pocket, "that I tasked Mr. Reardon with a week ago. I'm glad to hear you were successful."

Jack very carefully didn't yell in relief. Tan came forwards and, while the other pair watched him with cold-burning rage and worried confusion, unlocked Jack's restraints.

"What the hell is going on, Alex?" Harraway demanded, and it was the most life Jack had heard from the man.

While Jack shook free of the cuffs and stood to stretch the kinks out of his muscles, Tan graced his peers with a smile Jack imagined a limping gazelle might find on a lion's face.

"It's all rather straightforward," Tan assured them. "Perhaps Mr. Reardon could explain." His expression was clear—*I've stuck my neck out for you. Live up to it.*

"It's simple," Jack said. "Director Tan had some concerns that Omega Subject didn't surrender himself just to exchange information for political asylum."

McIntosh's icy regard shifted from Jack to Tan. "Truly?"

Tan was, thankfully, playing along with admirable aplomb. He nodded with an air of smugness. If he had any doubts about Jack's motives, he was hiding them well. For a man who claimed to have liberal ideas about how his assets worked, he had to have perfected a poker face. Jack decided to never play cards with the man.

"However," Jack continued, "it was clear that if Blade was here with ulterior motives, he wasn't going to reveal them in an interview, or even under stricter interrogation. Like me, he's been trained to resist it. If we were going to find out why he was really here, we had to go . . . outside of the box."

Harraway's earlier shock had morphed into a lazy smirk. "And that required breaking him out of his cell, marauding through the building, and then smashing a car through the front wall?"

"Call it a trust exercise," Jack said just as dryly.

"And?" McIntosh asked warily, looking between Tan and Jack as if she suspected one of them might spring another surprise attack. "Did it work?"

Jack looked from Tan to Harraway and, finally, to McIntosh.

She met Jack's gaze fearlessly.

"Come on, son." Harraway shifted against the wall. "Get on with it. Did it work?"

Jack braced himself. "Yes. I know why he came here."

"Well?" Tan demanded. "Why?"

Trying to watch all of them at once, Jack said, "Blade believes there is a traitor within the Meta-State. Inside the Office. This Office. He planted several invasive programs into the systems, which have been feeding him information for the past week."

Tan scowled. "We discovered them and eradicated them three days ago."

"How many?"

"Three."

"There were four. The one you probably haven't found is a Matryoshka program."

"Fuck," Tan snapped and immediately pulled out his phone.

Harraway looked from Tan to Jack, frowning hard enough his old, bushy eyebrows looked like a single entity. "Matryoshkas are very targeted. What was this one after?"

"The name of the person who was protecting Samuel Valadian. Whoever it was in the Office making sure the information about the size of his organisation was kept hidden. Who redirected any investigations into his activities by domestic law enforcement. There would have been an electronic footprint in the data, small enough to go unnoticed unless someone was looking for it."

"It would take a team of techs months to go through that much information," Harraway murmured.

"Twelve months," McIntosh said just as softly. "Hence the Matryoshka program."

"Well?" Harraway asked. "Did Blade find his traitor?"

Tan had finished his call and he looked at Jack, eyebrow quirking. "Yes, Mr. Reardon. Do we have a name of this supposed traitor?"

Three pairs of very intense eyes focused on Jack. His back prickled, the ghost of Jimmy coming up behind him again. Only this time, Jack was the architect of the ambush. He just hoped he didn't fall into his own trap.

"I don't," Jack said very clearly, "but Blade does."

He watched them closely for reactions, getting only a raised eyebrow from Tan and a long-suffering sigh from Harraway.

"You mean, after you broke him out of a highly secure cell," the Intel director said, "he didn't trust you enough to tell who he was going after?"

Jack shrugged. "He's a Sugar Baby. They're not entirely rational, remember." And just in case that didn't do the job, he added, "He's got this code. Not an *assassin's* code, just a personal one. Finish the job, no matter what. Add to that the Sugar Baby factor, and 'no matter what' gets doubly scary."

The silence following his final words was brittle. It was broken by Tan and for once, there was no hint of a smirk in his serious tone.

"Did Omega Subject give you any hint as to whom his target may be?"

"None, sir. Which is why I couldn't risk him getting free inside the building again. I needed him to think I was on his side to get him back here, but now that he's confined, we'll be able to find out who his target is."

Harraway eyed Jack thoughtfully. "Once he wakes up."

With an agreeing nod, Jack said, "Of course."

McIntosh was the first to leave, giving Jack a parting expression full of chilly betrayal. Then Harraway, head down, still frowning. Tan lingered a moment, waiting until the door was closed behind the Intel director before speaking.

"You took a risk."

They might be alone, but the room was fully monitored, so they couldn't say anything too revealing.

"Thought it was worth it, sir."

Lips quirking, Tan said, "Let's see how it all plays out first." Then he too left.

On his own again, at least Jack could pace this time. He'd done everything he could. The rest was up to Ethan.

It was fifteen minutes before he got his next visitor.

"Reardon," Maxwell said gruffly.

"Maxwell," Jack returned in kind. "Sorry about the nose, sailor. All part of the job."

The HoS touched his bruised cheek self-consciously. "So Tan assures me. Doesn't stop it hurting, though."

"No, I don't imagine it's much of a balm."

Maxwell shrugged, then looked Jack in the eyes. "Before it's over, I have to know. What was it? Am I not pretty enough for you? Not crazy enough?"

Before it's over? What the . . . Jack eased out of striking range, saying steadily, "None of those. You're just not my type, Gerard."

After a moment, Maxwell nodded. "Pretty much what I thought. Techs say your implant is dead."

Thrown a little by the non sequitur, Jack felt his stomach begin to churn with that pre-combat queasiness. "Yeah, I killed it so no one could track me. Had to make it look good."

"Room monitoring is down too," he said casually, then blindingly fast, his Glock 19 was pointed at Jack's head. "Sorry, soldier. Orders. You're not going to get out of this one scot-free. McIntosh isn't going to save your arse again."

Christ. What the hell was happening? Maxwell wasn't a part of this. *His* name hadn't been anywhere in the retrieved information.

Jack kept perfectly still, as nonthreatening as he could be. "What do you mean? Save me again?"

"You went rogue in the desert, Jack. They don't like that. But McIntosh stepped in and said it wasn't your fault. You were forced into extenuating circumstances. She's not getting the chance to do so this time."

"But Director Tan—"

"Is generally full of bullshit. You know it, I know it."

Nodding along to show compliance, Jack risked raising his hands in a peaceful gesture. "Who gave you the orders to do this, Gerard?" Did this whole mess go further than the single traitor? Or was it really policy to kill assets of doubtful loyalty?

"Not that it matters, but—"

The door opened behind him. "Jack, we need to—"

Maxwell spun towards McIntosh. Jack threw himself across the room and tackled Maxwell. They hit the ground and the gun skittered away.

It was over quickly. Between Jack wrestling him and McIntosh pulling her gun while kicking Maxwell's firearm further away, the HoS surrendered rather than get his face smashed in again.

"What the hell, Maxwell?" McIntosh demanded, keeping her gun on him as Jack scrambled back to his feet.

"Orders, ma'am," he growled, slowly getting to his knees. "Reardon should never have been allowed back in after he went rogue in the desert. You know that as well as I do."

Jack picked up Maxwell's gun. "Is it true, ma'am?" God. If he'd been living on borrowed time for a year, then he'd made the wrong decision. He should have agreed to run with Ethan.

"Of course not." She blasted Maxwell with the full force of her icy glare. "Who told you that? It's never been Office policy, and never will be."

Maxwell suddenly looked sick. Pale and sweaty, a tremble in his hands as he held them much as Jack had a minute before, open and empty. "It was Harraway, ma'am. He wanted me to take care of Jack eleven months back, but you kept him under review for so long I couldn't get to him. Then Harraway said not to bother. Jack was your problem; you could take the fall for him."

McIntosh went even chillier. Slowly, she lowered her gun. "You're an idiot, Maxwell." To Jack, she said, "You got a name, didn't you."

Jack nodded. Then it hit him. If Maxwell was in this with Harraway and was here . . .

Without a word, he sprinted past McIntosh, out of the room, and headed for the stairs.

FORTY-ONE THEN

Two days he waited, sleeping through the hot days, working at night. Sheila followed him around like a lost puppy. She butted his back if he didn't pat her at least twice a minute, occasionally galloping off, only to return to her pestering after an hour or so. Jack started the buggy up every evening, making sure it was ready for a quick getaway.

It wasn't that he thought Blade would lose. He just had to be ready for every possibility.

There was no coffee in Blade's stockpile, but there was tea. Jack did without caffeine rather than drink it. He was leaning against the stable wall, mug of water in hand, watching the sun come up on the third day, when he saw him.

A thin spear of darkness against the rising sun, slowly growing into the shape of a limping, weary man as he got closer. Sheila, who'd been dozing under the tail of the chopper, came awake at some unknown signal. She galloped off excitedly to greet her master. Blade had an arm slung over her neck when they reached the stable.

The assassin was dirty, bloody, exhausted, and a sight for sore eyes.

Wordlessly, Jack took his weight from the camel and steered him into the stable. He shooed a worried Sheila out, then cared for Blade as Blade had once cared for him. Laying a mostly clean, bandaged, and dehydrated assassin down on the bed, Jack was caught by his hand.

"Thank you," Blade rasped.

"Just repaying a favour."

"I wasn't sure you'd be here."

"Couldn't get much further. I busted up the chopper again." He loosened Blade's hand from his arm and put a bottle of hydro-lyte into it. "Drink slowly."

Blade was up that night, still a little dizzy, but awake and rational. So they talked, and as they did, Jack came to a bittersweet conclusion. Yes, Blade'd had his ulterior motives for getting close to Jack, but not everything had been made up. Here and now, with no need for deceit, Jack found the truths amongst the lies. Blade's cars were all real, lovingly described in detail and all named—all of them female. How he'd found Sheila wandering alone and starved of attention, an instant devotee the moment he patted her. His sweet tooth and his dislike for being subject to the controlling whims of a bureaucracy. They didn't talk about the immediate situation at all.

The next night was different.

"You killed Valadian?" Jack asked softly.

Cup of steaming tea in hand, Blade nodded. "He died before he could tell me anything, though. Threw himself on my knife. I guess he had some courage about him, at the end."

"I guess." The question he really wanted to ask burned his throat, but he pushed it down. "So, what's next?"

"Next, I will have to find another way to discover who his protector was."

Jack snorted. "Good luck with that."

Blade smiled. "I have my means." He put aside his cup and stood, stretching.

Jack tried not to look, but his gaze caught on the exposed strip of lean, pale skin between top and pants. Too late he realised Blade was watching him, as well.

"Jack," he murmured, coming closer. "I did mean it, you know. I don't regret it."

"Do you regret letting Valadian fuck you?" It was out before Jack could stop it.

Blade's advance stalled. He looked away, his strange gaze taking in the night outside the stable. "No."

"I see." Jack pulled his sleeping bag around his shoulders. "I think that closes that conversation."

"No, Jack, it doesn't. I don't regret Valadian for entirely different reasons. He was just part of the job."

"And I wasn't? Isn't that what this whole bloody mess was about? Me?"

"Will you let me explain?"

"You can try."

Blade's shoulders stiffened briefly before relaxing. "I needed Valadian to trust me, and with his personality type, he only trusts those he controls. I had the rumour planted I was submissive in bed, and he did only what came naturally to a man of his type. He tried to dominate me. I can't regret that because it was part of the plan and it went perfectly."

"Brilliant. And me? What does my personality type respond to?"

"Respect," Blade said immediately. "You will only trust those you respect, but they must earn your respect and if they lose it, then you will be merciless with them."

Jack felt like a fly pinned to a board. "Yeah? So you think you earned my respect?"

"Not entirely. You don't trust me, Jack, and I don't blame you for that. I treated you very unfairly in this." He swallowed hard. "But I *do* trust you. And that's why I don't regret that night."

"Liar. You hated it. I drove you beyond your control and you don't like that."

"That's true. I don't like losing control. There is so much about my . . . about the world I have no control over, that what control I do have, I won't give up."

Blade came a step closer, so Jack could smell him—sweat, tea, and antibacterial cream. Tentatively, Blade nudged at Jack's knees.

"What you did, that's never happened before. And . . . I liked it. An awful lot."

Jack really wanted to believe him. "So the awkwardness after, the way you turned away, that was . . . you realising you still had to betray me to Valadian." Involuntarily, his knees parted.

"Yes." Blade eased between his legs and, after a moment's hesitation, took off his shirt. "I'd like to make it up to you."

"No." It was out, like his knees parting, without a thought.

The assassin slowly ran fingers through Jack's hair. "Why not?"

So many reasons why not, but what Jack said was, "That's not a good reason to have sex."

Blade's lips twitched. With deliberate slowness, he shifted one leg to outside Jack's, then the other. He sank down to Jack's lap. "Then what's a good reason?"

Carefully keeping his hands to himself, Jack asked in what he hoped was a level tone, "What are you doing?"

The smile almost reached those impenetrable eyes. "Seducing you. Turnabout is fair play, after all."

Jack's laugh was as involuntary as everything else he'd done in the past five minutes.

"So," Blade said, sliding an inch closer, "a good reason?"

Why was he fighting this? Wasn't he already drowning in all the bad things? What was one more wrong decision?

"Well," he said, drawing it out as he put his hands on Blade's hips. "One I've always found to be good is . . ." Fingers tightening, he pulled the man closer so their erections met. "Mutual attraction."

Ethan slid a hand around Jack's neck, his fingers questing up into his hair. The other he pressed to Jack's chest, right over his heart. The assassin smiled almost shyly when the beat tripped and then pounded harder. It was echoed in Jack's dick as Ethan rocked against him slowly. Looking up into those strange, empty eyes wasn't quite the disturbance it had started out as, not now Jack knew to look beyond them. The gentle dip of stupidly long lashes, the flush on his pale cheeks, the way his full lips parted on a low moan. Ethan's dick rubbed over his own, hard and insistent.

And this, too, *wasn't* a lie. This wasn't retribution or returning a favour. Ethan wanted him. Maybe even as much as Jack wanted him right then.

"I think," Ethan murmured, tilting his head towards Jack, "that requirement is fulfilled."

Of their own accord, Jack's hands slipped from Ethan's hips around his back, running his fingers over all that smooth, warm skin. Over the faint scars that had broken Jack's restraint back in the cave.

"Yeah," he whispered. "More than."

In his position, Ethan had the chance to take charge, to direct and dictate. The fingers in Jack's hair curled and tugged, lifting Jack's face up to Ethan's. His white eyes fixed on Jack's mouth. Chest heaving, Ethan licked his lips, then lowered his head.

Jack didn't move. Couldn't move. The image of Ethan kissing Valadian flashed before his eyes, and yet he didn't move. There was still anger at that moment. At Valadian for taking something he should never have had in the first place. At Ethan for letting it happen, for encouraging it, even. But here and now, all Jack could think was it had looked like kissing Ethan Blade had been amazing. Of all the wrong, bad decisions he'd already made, this would be the worst, but he didn't move.

Ethan kissed Jack's jaw.

Relief and regret warred for a nasty moment, and then Ethan nipped his skin before licking away the sting. He pressed his body to Jack, sleek and limber, thighs clamping tight to Jack's hips. Jack forgot the moment, forgot the bad decisions, forgot the world, and wrapped his arms around Ethan, moaning as the man devoured his stubbled jaw on his way to Jack's ear, to his hair, to his neck, and back again.

"Jesus," Jack hissed as he turned to give Ethan access to the other side.

"Should I stop?"

"Hell no."

"Good. Shirt off."

Between them they wrestled Jack out of his shirt. Then Ethan was draped all over him, skin to skin, his mouth working across Jack's shoulders, his throat, his biceps. Ethan touched and traced every inch of his chest, then skimmed over the desperate bulge in Jack's pants, never quite getting there.

Deciding he needed a lesson, Jack slid a hand between them and cupped Ethan's dick through his pants. Ethan ground into his hand, then groaned and melted when Jack squeezed.

It was all too much and not enough.

"God*damn*," Jack muttered as he went for the fastenings of Ethan's pants.

Chuckling, Ethan helped him and retreated long enough to shuck the pants. Then he was right back, straddling Jack and holding on for his life as Jack wrapped his dick up again in his hand.

"Jack," seemed about the only word in Ethan's vocabulary as he writhed on Jack's lap. All of his coordination and control was lost as he clutched at Jack's shoulders, back arching as he thrust into Jack's fist roughly.

And still, nowhere near enough.

Ethan let out a startled yelp when Jack pushed him off his lap. Jack stood and caught him around the waist, then pulled their bodies flush. More contact, more skin, more of everything.

"Bed," Jack growled.

With a huffed laugh, Ethan agreed, and they stumble-danced into the other room of the stable. Thankfully, Sheila was out roaming. Jack was so desperate, however, he probably could have lifted her physically and thrown her out.

There was a sleeping bag already on the bed and, after Jack all but dropped him onto it, Ethan watched avidly while Jack stripped in record time. By the time he tumbled down on the bed, Ethan had produced a condom and lube from somewhere. Now that he knew why Ethan had them on hand, Jack hesitated, but a single stroke from the assassin obliterated his doubts. He took the gear and put it aside for later use. Right this moment, he needed to touch, to taste, to drown.

Christ. So much of everything, right here. Hot skin and sleek muscles, dextrous fingers and strong hands, debauched moans and wanton kisses. Everything was in motion, falling into rhythm, and Jack lost himself in listening to Ethan losing control.

He fell so deep into it that when he reached Ethan's dick, he had no capacity to tease or linger. He just swallowed him down and sucked long and hard. Ethan bucked and writhed, begging within minutes, coming with a strangled shout minutes after that.

Jack barely stopped to lick his lips. He grabbed the gear off the crate, covered two fingers in lube, and slid one into Ethan's relaxed body. Ethan submitted with a throaty purr and hooked his ankles together at the base of Jack's spine. Jack tried to take it slow, to make sure Ethan was ready, but the man under him was impatient.

"Now, Jack, please."

When the tone of the words went from begging to threatening, Jack complied. He stroked on the condom and more lube, then sank in.

"God," Jack hissed, burying his face in Ethan's chest.

This was so completely wrong, but he didn't care. Later. He would care later. When he couldn't feel this dangerous, crazy man all around him, couldn't feel him shake and quiver. Or hear him breathe Jack's name, or taste his sweat and skin and musk, or watch the long curve of his neck as he tossed his head back, or the way his legs wrapped around Jack's hips. He would care and worry after he'd come.

At least twice.

Several hours of sated sleep later, Jack roused to the strange sensation of another person wriggling against him. It had been a very long time since he'd actually *slept* with someone, so the feel of Ethan rolling over was odd enough to wake him. Conversely, it didn't prompt a violent response, his body already adjusting to the other man's presence.

"Jack?"

"Mm?"

"Come with me."

Intentionally misinterpreting to give himself time to comprehend the words, Jack mumbled, "Didn't I already do that? Twice."

Ethan snickered and burrowed under Jack's arm to press his lips to a bared shoulder. "Yes, and as good as that was, I mean leave with me. Help me find the person protecting Valadian. I think we'd make a good team."

Jack unwound Ethan from around him and put as much distance between them as he could without slipping from the warmed sleeping bag into the cold night. He didn't want to be distracted by Ethan's naked body, but neither did he want to be uncomfortable.

"You do?" he asked.

"I do. We worked well together at the torture shack and against the dingoes. It would let you finish your job, as well."

"No," Jack murmured. "No," with more conviction.

Ethan gave him silence to fill but when he didn't, prompted with, "Why not?"

Jack wanted to say, *Because I'm not like you. I can't kill a man, then step over his body as if he doesn't exist anymore. I can't walk away from all the moral corruption and bad decisions as if they mean nothing. There's too much inside my head. Too many bad memories. If I don't let them go, it'll be worse than marching into my CO's office and punching until they pull me off,* but couldn't. Not while Ethan looked at him with wounded innocence.

Instead, he said, "This job is finished for me. I was here for Valadian. He's gone and I have all the information we need to make a start on tracking down the rest of his partners. It's time I went home."

Ethan met his eyes and, as if he could see the words Jack didn't say, nodded. "I understand."

They didn't move back together, but didn't move any further apart either.

The next time Jack woke up, he was alone. Rolling over, he saw Ethan, dressed and packing tins of food into a backpack.

"What are you doing?"

"Leaving. I think it would be best I got started sooner rather than later. Element of surprise and all. And speaking of which, I would prefer if you could keep the matter of Valadian's protector to yourself. If he or she is alerted to my search, it will only make my job much harder."

Whether it was the combination of the orgasms and the lingering warmth of Ethan's body, or because he simply didn't want to believe in the possibility of a traitor, Jack said, "Yeah, no worries. I won't mention you at all."

Ethan's smile was glorious. "Thank you, Jack. I'll take the buggy." He stilled Jack's protest with an upraised hand. "If it breaks down, I can fix it. You can't. Sheila will be here for you. If you go due east, you'll find a mine within four days. Once you're safe, Sheila will find her own way home."

He was right, and the last several days had allowed Jack to form an uneasy truce with the dumb lump of a camel.

Ethan was ready to go in short order. Jack followed him out to the buggy.

"How long do you think it'll take you to track down this person?" he asked as the assassin settled into the driver's seat.

"I shouldn't think more than six months," Ethan said confidently. He fussed with the seat for a moment, then looked up at Jack again. "Paul St. Clair."

"Who's he?"

"Me."

Jack stared at him. "You?"

"You were right when we first met. Ethan Blade is a name fit for a circus performer or an assassin. Paul St. Clair fits neither of those professions. It doesn't strike fear into a stout heart. Don't try to look him up in any of your databases. He doesn't exist anywhere other than here." Ethan tapped his own chest.

Stunned by the offer of confidence, Jack asked, "Then why tell me?"

"So the next time you hear it, you will know it's me."

Jack swallowed the sudden rise of emotion in his throat. "The next time I hear it, or see you, I'm going to . . ." He couldn't finish it, not with Ethan looking at him so openly and honestly.

"Going to . . . what?"

Floundering for something not pathetic, he found, "Arrest you."

Ethan grinned. "Won't that be fun."

Then he was gone, disappearing into the shimmering distance.

FORTY-TWO NOW

"**M**onitoring's down in the cell, as well," Maxwell called out from behind.

"You're an imbecile," McIntosh yelled back at him as she raced after Jack.

He paid them no heed, fixated on getting to Ethan in time. He leaped down the stairs recklessly, then barrelled around the last corner and slammed into the door to the next level.

"Open it up, fucking now!"

"Do it," McIntosh commanded, pulling up behind him. She was speaking into her phone. "Now!"

The door clicked open, and Jack was through and pelting down the corridor to the cells. Thank God the door to Ethan's cell was sliding back by the time he reached it. He grabbed the edge of the opening, then swung around and into the cell.

"Jack, so nice of you to come."

Panting, Jack took in the scene.

Harraway, against the wall, limp and defeated. Ethan, awake, in scrubs, barefoot and regarding Jack grimly, his lip split and cheek reddened. He was pinning his target with one hand to his throat, the director's own gun pressed into Harraway's stomach.

"He's awake," Maxwell gasped from behind Jack.

"Well observed," Ethan murmured. "I trust the plan went swimmingly, Jack."

Not quite able to form words, Jack just nodded.

"Ms. McIntosh." Ethan let Harraway's throat go, but kept the gun trained on him as he stepped backwards. "If you would care to take this man into custody. I think you'll find he's been very dishonest in his dealings for the Office."

McIntosh, barely even breathing hard, looked between Ethan and Harraway.

"We can prove it, ma'am," Jack said. "I have the data that pinpoints Harraway as the one covering for Valadian. It might take a while, but I bet when we start looking, we'll find other persons of interest he's been protecting as well."

Finally, McIntosh nodded. "We probably will. Glen? Honestly?"

Harraway sagged even further, then sighed and straightened. Pulling his shoulders back, he smiled smugly. "I had a good run. Earned a lot of money none of you will ever find, and I had fun watching you all scramble at the crumbs of information I let you have. Frankly, I'm tired of it all. We work and work and still, the bastards are out there. As long as they're running the show, why not make some money off it."

"Was it fun killing Maria Dioli?" Jack asked bitterly.

"No, son, it wasn't. You tried to warn her off, but she didn't listen. She found discrepancies between what information Intel passed on and what she'd discovered herself. When she confronted me about it, there was little else I could do."

McIntosh shook her head slowly, disbelievingly. "I knew you were losing patience for the job, Glen, but *this*? Couldn't you have retired?"

"On the pension this place gives you?" There was no malice in Harraway's tone, just weariness, as if now that he was exposed, he didn't want to linger. "Trust me, Alex will start to feel it in a couple of years, when all this stops being a big game to him. You, Donna, you probably won't care. You're here for the righteousness of it all."

"Glen," McIntosh murmured, as if she still couldn't quite believe it.

Harraway turned that apathetic smile on Ethan. "Was this why Valadian hired you, son? To get rid of me before I could give him up?"

Ethan returned the smile, chilling and empty of compassion. For a moment, Jack thought he was going to pull the trigger.

"No, Director Harraway." He lowered the gun. "Jack frowns on unnecessary death." He faced Jack, his smile just as dead as the one he'd given Harraway. "You were right, Jack. My plan wouldn't have worked. This was much better."

Some of the anxiety coiling in Jack's stomach eased. "You forgive me, then?"

"No."

Jack tensed right back up. It was the buggy and the cave all over again. Jack had put himself between Ethan and his objective, had prevented the assassin from completing his meticulously detailed plan. The man still held a gun.

"Not until you apologise for punching me in the face." Ethan winked.

On an explosive gasp of relief, Jack managed a half-hearted, "Fuck you, Blade."

"Good enough, Jack."

While two of the sublevels' security personnel came in to process Harraway, the rest of them retreated to the corridor. Ethan was asked, extremely politely, to surrender his weapon, which he did. Jack, too, had to give up Maxwell's gun. Maxwell was also stripped of his gear and, via McIntosh's clipped, cold words, stood down as head of security. By the time Tan showed up, McIntosh was promising Maxwell he'd be spending at least the next four months on review, and in hearings for probably the next year. Jack's smirk was wiped away when she threatened him with the same.

The oddest moment, however, was when Tan approached Ethan. It was then that Jack understood what Tan had been after in his interview with Jack. Tan wanted Ethan. Wanted his skills and methods. Someone like Ethan, highly trained, capable of working in so many different theatres, somewhat morally ambiguous, would probably fulfil all of Tan's wildest dreams and hopes.

"Mr. Blade." Tan oozed respect. "Thank you for your help in this matter. The Office is in your debt."

McIntosh looked like she wanted to call Tan an imbecile as well.

"Not at all, Director Tan," Ethan said urbanely. "I was merely doing my job. Which will be completed once Jack hands over the data stick he took from me earlier."

"Oh, yeah," Jack muttered as all eyes turned on him. "Forgot about that." He reached into his hair, found the stick, and unclipped it from where it had nestled, camouflaged in his black curls. He handed it over to McIntosh, who closed her hand around it as if it were the last vial of antidote to the poison running in her veins.

"It holds all the data that proves Director Harraway was protecting Samuel Valadian," Ethan confirmed. "As well as the key to shutting down the Matryoshka program."

"Thank you," McIntosh said, still icy.

"What now?" Jack asked, wondering just how Ethan planned on getting away this time.

"My job is finished," he said simply. "Time for me to leave."

After a long, tense moment and exchanged looks filled with silent arguments and counterarguments, Directors McIntosh and Tan stepped back and waved Ethan between them, in the direction of the stairs leading out of the sublevels.

As relieved as he was to see Ethan given his freedom, Jack had to wonder just how Tan would justify it to the minister.

"Cheers," Ethan said happily and, with a parting smile for Jack, walked away. The guards and assets who'd been milling at the far end of the corridor peeled aside to let him go.

"Wait, Blade!" Tan called just as Ethan was at the door.

"Yes, Director Tan?"

"How will we contact you, if we have a need for you in the future?"

Jack hid a smirk at his thoughts being proven correct.

"It's simple. Ask Jack. He'll know how to get in touch."

And he was gone.

Things went both blurredly fast and agonisingly slow after Ethan Blade left the building. Glen Harraway was officially arrested and recorded his confession. Jack was plonked into a chair in an interview room and forced to repeat the whole tale over and over. Around the twelfth time, he nearly admitted to fucking Ethan so hard he went blind in one eye for a minute. Escaping that potential pit of madness, he was released into building detainment again. His request for clothes was rejected, as was the one for fudge. The Aston Martin was found abandoned on the side of a road halfway to Newcastle, the passenger seat full of shopping bags containing the intel that originally led Ethan to the Sydney branch of the Office. The car was impounded and the driver never found.

On the fourth day of Jack's confinement, he was summoned to McIntosh's office.

"Sit, please," she said, cool but solicitous.

Jack did so, a little self-conscious. He was still in his black combat attire, which had stopped being tolerable around noon on day three. Perhaps the smell might help them reach a decision about his future prospects as a gainfully employed asset.

"Before you ask, your actions are still under review by DIC Lund and Minister Simmons," McIntosh said. "Hopefully their deliberations won't take much longer. Both Director Tan and I have made our statements. I don't know exactly what Tan said, but I gather it was generally supportive."

Her ice-blue gaze drilled into him. Just as she didn't like Tan's propensity for retroactively approving the reckless actions of his operatives—and now one of hers—she'd made it clear she wasn't happy with Jack's show of initiative during this whole thing.

Jack was thankful for Tan's backing, but had to wonder if McIntosh had been as supportive. Her stony expression gave nothing away.

"For my part," she continued in the same steady tone, "I studied your interviews and reports, and spoke with Dr. Granger."

They'd given him a break from the interviews on day two for another psych evaluation, which had been rough. Jack was halfway certain the doctor had come to all the right conclusions about his relationship with Ethan. Right then, he wasn't sure if he cared.

"And?" he prompted, wanting this finished.

McIntosh regarded him for a long moment, and then her gaze actually warmed up several degrees. "And," she said, almost grudgingly, "I believe you. You were in a difficult position and you did, if not exactly the *only* thing you could have, at least what you felt to be *right*."

Jack carefully closed his mouth and took a few moments to order his thoughts. "Thank you."

"I won't pretend to be pleased with any of it," she clarified, "but I am willing to admit my own culpability. I put you in that position to start with."

"Because you suspected me of having turned."

"No, not exactly." A small smile flittered across her face at Jack's confused frown. "I've suspected for some time *someone* was acting contrary to the Office's purview. The flow of intel through every department has been sluggish for a long time, but it wasn't until we stumbled across the extent of Valadian's operation I realised just how compromised it was."

Pieces falling into place, Jack nodded. "That's why you sent me in so fast. You didn't know who you could trust, so you had to act alone."

"Exactly. I've been investigating it on my own since you went undercover. If we'd received all the intelligence on Valadian, that operation would never have ended as it did. Or been necessary in the first place. I'm sorry, Jack, but I used you shamelessly this past year. If everyone thought I was suspicious of you, they wouldn't look too closely at what else I might be doing."

"Did you discover Harraway's part on your own?"

She shook her head. "I *suspected* him, but hadn't yet found the proof. Blade's use of the Matryoshka program cut through hundreds of hours of man time. You were right about him, Jack. His methods are blunt, but he did surprise us. The only damage to the staff he caused during his escape, apart from bruises and a lot of headaches, was a broken arm."

"It's that personal code of his," Jack said wryly. "He does the job he's paid for, nothing more, nothing less. Is Tan serious about using him in the future?"

McIntosh startled him with a sudden laugh. "I'm not sure, but I'm looking forward to seeing his capital expenditure request if he does."

Jack chuckled, pleased to realise it was genuine. Perhaps he and McIntosh weren't in such a bad place after all. Which was why he said, "Ma'am, I understand the concerns you had regarding my loyalty."

The amusement faded away and his director regarded him steadily, her gaze warm and patient, though, encouraging him to go on.

"And I wanted to let you know that *I* trust myself again. I have accepted the fact that what I did while in the desert was the only thing I could have done." He'd been unable to say this to Ethan, but now, in regards to his future career and relationship with McIntosh, it was easier to admit. Less . . . important. "I'm back, ma'am. This is where I belong."

McIntosh was quiet for a long moment. Then she nodded. "Dr. Granger agrees with you. And so do I. Welcome home, Jack."

On that heartening note, McIntosh let him go. Day six saw him in Director Tan's office, feeling even more unclean and rumpled compared to the neatly suited director.

"That was a big risk you took," Tan said without preamble.

"I didn't think it was that big a one," Jack replied. "After all, you had gone to some length to tell me how your operatives were given more leniency than those of ITA."

Tan steepled his fingers. "You're not an ETA asset, Mr. Reardon. Would you like to be?"

Before his conversation with McIntosh, Jack had seriously considered transferring. No matter what she said about her motivations, McIntosh *had* doubted his loyalty. After their talk, however, his worries had vanished. He hadn't lied to her, or himself. He was feeling more settled at work than he had since returning from the desert, despite the impending decision from the DIC and minister. McIntosh had dangled the promotion to Field Leader in front of him again, this time stipulated on whether he had a job after the handing down of the initial judgement. Field Leader would give him more control over where and how he worked. And right then, control over his own destiny seemed like a very good thing.

"No." But because the idea of options in the future appealed right then, he added, "At least, not now. Ask me again later. If I still have a job here, that is."

Tan nodded sagely. "Why did you turn down my offer of a position with ETA when you first joined us?"

Jack considered fobbing him off once again, but decided to tell the truth. If he ever did end up working for Tan, he needed this to be clear from the start.

"I won't go back to India, sir."

With his heritage, his knowledge, there was no way Tan would have ever *not* sent him there. Seven years ago, fresh from the nightmare of Jharkhand, he would have killed anyone who tried to send him back. Now, his feelings weren't quite so desperate, but had settled into a deep-seated *need* to never return.

As if reading those thoughts in Jack's eyes, Tan was silent for a moment, then nodded. "I understand. I have my fingers crossed the DIC and minister will make the right decision regarding your future with us. You may go, Mr. Reardon."

"Thank you, sir." Jack stood. "One more thing."

Tan waved at him to continue.

"Should Blade ever contact me again, how do you want me to play it?"

McIntosh had washed her hands of the whole concept, leaving it solely in Tan's hands.

"Well, Mr. Reardon, whether or not he's Ethan Blade, he's a remarkable individual, and it would only benefit us to keep him on side. If he contacts you, I suggest you do whatever is required to keep him happy." He smiled that lion's smile again. "Within reason."

Jack snorted. "Whose reason, sir? Yours, mine, or his?"

Tan just laughed and sent him on his way.

Day nine saw Director In Charge Lund and Minister Simmons hand down their initial judgement on Jack's conduct during the whole disastrous affair.

That night, Jack went home a Field Leader. He took a long, hot shower, then fell into his own bed and slept for ten hours.

When he woke up, it was to the scent of strongly brewed tea.

Dear Reader,

Thank you for reading L.J. Hayward's *Where Death Meets the Devil*!

We know your time is precious and you have many, many entertainment options, so it means a lot that you've chosen to spend your time reading. We really hope you enjoyed it.

We'd be honored if you'd consider posting a review—good or bad—on sites like **Amazon, Barnes & Noble, Kobo, Goodreads, Twitter, Facebook, Tumblr,** and your blog or website. We'd also be honored if you told your friends and family about this book. Word of mouth is a book's lifeblood!

For more information on upcoming releases, author interviews, blog tours, contests, giveaways, and more, please sign up for our weekly, spam-free newsletter and visit us around the web:

Newsletter: tinyurl.com/RiptideSignup
Twitter: twitter.com/RiptideBooks
Facebook: facebook.com/RiptidePublishing
Goodreads: tinyurl.com/RiptideOnGoodreads
Tumblr: riptidepublishing.tumblr.com

Thank you so much for Reading the Rainbow!

RiptidePublishing.com

ACKNOWLEDGEMENTS

I only have a couple of folks to thank here, but it is heartfelt. Firstly, Catriona F, for all the support and advice. The story may have changed a lot since you read it, but everything you said helped me move forward and end up here. Secondly, Jenny Blackford, for listening to my neurotic ramblings and always having the right response. Lastly, the team at Riptide and especially my awesome editor, May Peterson. Massive thanks for all your patience and expertise. Yay, we made it!

ALSO BY
L.J. HAYWARD

ABOUT THE AUTHOR

L.J. Hayward has been telling stories for most of her life. Granted, a good deal of them have been of the tall variety, but who's counting? Parents and teachers notwithstanding, of course. These days, the vast majority of her storytelling has been in an honest attempt to create fun and exciting ways of entertaining others (and making money).

As such, she is still a mad (always provoked!) scientist in a dungeon laboratory (it has no windows—seriously, the zombie apocalypse could be going on outside and she'd have nary a clue) who, on the rare occasions she emerges into the light, does so under extreme protest and with the potential hazard of bursting into flames under the southeast Queensland sun.

Visit L.J. at her website, ljhayward.com; at her blog, l-j-hayward.livejournal.com; on Twitter, @ljhayward; or on Goodreads, goodreads.com/L.J.Hayward.

Enjoy more stories like
Where Death Meets the Devil
at RiptidePublishing.com!

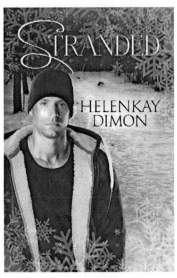

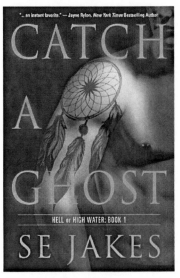

Stranded
ISBN: 978-1-62649-364-3

Catch a Ghost
ISBN: 978-1-62649-039-0

Earn Bonus Bucks!

Earn 1 Bonus Buck for each dollar you spend. Find out how at
RiptidePublishing.com/news/bonus-bucks.

Win Free Ebooks for a Year!

Pre-order coming soon titles directly through our site and you'll
receive one entry into a drawing for a chance to win free books for
a year! Get the details at RiptidePublishing.com/contests.